THE FIFTH RACE OF FEAR

CLIO GRAY

THE FIFTH FACE OF FEAR © 2023 CLIO GRAY

Clio Gray asserts the moral right to be identified as the author of this work in accordance with the Copyright, Designs and Patents Act 1988.

This is a work of fiction. Names, characters, places and incidents are either the result of the author's imagination or are used fictitiously. Any resemblance to actual persons, living or dead, business establishments, events or locales is entirely coincidental.

All rights reserved. No part of this publication may be reproduced, stored in or introduced into a retrieval system or transmitted in any form or by any means (electronic, mechanical, photocopying, recording or otherwise) without the prior written permission of the author.

Isbn: 978-1-914399-73-2

This book is sold subject to the condition that it shall not be resold, lent, hired out or otherwise circulated without the express prior consent of the author.

Printed and bound in Great Britain by Bell & Bain

Cover Design © 2023 David McKinley Mercat Design. Images courtesy of Dreamstime. All Rights Reserved

SPARSILE BOOKS LTD

Thank you, John, for forty years of friendship and beyond.

By the same author

The Stroop Series
Guardians of the Key
The Roaring of the Labyrinth
Envoy of the Black Pine
The Brotherhood of Five

The Scottish Series
Deadly Prospects
Burning Secrets
Hidden Pasts

The Troubadours Series
Stumblestone
The Fifth Face of Fear

The Bookfinders Series
Legacy of the Lynx
The Juggler's Box

Other books
The Anatomist's Dream
Archimimus
Types of Everlasting Rest
Peder and the Skincatcher

A Sea Without Tides

1851 The Far Edge of Mecklenburg

A quiet village on the edge of a forest; hard white frost three days lying; freezing fog closed over the heights of trees, barns and roofs; thin wisps curling down corners and boles.

Everything still.

No wind.

Water barely moving, lapping gently against heaps of stranded kelp sprinkled over with hoarfrost, sparkling like the sand clearly visible beneath the imperceptible shiver of the waves.

Soft sound of oars, creak of wood as feet brace, a body moving with the rowing; long white necks of goose barnacles swaying beneath the ramshackle pier that has lost half its planks, is more spirket than spar; rusted nails worked loose, square heads bent and broken; two swans paddling slow circles beneath.

Beyond the Joshua Tree—an ash pollarded into the shape of the cross, sprouting new growth in spring, dropping leaves in winter as it is now—a fog bow materialises as the newly risen sun refracts from the mist. And from the dark maw of the forest comes a small sow, red pelt raddled, snout greying with age. On her heels a young man, quick-stepping, sharp-featured, head uncommon—large protuberance, like a hard-swollen bladder, growing from the base of his skull and all up one side—hidden beneath a wide-brimmed felt hat. Pig and man careful about the village, passing beneath the fog bow, heading down to the pier.

Oars drawn in, the boat allowed to drift silently towards the shore on the slight rock of waves, the two swans keeping to the shadows as the erstwhile rower puts out his hands, guides himself in, holds his breath. Watches and waits, looks and listens. Hears a soft tread on the shingle bank.

'Is it you?' he asks, using no names.

After a few moments, the reply.

'It's I.'

Making his way through the fog to the water's edge, lifting up his pig and getting them on board, the rower pushing off with an oar, then forward-stroking, taking them out into still waters and away.

The inhabitants of the quiet village on the edge of the forest beginning to wake, rustling up their fires, rubbing cold hands, blowing into them, holding their clothes up to meagre flames to warm smocks and shirts before shrugging them over their shoulders.

The inhabitants of the quiet village sighing as they glance out of their small windows, open their doors to frost and fog wondering how much longer both could stay, and both so uninvited.

No idea that a man on the run has filtered past them only minutes previously, only sign of him being the tracks he's left in the frosted grass if they were looking, which they were not.

No idea he is being rowed away by his rescuer out there beyond the pier.

No sound coming from the sea as on clear days, when you can hear men talking five hundred yards from shore.

They make their salutary genuflections to the Joshua Tree and head through the disappearing fog bow into the dark forest to whistle up their sheep and goats.

To start their day as they always did.

Normal folk going about a normal day.

Quiet folk in a quiet village on the edge of a quiet forest.

No notion of what will be set in motion because of the young man who has passed unseen about their village and boarded the boat that is taking him over the water to the island.

Told once, by a travelling theatre who'd passed through their village a few months previously, just after Michaelmas, that everything was connected, that actions here have consequences there; one small happening able to turn into a huge one, like a snowball gathering mass and speed as it rolls down a hill. A play that hadn't gone down well, because no one in this quiet village quite believed it.

They'd not booed; neither had they clapped.

They simply couldn't understand it.

History seeming to have passed them by.

Their village on the farthest edge of Mecklenburg: an isolated fringe on Germany's sprawling shawl, the outside world of no concern to them, nor them to it.

Folk waking to frost and fog, as today, or maybe to light and sunshine, maybe spring and all the new growth spring brings with it; or maybe a high winter wind whipping up the water, rolling spindrift over the shingle banks and up into their streets and, on occasion, into their homes.

Simply the way things were, and always had been.

No mystery to it, no matter what the Pfiffmaklers had tried to tell them.

Folk merely getting on with getting on.

Folk waking into a morning no different from any other.

None the wiser a week or so after the young man had been and gone, the fog down again, when two more strangers fetched themselves out of the undergrowth once the village folk had departed into forest gloom; strangers who'd followed tracks and traces, scattered conversations, leading them to here: to the path skirting the Joshua Tree and its village, strangers going down to the shingle and the dilapidated pier.

The older man shaking his head, growling, anger never far from him, rage his natural bent.

'We almost had him.'

'Almost,' his companion agrees, gazing off towards the fog-bound sea, cocking his head, hearing the shockwaves hitting the rocky outcrop to their left caused by gannets' distant diving a couple of seconds after they've gone plummeting into the sea. Stray birds brought in by recent storms, far from their normal course. Soft noises but distinct, once you'd figured out the timing, linked the action with the consequence.

As they'd done with their fugitive.

Follow a crow long enough, Mergim had once told the older man, *and you'll find carrion.*

Some Albanian saying from Mergim's homeland, and he'd been right.

Only weeks, or even days, behind their prize and closing fast.

Only the fog, rolling in from the Baltic with seasonable regularity, slowing them up.

Yet here they were, all the same, standing by the dilapidated pier of this quiet village on the edge of a forest at the very edge of Germany, as the sea lapped against its shores and the gannets dived and the swans paddled and the Joshua Tree threw off a few more leaves as it stretched its arms towards an unseen sun.

Madness Foreseen, Massacres Remembered

And here are those Pfiffmaklers who'd so under-impressed the Joshua Tree villagers a few months back.

Die Kunterbunt Trudelndschau, The Higgledy Piggledy Travelling Show.

Purveyors of Theatre and Entertainment for four generations, founded by their querulous and dictatorial Old Grandma who'd left them to it a decade back after Old Grandma found a new calling.

Here is Wenzel, Father of the Fair since grandma's leaving, puffing at his rancorous pipe, studying the details of their upcoming performances. And there, tending to the fire and a breakfast soon to come, is his wife Rosa. At her side is sister-in-law Yssel and down by the water's edge is Yssel's husband Peppe who is also Rosa's brother.

An unusual lot, these Pfiffmaklers. Tight-knit, as self-sufficient as those villagers although unlike those villagers—who are grafted to their land like lichen to a rock—the Pfiffmaklers have travelled farther and wider than most. Have been from the Voralbergs in Austria, where Old Grandma originated, to the wildest hinterlands of Italy, Serbia, Croatia and Albania, and a hundred other places in between. They've met more people and odd situations than there would be crumbs if you grated up several large loaves of bread and scattered them about your feet.

They've been embroiled in histories not their own.

Been diminished and enriched by them.

And here comes Hulde, adopted into their ranks because of those embroiling histories. Only survivor of a massacred village on the outposts of Albania; a village, one might have supposed, as inconsequential as that of the Joshua Tree over the water.

Snowballs rolling down hills the Pfiffmaklers had told those Joshua Tree villagers, which allusion they hadn't understood, couldn't grasp, couldn't see the beginning of nor the end. Snowballs once more beginning to roll for the Pfiffmaklers, someone else's history about to overtake their own.

Last to introduce are Pietro and Livia Benedetta who rise as one, roll up their bed mat; Livia sitting as Pietro takes out the lacquer-backed brush he'd presented her with on their wedding night ten years previously, stroking the bristles evenly through her silvery-grey hair as he'd done every morning and every night since. Taking up a small pot of ointment, rubbing it gently into the half of his wife's face stricken with burn-scars, and next into the unblemished part, smooth as a bullace. Livia taking Pietro's hand once he's finished and kissing it gently, before dividing her hair at the nape of her neck and deftly plaiting each length, tying their ends off with ribbons.

'Big day,' Pietro murmured, as Livia returned his ministrations, laving his chin and cheeks with soapy water.

'Big day,' she agreed, setting to with her razor and scraping away the bristles. 'Think we're up to it?'

The pair not married in the strictest sense, but as bound together as a sole is to its boot.

'I do,' Pietro said. 'And you're not feeling sickly?'

Putting a hand to Livia's belly, a thrill passing through both to know what was growing there, neither of them being in their youngest years. Livia shaking her head.

'Feeling fine,' she mollified. 'Just wanting to do everyone proud.'

As did they both.

Two people brought together by the most extraordinary of circumstances come from the finding of Hulde. Pietro—ex-carriage driver for the Archbishop of Ravenna—who'd taken to acting on Pfiffmakler stages, and the Janus woman who'd been on stages not of her own making her whole life.

Eleven years they'd been with Die Kunterbunt Trudelndschau, who'd taken them in, made them their own; today the two presenting their own set of plays, a schedule entirely of their own devising, both nervous because of it.

They'd learned a lot, since being with the Pfiffmaklers, about stagecraft, scripts and plots, this the first time they'd been put in charge of the whole show. Pfiffmaklers born to it, brought up in it. Not so Pietro nor Livia, stunning debuts as both had made. It had taken them this long to have the confidence to present to Wenzel Pfiffmakler an entire set, instead of merely an idea here or there to be incorporated into whatever the Pfiffmaklers had already scheduled.

They'd planned for several years, honed and polished, thought and re-thought, made account for where the Higgledy Piggledy Travelling Show might take them. Seizing the opportunity when they realised they'd be on a small island for the first week of Advent, and taking their ideas to Wenzel.

Wenzel studying their scripts studiously, raising his eyebrows as he read—eyebrows grown and thickened over the years since they'd known him, sprouting white hairs as the Joshua Tree sprouted new growth in spring. Wenzel impressed. Wenzel always having to steer the line between secular and religious as situation, place, and time of year dictated. This exactly right for where they were going, which was St Mary's Church, modelled on Lübeck cathedral, in the small town of Bergen on Rügen Island.

'I'll need to speak to Rosa,' Wenzel said, 'but this, Benedettas, seems exactly right.'

Wenzel calling them to his tent a few days later, giving them back their scripts with a few additions, a few subtractions. Wenzel smiling—as much as could be detected through his beard.

'You've done a real fine job,' he praised them, 'concocted a really exciting Advent Cycle. This piece about the life of St Hildegard is inspired. The Sibyl of the Rhine no less. And you say this is her actual music? Songs she wrote herself? Well, well.'

'We found an old manuscript,' Livia said, 'when we were travelling near Bingen.'

'The place she was Abbess of?' Wenzel asked, having read as much in their script, realising how long these two must have worked on it given it had to be almost three years since they'd been in that particular neck of the woods.

'We thought at first to buy it for Heraldo,' Pietro explained, 'what with all the musical notations and that. But then, when we started in on it...well...'

He coloured, stammered to a stop; Wenzel relieving him of the burden.

'I can see why you'd want to hang onto it, and you made the right choice.'

'Heraldo helped us with all the songs,' Livia went on, 'and he's even constructed some of the instruments played way back then.'

'He's made us a *Geigenwerk*,' Pietro butted in. 'It's like a hurdy-gurdy with wheel cymbals that can be operated by a keyboard...'

'Cutting out the need for a second player,' Wenzel interrupted, proud of his eldest son's obsession with creating new instruments from old like other boys might engineer animal traps, or new ways of netting birds.

He narrowed his eyes, looked about him.

'Speaking of Heraldo,' he paused the conversation. 'Where is he? I haven't seen him all morning.'

Wenzel taking out the fine pocket watch he kept scrupulously clean and wound at all times; Pietro and Livia exchanging a quick glance.

'He was down by the shore earlier,' Pietro offered quietly, aware Wenzel might not take this well. Which he did not. Wenzel clamping his lips tight, leaning his head back upon his neck to stem the anger.

'He didn't...' he got out in a low rumble, although one look at Pietro and Livia told him all he needed.

'Ludmilla!' he yelled, pushing himself out of his tent. 'Ludmilla! Get yourself here, right now!'

His niece appeared before him a few moments later, her long luxuriant hair swinging in a loose plait down her back, Ludmilla holding up her hands against the expected onslaught which wasn't long in coming.

'Don't tell me he did what I specifically told him not to do,' Wenzel started, halted by his wife Rosa coming up on Ludmilla's heels.

'Now let's take a moment,' Rosa said.

'I'll not take a bloody moment, woman, not now nor anywise!' Wenzel argued. 'We don't need this kind of trouble. I thought I'd made myself absolutely clear on that front not three weeks since!'

Rosa raised her eyebrows, put her hands defiantly on her hips, clearing her throat with menace.

'Well, yes you did. But ever since grandma left you've also made it clear that we are no longer to be dictated to, that we operate as a plebiscite, that the views of the one are...'

'Equally as valid as another's,' Heraldo finished for his mother, stepping in lightly, taking the hand Ludmilla put out to him and squaring up to his father. 'Which is what I've done.'

Wenzel shaking his head.

'It's madness,' he argued. 'We can't possibly hide him. What if folk are still after him? We know too damn well what happened last time someone got close to finding him.'

'If we're certain he was why that happened,' Heraldo put in, 'which we aren't.'

'But it was a massacre, son,' Wenzel reminded him. 'Maulwerf's Fair of Wonders decimated, and Maulwerf one of the finest men I've ever met.'

'So we're to turn our backs on him?' Heraldo bridled. 'One of our own who needs help? What would've happened to Hulde if we'd done the same to her?'

Wenzel taking a breath, rubbing at his nose with the back of his hand, for what might have happened to Hulde if they'd not found her didn't bear thinking about. Wenzel admitting defeat.

'So where've you stashed him?' Wenzel asked. 'No small feat to hide a head like his, never mind his blasted pig.'

Heraldo smiling, having thought all this through. Fairs' folk up and down the land cognisant of the plight of Philbert and the legends attached to him; how, after the 1848 uprisings, he'd been branded a wanted man, or a wanted boy as he'd been back then. Heraldo storing it all up, recalling it, certain he'd caught sight of the fugitive several weeks back in Rostock and brought it up at family council.

'It's him,' Heraldo had been sure, Philbert by then a hero of the failed revolutions, a martyr to the cause, still on the run. 'Saw him plain as day!'

'If you saw him plain as day then you can be damn sure other people did too,' Wenzel had protested. 'Please tell me you didn't approach him.'

Heraldo shaking his head.

'Wanted to speak to you first, father,' Heraldo had said.

'We've to leave him be,' Wenzel decided. 'He's got along well enough on his own all this while. Doesn't need us to go rattling…'

'What if it was me? Or Lupercal or Jericho?' Heraldo speaking of his brothers; Heraldo always on the side of the downtrodden, the disregarded. 'And we're already going to Mecklenburg. We could get him over the Baltic to…'

'Enough!' Wenzel had stated. 'We're too small an entourage to take such a risk. If Maulwerf couldn't protect him then how are we supposed to do it now? No. That's my final decision.'

Wenzel's final decision, if not Heraldo's. It wasn't often he went up against his father, rarely went up against anyone, but this was different; this was someone whose life and actions had been acted out by street theatres up and down the land, about whom songs had been sung, who walked like the ghost of revolutions past in ballads and broadsheets.

Heraldo taking a unilateral decision, not without forethought, nor without discussing it with Ludmilla, nor without forming a half-decent plan: a plan predicated on all they knew about this remote part of Germany. A plan he now outlined to his father.

'We're the only ones knew we were coming back this way, and only because we heard…'

'Quite by chance,' Ludmilla put in, Heraldo smiling at his wife.

'Exactly. Quite by chance, because we heard the island hadn't seen an Advent Cycle in years, if ever, and decided to fill the gap. So who's to follow us? And for what reason?'

'Because someone saw you conspiring with a fugitive?' Wenzel ground out his own question in answer.

'Ah, but no one did,' Heraldo replied brightly. 'That's the beauty of it!'

'We sent him a coded message,' Ludmilla got in, 'which no one would understand if it wasn't him. Got a boy to slip it to him, so he never even saw us.'

'Wasn't sure he'd turn up,' Heraldo went on, shrugging his shoulders. 'We left it all a little vague…'

'Like a puzzle!' his younger brother Lupercal joining the conversation.

'Ooh, I like puzzles,' added Jericho. 'What was it? What did it say?'

'It doesn't matter for the moment,' Wenzel cut his boys short. 'I take it he did turn up? That he's somewhere here on the island?'

Heraldo nodded.

'He is, father. But he's hidden, and won't come anywhere near us.'

Heraldo and Ludmilla outlining their plan in turns, Wenzel listening, the fog clammy about them, come from low cold clouds rolling in from the north, settling onto this island like a swan folding itself down upon a warm nest. The sun beginning to burn through the fog, Wenzel hearing the dripping of water from nearby branches.

And, as plans went, he had to admit it was a decent one.

The beech forests of Jasmund Peninsula on Rügen Island were vast; the trees skeletal with winter, eerily ethereal in the fog drifting in sprites and wisps between and above them. So calm, so utterly beautiful, Philbert—the fugitive Heraldo had fetched from across the water—had to put his fingers to his Adam's Apple to keep himself from weeping. Kroonk, his companion pig, having a fine time snuffling through the leaves, pushing them up in pluffs with her red-bristled old snout to get at the mast. Philbert recalling Tomaso, the three-eyed boy he'd never liked, trying to teach Kroonk the arts of truffle hunting. A miserable failure, which was a mercy given how it had soured Tomaso's fragile friendship towards Philbert beyond repair, neither of them any longer pretending care.

Maulwerf and his Fair of Wonders.

It seemed a lifetime ago.

Philbert turning his back on them so they could preserve what little they had left, in case all that had happened in Schleswig-Holstein really had been his fault. All flowing like a river tumbling and boiling with the waters pushing in from the too many tributaries of the history of those times. The workers of Silesia overthrowing factories, burning down their workshops; craftsmen all over Europe being forced out of their trades by the new machinery they'd welcomed in, believing it would deliver them from the worst of their work and instead had lowered their wages, forced them into penury and bonded labour. A vast number of newly impoverished labourers jumbled in with all the rest, until those years-old banks of class and division had burst.

Too much, the downtrodden had eventually called out, their burdens too heavy to bear.

Too much, the intellectuals eventually agreed, spearheading the campaign for the labourers against the princes, politicians and principalities who had seen fit to allow and encourage all this to pass as if it would have no consequence.

An enormous outpouring of anger into which pot of unrest Philbert had been stirred.

His part in it accidental, and unintendedly enormous.

Philbert right there when the greatest of those intellectuals agreed to meet a coterie of like-minded men in a subterranean cellar called the Westphal Club in an obscure town in Germany. Von Ebner, Man of the People, scourge of the rich and wealthy, and particularly of Prince Clemens Lothar Wenzel Metternich whose rise to power had dovetailed with—been responsible for—the autocracy and police despotism leading directly to much of this political unrest in the first place.

Philbert breathed deeply. Tried to close the door to these memories, instead had the door ripped off its hinges as they coursed through unbidden.

There he was again, the boy with the big head, with the taupe, being brought into a smoky fug-filled room crowded with tables and talk, ready to be assessed by various Great Men who knew about his condition but had never witnessed it for themselves.

The Anatomist's Dream, they were all saying, marvelling, treating him as special and him feeling proud because of it.

Until the new special marvel came into the cellar: Von Ebner himself striding in with his stovepipe hat, and Philbert no longer the centre of attention for, on Von Ebner's heels, came Metternich's men who had been waiting for such a chance. Von Ebner so careful where he went, what he did, and in this tiny place, in this unknown town, had believed himself safe. With Philbert was Dr Ullendorf, who had brought Philbert to the Westphal, organised this meeting of minds. Dr Ullendorf standing up, waving a hand.

'Von Ebner, my dear fellow!'

Next second Von Ebner skewed sideways by a bullet, and Ullendorf crashing down onto the table under which Philbert had been dragged. All a stramash of confusion, pistol flares, tumbling chairs; candles and lanterns rolling to the floor; glasses smashing, spirits catching light; men pushing, shoving, falling.

You've got to get out, Philbert, you've to go right now!

Philbert pushed on by his mentor, crawling out from beneath Ullendorf's body and the splinters of the table, scuttling through the mess and blood, the shouts and shots; off to the kitchens, clambering up sacks of cabbages and potatoes and out the tiny window, catapulting himself onto the wet street like a rat from a ginnel, running and running until he ran out of breath.

Giant head buzzing, heart beating a drum roll.

Then as now.

'Well, my dear, what do you think?' Wenzel asked his wife as he puffed at his pipe, Rosa pouring hot water into the bucket in which he nightly soaked his feet. Rosa twitching her lips.

'Sounds fine to me,' she replied, adding mineral salts to the bucket, giving the water a swish with her hand. 'Heraldo didn't do this lightly. And think of that poor boy, Wenzel. On the run these several years. Do you really think people still care about what he did?'

Wenzel pulled at his beard, flexed his toes in the water, had no doubt a man like Metternich would never let such a matter go. The revolutions of 1848 raw and recent, deeply unsettling, tipping kings and princes from their thrones, toppling the government in Vienna, unseating men who'd believed themselves all-powerful, invulnerable. Including, incredible as it seemed, a man more all-powerful and invulnerable than anyone in Germany: Metternich himself. Metternich forced to flee into English exile like a mangy old dog being pelted by the ideological stones of the rabble he despised.

Hubris and humiliation making the very worst of bedfellows. Metternich bitter to the core, hard of nerve and will, and would never let those he held responsible for his demise to fizzle away into ordinary life. Philbert being a very notable one of them. A few years here or there would not matter a jot. More worrying for Wenzel being a snippet of news he'd picked up the previous week:

Metternich was no longer in England.

Metternich was back on German soil.

Had taken up residence in a castle on the Rhine at Johannisberg, near Wiesbaden.

Metternich no longer the pelted dog, become instead a mastiff baying for blood.

And, in particular, for the blood of the Anatomist's Dream.

A Man Walking Free

Mergim went over the loose cobbles of the prison yard for the last time, ducking as someone chucked a load of stale bread and scraps over the wall; regarding the men who scrambled to scoop them up and stuff them into their mouths with slight disgust. Every crumb welcomed, a paltry addition to their daily rations.

Any other day than this he'd have been doing the same.

Ten years he'd been here, in the prison of Kragujevac on the banks of the Lepenica River, shacked up with the worst of men. Men who'd murdered their women by shoving them headfirst into a cauldron of boiling stew because their buttons hadn't been sewn on properly; men who'd murdered mistresses, having deluded themselves into believing those pretty young women were their property and not merely carrying out transactions to keep themselves alive; men who'd set their own children on fire because they'd let down the family name or stepped out with the wrong person, or merely because they were there when such men had been too angry, too drink-sodden, to recognise the difference between real life and nightmare. Men who routinely bashed their heads against the walls of their prison cells unable to bear what they'd done, who acknowledged their misdeeds even if they couldn't remember doing them; and some kind of honour in that.

Going at hard graft every day without resentment because they understood it was deserved: breaking down coir for ropes, binding those ropes, twisting them together to better purpose, making them thicker and thicker for the ships needing them, using winches and pulleys for the largest when they were the width of a man's waist and had to be stretched and tarred. Mergim's hands bloodied within days, his companions lending him pots of diluted lye and mixtures of vinegar in which to soak them every night to heal them, harden them, until he had no feeling left in hands or wrists; fingers working to lace and tie his boots through mechanical memory alone.

Playing chess of a night, after learning the rudimentaries. Finding pleasure in it.

Pouring out their bitter coffee brewed in tins over small fires, sharing their rations, donating small portions to anyone who was sick or looked like he might drop.

Honour, then, amongst murderers if not amongst thieves, with whom the murderers did not mix, being different kind of men and partitioned off by high prison walls and fences; hearing the thieves bickering and arguing the whole night through, maybe because they had hope of release in a few years and believed there was gain in proving themselves nastier, more vicious, than the rest.

Of all the murderers in this prison Mergim was the only one who would see time served and get out again. Making him a valuable commodity, a person who might, if he was so inclined, be able to get word and letters out to families. Mergim respected not for the crime he'd been charged with but for what came after it: how he'd personally prevented the escape of, and delivered back to Serbia, a war criminal, a man reviled by a great many during Serbia's fight for independence.

And now, ten years later, Mergim has his freedom, a guard accompanying him across the yard, past the gun-tower, through several heavily bolted gates and over the short bridge across the moat surrounding the prison which swirls thick with the detritus of every inmate's crap-bucket: a vile clog of stool-thickened water which murmurs and moves, black with flies. Suicide to go into it, if you'd managed to get that far in your desperate attempt to escape; though still, every few months, someone tried when the guards were too lax or too drunk or both, guards unconcerned, knowing that even if you drew in enough breath, had strength enough to drag your bones out the other side, well. What the hell. All that had gone into you in your desperate swim across the moat would have you dead within the month.

Mergim had never thought about escape. He knew what he'd done and regretted it, taking part in the pointless massacre of a group of Albanian Christians hoping for a better life. Only allowed to live that better life for a few days before Mergim and his fellows fell upon them with billhooks, daggers, and too few bullets to carry out their plan with any modicum of mercy.

And it was to that village Mergim headed after he left Kragujevac.

Mergim going from Kragujevac down the Ibar River to Kostrovka Mitrovica, and from there along the borderline between Albania and Montenegro. Finally reaching the meagre track skirting the Adriatic coast, walking down the wide street lined with ancient fig trees whose roots wrapped about their bases like thick brown snakes. Walking past the rusted pump, the cottages now decrepit beyond feasible repair, coming upon the village-green thick with rotting hulms of hemlock and angelica, goats-rue and grasses.

He pushed through the tangles, finding the sundial he sought and sat upon it, surveying a scene so peaceful it didn't seem possible this place held such history. He closed his eyes, held his face up to the late spring sun, smelling the sea lapping on unconcerned a few hundred yards to his left. He'd paid his dues as far as the Serbian authorities were concerned, as had been apparent at his trial when he'd been given leniency far exceeding his expectations, and far more so than he believed he'd deserved.

But such joy in being here where so much for him had started, and such joy in being alone. Never alone in prison, not for long, not unless he chose to wander the yard from one perimeter to the other as night began to fall, as he'd often done. Even then that aloneness never lasting long before he'd be joined by one or another of his fellow inmates falling into step beside him. No words, merely a silent striding from one wall to the next and back again, the men believing they were lending him solidarity, currying favour, not understanding they were crushing the one limited freedom in incarceration he'd ever found. A lack of freedom compounded by the prisoners on the other side of the wire, the thieves and smugglers, pimps, and beaters-upper of men and women, calling out to him. Asking his advice. Men far worse, in his opinion, than most of his companion murderers.

Follow a crow long enough and you'll find carrion.

And true enough in Kragujevac.

But no more.

Mergim liberated, unlike his fellows.

Free to pursue whatever chance at life he had left to him.

And an odd feeling, as he sat on the sundial in the middle of the overgrown green at the end of the village and its wide street lined with fig trees, to realise there was only one goal he wanted to pursue.

He wanted to find the Pfiffmaklers, wherever they might be.

He wanted to find out what had happened to them after he'd been incarcerated. And most of all he wanted, he needed, to find out what had happened to Hulde, the only inhabitant who had come out of this ruined village alive.

'Surely there's no harm to us?' Rosa asked, having heard Wenzel's snippet of news concerning Metternich as she gently laved her husband's feet, regarding the dirty water with disgust. Remembering a Tibetan contortionist who'd travelled with them for a while who, on watching this same domestic scenario between husband and wife, informed Rosa how back in her home village the women—once their men's feet were cleansed and dried—were made to drink the filthy water as a sign of respect to their husbands. Rosa appalled, thanking God her Wenzel was as appalled as she.

'It seems to me,' she added, as she lifted the bucket away, 'that the weakest part of Heraldo's plan is the end of it, when it will have to be one of us who hires the boat to take the lad over to the Danish Isles.'

'Exactly,' Wenzel agreed. 'We've to figure a way around that. We can't have our name attached to any of it.'

'Do you really think people are still tracking this Philbert?' Rosa asked, rubbing a towel about Wenzel's feet. Wenzel shrugging.

'I don't know. But if they are, and if they discover he was heading to Stralsund the same time we were there... well. They're bound to think Fairs Folk. From Maulwerf's Fair of Wonders to us. And no getting that hare back into the box.'

Wenzel casting a glance towards the other members of his troupe who were gathered about the fire, every one of them his responsibility; noting Livia's outspread hand resting on her swollen belly. A complete surprise to him, if not to Rosa, when the ex-coachman and the Janus Woman got together.

'You're such a dolt sometimes,' Rosa had commented, 'for if ever two people were likely to strike it up then it was them.'

Wenzel constantly amazed by his wife's perspicuity in such matters.

Ludmilla and Heraldo marrying a few years previously had been even more of a shock, despite them being thrust into the role of joint parents once they'd taken Hulde in, which was maybe as well for they'd had no other bairns since.

He looked again at Livia, that protective hand upon her belly.

A new life about to be born into the world. A new life he would be required to protect.

He was prevaricating.

Heraldo's plan had seemed foolproof at first glance, but all plans had flaws. Hidden weaknesses someone with the right information could exploit.

The smart move being to get Philbert away as soon as they could, except they'd Advent Theatres to perform. Folk like the Pfiffmaklers always hand to mouth, reliant on one performance to get funds enough to move them on to the next. And they would need funds to get Philbert passage, which meant time.

Which meant they were vulnerable.

He knew what his Old Grandma would have done had she still been at the helm. She'd have thrown the lad to whatever wolves were trailing his spoor, taken whatever reward was still on his misshapen head; had his blasted pig carved up and chucked onto the fire for dinner.

But Wenzel was not his grandmother.

And unlike her and Metternich, Wenzel believed in equality and democracy, the rightness of the fight to relieve the burdens of the common man. As excited by the revolutions a few years back as he had later been disgruntled and ired as the next man when their successes had been so paltry and brief.

And whether this Philbert, this Little Maus, this Anatomist's Dream, had been the one to reduce Maulwerf's Fair of Wonders to rags and ruin because of it, he understood there was no undoing what Heraldo and Ludmilla had done. Philbert had, by their actions, become Wenzel's responsibility whether he liked it or no. Which he did not. But there it was. Hares and boxes.

Time to state his case, add his own adjunct to Heraldo's plan.

Time also to make his own enquiries, see what sifted out of the barrel.

The Island Of The Damned

'St Mary's church is a special place,' Livia was saying, 'so we'll need to get everything exactly right.'

'Special, how?' Hulde asked, her serious face creased in concentration.

'Because, my little linnet,' Livia smiled at Hulde, 'it was the very first church to be built on these islands not long after the Danes converted the pagans here, way back in the 1180s.'

'That's a really long time ago,' Hulde agreed, doing a few quick calculations in her head, 'about as long as I've been alive times forty.'

Livia raising her eyebrows as much as her scars allowed the lifting. Hulde an odd child, given to weighing situations up comparative to her own survival. Perhaps no surprise, given how close to dying she'd been on several occasions and in such awful ways.

'It actually doesn't sound so long when you put it like that,' Livia commented, running her fingers through Hulde's hair. 'Forty of your lifetimes! Imagine that. You're a mighty deep thinker for one so young.'

'Not so young now,' Hulde argued. 'Eleven years since Ludmilla and Heraldo found us.'

True enough, Livia thought. She and Hulde adopted into the Pfiffmakler clan about the same time. No one celebrating birth dates, no one paying their age much mind, but every year she and Hulde holding their own small celebration of thanksgiving, picking the third of May as their common starting point, the day that had brought them all definitively together. The two taking a long walk together, usually spent in contemplative silence as each appreciated the sky, the trees, the flowers, the birds, the happiness they'd gained at the very moment in both their lives they'd believed all was lost.

At the furthest point of their walk they always stopped for a picnic, exchanged small gifts. Livia fingering the bracelet Hulde had given her on their most recent outing, made of pieces of glass threaded on a thong.

'This is wonderful!' Livia had exclaimed. 'You must have been collecting them for months!'

And polishing them, she'd thought, and spending hours carefully boring a hole through each one.

'There's eleven,' Hulde explained, 'one for each year we've been together.'

Livia's eyes filling with tears to be given such a considered gift so long in the making.

'Forty of your lifetimes,' she said, with a sniff. 'I'm glad to be sharing one.'

Rewarded by one of Hulde's rare smiles breaking across her face like a rainbow suddenly appearing, quieting the storm.

'I really like the Hildegard songs we're doing this year,' Hulde said, 'and isn't it real odd they must have been composed about the same time St Mary's was built?'

Livia frowned. It hadn't occurred to her, yet Hulde was right. According to the booklet Pietro had garnered St Mary's foundation stones were laid in 1185, the church completed in 1193, and Hildegard dying in Rupertsberg near Bingen in 1179 just past her eighty-first year. Over forty of Hulde's lifetimes ago, which meant less than twenty of Livia's own.

She shivered.

It seemed impossible seven centuries could be calculated to appear so near, yet that's what Hulde had done, as if Hulde were tying all those years together like she'd threaded the polished pieces of glass onto the thong about Livia's wrist.

'Come on you,' Livia said, trying to shake the thought. 'Let's get Ludmilla over and run through your first song. Your descant's really coming along.'

'Do you think so?' Hulde looking up at Livia, expectant. Ludmilla teaching her how to sing being one of the greatest joys of this new life, never mind it had put Longhella's nose completely out of joint, and Longhella, Ludmilla's sister, never her greatest fan.

'I do,' Livia assured and, right on cue, Ludmilla appeared waving a piece of paper in her hand.

'You'll never guess what Heraldo's just found out!' Ludmilla exclaimed as she approached them, looking a little strained as she always did whenever she found Hulde and Livia together, never quite understanding their bond and certainly not their May-Day trysts from which they shut everyone else out. Rallying quickly.

'I'm sure you're going to tell us,' Livia replied, getting to her feet, Ludmilla obviously excited.

'It's extraordinary!' she went on. 'You know the Jaromar fellow who was made first Danish overlord of this place? The one who built St Mary's?' Not waiting for Livia to answer. 'Well he only went and married someone called Hildegard, illegitimate daughter of King Canute of Denmark. And both Jaromar and Hildegard are buried in St Mary's, their gravestones embedded into the walls!'

'Don't see what you're getting so worked up about.' Longhella appeared, trailing on her sister's heels. 'It's only history and dust, folk long dead and gone.' Shaking out her skirt as if to rid it of them. Ludmilla tutting beneath her breath, trying to be patient. They'd used to be so close when they were younger, but these last few years Longhella had soured like a lemon fallen too quickly from its branch. All to do with Old Grandma leaving and Hulde joining them, both facts ripping Longhella's life down the middle, dividing her from the rest of the family. A distance Longhella seemed to deliberately cultivate despite everyone trying their darndest to put it right.

'It means we've a connection,' Ludmilla sighed, the joy sucked out of her revelation, keeping it short. 'Their Hildegard and our Hildegard.'

'Why should they care?' Longhella demanded. 'They're two completely different people who never even met.'

'Names are important,' Hulde began in Ludmilla's defence, lowering her eyes as Longhella swiveled her gimlet gaze towards the girl.

'Don't you start all that Beloved nonsense, you little toad,' Longhella shot back. 'We only picked Hulde because it was the first name that came to mind. And we had to call you something, seeing as how you never volunteered one of your own.'

Hulde hung her head, for it was true. Huge tranches of her past missing, her name only one of them. Heraldo had explained it was no wonder, her being so young when they'd found her and in such unusual circumstance; how children rarely have any coherent memories before the age of five, their brains not wired that way, needing room to accommodate new experiences coming along on a daily basis.

'It's all about learning when you're young, not memory,' he'd assured her. 'Why, I can't recall anything at all before I was about six or seven, when father and some mad astronomer had me sitting on a freezing cold mountain where we saw a meteorite strike the moon.'

'Your first ever memory?' Hulde had asked. 'Are you sure?'

'Sure as my second is Ludmilla trying to shove an entire apple inside my mouth to see if it would fit!'

Heraldo had not been lying. He'd never met anyone who had more than fragments of their early childhood and, even then, no more than vague flickers across a blurry screen. The single exception being a master mnemonist who'd claimed very little was lost from him, and proved it plenty of times, and even he only went back to the grand old age of three.

'We were just about to practise our first song,' Livia intervened. 'And Longhella, I've been meaning to ask. How would you feel about doing a solo at the end of the first set?'

In the old days Longhella would have jumped at the chance. Now she recognised that chance for what it was: scraps from other people's plates.

'Oh, don't mind if I do. If you're sure I'm up to it.'

Livia shook her head.

'We all know you've a beautiful voice,' she countered. 'We're just never sure you can be bothered to learn all the words.'

Longhella pouted, which did no favours to her otherwise pretty face. Even Lupercal, her cousin, who'd formerly fawned on her every word, no longer sought out her company and instead—which

Longhella found hard to swallow—was beginning to find Hulde a better target for his admiration.

'Best make sure it's short, then,' Longhella replied, before heading off on her way.

'That girl,' Livia muttered.

'That young woman,' Ludmilla corrected, 'and don't judge her too harshly, Livia. She's never been one for change, ever since she was little. Thought things would go on and on as always. Hated it when I differed how I plaited my hair and she felt she had to follow suit.'

Like a rock on top of a mountain, she thought, *who suddenly finds herself at the bottom and can't understand how she's got there, and can't figure out how to get herself back up again.*

Understanding Longhella better than Longhella did herself and pitying her for it, for being unable to forgive Hulde, or Ludmilla come to that. Longhella could have left the Pfiffmaklers several times, had been given generous offers of courtship despite her being prickly as a hedge of blackthorn, but no. Intimacy was not for her. Longhella had made that clear and plain. Seemingly unable but to stay put with the Pfiffmaklers despite herself, as if her bitterness towards them was all that got her up in the morning, wound her up and gave her the grace to move and breathe.

You'll never find white flour in a coal sack.

One of Old Grandma's sayings, and never so true as now.

Longhella blacker than coal and getting blacker with every day.

Ludmilla needing to know it would not always be so.

That Longhella could be saved.

The ghost of an idea taking shape in her head. An idea as insidious and vague as the fog rolling in from the Baltic, but there nonetheless.

In the forest of Jasmund, Philbert, like Wenzel, had been having hard thoughts.

He knew nothing, unlike Wenzel, about Metternich's repatriation to German soil.

Had he known that fact he would never have taken Heraldo up on his offer of help.

Would have carried on his nomadic existence, he and Kroonk together and nobody else. Should have abandoned Kroonk way back after the disasters at the Westphal but could not, despite her being with him an obvious aid to anyone who might still be tracking him, if anyone still was. Which he doubted. Could not be sure if anyone had ever been tracking him in the first place. Had thought long about the presumption of guilt the massacre at the Ice Fair in Schleswig-Holstein carried with it, and still couldn't make up his mind. Still reasoned how easily it could have been coincidence and nothing whatsoever to do with him.

Nevertheless prudent to assume it was.

In the first year, following the winter of 1848, he'd disguised his little Kroonk, made for her a coat of fur so she could pass for a dog at a distance; a disguise cobbled together by killing a couple of strays and taking their pelts, sewing them crudely to form a covering he had strapped about her. Not a pleasant job, but nothing had been pleasant back then. And a disguise only working at a distance, which was the closest to anyone he ever chose to be.

Until now.

He unfolded the small piece of paper that had been thrust into his pocket by a street urchin in Rostock, gone without comment or need of any tip. Which was as well, for Philbert had nothing to give. Had been living off the land all this time, him and Kroonk getting gaunt and skinny. Muscles locking in, all fat gone. Had been thinking it might have been a long enough time that he could return to the places he knew well, look up whatever remained of Maulwerf's Fair of Wonders, thank them for all they had done for him.

His missive from Heraldo changing his mind.

Had been at first unsure what to make of that little scrap of paper.

Immediate thought being to crumple it up, chuck it away and would have done so had not two things happened: firstly, looking at Kroonk in her pathetic ill-fitting fur pelt, replaced several times over, each a little more artful, but a bad ruse all the same. Latterly he'd constructed a small handcart-come-crate in which he could hide her whenever they had to pass near towns or large bodies of people.

Secondly, and more chillingly, was what he'd heard that very morning. Balladeers singing their songs, his humming trailing to a stop as he caught the final verses:

The prisoners cried and protested in their gaols
As the prisoners wept for their travails;
The soldiers levelling their guns

At the heads of fathers, brothers, and sons;
Until came the Little Mouse with his Fair,
Who had no fear for Metternich the bear,
Who crept into the gaol at dawn
And freed the brave heroes of Lengerrborn.
The Little Mouse who poisoned the Schupos with his wine
As if led by hand Divine.
As if led by hand Divine,
Our Little Mouse with his poisoned wine.

Philbert's legs shaking, heart pounding so fast he'd almost fainted. Unaware his life-story had become the backdrop to many of the legends following the revolutions of 1848. The Little Maus, as he'd been dubbed back then, arriving at the prison in Lengerrborn where the survivors of the Westphal Club had been brought. Every last one of them due to be executed at noon, all deemed traitors, followers of Von Ebner. Edict issued on the orders of Prince Metternich, arch-autocrat, who had hated and despised Von Ebner for the very many years Von Ebner had been working against him.

None of this known by Philbert, who had never heard of Metternich.

Knew Von Ebner only by name, and that brief sight of him in the Westphal when all had gone so wrong.

Knew not what he was handing over to the prison guards, nor what Metternich had ordered to be done.

His old mentor, Kwert, scooped up with all the rest; Kwert the one to urge Philbert away from the Westphal, pointing him in the direction of the kitchens. Philbert performing a paltry kindness in return, scraping up some cold meat and a bottle of wine to ease what for Kwert was going to be dreadful morning before, Philbert naively assumed, it all got sorted out and Kwert was released. Handing his gifts for Kwert to the gaolers.

Oh Philbert, you innocent! You truly believed they would pass them on to your friend!

But of course not, maybe the meat, but never the wine, given what the gaolers would soon have to do. Which did not sit well with them. Would make of them pariahs in the town. Cursing Metternich's soldiers for tasking them with the execution of a yardful of prisoners on Metternich's personal orders; a spiteful, vengeful whim designed to terrify any more of Von Ebner's followers who might choose to rise up against the puffed-up prink Metternich.

So no.

Not the wine.

And the wine—the balladeers having it right—poisoned.

Philbert knew not how nor why, only that two of those gaolers died hideously right before his eyes and the other become severely incapacitated. Kwert, who'd been brought into the Guards' Room ostensibly to receive Philbert's gifts, in reality to say his goodbyes to the lad—those guards still having hearts—as horrified as Philbert. Which did not stop Kwert drawing back the heavy bolts and heaving open the doors to the yard, whereupon all those prisoners who'd been counting down the minutes, shaking and sweating, skin the colour of flour that has not been in a coal sack, were released. A thousand hurried thanks upon their bloodless lips before they flooded out onto the streets of Lengerrborn, from where they drained away like so much water down a sinkhole.

A farcical, bathetic end to what should have been one of Metternich's major strikes against the insurgents. A personal insult and injury to his perceived power base, which incident had precipitated his road to disgrace and exile, to wrath and dire retribution towards the Little Maus who had poisoned the Schupos with his wine as if led by hand Divine.

The entire scenario flashing through Philbert's head as the small audience began to clap their loud approval for the balladeers' recitation, shouting out the last lines several times.

Philbert getting out of that place as fast as he could, keeping his hat down, keeping his head hidden, keeping Kroonk within her crate. So all the more reason to mistrust the message he'd found thrust into his pocket later that day referencing that same song.

To our Little Maus with your poisoned wine. If it's really you, we want to help.

Get yourself to the village nearby Stralsund that has the Joshua Tree. We'll be there two days before Advent. Wait in the forest. Go down to the pier before dawn and we'll take you over the water.

From a Higgledy Piggledy friend.

Would have ignored it had he not recognised the last reference, for he knew Higgledy Piggledy. An outfit Maulwerf's Fair had occasionally come across in the old days.

Philbert's past life, given the enthusiasm of that overheard song, possibly catching up with him, and only this little scrap of paper, these few cryptic lines, standing between himself and the maw of history ready to swallow him and Kroonk down its fearful gullet.

Maybe his last chance of getting out of its way.

Taking that chance.

Heraldo Pfiffmakler true to his word. Heraldo at the jetty of the Joshua Tree village, taking Philbert, the Anatomist's Dream, the Little Maus, across the water to the Island of the Damned.

The First Face of Fear: Tiny Portraits, Tiny Lives

St Mary's was packed wall to wall, pew after pew.

First day of the Pfiffmaklers'—of the Benedettas'—Advent Cycle, and everyone in Bergen up for it, everyone excited.

'Welcome ladies and gents!' Wenzel begins his spiel. 'We're honoured to be here and hope to do you proud, give you the greatest Advent Cycle you've ever seen!'

Not hard, given there'd been no Advent Cycle here in living memory. The Pfiffmaklers making best use of that knowledge and adapting, as always, to local circumstance.

'We've been amazed by your island, by your church, your extraordinary history,' Wenzel continues, to murmurs of approval from the crowd, 'and so we'll begin with one of your very own folk tales. Follow me,' he says, as a large bright star ascends behind him into the darkened eaves, its supporting wires so thin they're invisible, 'to narrow dwellings, where the heart grows faint and weary. To dreary places where men have lost their names.'

His audience shivering as the first backdrop is illuminated: a grim place, shadowy ginnels, high prison walls.

'See the windows set in the walls, long rows of them, like the deep-set eyes of sleepy old men, and yet, and yet...'

A light comes on behind one window and then another and another, the audience audibly intaking breath as they begin to recognise the tale.

'And what are behind these windows?' Wenzel asks and then informs them. 'Prisoners. Rules and regulations to be rigidly observed, numbers and crimes...'

A curtain lifting to reveal Pietro cowering in his cell.

'And what is he dreaming of, this nameless man?' asks Wenzel.

'I'm dreaming of what I've done,' Pietro answers dully. 'On a Christmas past when I—'

'But wait! Who is this?' Wenzel demands as Livia comes on stage with her visibly swollen belly, leading a lamb on a tether.

'Oh my Lord!' she cries out. 'What am I to do? My child is so close to entering this world and I've no home to provide for it, and no father...'

The veiled Christmas lesson lost on no one.

'She's to sell her most precious of possessions,' Wenzel goes on for her.

Enter a swirling crowd of Lupercal, Jericho, Peppe and Ludmilla, all shouting loudly, offering money, keen to get a lamb they can slaughter, gut, and roast for their Christmas table.

'And so she gets her money!'

Bickering and bartering, Livia holding up a handful of paper notes in triumph; the reveling crowd swaying to one side, holding their lamb aloft in triumph.

'So all is well for her...until...'

Pietro up from his cell, re-enacting his crime, running through the crowd, snatching the money from Livia's hand and leaping off stage, the crowd of barterers chasing him, baying on his heels.

Stop thief! they're yelling. *Stop and stop!*

'But he's stolen it! Stolen everything!' Livia quails, unable to bear the loss. 'What is to become of me?'

Huge bang, and a pluff of purple smoke as the crowd drags Pietro back on stage in irons.

'Our prisoner,' Wenzel shouts. 'Denied a name! Called only Number 101. A spoiled man! A spoiled life! Narrow years condemned to be lived in a narrow room, sleeping on a narrow bed in a narrow cell. So what do we do, ladies and gentlemen? Because right now, right here, on this very day, he's served his time. He's done his years! Do we condemn him further, or do we set him free?'

The crowd in St Mary's don't know which way to turn.

They've been challenged, and the star in the firmament up above them has begun to glow, to spit out sparks, and they're transfixed, turning their eyes up towards it.

'We've to let him go! He's served his sentence!' someone shouts.

'We've to let him rot,' another argues. 'He's Prisoner Number 101 and it always ends badly in every tale I've ever heard.'

'Just as his stupid dreams of bringing a white-wooled lambikin back home with a golden collar, is what I remember,' a third person adds.

'And dreams is only dreams,' yells a fourth, 'and no good ever comes of them.'

'What about the poor woman he stole from?' shouts a lone voice. 'Surely he might as well have condemned her and her child to death!'

Darkness rolling down over Pietro, now back in his cell, until cries out a further voice: the woman in her raggedy dress reappearing, the pregnant woman from whom he'd stolen the money after she'd sold her lamb.

'But it's Christmas,' the raggedy woman pleads, beatific, holding out her hands to the audience.

'Not yet, it ain't,' some wag reminds from the crowd. 'Let him hang, is what I say.'

'And what of the rest?' Wenzel tasks the audience. 'How do you judge? And what says the star that has led us to this place? Shone its light into the darkest places, into the narrow room, onto the narrow bed and the shallow man who has no name?'

'It's telling us forgiveness,' says a woman close to the scene of the action.

'It's doing nothing of the sort,' retorts the man sitting next to her, who would have skelped her royally had they been at home.

'Isn't it telling us,' Wenzel asks, in the spirit of the season, 'that we're all human? That desperate situations bring on desperate actions? That we all make mistakes, all of us a hair's breadth away from being the raggedy woman or Prisoner Number 101?'

'My name is Jaromar!' Prisoner Number 101 suddenly yells out, and the audience look intrigued, for the tale has taken an unexpected turn into their most sacred history. 'My name forgotten by all but you!'

Sweeping out an arm to indicate the audience.

'My name is Jaromar,' he repeats, 'the man who converted us from our pagan ways, brought us into the light!'

And the light is really shining now, the star become a sun, glittering with red and orange halos, illuminating the darkened scene below. The audience entranced, no idea how the pyrotechnics are being done.

'And my name is Hildegard.' The raggedy woman moves forward, puts her hand through the bars of the prison window, Pietro standing to grasp it, kissing it with such unfeigned tenderness the audience are torn.

'She's forgiving him,' a woman sighs, 'so shouldn't we do the same?'

'She's a blasted idiot!' a man cries out. 'He's skinned her once and he'll skin her twice, first chance he gets.'

All this time Livia has been in profile, showing the good half of her face; now she turns towards the audience who gasp to see her so divided, the Janus Woman fully revealed, her scars livid, ugly, and unquestionably real.

'I've already been skinned,' she explains, as she brings Pietro/Jaromar to her side. 'Like the pagans here of old, when our lives were darker than these streets, narrower than these cells between these narrow prison walls. Like we all were before Jaromar lifted the veil and set us free.'

'And set us free!' Jaromar echoes loudly by her side, 'and wed me to Hildegard and to the truth, and to the Way of the One True Overlord, to our Saviour Jesus Christ.'

'By the light of the star,' Wenzel begins to wind up the first part of the show, 'and by the wisdom of your very own folk tales, here is our first Advent lesson…'

'To trust in our Lord,' Livia/Hildegard says.

'To believe in our hopes and dreams,' Pietro/Jaromar avers.

'To know the Christmas spirit begins right here and right now!'

Wenzel is in no doubt, nor is the star above him which explodes, firing out great arcs of light as it disintegrates. The backdrop quickly changing, Jaromar and Hildegard now on their knees, holding hands, plighting their troth, and so obvious the love between them that even the blackest heart within the audience is momentarily mute.

Ludmilla and Hulde piping up in the wings, performing one of Hildegard of Bingen's songs from her *Symphonia Armonie Celestium Revelationum*. The entire church stilling as they sing.

How precious her womb,
A closed and lifeless tomb
Until flooded by warmth divine,
When sprang a flower from within

Pietro placing a gentle hand upon Livia's swollen belly, a sight so moving many of the women present shed a small tear...

The Son of God coming like the dawn
To her chamber on Christmas morn.
So behold the green shoot of Christ and arise,
For He alone can bring us into Paradise.

Pietro and Livia rising slowly up and up—timing is everything—so it seems they're floating above the makeshift stage as a swirl of green smoke envelops them from their feet upwards. Last sight for the audience being Jaromar and Hildegard exchanging a chaste kiss—for they're in a church after all—and the backdrop is suddenly transfigured into a bucolic scene that might have been the Garden of Eden itself, Jaromar and Hildegard thereby become Adam and Eve, the first truly Christian souls to walk upon the earth of the Island of Rügen.

Paradise brought inside the walls of St Mary's, and a cracking start to their Advent Cycle. The audience enthusiastically joining in the chorus lines to what should have been Longhella's starring solo:

Down in yon forest I saw a hall,
   —and the bells of Paradise,
   I heard them ring—
Covered all over in purple and gold
   —and I love my Lord Jesus above everything;

And in that hall there stands a bed,

> *—and the bells of Paradise, I heard them ring—*
> *Covered all over with scarlet so red,*
> *—and I love my Lord Jesus above everything…*

Purple and gold, scarlet and red: the sunset glowering and intense, as seems only to occur in winter. Bells ringing out from the village Mergim has tramped towards these past few weeks on his roundabout route, the last letter he has to deliver tucked inside his jacket pocket. All the way here he's visited the families of those sons, husbands, fathers, brothers, lost to them behind the vast walls of Kragujevac, and blesses now the duty, for when he'd flipped through the letters, addressed usually with only name and village or town, he'd come across this last and his memory jogged, heart jagging with hope, finding a place to begin his search: the place the Pfiffmaklers had started from before they'd found Hulde. A place whose name he might not otherwise have remembered.

Mergim arriving in Osijek on the River Drava as the *fašnik*, the Croatian Christmas season, is almost over; the men packing away their stilts, the masked processions done, the night closing down the lid upon their Shrove Tuesday celebrations.

He doesn't really expect the Pfiffmaklers to be here, but does the rounds looking for them, asking about them, if anyone has seen them recently, where they might be, where their annual circuit might take them.

'The Pfiffmaklers!' says one old cove. 'Now there's a name I haven't heard in years!'

He takes a good pinch of the tobacco Mergim offers him, eyeing with covetous curiosity the pouch made from the webbed foot of an albatross gifted to Mergim by one of his fellow inmates in Kragujevac.

'But you know them?' Mergim persists.

The old cove laughs, croaks like an ancient toad newly emerged from winter mud.

'I'll say! The stories that went the rounds after they came back from Italy which was…well, I don't know when. Quite a few years back.'

'But you've heard of them since?' Mergim asks.

The old man gets his pipe going, weighing up his reply.

'Well, yes and no is the answer to that.'

Mergim waits. Has learned a lot about waiting in Kragujevac where it seemed waiting was all he'd done: waiting for bad coffee to boil on the tiny flame of their burner, waiting for someone to make a chess move, waiting for the loud report of a bullet as one or another of their cohorts were put against a wall and shot for contravening some petty rule.

Waiting for release.

'Now let me see,' the old man says, puffing placidly at his pipe. 'They come back here the year following all that broo-haha, and we was mighty glad to see them. Heroes, they were, after delivering up that war criminal. He always was a black-hearted son-of-a-bitch.'

Spitting from the side of his mouth.

Mergim's heart beating a little faster.

'Fought with him, I did,' the old man went on, 'back in the day. Back in the bad old days, and he was wily as a fox outside a chicken coop.'

And so much Mergim could have said on that front, but did not.

Mergim waiting.

Mergim not disappointed.

'Well, like I said,' the man explained. 'Back they came, but this weren't never their natural stamping grounds. Seem to recall they was heading back into Germany, going up the Danube. Ain't never seen 'em from that day to this, more's the pity. Real fine girls they had with 'em. Was hoping to marry off one of me grandsons to the oldest, but she wasn't having none of it.'

Another cackle of toad-laugh.

'Not that I were surprised,' the man added, 'them lads being no lookers, and couldn't none of them recite a wooing poem if I'd inscribed it on a brick and hung it about their miserable necks.'

Another puff, another cackle.

'But know who you should speak with? Man named Valter Poppelmann. And he'll be just around the corner. Find the nearest tavern and you'll find Valter. Look for a pool of puke, and he'll not be far.'

Mergim so surprised it was all he could do to keep his footing. Couldn't believe his luck. Tapped at his throat, at the string from which he kept another keepsake from Kragujevac. A tiny embroidered picture of St Leonard, patron saint of prisoners, barely the size of his thumbnail. Created by a man who spent his nights carefully unravelling the threads from a multi-coloured sock and poking those threads in and out through scraps of linen with a sharpened nail. So detailed you could see the prison walls rising up behind St Leonard's head like a dark halo, with tiny pale pinpricks of windows and, at one, a minute face that might have belonged to Prisoner 101, or Mergim, or the man who had created such a miniature wonder from weave and weft.

'I thought he travelled with them? With the Pfiffmaklers, I mean,' Mergim finally got out, for that had certainly been Valter's intent as he recalled it.

The old man looked pointedly at Mergim's tobacco pouch, hanging like a tantalising fruit from Mergim's belt. Mergim took the hint, offered it over, the man taking as much as he could get between finger and thumb and stuffing it into the bowl of his pipe so hard it extinguished what was already burning and would have to be loosened, repacked, to get any smoke out of it again. Mergim smiling tightly. Let the man have his tobacco. He was earning it.

'Well then, thank you,' the old man said, without a lick of shame. 'And yes you're right. There was that big trial, and my, that was a spectacle, right and proper. Didn't get to attend it meself, not with me bones the way they are and not fit for travelling, but heard about it from plenty others. Place packed from floor to rafters. That bastard traitor finally getting what he deserved.'

No need to tell Mergim, who'd been there, been a witness; had his own trial conducted back to back. And the old man right. You couldn't have slipped an eel or the lithest of otters into the crowd who'd gathered in Kragujevac Courthouse once word was out.

'Like I said,' the old man went on, sucking at his extinguished pipe, 'Valter was kinda the star witness, along with some other fellow whose name I don't mind...'

Mine, Mergim could have informed him. *It's my name you don't mind.*

'Anywise, he come here with the Pfiffmaklers the following year, like I already said, and looked fit to stay with 'em. Then came back a few years after with his tail between his legs. Seems his uncle died, far as I recall. And he's kinda been here ever since.'

Valter Poppelmann knew he was going to be sick. Again. He didn't know why he still did this. Didn't know why he had to keep drinking so much his own body was coerced to be prison guard, force the drink back up and out of him to keep itself from dying. Felt wretched every minute of every day, every minute of every night, except when he was lying passed out on a bench or a floor, or in some decrepit barn that would have felt as wretched as himself had it been sentient.

He knew he'd always been weak, and despised himself for it. Should have felt liberated after he'd joined the Pfiffmaklers, should have come back to life.

Not the way it had gone.

The trial making him a pariah, even amongst the Pfiffmaklers who already knew the worst and still welcomed him with open arms. Or most of them. He'd thought that staying with them, staying with Andreas, the man who'd become his guardian, might allow him to become a normal human being, but he'd learned that no. That was never going to happen. He was never going to be one of their happy clappy family. Not then, and absolutely not after Andreas had died so wretchedly, his limbs twisted with arthritis so he could no longer walk, let alone do up a belt buckle or take off his socks.

'It's time,' Andreas had whispered to Valter one night as Valter came in to lift Andreas onto the bucket he used as a toilet. 'I can't go on. I won't go on. Not like this.'

'Please don't leave me,' Valter had pleaded, cradling Andreas in his arms as he took him from bucket back to bed. 'I can't bear to be alone.'

'You're not alone,' Andreas soothed. 'You've all the Pfiffmaklers. But me? I've only you, Valter. No one else to see me right.'

They'd talked about it often, about the time Andreas would find going on harder than the alternative. Andreas making the going easier by pointing at the pocket his crabbed fingers could no longer reach into, at the vial he could no longer grasp and certainly not take the lid off. A vial whose contents Andreas had prepared a long time back for this precise moment.

'I don't want you to go,' Valter had whispered, Valter kneeling at the side of the bed of the man he'd called uncle for so many years. Andreas placing his hand upon Valter's stark red hair that stood up like the spines of an irritated hedgehog.

'Iritch,' Andreas replied. 'I'm all hedgehoggery. Promise me you'll never go down that road, for it's not been a good one.'

Valter brimming with tears.

'Please don't leave me,' Valter tried again. 'Please don't make me do it. I'll get Wenzel or Heraldo…they're strong. They're—'

'It's me and you,' Andreas made the situation clear. 'It's your gift to me. And no greater gift you could be giving.'

'I don't want you to go. I can't bear it!'

Valter sounding like the turbulent child he'd always been, all broken up inside, grown into a man devoid of common purpose or common need. A boy smashed to pieces long before he'd become a man, Andreas the only anchor to his wretched life. And now Andreas choosing to leave him to it.

'It won't take long,' Andreas assured him. 'It'll only be minutes.'

Valter giving in. Valter taking the vial from Andreas's pocket and the cork from the vial, pouring the contents into a glass of wine. Andreas certain on that point.

'Has to be something I like drinking, and you and me? We've swallowed our fair share.'

'Please don't…' Valter tried again. Andreas would not be moved.

'I can't get to the toilet on my own. I can't buckle a belt or tie a shoe. I'm no longer a showman but a burden. And I've never ever wanted to be that. Goodbye, my fine young boy. And remember that I always thought you fine. Time to make your life what it should have been.'

'Uncle!' Valter calls, but Andreas has grasped the glass between the twisted fingers of both hands and brought it to his mouth, tipped its contents down his throat. One last act he can do for himself.

'Be a good boy. Make me proud.'

'Uncle!' Valter shouts, several members of the Pfiffmakler crew running towards his tent because of it, the several members of the Pfiffmakler crew getting there to find Andreas taking a God Almighty fit that has his eyes rolling up into his head so all you can see are the whites crackled over with blood like an old oil painting, feet kicking hard enough to dislodge his boots. And then dead. Nothing to be done but lever up a weeping Valter from his side, get the body wrapped and into the ground.

They were in a pretty spot, halfway between Black Forest and Black Sea, between Vienna and Budapest. A soft-leaved glade of linden and sweet chestnuts, which was where they buried Andreas, on the edge where the soil was easiest dug and a cairn easily erected so they—if no one else—would know where he lay if they ever passed this way again. Peppe topping the cairn off with a hedgehog he'd carved from a lime bough, with the initials AZ on its flat base.

Valter going with them when they left the following morning, and staying with them a few months more although it was obvious he was floundering.

'We've got to help him,' Ludmilla said to Wenzel, to Heraldo, to anyone who would listen. No one knew how. Everyone recognising the truism that one straw can become many, becomes too many, and eventually collapses the roof. Valter collapsing right before their eyes. Last straw for Valter being the awful pity Ludmilla poured on him at every turn, with every glance, with every light-hearted conversation she tried to engage him in.

'You've to stop it,' Livia advised Ludmilla. 'I know you mean well but, honestly, you're only making things worse.'

'How can I stop it?' Ludmilla, soft-hearted creature, had argued. 'He's one of us, he's part of—'

'Isn't that the point?' Livia interrupted. 'He's not one of us. He's so far from being one of us that—'

'But you managed it,' Ludmilla was adamant. 'You and Pietro. You've seen terrible things, suffered terrible things. Maybe you should speak to him. In fact that's it! It should be you who—'

'You can't fix a person by wishing it,' Livia cut her off, no one knowing the truth of it better than the Janus Woman. Time to spell it out. Put the girl straight. Raising her voice, sharpened by anger and impatience. 'He's not a child, Ludmilla, and neither are you. People aren't puppets who can be given a new lick of paint, get their strings fixed, dance to whatever tune you choose to give them.'

Ludmilla blinking at the rebuke, about to remonstrate. Livia getting there first.

'I know I sound harsh, but that's the truth of it. Do you think I'd look like this if I could have wished it away?'

Ludmilla looking at Livia, at the scars that had boiled off half of her face.

'No, is the answer to that,' Livia went on. 'But if I could have, and if I had and if it had succeeded? Well, where would I be now? Answer me that.'

Ludmilla frowned.

'Back home with your family?'

'Back home with my family. Precisely,' Livia agreed. 'And what would that have gained me? What would my life have been like if I'd stayed?'

Ludmilla shook her head, bewildered by the question, for who wouldn't want to not have a face like Livia's? Who wouldn't choose instead to be with their family? Livia explicating the situation for her.

'I'd have had a dull and boring life. I'd have married whichever man my parents thought me suitable for. I'd have worked on the farm, pushed out children who would have carried on living dull and boring lives just like I would have done. So tell me this, Ludmilla, and think about this hard. Which life do you think I would rather have lived if I'd had the choice at the start of it? If I'd known everything that would happen? That one, or this?'

This one, was Ludmilla's immediate reaction. *This one, where you've found us and you've found Pietro and are happy, joyous at the breaking of every day.*

'This one,' Livia concluded the lesson for her. 'No one knows what will occur around the next corner. No one knows what might have been if only this or that had or hadn't happened. Fact is,' Livia said, 'that's how life is. And how it's got to be for Valter. You can't tell him how to live his life. He's his own corners to go around and for Christ's sake, child, you've to give him leave to do exactly that.'

And several weeks later Valter had done exactly that.

Left the Pfiffmaklers, turned from the way they were and the way they were going, retreated down the Danube, lingering by the cairn beneath which Andreas was buried like Valter was some old dog who couldn't bear to leave his master. Spending long days leaning against the stones, chewing lime leaves and dry chestnuts for sustenance, trying to find the core of himself, the fine young boy Andreas believed he had been, how to become the fine young man Andreas believed him capable of being, who would make Andreas proud.

The task proving too onerous and unfathomable. Valter retracing his steps back to Osijek. Valter unable to find his own path out.

No lick of paint nor mended strings for Valter.
Valter as pathetic a man as he had ever been.

Carols, Hummingbirds And Bad Disguises

'They only went and killed my blasted solo,' Longhella was complaining, for the third or fourth time.

'Oh do be quiet about it,' Rosa admonished. 'It's a grand thing they knew the carol and felt moved enough to join in.'

'Blasted bells of blasted Paradise,' Longhella muttered. 'Might as well have had the real thing, the racket that lot were making.'

'That lot,' Rosa replied shortly, 'are paying our wages, so best button your lip.'

Lord, the girl was infuriating.

'And what's it all about anyway?' Longhella wasn't to be stopped. 'Barns and beds, moonlight streaming in through windows over thorn trees? What's any of it to do with Christmas?'

'It's a transposition of an old chivalric poem,' Pietro explained. 'In the original the maid on the stone is mourning her dying knight; in the carol the dying lord becomes Christ and the maid becomes the Madonna—'

'Oh that's so wrong I don't know where to begin!' Longhella interrupted. She might be infuriating, dull-witted she was not. 'That means the lover becomes the mother. Doesn't anyone else have a problem with that?'

Pietro smiled.

'It is a bit of stretch,' he agreed, 'but that's the way with Christianity. Gobbles up everything in its path and adapts it to circumstance. Like we do.'

'Like the Pfiffmaklers do, you mean,' Longhella countered, although no bitterness there, no real meaning to exclude him, for she liked Pietro. She hadn't meant to like him, had gone out of her way to find something wrong with him, especially after he'd hooked up with Livia Benedetta who she couldn't stand. The fact remaining that Pietro was a likeable fellow, the person who'd spent the most time with Old Grandma Pfiffmakler after she'd chosen to leave the Kunterbunt. Pietro the one person who'd recognised Longhella's deep loss at Grandma's leaving and knew a fair bit more about that leaving than the rest. Pietro delivering Old Grandma to the Redemptorists and, afterwards, deciding to transform himself from carriage driver to actor upon the stage.

A decision Old Grandma had been a part of, directing him on his path.

And anything that was a part of Old Grandma was a part of Longhella.

The two always close, far more so than any of the other Pfiffmaklers understood.

The two of them scattered from the same corn, grown from the same seed.

Longhella thinking often on what Old Grandma had told her before she went:

Be good, my dear. You're the one I shall miss the most; and don't throw yourself at the first fancy man that takes your sway, and don't let anyone—not anyone—tell you what you thinks is wrong.

Pietro confirming it.

'She talked about you a lot,' he'd said to Longhella, a few nights after he'd caught the Pfiffmaklers up after months of tracking them, long after Valter and Mergim and the prisoner they were taking had departed for Serbia—about which Longhella cared less than an owl does the mouse it spears up from the gloaming grass.

'And let me tell you this,' he'd confided. 'She's an extraordinary woman.'

Longhella's throat constricting so much she couldn't speak. Pietro carrying on.

'And not only because she met a saint, or the man who would become one, and not only because she was witness to his miracles, or because the Archbishop singled her out; but because she's her own miracle. An extraordinary woman in her own right, and maybe her own saint in the making.'

At which Longhella could have laughed out loud, for the idea was too ludicrous, until Pietro said what he did next, not working for an Archbishop without some of the religious in him taking hold.

'That's when it happens, Longhella, right at the end of life. Right at the end, when you finally weigh up what you've done, when you deem what has been worthy and what hasn't, when you've enough perspective to sift the good from the bad. And do you know what she told me?'

Longhella didn't, feared she was about to be thrown headlong through the gates of hell.

'Of all of you, of all you Pfiffmaklers, you were the one of whom she was most proud because you're strong, know your own mind, just like her. And of all of you, and I know I'm not one of you, that I've only just found you…' Pietro a thirty-year-old man with a straggling beard who'd only recently taken part tangentially in one of the Pfiffmakler dramas and fervently wanted to be part of them again. 'Of all of you,' he went on, 'I feel I know you best, because Old Grandma talked on you, spoke on you, worried about you.'

Told me, in no uncertain terms that if ever I hooked up with the Pfiffmaklers it was you, Longhella, I was to oversee. Take your side, listen to your reasoning, now she isn't here to do it herself.

'What did she say?' Longhella asked, trying to stop her tears because she was truly moved, and it took a lot to move the likes of Longhella who'd always been the centre of her own universe, who always saw the world in black and white as if there were no different shades of horses, only zebras stamping through her world.

She's going to fall hard one day, Pietro, Grandma had said. *One day she's going to meet the wrong man, or maybe the right one, but either way, when it hits her, it'll be to her like she's fallen down a well. No getting back out. All or nothing, will be how she sees it. And that's when she'll need you most.*

'She told me to look out for you,' Pietro said simply. 'Told me to be her eyes and ears and that, Longhella, is what I intend to do.'

And so he had, taking Longhella's side when no one else would, a fact that had mystified many of the Pfiffmaklers, excepting Longhella and, although Longhella would never have admitted it, Livia Benedetta too. A woman who, in Longhella's view, had no reason to exist at all. A woman who should have been left to rot. A woman doubly guilty, as Longhella saw it, for not only being alive and with them but—at the disgustingly old age of what had to be nearly forty—becoming pregnant by Longhella's protector Pietro. Longhella hoping the little monstrosity inside her would never see the light of day.

Philbert was seeing a long stream of faces: Little Lita, Frau Fettelheim, Hermann, Tomaso; Maulwerf, with his round spectacles and brushed waistcoat; Hannah, with her speckled arms; the Turk and the Clockmaker, and Kwert. Kwert the hesychast, reader of murfles and mottlements. Kwert his mentor, teaching Philbert the art of reading, guiding him from one stage of life to the next. Philbert seeing Kwert's long fingers taking out his *Philocalia* and turning the pages. Philbert listening to Kwert's soft voice as he read from Gregory of Nareg's Lamentations:
When rise the rays of Your mercy and Your glory
Then are my sins melted away,
All transgressions dissolved;
They make flee the shadows, disperse the mist,
Sweep away the fog...
Philbert's mind as clear as the raindrops dripping from the leaves about him. Philbert as filled with memories as the sky above him was filled with clouds, as the night sky is with stars. Every point in time fixed, able to be visited at will, all stored up in his misshapen head like sacks of grain in a vast barn; every individual ear of corn precisely recorded and placed with its right fellows.

It had been the way with him since Doctor Ullendorf drilled through his skull, enriching his world with a thousand points of light, one memory sparking off another and another and another in a dazzling cascade, making of his past an unending tapestry of scenes and words and deeds. Like the master mnemonist Heraldo had told Hulde about, Philbert was a prodigy in that respect. The Anatomist's Dream. Later physicians might have posited that Doctor Ullendorf had been imprecise with his trepanation, that his drill had somehow stimulated parts of Philbert's brain which in most people remained a shunting yard, one memory shoving another into oblivion so they would not overwhelm their hosts, flood them with recollection at every scent, every taste, every face, every action viewed. Not so for Philbert, for whom it had been the greatest of gifts, keeping alive those he'd lost.

He lay on his back at the very edge of the forest of Jasmund Peninsula, the sheer chalk cliffs dropping away a few yards to his left, the sound of the sea a comforting murmur below him. Up above, an osprey nest, a large unwieldy habitation of sticks and stems a full four yards wide so had to be old. The birds returning every spring to add a little more and a little more, until the whole would become too heavy for the branches bearing it and would collapse, when the birds would start their building all over again. Maybe not often in their lifetimes, assuming they got to their limit of twenty-nine years—as Philbert knew they'd been recorded as reaching. Living longer than many people did. An astonishing thought, how a bird could outlive a man. But astonishing thoughts were for Philbert the order of the day.

Not least the fact that he was here on Rügen, brought here by the Pfiffmaklers.

He'd known them the moment he'd seen them in Rostock, and for that very reason had steered well clear. When he'd grasped the meaning of the note given him he'd tried to figure where he'd made a slip, where one or another of them had not only seen him but recognised him. He'd been so very careful. Obviously not careful enough.

He and Heraldo had spoken very little on the boat journey out from the Joshua Tree village, both recognising the need to stay silent in case someone else was abroad in some other boat they couldn't see in the fog. But eventually Philbert had to ask.

'How did you know me?'

No sound except the dipping in and pulling out of oars, the slight dripping as their blunt blades left the water, the soft plash as they went back in again. A mechanical sound, not unlike one of the Clockmaker's intricate automata-like time-keepers marking minutes by a bird pecking at a piece of wood, a child bouncing a ball, a tiny bee emerging from one flower and settling upon another. Maulwerf's Fair of Wonders in miniature.

'You're hard to forget,' Heraldo had said. 'Remember when we met you? Not the first time, but the second?'

Philbert didn't hesitate.

'The opening of Magendie's Sylvean Aqueduct.' Philbert detecting a faint movement as Heraldo shifted his feet along the holding board, the fog having thickened the further they'd gone abroad so neither could see the face of the other.

'You were one of the last folk went up the steps to the lodge,' Philbert went on. 'Seem to recall you got booted.'

Rewarded by a soft laugh from Heraldo.

'Well, you could say that. Booted, as you said, right at the door. Think you kind of spoiled it for the rest of us.'

Philbert saying nothing. Philbert seeing the dark interior of that vast wooden lodge, the wrinkled walnut of a man as he sat in his wrinkled walnut of a throne; a man who might have created the wonder of the Sylvean Aqueduct but who had also insulted and belittled the people Philbert held dear.

So what do you keep inside your head, nut boy? Magendie had asked Philbert, when it was Philbert's turn to approach the Master; Philbert so angry at the way Magendie had treated the White Jester and his hairy faced but beautifully singing wife he had ignored Maulwerf's warning glances and answered in kind.

You don't want to know. There are memories in here that span the world far more than your aqueduct will ever do, and violence enough to make your hair curl, if only you had hair enough to make the exercise worthwhile.

Lord. That had been a moment. The Great Magendie staring at Philbert as if he'd been bitten. Philbert staring right back about ready to kill the man, seeing in those tawny eyes that the Great Magendie knew it, that Philbert might have done it had not Maulwerf pulled Philbert back. Magendie summarily dismissing them all. Philbert and Maulwerf passing the last dregs of show people ordered up to his lodge to entertain him.

The girls with their long, braided hair and their orange skirts, the younger grumbling as she passed him by.

'How many of these godforsaken steps are there? I'm only going to have stumps to dance on if there are too many more.'

Heraldo with several musical instruments piled upon his back.

A couple of young boys.

A few older folk dragging up a cart that no doubt would unfold into a puppet theatre.

Then the lot of them coming back down the steps a few minutes later, two green-hatted boys prancing on behind them telling the world their master was tired and would entertain no more visitors.

As if the world cared.

Philbert suddenly realising the Pfiffmaklers might have cared. That he might have spiked their remunerations for the night.

'Sorry about that,' Philbert said into the fog. 'I mean if what I did...'

Another laugh. Heraldo mirthful, Philbert frowning.

'Bet you don't know what the White Jester said to me,' Heraldo went on, 'when we got back down I mean.'

Philbert unable to answer. The White Jester Alarico and his wonderful wife all he could see, all he could hear: Alarico telling his awful jokes, her singing her soul-shifting songs. Philbert still wearing the waistcoat she'd made him, although it was threadbare and faded; the matching one she'd made for Kroonk long gone.

'Said you speared that god-awful Magendie through and through by words alone.'

Heraldo could not see Philbert's face through the fog, might have stopped if he had as Philbert remembered another spear, made of steel instead of speech, that had gutted poor Frau Fettelheim side to side, right at her moment of glory.

Good God, the memories kept on coming: the Ice Fair, the knick-hedges, the tumbled tombs of the Angles, the dunes rolling down to the sea; the snow-filled night when Philbert had lifted the flap of his tent and looked up at the white-bricked walls of the palace where the Aethling Rupert had been preparing his Christmas Gift for his people; the masked harlequin in his motley costume shouting out:

Die Winterfreudenfest is begun!

The wolves of men girding themselves in the surrounding forests, maybe brought to the palace on Philbert's tail or maybe not. He would never be certain. Needing to be certain he was not being tracked now. He'd not truly entertained the possibility anyone was still looking for him but, after getting Heraldo's note, after Heraldo had apparently recognised him with such ease, he had to be sure what had happened to Maulwerf's Fair wouldn't happen to the Pfiffmaklers.

Not because of him.

And so, after the boy sent by Heraldo had first approached him in Rostock, he'd stowed Kroonk in her crate, left her in the moss-and-wattle covered hide he'd created. Hated to leave her, and every moment away from her fearing she'd be discovered, for if that happened, well, bacon haunches all round. But needed to find out. Had returned to Rostock, hung around the fair ground for a day and a night, listening, always listening; and asking, always asking.

Had taken on the pretense of an old man, the lessons of Maulwerf's theatre paying its dues; his face grimed with dirt and dust, crabbing his body so he never had to look people in the eye, because the eyes of the young can never be mistaken for those of the old. Even if you rubbed them with onion and peppers the effect doesn't last long. Philbert shrugging up a shoulder, keeping hat and head lolled down to mask his taupe, as if in arthritic agony. And it had been agony to keep that pose up hour after hour, and had got far closer to folk than he would have liked, talked to more people in that one day than he'd done in the past two years.

'Excuse me, sir; excuse me, madam,' he'd croaked in his old man's voice, 'I'm looking for my grandson. We got parted before we landed here, and it's such a crowd. A boy with a pig? He's got a rather large head, I'm sorry to say. I really need to find him.'

Rewarded at the eleventh hour by a woman who kept a glass case of stuffed hummingbirds: the most glorious flitter and flutter of colour Philbert had ever seen; a winter sunrise on the wing, even if those wings no longer moved.

'Funny you should ask,' she'd said, not bothering to look at old man Philbert, too concerned with taking money from paying customers, 'you're the second person to ask about him in the past few days.'

Old man Philbert almost having a heart attack despite his youth, recovering quickly.

'That'll be my other grandson! Oh thank the Lord!'

The woman stopping then, turning from her hummingbirds, staring intently at Philbert and his disguise. Philbert and his disguise taking an involuntary step backwards.

'I hardly think so,' she said, 'unless he was born in Serbia fifty odd years back.' fixing a beady eye on Philbert. 'I spent a long time in that part of the world when my bones were younger. Got a real distinctive accent, those folk.'

Philbert so shocked he'd allowed his disguise to slip, lifted up his head as the woman gave him a piece of advice.

'So let me tell you this for free. Best tell your…grandson…to get himself running, because that was one bad son-of-a-bitch, and he was on the hunt. And ain't no part of any of us.'

Philbert away, Philbert knowing he'd been rumbled, that the hummingbird woman knew precisely who he was and was giving him a chance; and if she knew him then most likely others did too—and not only Heraldo— and them maybe not so inclined to protect one of their own.

Philbert not bothering to question Heraldo further on how he'd picked him out from the crowds he'd tried so hard to avoid, for plainly Philbert had been spotted on many occasions, had made bad stratagem, should maybe have woven himself into those crowds as often as he could and not stuck to the periphery where he was as obvious to the falcon as the one starling, the one sparrow, the one knot, who couldn't keep up with the flock.

A terrible tussle taking hold.

Someone else asking after him and his whereabouts, apart from Heraldo.

Choice being to go with the Pfiffmaklers or to go on alone.

Did not want to put the Pfiffmaklers in danger, nor himself and Kroonk come to that.

On the other hand, how was anyone going to connect him to them? Could not think of any logical reason how they possibly could.

And so he made his decision, took the only chance ever offered him on his sojourn of exile.

First Face of Fear presented, and ignored.

Wobbly Nails, Wobbly Minds

That bad son-of-a-bitch from Serbia interrogated every last inhabitant of the fog-bound village.

Was there another Joshua Tree hereabouts?

Had anyone seen strangers?

A lad with a pig?

Where would someone be going if they came from Rostock to here?

The villagers startled.

Answering no, no and no to the first three questions, and maybe on to the Stettiner-haff to the last, where the river Oder ended and folk often went to see the wooded islets of Usedom and Wollin, and especially the *nehrungs*. Long tongues of sand, finger-thin comparative to their length, some flat, others undulating with hillocks of sand shifting and twisting according to the direction of the wind. Or maybe to the pouring out of the Vistula, whose estuary was enclosed on the north-west by a sandy promontory stretching out eighteen miles though was barely a quarter mile wide. Folk travelling up its spit as on a pilgrimage to visit the lighthouse of Hela at its very end.

'And over there?' the son-of-a-bitch had asked, shoving his thumb in the direction of the foggy sea. 'What's over there?'

'Rügen Island,' he was told by the puzzled villagers. 'And no reason on earth why anyone would want to go there.'

'Which is precisely why he'd go there,' the son-of-a-bitch confided to his companion as they bided a while on the circular seat collaring the Joshua Tree, Rasvlach one side, Diderik the other. Its religious significance completely passing them by, the son-of-a-bitch's younger companion busily scratching a few marks in its wood.

'Bit of a gamble though,' the knife-wielder commented. 'Gotta think maybe he's heading to Berlin which isn't...Ouch! What the hell!' he exclaimed as he received a hard thwack to the side of his head from his companion, who had his own ideas.

'He's gone over to Rügen, I'm damn sure of it.'

Diderik rubbing his temple.

Getting really fed up with being treated like a second-class citizen. Had only gone into this bounty business because Rasvlach had convinced him, back in Kragujevac, it would yield good money. Which it had, until Rasvlach heard about the newly repatriated Metternich and the Little Maus business, which had really got Rasvlach's blood boiling. The hummingbird woman slightly wrong on one point, for the son-of-a-bitch Rasvlach was a Croatian through and through, despite spending most of his days in Serbia and ending up in a Serbian prison, sounding like one of Serbia's own.

Rasvlach a hard-arsed nationalist all his days. Rasvlach fired up with Croatian zeal on the tail of Serbia's independence, caught up in the delusion Croatia would be as liberated as Serbia when the Habsburgs crumbled under revolutionary pressure. Rasvlach a loud-mouthed follower of Josip Jelačić, first leader of the semi-autonomous Croatian State in 1848, the year of revolutions.

Rasvlach celebrating with all the rest.

Rasvlach three days drunk with it, and side by side with Jelačić when he declared war on Hungary; there with Jelačić when the Hungarians pushed them back to Vienna. Which was when logic disintegrated. Jelačić and Prince Windischgrätz bombing the hell out of Vienna, executing all the revolutionary leaders. All of which stramash led to the abdication of the Emperor Ferdinand who'd appointed Jelačić in the first place.

Rasvlach completely confused ever since, befuddled by the politics: the tangling up in their fight of Hungarians, Turks and Russians; everything going arse over tit. Jelačić's power-base eroded as the Viennese court re-established itself and threw Croatia to the dogs. Rasvlach disgusted, Rasvlach made into a man dedicated to violence. Rasvlach venting his rage on some Serbian idiot who'd declared that at least the Habsburgs had been better than the Turks.

'Those Habsburgs are all bastards!' Rasvlach had yelled right into that man's face. 'They've gone back on every promise they ever made us!'

That man, Rasvlach's drinking companion, more sanguine, providing a new example.

'Ever hear about the Little Maus?' he'd asked.

Which Rasvlach had not.

'He was a fair's turn,' the man explained. 'Had a huge growth on his head. Became a bit of legend. Got caught up in the riots in Germany, was right in the middle of it when Von Ebner got killed and managed to free all his fellow revolutionaries the morning they were about to be shot.'

'So what?' Rasvlach didn't care tuppence about any of it. His companion not of the same opinion.

'Point is this: he was like the loose nail in the horse's shoe niggling and naggling; same horse who went on to break down the stable doors and made a bolt for freedom, made the men who believed they'd owned him spitting mad and ordering armies after him, for the sake of that single nail.'

'What the bugger are you on about?' Rasvlach complained, disliking intellectuals of every stripe, folk who believed themselves better than him because they'd a bit of learning.

'I'm on about the fact,' the man explained patiently, 'that 1848 was like that all over: wobbly nails causing separate horses to bolt off willy nilly when what was needed was the whole lot stampeding at the same time. Like we did in Serbia against the Turks. Like your lot should have done against the Habsburgs instead of palling up with them.'

Rasvlach narrowing his eyes, for palling up with the Habsburgs was absolutely not what he and his fellow Croatians had signed up for.

'Got to know where and when to pick your enemies,' Rasvlach's newly picked enemy concluded. 'And got to go at them full on, get all your wobbly nails wobbling at the same time.'

Rasvlach believing himself accused, believing himself denigrated.

Rasvlach exploding.

'My name is Georg Rasvlach!' he'd yelled as he stood up, swept all the glasses from the table, unsheathed his knife. 'All you buggering Serbians should be down on your knees begging us Croatians forgiveness for what you've done!'

Rasvlach ending up in Kragujevac because of it, the blabbermouth philosopher he'd attacked surviving by a thread. Rasvlach given ten long years, which was ten years longer than Rasvlach wanted to stay in prison.

Rasvlach engineering his escape and taking Diderik with him, for every henchman needs his sidekick, for which Diderik had to give the man full points.

My god! Who else would have dared it!

Neither the two of them locked up with the worst, with the murderers; Rasvlach nevertheless making contact with those men, seeking them out across the wire partitions and walls to glean advice, for they had been here the longest, knew all the ins and outs.

Diderik quivering with consternation when Rasvlach first approached him, saying Diderik was central to his plan because Diderik was only in for pilfering and only had another year to go and when that year came up, well. That was when Rasvlach would spring his trap.

And blow him if it hadn't worked; Diderik sitting on the banks of the moat as soon as it was dark. Sitting out one night, two, three, and on the fourth there came his signal: a tiny pinprick of candlelight on the other side, meaning Rasvlach had evaded the guards—undoubtedly drunk after playing cards, for guarding prisoners was tedious and thankless work, and entertainment at the end of day well-earned and due—and Diderik had chucked over his rope, grabbed at the other end by Rasvlach who'd secured it about a stake driven into his side of the bank and over he'd come, thrashing his legs through the filthy mire, hands wrapped in sacking clutching at the rope to keep his head above the surface, crawling out muttering under his breath, instantly discarding his spoiled clothing, kicking it with venom back into the moat. Sluicing himself down with fresh water from the pail Diderik had to hand, as ordered; donning the new garb Diderik, as ordered, had brought with him.

'You did it, boss!' Diderik had whispered in awe.

''Course I bloody did,' Rasvlach growled back between clenched teeth. 'But can't be hanging around here like tired washing. Let's be gone.'

The start of Diderik's new life; one imagined as dashing and heroic: tracking down malefactors, no one better equipped to do it than two ex-malefactors such as themselves. Rasvlach proving himself adept at the task, seeming to know every place low-lifes went to lie low; able to sniff out those places wherever they went, in every new town or city; Rasvlach locating within hours of their arrival the darkest, narrowest of streets, where scrawny whore-faced women screeched and took in the worst of the worst: feeding them, hiding them, servicing their every need for a couple of coins.

Diderik's mother would have wept to know the armpits of places Rasvlach had taken her son. The shine soon gone from Diderik's new vocation, which was not so much dashing and heroic as vicious and vile. Rasvlach of the view that a dead felon was far less trouble than a living one and delivery, alive or dead, of no concern to the authorities who'd commissioned their finding. Glad to be rid of the expense of holding a trial. Payment to the men who'd apprehended the offenders easily the more affordable option.

Travelling from one place to the next, gone from Serbia quick as they could in case someone like them was on Rasvlach's tail. Soon enough established in Vienna, and sent from Vienna on to Prague, and from Prague to Berlin. Letters of recommendation piling up in their pockets, and a bit of cash. Living well, if always on the move. Until the son-of-a-bitch Rasvlach heard about Metternich's renewed reward for the finding of one Philbert, also known as the Little Maus, who'd poisoned a load of schupos a few years back in some nowhere place called Lengerrborn.

Rasvlach really worked up about it, gabbling on about nails and horses and how it had been this Little Maus's fault the 1848 revolutions hadn't amounted to more than a pile of shit; Rasvlach's beloved Croatia coming out worst of all.

'This is it,' Rasvlach had announced. 'This is our gold mine, Diderik. Find this little bastard and deliver him up to Metternich and we'll never have to work another day in our lives. Not to mention I'll have the great pleasure of slicing his bastard head from off his bastard neck, get it pickled and presentable. And it'll only take his head, mind. Can't be another one like it anywhere we're likely to see.'

Rasvlach apparently having heard of this Little Maus somewhere before, and taking it personally.

The Anatomist's Dream.

Rasvlach's dream.

Diderik, having nothing more lively than a pile of dead moss between his ears, nevertheless recognising obsession when he saw it.

'Are you sure, boss?' he'd queried. 'It's going to take us right out of...ouch! I really wish you wouldn't do that.'

The first of many hard clouts when Diderik had the temerity to question Rasvlach's new mission, though not so bad as the methods Rasvlach employed in following his new quarry, which had included chopping off the hand of someone Rasvlach was convinced knew more than he was telling them.

'You're on the Fairs' circuit,' Rasvlach had said to the man he was interrogating. 'And I knows you was in Schleswig-Holstein when it all came to an end on the Ice Fair. Got it on good witness, so might as well spit it out, save yourself a load of pain.'

Where Rasvlach had got his information Diderik didn't know. A lot Diderik didn't know about Rasvlach. They'd spent weeks tracking down this bald-headed old man who had an old tattoo fading into the bald skin of his skull looking like some ancient turtle-necked fish dragged up from the depths.

'I don't know anything,' Herr Himbeere had pleaded, late practitioner of interpreting the future from the intestines of newly gutted lambs. Now a broken old man who didn't understand why men did what they did. A refrain oft repeated after he'd been brought out of the wood-cellar of Rupert's palace where he'd managed to lock himself in, evaded the worst of the attack on the rest of the fairs folk on the ice. Coming out dehydrated, starved, and nowhere near normal. Nor ever would be again.

'And yet you do know Philbert,' Rasvlach had persisted, 'also called the Little Maus.'

Herr Himbeere screwing up his eyes because yes, he vaguely remembered the name: the lad who'd helped him out on that worst of nights, the Ice Fair; the lad who'd chucked the lamb's guts down the chute when he'd told him they were bad, that he hadn't told Prince Rupert what they really meant.

'He went off into the forest,' he tried. 'I've never seen him from that day to...but what are you doing? I don't know...'

Rasvlach pulling Herr Himbeere's right hand across the table outside the mean tavern Rasvlach had tracked the man down to.

'You must have,' Rasvlach insisted. 'He was your helpmeet.'

Herr Himbeere's eyes widening, flicking towards Diderik, looking for help.

'Only for that one night,' Himbeere said. 'His own man was sick. I'd only met him once or—'

'Not true,' Rasvlach dictated. 'Been told he helped you out on previous occasions, so why not afterwards?'

Herr Himbeere sweating badly. So much about that night, about that time, he couldn't recall with any clarity. Several nights in the wood cellar without food or drink doing his mind no favours. Memories scrambled ever since. Taking his show on the road as usual, but never again intersecting with Maulwerf's depleted Fair of Wonders, in fact running hightail if he'd heard they were in the vicinity.

'I can't tell you anything,' Herr Himbeere implored. His interrogator not believing him. Rasvlach gripping hard at Herr Himbeere's arm, positioning it just so.

And down came the thwack of Rasvlach's broad-bladed short-axe, right through sinew and bone; Herr Himbeere not believing what he was seeing, not believing this was being done, watching his fingers pulse out a last dance of their own making, and then a dreadful chill as Rasvlach released him and Herr Himbeere held up his arm and realised the truth of it. Too shocked to feel any pain, but screaming and screaming, though no one on the other side of the wall of that dark tavern paid any mind. Herr Himbeere still screaming as he ran from his torturer, gripping his severed wrist, blood pumping from it as if it would never stop, leaving his hand behind upon the table.

Herr Himbeere falling to his knees, screams become moans, become groans, become a dreadful whimpering that had Diderik running on behind him. Diderik shivering, horrified, shoving a dirty handkerchief over Herr Himbeere's severed wrist, tying it off with a twist of string he'd fished from his pocket with shaking fingers—so glad he still had his own fingers—telling Himbeere to get to a doctor or the hospital on the edge of town where folk with contagious diseases went.

Herr Himbeere unable to comply.

Herr Himbeere tipping over into the dust and bleeding to death before Diderik's eyes.

Rasvlach coming on behind, wiping his blade on his trousers, chucking Herr Himbeere's severed hand to a small pack of scrawny dogs who'd appeared from the other side of the tavern, enticed by the smell of fresh blood.

'That's what happens when you don't tell the truth,' Rasvlach informed Diderik. Diderik crying, Diderik as weak as was Herr Himbeere. Diderik trying to stop the bleeding, trying to drag Herr Himbeere away. Diderik stopped by Rasvlach's boot coming down hard upon his back.

'Leave him, boy,' Rasvlach commanded. 'Trash like that ain't even worth the breath.'

Trash like that.

The dogs growling and snarling as they fought over their handy prize. One of them slinking from the crowd with it, the others nosing around Herr Himbeere's prostrate body. Not that Diderik ever learned the man's name, nor how Rasvlach had found him and singled him out.

Diderik leaving the trash to the dogs, unable to rid his mind of what the trash had been murmuring as he'd gone:

'Didn't see him after…didn't even really know him…didn't…'

Didn't nothing.

Unknown man, as far as Diderik knew, dying like a flounder flung onto the sand by the sea.

No reason for it. No reason at all.

Diderik beginning to rethink his relationship with his cohort.

The reason he scratched his initials and symbols into the Joshua Tree seat when Rasvlach wasn't looking.

Something left at least, when his own time came.

And no doubt in Diderik's mind that day would come. Diderik having the sudden revelation, as he'd watched the bald-headed man dying in the dust, that he, Diderik, was about as valuable. Which meant he was worth nothing at all.

Diderik the dispensable.

Diderik distraught.

Diderik watching his back ever since.

Judgements Made On Jewels Resplendent

Mergim shoveled Valter up from the tavern floor. Valter protesting feebly, flapping his arms like an ancient chicken about to have his neck wrung by the tavern owner.

'Floor's one thing, puking on a table top's another,' the man was saying as Mergim stepped into the dark interior; immediate stench of beer-soaked sawdust in his nostrils, undercurrents of unwashed men, sour breath, cheap tobacco, vague hints of spiced meat marking the top notes.

Mergim seeing Valter's bright red hair through the sawdust and smoke as the tavern-owner stepped forward and began to kick Valter physically towards the door.

'That'll do,' Mergim barked. 'I'll take care.'

Putting out his hands to haul Valter away by his shoulders. The tavern owner leaving be, seeing the long curlicues of a prison tattoo going from Mergim's wrist right up his forearm and disappearing into Mergim's sleeve. Another gift from the sock-puller and his deft needle, a man so clever with his hands he'd needed only charcoal from the fire and a few boiled-up onion skins to mark the tendrils of a columbine onto Mergim's arm.

'Sign of healed sins,' the tattooist had informed Mergim. 'Seems kind of apt in your case. Of course I could do ivy or mistletoe if you're preferring.'

'For why?' Mergim had enquired.

'For them being always green,' came the quick answer. 'Gives hope we'll all one day be resurrected, in the next life if not in this.'

Mergim laughing.

'Jesus! Hardly think us lot are going anywhere but down.'

The needle-wielder pausing as he traced his design on Mergim's skin with a fine sliver of graphite, leaning in so close Mergim could see several lice pushing their tiny claws through the man's thin hair.

'Think you're wrong there, friend,' the man corrected. 'Never met a more godly crew than I have in here. Sheep with black jackets don't need half the amount of scrubbing as white ones do.'

Mergim reconsidering, for he had a point. Most of the murderers in Kragujevac truly repentant of their crimes, sanguine about spending the rest of their days behind walls and bars, believing they'd no right to be anywhere else; spending a fair bit of their time in the tiny chapel kneeling before a chipped statue of the Piéta so the stone there was worn smooth, cupped by many knees. The Madonna's mouth wide open with a silent howl as she cradled her dying son. As some of the men had cradled dying wives, friends or children the moment after they'd struck out in blind and drunken anger and realised what they'd done.

Most pitiful were the few who ranted and railed about their imprisonment, banging their heads against the stone walls in their impotence, or standing still in the yard holding their faces up to the sky like wolves about ready to skirl their grievances to the universe, who would have killed every last man in the prison if it would earn them one more day walking freely down a street, or smelling the damp mushroom-springing leaf-littered floor of a favourite forest, or spreading their pale limbs in a blue pool nestled out of limestone by a waterfall cascading down on the rocks for thousands and thousands of years.

Pitiful, certainly, but no more pitiful than Valter was as Mergim hauled him from the tavern and out into the dark street, plunging his head into the cool water of a fountain just down the way. Valter coming out burbling and crying, wiping his eyes in disbelief and despair.

'Valter,' Mergim stated. 'It's me. It's Mergim.'

Valter shaking his head, the water making his hair stand up in points. Valter pushing his chin forward and back several times like a merganser sometimes will in the sea as it chases a shoal of fish with its serrated beak. Valter nowhere near as able to grasp anything so slippery.

'Who're you?' he slurred, tongue white and furry with beer and tobacco, a sight that had Mergim wanting to retch, wanting to hand Valter one of the rough-barked twigs he kept in his pocket to clear away all that slurry.

'It's me. It's Mergim. Came back with you from Italy, after we met the Pfiffmaklers.'

The last name, if not the first, making Valter twist up his drink-sodden head.

'Fucking Piffelmakkels,' Valter mumbled, before suddenly retching, though nothing came out but dribbles.

'Christ, but you're in some kind of mess,' Mergim observed. They'd not been without drink in Kragujevac, far from it. The inmates encouraged to brew up whatever they could if it would keep them in somnolent stupor, and if one of them killed another because of it then no harm done. One body dragged out and soon enough another dragged in. Kept the bed spaces tidy.

'What do you know about the Pfiffmaklers?' Mergim asked, as he got Valter up on wobbly pins. 'Know where they was going when you left them?'

Valter letting out a bitter bray of laughter.

'Don't talk to me about them! Don't never want to be around anyone so happy ever again. Gave me the bloody creeps.'

And so it went on, Mergim asking Valter what he knew, Valter reluctant to give details. Valter managing to direct Mergim to some old shack Valter had been sleeping in; Valter collapsing in a heap upon a load of old straw. Mergim firing up the tinder Valter had left ready beneath a billycan of water and bad coffee, so Valter not completely useless after all. Valter able to figure out and plan for a next day, although Mergim wasn't sure how many next days Valter could have, given the state he was in.

Mergim reminded of another inmate who spent his days and nights capturing butterflies and moths, for everyone needed some kind of occupation—more so than did men on the outside—pinning them onto a piece of cloth, leaving them to dry on a sun-pooled wall. A beautiful patchwork he would spend hours working at, repositioning one insect, replacing one with another like a tailor arranging mother-of-pearl buttons on a fine silk suit. The man heart-struck when one of the larger hawkmoths began exuding a greasy compound from its abdomen that crept up and over the circles of pink and black fur; ended up covering the entire insect, dulling outspread wings previously resembling thin slices of delicately engraved wood. In this case alcohol had actually helped, someone suggesting dipping the insect in the hard stuff, which acted like a solvent, and a few days later the hawkmoth had been brand new.

Yet another use for alcohol inside those walls besides its drinking: a solute for tattoo pigments, a cleaner-out of wounds, a cauteriser of lanced boils, an anaesthetic for toothache and gum rot, a useful ointment for anything and everywhere once mixed to a paste with chalkdust and various chopped-up herbs; a sleeping draught; a cure for moth grease.

None of these uses applicable to Valter, apart from being a general anaesthetic for a life he no longer seemed able to bear. Mergim despising Valter for throwing away what for most men, Mergim included, was so hard won. A spell in Kragujevac might have been the making of Valter, as it had been for Mergim. A situation that made you weigh yourself up on a daily basis, made you acutely aware of the value of a blue sky, a heavy-bellied pelican flying low towards its nesting ground; a warm sun, a cooling wind, a friendly word, a hawkmoth, the awe of waking to a sharp-edged world of walls and wires softened into cleansingly beautiful white and light by an unexpected snowfall during the night.

A transformation as evident in Mergim as any of those snow-lit mornings.

Mergim dozing quietly the night through as Valter snored and belched. Valter moving only once, when he put out a bleary hand and got hold of a flagon of water, shuggled it down his throat, glug after glug, until it was emptied. Mergim, waking to witness this small act of healing Valter had prepared for himself, finding in it an indication that Valter knew how low he'd got and yet was putting in place some remedial effort to ward off the worst.

So Mergim would wait a little longer, wait to see what the new morning would bring, what Valter could tell him about the Pfiffmaklers once his brain had been unscrambled by the passing of the night.

'Hope and revelation, ladies and gentlemen,' Wenzel begins, the second tranche of the Advent Cycle at St Mary's running on apace, 'is what the life of St Hildegard shows us. For it was during her long life that this very special island—last stronghold of the Western Slavs, last pagan foothold in our great country—was finally brought into the Christian fold.'

A fast-travelling narrative illustrated by means of a moving picture panorama Livia and Pietro had witnessed a few years previously. No more switching backdrops, instead a continuous screel of painted linen wound from one vertical roll to another. The effect astonishing the patrons of St Mary's as Hildegard's life scrolled out before them, as if they were travelling it with her.

'A high birth,' Wenzel informs them, 'but a late child, the last of many, so one of necessity dedicated to the grace of God. Sent to the lonely hill-top anchorage of Disibodenberg.'

The audience seeing it as the child Hildegard must have done on her first arrival: a bleak and forbidding place.

A terrible place for anyone, Wenzel intones, *let alone a child as young as she.*

Audience locked with Hildegard inside her cold stone cell.

Where she remained for twenty years and more, ladies and gentlemen. Twenty years in her tiny cell, not one footstep outside it in all that time. But not without protection.

The audience introduced to the blessed Abbess Jutta, a towering vision of blue and gold whose robes seemed to fold and flow about her like living clouds.

Who took care of Hildegard as she might have her own daughter, until the blessed Jutta died…

A mournful, rain-soaked scene: a coffin lowered into the depths. Ringing of hand-bells, soft lute playing.

…when Hildegard was elected to take Jutta's place as Abbess, and brought out from her cell. Hildegard walking in blessed sunshine, her feet upon the grass!

A beatific Hildegard, now a woman, striding towards Rupertsburg.

Where she founded her own holy monastery and revealed to the world her visions, began to write her songs and her great works of theology.

The rolling canvas revealing Hildegard's visions, giving them form and substance, Heaven opening itself to her and her audience.

Flooding her with a fiery light of such brilliance it permeated body, soul and breast.

Swirling circles of colour growing and pulsating as the linen is pulled from roll to roll, giving the visual illusion of depth and dizzying inclusion; the Virgin Mary herself fully dimensional and real, her arm appearing to move in blessing, her lips to speak and breathe. The Madonna as real to her audience as she'd been to Hildegard: a miracle of revelation.

The Mother of all joy, Wenzel tells them, *as drenched in God's blessings as the green grass is with dew.*

And hardly had one spectacle gone before another appeared: the linen winding on, splashed with vivid likenesses of the emperors and high statesmen who came to seek her opinions, Hildegard become a Feather on the Breath of God, the conduit who passed on His wisdom to His flock.

And oh my, the singing by Ludmilla, Longhella and Hulde of Hildegard's songs throughout this show had the audience in tears. Never had they heard anything so beautiful, nor seen anything so marvellous: living landscapes moving before their eyes, drawing them in, taking them with it as it progressed down the years of Hildegard's long life.

And so poignant to their own affairs: the last scene of the panorama being none other than their own Church of St Mary's, the linen stopping its movement, settling like the Black Lake in the beech forest, augmented with holiness by Ludmilla's interpretation of Hildegard's antiphon to the Blessed Virgin, *Oh Jewel Resplendent*, with its modulated highs and lamenting lows, accompanied by softly hummed notes sustained by the rest of the Pfiffmaklers which could have been the voice of the sea surrounding them on every side. The words of the antiphon remaining with them, for Livia and Pietro had taken care to translate the Latin into the islanders' own language throughout the performance, bringing them inside the circle of grace usually preserved for priests.

Oh jewel resplendent, flooded by the bright glad beauty of the sun,
A fountain leaping from the Father's heart
Bearing the Word that created the world,
Making of the Word a living person
And bringing Him to live amongst us…

The islanders of Rügen their own leaping fountain as they poured out of St Mary's once the day was done, some silent in their meditations, most not; most chattering like goldfinches, all believing themselves blessed, immersed in the spirit of Advent and the Christmas soon to come.

Philbert was having his own thoughts on Christmas as he bivouacked in the woods of Jasmund, another night slowly taking hold. Philbert not fearing the darkness, instead comforted: no need to catch his breath every time he heard the crack of a twig, the sudden up-flurry of birds, a woodpecker stopping its hammering. All of which might have signified someone wending their way through the trees, tracking him, tracking Kroonk.

Nighttime a safe time.

Advent not so much, with all its associations.

Philbert having his own panorama of *peintures vivants* scrolling through his head: scenes of the Ice Fair, of the bowls on poles flaming out light; of Rupert's Christmas Extravaganza unfolding at his feast: theatre, grandeur and entertainment. Of Philbert at the very top of the highest tower of the palace looking down on the Ice Fair; the sounds of heavy boots hammering on the stone staircase, of the blood in the snow, of himself emerging onto the worm-eaten wood of the rickety minstrel gallery and seeing the devastation down below. Rupert's pale exsanguinated face apparently looking right at Philbert as the lance that had pierced and fixed him to his wooden throne wobbled with his last few breaths. Philbert wondering ever since how alive the man had been, how cognisant, whether he was looking at Philbert with the faint expectation of salvation or with blame.

Another Feather on the Breath of God.

Hildegard's words woven into him from Kwert's *Philocalia*. Philbert finding them applicable to the moment as a murmuration of starlings rose up from the shingle below the cliffs, desisting their poking in the strand-line for scraps of food, and began to weave and wind, blow themselves into smoke above the trees before settling as one onto the osprey nest above his head. Kroonk stirring at the movement, Kroonk laying her head upon Philbert's knee, happy in the moment as Philbert hadn't been for a long, long time.

The blessing animals gave you.

Their belief in you, their absolute and unadulterated trust not many are truly worthy of. Philbert wondering how truly worthy he was. Philbert lauded, as he'd so recently learned, by many for his past actions in Lengerrborn in freeing all those Westphal men. Philbert loathed by a few for the same as he knew, and hated by a specific man, by Metternich, which he did not.

Philbert thinking on the Pfiffmaklers, what they might be risking by taking him in.

Had to believe, had to hope, that risk as negligible as Heraldo had assured him to be the case. And no one Philbert would rather put his trust in than Heraldo Pfiffmakler.

Mice Maybe Happier Than The Men Who Feed Them

'Oh God,' Valter groaned, his eyelids flickering as several beams of sunlight penetrated the holes in the rusted roof of the shack he'd latterly called home. Valter about to go through the automatic routines of his morning: checking his clothes and body to see if he'd been robbed or beaten. The first not usual, never having anything worth stealing; the second more common. Valter normally a solitary drunk though on occasion utterly obnoxious, picking fights during what passed for Valter as conversation.

He coughed harshly, like a heron interrupted. Belched once, twice. Farted loud and wet, screwing up his eyes against the stench. Waking up being the least favourite part of his day, if any of it could be called favourable. Merely another long line of hours to be got through, Valter spending most of them wandering at random around the countryside to hawk the carvings he was adept at. Nothing so intricate as the chess pieces he used to make, but he made damned good door-knockers and boot-hauler-offers, and any number of knife hasps, shovel and hoe handles, shepherding crooks, walking sticks, and anything else made of wood he was asked to fashion. He was unreliable as to time of delivery yet in the end he always did; folk forgiving him his tardiness for the quality of what he produced. Perfection for its purpose, made with the exact kind of wood to suit that purpose best.

Valter lying on his scrappy uncomfortable pallet as usual, putting out his hand for his water jug and finding it empty—as usual. Felt the fullness of his bladder, the burning in his bowels telling him to get up and at it—as usual. What was not usual was the smell of brewing coffee, of sausages sizzling in a pan. And not the cheap scrap-ends he usually bought; not from them could come this rich, deep aroma permeating the stale air of the shack, the scents of fat rich with spices and pepper sharpening its edges. Valter having the oddest feeling in his stomach.

Hunger.

He couldn't remember when that had happened last.

Pushed himself up on his elbows, blinked a few times, sniffed, hawked out a gob of phlegm, focused on the man tending to his fire, his kettle and his pan.

'What the blazes?' Valter croaked, the man turning towards him. Valter leaning his neck forward. Vague tingle of recognition, though nothing certain.

'Who are you?' Valter demanded. 'And what the hell are you doing in my home?'

That Valter considered this broken-down shack his home was not lost on either of the two occupants.

'Mergim,' said the interloper. 'I brought you back from the tavern last night. Thought the owner was about to bust your head.'

He stopped, shrugged his shoulders.

Valter slow to take the information in, taking a minute to answer.

'And so you're what? You're cooking me breakfast?'

'I am,' Mergim replied. 'I've coffee on the go; flatbreads and eggs ready to bubble up in the sausage fat when you're needing.'

Valter rolled himself to the side of his bed and sat with his elbows on his knees, brushing the base of his scrubby chin with his fingers.

'I know you,' he said, shuffling the mosaic of memory in his head. Most of the last few years mince if not so much what had gone on before, which was the reason for all that mince in the first place. 'You're Mergim,' he finally fished up the name, despite already having been given it. 'Jesus. They finally let you out.'

Mergim shrugged.

'Want to eat first, or get cleaned up?' Mergim asked. 'Entirely up to you.'

Valter twisting his lips. Valter remembering Mergim, and that Mergim must have spent many nights in places worse than this; this place bad, but surely no worse than prison.

'Kind of like to eat first, if it's all the same to you,' he said. 'But gotta take a piss.'

Mergim shrugged again and Valter got to his feet, staggering a little until he got his bearings; couldn't figure for the life of him what Mergim, of all people, was doing here. Tried to struggle through the fog of the previous night, seeking pointers. Getting nothing. All a big black blank, same as it was most nights. Valter heading out of the shack to relieve himself; Valter hearing some faint echo in his head, a voice telling him he was in some kind of mess. Valter already knowing it, Valter told it a million times. Valter not such a numbskull he didn't know it himself.

But Mergim turning up on his doorstep or, more properly, right inside Valter's house, this was new, and unsettling.

Something other than hunger rumbling inside Valter's guts.

Faint sense of shame how Valter had wasted all these years Mergim had been inside, that Mergim would have swapped with him in a heartbeat and probably made a better go of it.

Sluicing his head with water from the burn, feeling the need to tidy himself up for his visitor. Had as much of a wash as he could whilst keeping his clothes on.

Returning to the shack to find Mergim carefully pushing the sausages to one side of the pan and slipping the eggs in one by one, spooning fat over them so they clouded over as if they were eyes too innocent to witness the state of the place they were to end their days.

The Pfiffmaklers were on the move.

Their triumph at St Mary's had done them well, Wenzel having a few letters of recommendation in his pocket as they went up country and across the narrow causeway into Jasmund Peninsula to other parishes where they'd be welcomed.

Rügen Island proving as fertile a place for their Advent Cycles as Wenzel had hoped.

First stop: camping up by the mile-long lake the other side of the causeway, while Wenzel and Pietro walked the last few miles into Sagard to make their petition to the Pastor of St Michael's.

'I'm finding it all a bit odd,' Pietro confided as they tramped up the track. 'This place, I mean, with all their churches being built so late.'

Referring to both St Mary's and now St Michael's.

'They're over five hundred years old,' Wenzel countered. 'Hardly makes them new.'

Pietro frowned, brushed his hand along a stand of thistles by the wayside, their stems and leaves wilted and dry yet the flower-heads still extant: soft, silky and yellow beneath his fingertips, as if partially alive.

'It's not that,' Pietro tried to explain. 'It's more how they all sprung up at the same time, and so late in the day. Not like back in Italy, where we've been Christians to the root since almost the very beginning.'

Oh Lord, Wenzel thought, *please don't tell me Pietro is going to turn into another Grandma Pfiffmakler.*

'This island feels so cut off, and all these people really Slavs,' Pietro tried again.

Wenzel smiled.

'Best not say that to their faces,' he advised. 'Never a good idea to bite the hand that feeds.'

'Of course not,' Pietro quick to reply. 'I just mean that for a thousand years the rest of the world was Christian and these people here were still worshipping pagan gods. And I find that... peculiar.'

Wenzel rubbed his beard. Nobody could call him a dedicated historian, yet the Pfiffmaklers had been to many places, learned many odd facts about this and that, and felt the need to put Pietro right.

'Rest of the world is a bit sweeping,' he said. 'Don't think you could include Persia, China or India in that bracket. Or Africa. Nor the Americas, come to that. Which is kind of the rest of the world, when you look at it in the round. Then and now.'

Pietro taken aback, feeling challenged. Never believing himself overtly religious but, being Italian, as drenched in it as grass is with dew—to use the phrase from the Hildegard play. The idea completely new to him, for how could it be that half the world—maybe more than half the world—had still not been Christianised a thousand years after Christ had died, and many more centuries since?

It seemed impossible.

'And don't forget Hulde,' Wenzel added. 'Half her folk Islamists, the other half Christian. Same all over that region. One lot massacring the other and the other lot firing back in kind. Both guilty of the same crimes which both their religions say is wrong, and yet they do it anywise. So who's to say which half is right and which half wrong?'

Pietro thinking about that as they carried on in silence towards Sagard.

Pietro's world view tumbling and crumbling; giving him a startling new idea to add to their Advent Cycle, if only he and the Pfiffmaklers could get it prepared in time. And oh, so much better than Prisoner Number 101.

Rasvlach finally managed to bully one of the Joshua Tree villagers into taking him and Diderik over to Rügen. No one keen, Rasvlach not exactly flashing the cash. Rasvlach down on funds since he'd abnegated his usual duties and gone all out after his loose nail, his Little Maus. Diderik spitting mad about that, though it would not do to mention it.

Bullying being Rasvlach's only way as the folk here quite simply didn't want to go over the water. Considered Rügen folk not of their own, a people apart: Danes and Slavs, all suspected of keeping up the old ways no matter what anyone said to the contrary.

'They're dirt,' one woman informed Rasvlach. 'No more use to anyone than the mud on my shoe.'

No minding that the mud on her shoe comprised good, sea-weed-enriched manure.

'They're not our blood,' weighed in another villager, 'and never will be.'

'And we've no more time nor more truck with them,' said another, 'than I have with the shit that comes out of the backside of my dog who, by the by, is of more use than any of them lot will ever be.'

'They're cursed,' an old woman added. 'They named their entire island after their old god, after it's quarter face, it's red face. And all four of them faces means fear, and blood. No good will ever come of it.'

To say that Rasvlach had been moved by these objections would have been a drastic overstatement, and even Diderik—so recently wavering under Rasvlach's yoke—had been a little proud when Rasvlach cut through the lot of it.

'I don't give a curse about you or your buggering opinions. And I don't give a curse about what you think or don't think about anyone out there. I want passage over, and I'm telling you this, folks, I'm telling you this right now: if I don't get over in the next few hours then one of yous is going to wake up with their throat cut from ear to ear.'

Brutal, and effective.

Several offers right there on the table.

Rasvlach and Diderik on the next boat out.

'I want you to help me find the Pfiffmaklers,' Mergim got to the nub of his visit, Valter scraping the last of the flatbreads about the pan, small rivulets of fat glistening on his stubbled chin. Valter not looking up.

'Ain't seen hide nor hair of them in years,' he mumbled. 'Not since Andreas died.'

Mergim seeing the flicker of pain in Valter's stooped shoulders, the slight tremulation of his head.

'I was sorry to hear about that,' Mergim said. 'Guess he was the closest you had to kin.'

'He was my only family,' Valter countered quickly, grief bubbling to the surface, Valter chucking the last scrap of bread to the corner of the shack where a nest of mice shared his abode; not bothering to ask how Mergim knew about Andreas, for the fact that he'd found him meant Mergim knew all about how Valter had spent his last few years once he'd retreated to Osijek. Valter clearing his throat.

'Don't know how you think I can aid you.'

Mergim going through the motions of cleaning out the pan with a rag, despite Valter's bread doing the job perfectly well.

'Have to admit I was mighty surprised to hear you'd turned up again in this neck of the woods,' Mergim changed tack. 'Sort of took it as a sign.' Fingers going to the embroidered talisman about his neck. 'And I know you might think it odd, but after Kragujevac, after prison—well, I got the notion to see how the child was doing, seeing as how most of it was all my fault.'

Valter let out a snort of laughter.

'No need to kid yourself on that front,' he advised. 'We all know how that particular set of circumstances came about, and you weren't no more to blame than the arrow someone lets loose from a bow.'

Mergim thought about that, had thought about it a lot in Kragujevac, always coming to the opposite conclusion.

'You're wrong,' he said. 'I didn't have to do what I did. Could've turned back at any point, could have—'

'Could have, should have,' Valter interrupted. 'You'd have had your belly split open if you'd done so, left to die in a ditch with your guts spooling out before your eyes. You know it as well as I do.'

Valter's face creasing up. Mergim unnerved by Valter's vehemence and his vivid description. Valter very likely right. Yet still the fact remained that Mergim had always had a choice. Sudden sight of all those white egrets nesting in the marshes when he'd considered flight, of taking Hulde with him and getting the hell away. How he'd argued himself out of it at the time, believing the probable outcome to be both himself and Hulde tracked down and killed, or maybe only him. Hulde too valuable a commodity.

A weak argument it seemed when he'd thought about it properly, because he surely could have dropped the girl off somewhere safe and gone on alone, drawn the wolf after him and him alone. Sacrificed himself for her. And if anyone should have sacrificed himself for Hulde it surely had to be him.

Cowardice. No more, no less.

Long, long time to come to that conclusion.

'But she's happy with the Pfiffmaklers?' he asked. 'Hulde's happy with them?'

'Oh for God's sake!' Valter wheezed out another laugh. 'Couldn't be happier! You did her a favour in the long run. The whole lot of them happy as can be.'

Mergim remembering Valter's words of the night before, as Valter patently did not, how Valter had found the Pfiffmakler life repellent. Valter unable to bear so much happy family life all around him on a daily basis. And no wonder. Valter a boy who'd grown up in the worst of times, who wouldn't know normal if it slapped him in the face. Not that the Pfiffmaklers were normal in the strictest sense: always on the move, going from here to there to entertain whoever they encountered. A family nonetheless, more hard-bound than most by the life they led; as tied together as moss and spiderwebs in a goldcrest's nest, keeping by necessity to their own. No outsiders needed.

Mergim could see how that would grate on Valter, because it would have grated on himself. Rubbed him right up wrong, as his father had once said when the two sides of the divide of their village had fallen into outright war; families ripped stem from stern.

Folk like him and Valter destined to be on the edges, always happier on their own.

Folk who would never marry, never have families, not trusting themselves to bring up children to be better than they were themselves.

Happiness did not come into it.

'I need your help, Valter,' Mergim repeated his opening plea. 'I need to find the Pfiffmaklers. Ten years I've been in prison. Ten years, Valter. And now I'm out, well. It's all I want to do. All I've thought about. I have to see that Hulde's all right. I have to.'

Seeing the hesitation in Valter, if not the words tumbling through Valter's mind like a stream in spate:

Be the fine man I know you can be. Make me proud.

Valter closing his eyes, nodding his acquiescence, saying the words Mergim needed to hear.

'They're up country. Went north. Said they weren't coming back this way in a long time. Said they was going to try their hand as far north as they could get.'

As far away from me and my mess as possible, Valter was thinking, *and who could blame them for that?*

Eavesdroppers And Poetisers

Philbert too was thinking on the Pfiffmaklers, the how and why of them helping him.

Heraldo's idea, he was certain. Wenzel a good man, but unlikely to stick out his neck for anyone less than family. Excepting Hulde, which had struck Philbert as a mighty strange tale when he'd heard it, about as strange as his own. Such stories travelling like weevils through soil when it came to fairs' folk.

He was gazing at the late afternoon clouds, how they seemed to radiate from a single source on the sea's horizon like spokes from a wheel. Had been told a person's sightline was limited to around fifteen miles. An opinion he knew to be false. How else to explain being able to make out snow-clad mountains you knew to be forty, fifty miles distant? All to do with perspective: how you looked, where you were looking from. Like his own story, and Hulde's too: single events, single perspectives, throwing out a whole world of possible paths and endings.

Philbert conjuring up a scene from the *Philocalia*: St Ephrem's imagined argument between Heaven and Earth. A ridiculous debate if ever there was one. Heaven claiming its clouds represented the blessing hands of priests, the watchers, embodiments of the awe and beauty of God's Creation. Earth retorting it took the upper hand for it contained the prophets beloved not only by God but by humankind, and therefore should take the prize.

Philbert had never understood Kwert's religion, but understood awe; the unequivocal release he'd felt on seeing the sea again, of walking along its edge after he'd emerged from the forest by the Joshua Tree. A sea not seen up close since he'd left those other forests and shores in Schleswig-Holstein. A sea that hadn't broken, merely lapped silently in the fog against great banks of seaweed that would lie and rot, either on the shingle or on the villagers' fields, this part of the Baltic too small and landlocked to have proper tides; going up and down by mere inches instead of many yards, or many hundreds of yards, like normal seas.

But oh the smell of it had set his heart thrumming, and a hundred memories cascading through his head. No horizon visible then, only fog and water, and a visceral joy to be putting his feet onto shingle, to smell salt and seaweed. A determination that wherever Heraldo was seeing fit to send him he would not be parted from the sea again. Would find a place where every day he could walk down to the water, study the tides, track their movements, their depleted highs and lows. A place where he could tread the sands, sift with the sanderlings through the strandlines, make up his own arguments between Heaven and Earth about who was the most righteous and who the most blessed.

Too much time alone, many might have said had they been privy to Philbert's thoughts that afternoon, if not Philbert, nor Kroónk, as they spent another day and another night lying on their stomachs, gazing out onto the unfathomable sea.

Heaven and Earth their purview.

Heaven and Earth.

No one knowing precisely where they intersected, only that at some point they did.

Rasvlach and Diderik were landed on Rügen. Joshua Tree villager away the moment their feet touched shore, quick with his oars, pushing himself off again, never minding Rasvlach's cursed commands that he get himself back to give direction.

No sir, no more commands from you, you foul-mouthed man.

Villager away back to his village, and good bloody riddance to Rasvlach and Diderik.

Filth joining filth on the island of the damned.

Valter and Mergim set out north following the Danube soon as Valter had finished up his business, delivered his last commodities. Valter adamant he could not go without doing so. Mergim surprised by the regret expressed by Valter's customers, who were genuinely sad to see him go.

'Gonna miss you,' one had said, summing up for all. 'Never had better hafts nor shafts for me hoes and scythes, nor ones that fit right in and don't give me blisters. And the wife'll be sore annoyed when one of them pan handles of hers splits and you're not here to do another.'

The man putting out his hand, shaking Valter's.

'Good luck to you. Hope you find yourself a better road.'

Everyone knowing Valter's main occupation was drinking himself to death, glad he might be being given a way out of it.

Mergim asking Valter how long he'd stayed with the Pfiffmaklers, if he'd any idea where he'd left them.

'Stopped a while with them,' Valter replied vaguely. 'Took that long to get ourselves to Budapest. Loads of villages and towns in those parts and Wenzel had passes to all of them, and they all had festivals and feast-days pouring out their ears. All those bloody saints.'

Valter getting quieter after they'd skirted Budapest and were halfway to Vienna, reaching the outskirts of a tree glade where Valter stopped short by a cairn, most of whose stones had been scattered about its base. Valter kicking through them, looking for something. Finally had it, lifted it up: a small rounded knob of wood worn away by years of adverse weather and being scuffled about by travellers' boots, but plainly of significance to Valter.

'I can't believe it's still here,' Valter whispered, stroking his fingers over its blunted edges, over the thin letters on its base.

Mergim choosing not to speak, for what this lump of wood represented he'd no idea.

'Echinos,' Valter explained. 'Igel, Iritch, Arichi, and all kinds of hedgehoggery. This is where we buried my uncle.'

Valter sinking down, settling his back against the loose remnants of the cairn.

'He's right here beneath me,' Valter got out. 'Sometimes wished they'd buried me with him. Didn't have no right nor left after he'd gone.'

Mergim understanding, Mergim moving away, setting up camp a few yards distant.

No more broken a man at the war criminal's trial than Valter, who'd shattered himself into a thousand pieces when he'd tried to explain what it was all about, crying like a strangled crow.

As Mergim might have fractured Hulde had the Pfiffmaklers not been there to pick up the pieces. Mergim more determined than ever to find her. This Mergim's task, and maybe providing Valter a way back into the world, if Valter would allow it.

Pietro was fretting they'd not get all done in time.

When he'd put his new idea to Wenzel and Rosa they'd agreed immediately that Prisoner 101 fell by the roadside in comparison. Pietro blushing to realise it had always been a little clunky and tortuous, despite it going down well enough at St Mary's with its swerve into Jaromar/Hildegard.

'We can mug up a script without much problem,' Wenzel said. 'I can think of several of our present ones we can adapt to the story, do it by patchwork so to speak. It's the backdrops are the problem.'

A real stumbling block to his mind, until his wife broke in.

'I think you've already put your finger on it, my dear,' Rosa commented mildly, Wenzel harrumphing.

'I don't see how,' he muttered, puffing at his unlit pipe.

'Patchwork!' Livia said, getting Rosa's gist. 'We've plenty spare linen. We paint it up and tack it over various sections... but will they dry in time?'

Livia suddenly anxious. Rosa responding by sucking a thumb, holding it up to the air.

'Good drying wind coming in from the south-west,' she said, with the absolute conviction of a woman who'd been washing clothes and linen all her life. 'And it's dry as a bone. We pin the new sections like hammocks between the trees and they'll dry within hours. No rain yet,' she added, sniffing the air, 'though reckon it won't be more than a few days coming.'

And no more than a few days they had. Sagard and the congregation of St Michael's eagerly awaiting their arrival after Pietro's and Wenzel's visit the previous afternoon.

The whole clan falling into well accustomed roles as they prepared, not at all disconcerted when a dozen youngsters turned up the following morning to see what was what. A labour force swiftly taken advantage of.

'Want to help?' Heraldo asked the crowd of curious children who didn't need asking twice, all running forward at his direction, agog to see the fairs' folk on their knees by various large rectangles of canvas laid out on the ground.

'You, you and you!' Heraldo commanded. 'Get yourselves over to the painting area. Need some sky-work blocking in, and some forest. And a couple off to fetch more water. And we need some binding twine. Know how to make it from willows?'

Several nods, and off the children went on a run.

'And you,' Heraldo signalled the straggler at the back: a skinny child, hollow chested, pock-marked face sucked in at the cheeks like a wilted gourd. 'What's your name?'

'Ortwin,' the lad sighed. 'S'alright, mister. If you've run out of stuff to do I don't mind just watching.'

The lad about to plonk himself down to do exactly that, adopt the role others had given him of being the un-useful one on the sole count of looking a bit different, running out of puff whenever they played games. The sort of lad who, early doors, his peers had played tricks on: hide and seek, with him hiding and them with no intention whatsoever of seeking, some helpful churl whispering the best places to hide—always claustrophobic, small and dark—where Ortwin would bide for hours, sometimes overnight. Good hiding places right enough, for no one ever sought him out, not even his parents or older siblings. A game soon tired of, and onto something equally despicable.

'No such luck,' Heraldo answered affably. 'I've special duties for you.'

Ortwin didn't move, knew a double bluff when he saw one. Someone holding out a hand to shake then cocking the snook, chucking a load of hard conkers or stinking fish guts into his face.

'I'll go back,' he said. 'Thanks anyway, mister.'

Heraldo frowning. Heraldo wanting to bring the lad in, seeing the outlier in him and sympathising.

'No, wait. I mean it. I was thinking—'

'Heraldo thinking! That's something to watch,' Longhella exclaimed, sauntering into their circle, spotting the lone Ortwin, seeing a mark for her habitual unrest, flicking her braids, twitching her skirts, zeroing in and letting fall her gracious smile.

'Don't give him any mind, my fine young lad, for this here man,' indicating Heraldo, 'is a two-tongued viper is what he is. Him and his father. Only given me a bit part, as usual. Cut me out of the main stuff. So what's he been asking you to do? Because let me tell you, my young piece of plucked chicken, it won't be no wise better than what they've asked of me, which is to tell your entire island they're no better than a common whore for choosing one master over another.'

'Longhella!' Heraldo protested. 'You know that's not at all what we're doing.'

Longhella smiling beatifically at Ortwin.

'Just you wait and see,' she said. 'Just you wait and see.'

Ortwin stood, feet bolted to the ground as Longhella swung her hips and was away.

Ortwin enchanted, watching her every move, heart thumping as she turned and winked at him. At him! At Ortwin! Such a woman casting her graces at him and no one else.

Heraldo shaking his head.

'Talk about vipers,' he commented. 'Come on lad, still want to help?'

Steering Ortwin towards the lakeside. Ortwin nodding dumbly, overcome.

'You've fine fingers,' Heraldo observed. 'Ever done any painting?'

Ortwin finding his voice.

'Some,' he croaked, eager now to impress, to see that young woman again, revel in her smiles and graces at close quarters. 'Got to grinding ochre pastes when they was touching up the murals in St Michael's. Used to mix them up with water and dry them out into sticks,' Ortwin added. 'Got loads of colours from berries and plants and that. Mostly from around here.'

'Aha!' Heraldo quick to respond. 'That's perfect. Got just the job for you,' leading his charge onwards, introducing him to Rosa and Yssel, who were in a tizz.

'Run out of red,' Rosa informed her son briefly, rubbing her hands on her apron. 'Lord knows how we're going to complete the battle scenes.'

'Red, is it?' Ortwin feeling he'd grown three inches in the last few minutes, as if his hollowed-out chest had been refilled. 'Then you'll be needing down the other end of the lake where the eel traps are laid. There's a spring a few yards out and all it does is leak iron oxide like there's no tomorrow.'

Rosa and Yssel delighted. Ortwin proving a willing aide; quick with his directions, quick with his hands, quicker still to mix up the paste needed, deft when it came to applying the newly ground paint to the canvases.

'So you're doing what?' he asked. 'You said battlegrounds earlier? What battlegrounds?'

'Just you wait and see,' Rosa said, as Longhella had done before her.

'And you will!' Heraldo clapped Ortwin on the back. 'For we're going to have you right with us in the wings. Give you a grand eye view, seeing as how much help you've been.'

Ortwin delighted, Ortwin proud, Ortwin ignoring all the other village children as they went scampering back and headed off to Sagard once night began to fall on that winter afternoon. Ortwin electing to play his own game of hide and seek, pretending away, circling around, locating the lightning-hollowed oak he'd visited before, deciding to bide there the whole night through. A small place and dark, if not for him claustrophobic, where he could stay out his night, watch the extraordinary Pfiffmaklers go about their duties, listen to their talk, watch for those orange skirts to come swishing into the brash light of their fire, for the sway of those hips, the twitch of those lips, the swinging of those plaits.

Ortwin smitten.

Ortwin watching and listening when the Pfiffmaklers lifted their bowls of pigments away from the fire, replacing them with several pans to heat up their evening repast; his stomach grumbling as the fish they'd caught from the lake simmered in their juices. Smells augmented by dried wild garlic and thyme, the charcoaled scents of the flatbreads Rosa and Yssel flipped from their hands onto hot stones and back up again and over.

Oh my; he didn't think his day could have got any better, but here came that young woman again, the one he'd been waiting for. Longhella quite a few years his senior, but no less alluring for all that. Longhella flicking over her shoulders her long braids seemingly sparkling with gold in the firelight and jumping with their embers. Longhella joining her folk by the fire as they ate. Ortwin cocking his ear, catching vague snippets of conversation, tantalising talk of his island's history the Pfiffmaklers were apparently about to bring to life. Ortwin shivering with cold as the night came down and frost began to harden in the crevasses of tree bark about him, getting a little cramp in his foot so he had to rub and wriggle it to ease the spasms away.

Ortwin pulling lichen and moss from about the tree's base to make himself warmer, more comfortable, though God knew he'd been in colder and more uncomfortable places than this—his sleeping quarters in the root cellar beneath his parents' house equally chilly. His nighttime job to set traps for rats and mice, chase off any that didn't go willingly to their demise. His parents not unkind, but every child had to earn their keep in a household as poor as theirs, Ortwin no exception. And he preferred it down there, away from the loud snores of his father, the shuffling and kicking of his siblings as they slept top to toe in their single wide bed.

Ortwin liking the darkness, the earthy scents of the piles of potatoes, the apples in their barrels bedded in with dried bracken, the strings of drying onions hanging down from hooks like strangled men, the rich aroma of curing blood sausages and brined cuts of meat that would see them through the winter months; appreciative of the faint glow coming from the mould covering the sausage skins, and the few thin fingers of moonlight eking through cracks in the upper slats of his cellar's walls.

He got the shock of his life when a couple of the Pfiffmaklers rose up from their fire and filtered themselves away towards him. Thought at first it was Longhella again, but no. Someone very like her but older, leaner, with the same braided hair and orange skirts though less extravagant, more measured in her movements. And with her came Heraldo, the two moving easily if somewhat furtively, Heraldo cupping the woman's elbow with his hand.

'I've been thinking we ought to get word to him,' Heraldo spoke quietly, the woman biting at her bottom lip before replying.

'Me too. It's been almost a week since we landed him. He might be thinking we've deserted.'

Heraldo shook his head.

'I told him it would be a while. Then again I don't want him getting itchy feet, and a week's a long time to be kicking your heels when you're used to being constantly on the move.'

Ortwin caught his breath, moved involuntarily back into his hollow.

Heraldo turning his head towards the slight sound, like an owl listening for the rustling of a vole.

'Did you hear that?' he whispered, holding his head quite still, clutching tightly at Ludmilla's elbow, Ludmilla leaning in towards her husband.

'I don't think I did. It's probably a fox, or maybe an otter. I saw some spraint back by the shore, and some fish bones.'

Ortwin impressed. He often came down to the lake at dawn to watch the otters, knew they came ashore at various fixed points not too far from their den; places they marked and guarded and left their detritus. He'd observed young spring-born kits trailing their mothers—the males gone away, not liking company—learning how to fish, how to sway their bodies and tails in the water to get up momentum; seen the youngsters plainly enjoying their play, sliding down a muddy bank into the water, wishing he could join them and do the same. He'd tried it once, on a sunny summer day, skimming down their mud slide, laughing as he went. Regretting it the following morning when he discovered the den deserted, his antics, his scent, having scared them away, made them secretive. Two weeks it had taken him to find the underwater entrance to their new den several hundred yards up shore in dense vegetation, well disguised by bulrushes and reeds, making it all the harder to observe the family he felt to be of his own.

'The fact remains,' Heraldo was saying, 'it's high time we got word to him.'

'I think we can say his name,' Ludmilla replied, 'unless you think these woods have ears.'

Heraldo smiled, but remained serious.

'I don't think we should. Just in case. He told me on the boat over that someone else in Rostock had been asking after him, but for goodness sake don't tell father that.'

Ludmilla let out a gasp.

'And this is the first time you've chosen to tell me?' Sounding angry, pulling herself away from Heraldo. 'And who exactly was asking? Did he know?'

Heraldo rubbing his eyes with his fingers, shaking his head.

'Some Serbian fellow is all he said,' Heraldo trying to ameliorate the situation. 'Though can't think why any Serbian would have... ouch!'

Heraldo wincing as Ludmilla jabbed him hard in the ribs with her elbow. No playing now.

'This is serious,' she said. 'I mean I know we always thought folk wouldn't have forgotten him. But someone asking directly? That puts a whole new edge on things. What if they've followed him? Followed us? Put two and two together?'

'How could they have?' Heraldo argued, louder than he'd intended, completely ignorant this wood really did have ears, namely Ortwin's. 'There's nothing to tie us to Philbert... I mean to... well, you know who I mean. There's nothing, Ludmilla. You know how carefully we've planned this.'

Ludmilla subsided, nodded in the meagre moonlight, looked off towards the lake, to the rest of the Pfiffmaklers sat about their fire. Listened to her cousins, Lupercal and Jericho, as they rehearsed one of the songs they'd need for the pageant Livia and Pietro had engineered so recently to reflect the history of this island. This their being, their lifeblood: the constant need to adapt to new circumstance as and when it presented itself. And she supposed Philbert's new circumstances were no different. But all the more need to communicate with him, tell him to bide his time, stay hidden until they were certain the coast was clear. Quite literally. The coast being clear integral to their plan.

'And you did set up with him the notion about the trees?' Ludmilla asked, as if Heraldo might have forgotten. The idea sparked by a poetiser they'd met a few months before they'd reached Rostock. A man who carved his poems into the smooth bark of trees, making a scant living from folk paying him to inscribe short verses, usually from lover to lover, or from a son to his mother as he left for war or to make his fortune, or to celebrate the passing of someone recently deceased. Some mundane, some rather beautiful, most impressive being the poetiser's masterpiece, carved over several months and still working on it when Ludmilla and Heraldo came across the man: a full forty lines of verse top down from a bole he'd carefully been pollarding and nurturing so the blank bark ran from the tree's mid-level branches to the ground. Eight long feet in which to inscribe his poem, the man balancing up top his ladder to get the first line done, and then the next, and the next, all the way to the ground.

Still four feet up when Heraldo and Ludmilla had happened upon him.

'My paean to the universe!' he'd cried happily as they came to see him at his work, throw a few coins into his cap as others had done before them.

'Won't all be lost when the bark heals itself?' Heraldo had asked.

'You might think so,' the poetiser replied, looking down on them from his ladder, 'except the way I'm putting in the words? The way I'm chiselling them in? What will happen is that yes, the bark will heal itself. Close itself over the gashes. But I've put them deep and wide so when the wood heals over it will leave thin scars on the surface and those scars will be my words. My words! Here for centuries!'

Privately Heraldo doubted it; then again he'd seen inscriptions on tree boles going back almost two hundred years, if the dates could be believed; so maybe if this poet had chosen just the right tree, the exact right bark, he might be on to something.

'Think on it!' the poetiser's enthusiasm had not been dimmed. 'I'm only going back to source. Paper comes from trees. Ink comes from pine tar. All I'm doing is stripping the middle processes away. Giving back to the trees what the trees have always given us.'

An elegant philosophy, Heraldo had thought then.

'I'm thinking we should send Longhella,' Ludmilla said, ignoring trees and verses not yet written. Ludmilla thinking back to her conversation with Livia a few days previously about Longhella being judged and yet having so much more to her than people thought—as far as Ludmilla was concerned.

'Longhella!' Heraldo exclaimed. 'Surely not!'

The words out before he could stop them. Ludmilla looking up at him with disquiet.

Heraldo qualifying.

'I just mean, well. She's hardly the most inconspicuous person in the world.'

'Quite,' Ludmilla answered shortly. 'So who's going to suspect her of doing anything other than going around collecting fungi and nuts for her family?'

'But to send her alone? Is that wise?' Heraldo not convinced. 'Perhaps one of the boys should go with her?'

'Perhaps,' Ludmilla agreed. 'But I was thinking not. I was thinking we should send her when the Advent Cycle is in full swing, when just about everyone in the entire district will be at St Michael's.'

Heraldo smiled into the darkness.

'So it was you who convinced Livia and Pietro to give her such a small part?'

Remembering how annoyed Longhella had been, though maybe not when she learned she had a bigger part to play in someone else's drama.

Ludmilla leant her head against Heraldo's shoulder, braced herself, knowing Heraldo was not going to like what she next said. Got it said anyway.

'I think she should take Hulde with her.'

Holding her breath, unsurprised when Heraldo's body heaved and flung Ludmilla away, holding her at arm's length.

'You can't be serious. Longhella and Hulde? Why on earth would you think that a good idea?'

Longhella's attitude towards Hulde unchanged in all the years Hulde had been with them; Longhella believing Hulde a cuckoo in the nest, Longhella never able to accept Hulde as the rest had done. Longhella believing Hulde to be the source of the events that had led to Old Grandma Pfiffmakler leaving.

'Don't you think it's time?' Ludmilla persisted. 'It might help them both. They've never been alone together. Never. Just think on that.'

Heraldo thinking, realising it was true, and how odd that was. Thinking too it was not such a bad idea after all and saying so. The two moving back towards the lake, decision made.

Ortwin's ears twitching, going red about their edges.

Ortwin quick to see the possibilities. Ortwin imbued with the tales told by the elders of his village of adventure, piracy and romance. Longhella seemingly made for the part of heroine: beautiful, strong, a temper quick and hot as fire. Longhella about to embark on a dangerous mission to carve words into trees to aid a hidden fugitive.

Of Hulde he knew nothing, and did not care.

Ortwin, the village boy whom everyone overlooked, privy to this secret, and swearing he would make certain his heroine came to no harm.

New Plays, Bad Eggs

On the outskirts of Sagard, the Pfiffmaklers are surrounded by crowds eager to take their burdens from them and steer them to the church. With the help of the village children all had been completed on schedule. And now the great day was upon them the children insisted on being the ones to push and pull the cart carrying the huge rolled up panorama—heavier now it had several sections over-sewn with the new linen panels they'd helped create. No notion in them what it was, how it would play out, yet keen to demonstrate their partial ownership. Pfiffmaklers happy for their help, freeing the Pfiffmaklers up to make a big entrance, playing their instruments, banging their drums, Lupercal and Jericho tumbling their acrobatics up the street. Several children trying to emulate their breathtaking leaps and tumbles, failing miserably. Luckily no broken bones, as had happened in other places at other times.

The whole town-ship a-jitter. Pfiffmaklers scarcely needing to advertise their wares; the two days they would be in Sagard already declared an Advent Holiday, and everyone keen to take advantage. Sagard men and women setting up their own meagre entertainments comprising barrels in which to bob for apples, a stall of hoop-la where folk could throw horseshoes onto sticks to win small trinkets; several trestles erected beneath canvas hoods, to keep off the rain Rosa had anticipated the coming of, laden with platters of food, bowls of drink, everyone anticipating the feast.

The Pastor of St Michael's having difficulty weaving a way through his excited congregation, finally managing to puff his way up to Wenzel, shake his hand.

'You're so welcome!' he enthused. 'I can't tell what an honour it is to have a real live Advent Cycle here in our church. We've heard such good things from your last port of call. This place is really rather parochial,' he whispered in an aside, 'gossip travelling free as the wind. But good gossip in this case. Very good. Come! Come!'

Leading the Pfiffmaklers into his church, pointing proudly at the stage he'd set up before the altar.

'I've had to push all the seats back,' he went on, 'but nobody will mind being a little short on leg room. Oh come on in! You're so welcome!'

The whole place rushing and twittering like the Pfiffmaklers were the grandest, strangest thing they'd ever seen. Which they were. Rügen not on any regular fairs' circuit, as Wenzel had accurately predicted. Wenzel overwhelmed by their welcome—no need for letters of introduction or passes here—and hoped they would not disappoint.

'What do you need?' the Pastor asked as he led his visitors towards his stage. 'I do hope I've adequately set it up. I've ensured all is propped, and you've two sets of steps, one to left and one to right. I know a little about theatrics,' he confided. 'Used to have a parish in Copenhagen before I came here. And no doubt you've heard of their famous harbour entertainments. Happy days!'

Propelling Wenzel on before him. Wenzel getting up on the stage, inspecting its length and breadth, its side-steps, the strength of its boards, the places they'd need to erect the panorama, where they could install buckets instead of fire-pits; how they could secrete a couple of shrouded booths in which to change costumes, set up instruments.

'You've done a magnificent job,' Wenzel complimented. 'We'll need an hour or so to get ready, but no reason not to give our first performance soon as.' Getting out his pocket watch and giving it an ostentatious wind. 'How does twelve noon sound?'

'Perfect!' the Pastor agreed with alacrity. 'We'll get the bells ringing a quarter hour before, although I suspect everyone is here already.'

And so it was.

Wenzel gathering his troops.

'All right, everyone. As agreed we'll lead with our new Island History first, give them Hildegard of Bingen tomorrow and end with our usual Creation of the World. Any questions?'

No questions, although Ludmilla and Heraldo requested a private word.

'It's about Philbert,' Heraldo began. Wenzel sucking in his lips, making it look like the bottom half of his face was entirely made of beard from nose to chin.

'What else would it be?' he asked, trying to hide his irritation. 'I've already said that yes, you've made a good plan, but it cannot be allowed to impinge on what we're doing here. You said yourself that if it's to succeed then we need to get ourselves—'

'I know that, Father,' Heraldo interrupted. 'And yes, of course it does. But we can't leave him hanging in the wind. We've to—'

'We've to nothing,' Wenzel stopped his son short. 'This is your plan, and yours only. I've told you before I've misgivings, and I'm not alone. Neither Yssel nor Rosa are happy.'

Wenzel stopped himself, tutted, shook his head.

Neglecting to mention how Peppe had stood up for Heraldo, and Philbert's plight; the only one to do so.

'I'm sorry, son. I know how much this means to you but honestly, for the rest of us? We're just wanting to make a good Advent Cycle and get on.'

Wenzel relenting slightly, seeing the disappointment on Heraldo's face.

Wenzel sighing.

'What do you need?' he asked. 'It better hadn't be much.'

Ludmilla smiling, never really believing Wenzel would deny them.

'Longhella for a couple of hours, and Hulde.'

Wenzel's eyebrows rising like twin grey clouds.

'Longhella and Hulde?' he asked, with incredulity. 'And when do you need them?'

'Soon as you can release them from the performance,' Heraldo said quickly. 'We're thinking during the first battle, get them away while no one's looking.'

Wenzel's lips twitching with amusement and admiration.

'So you've already planned this with Livia and Pietro,' he stated. 'And what if Longhella doesn't go for it?' Catching the glance between

Heraldo and Ludmilla, shaking his head, knowing as well as they that Longhella would rather do anything than sit on her hands, be forced to watch a play she was no great part of.

'Very well then,' he agreed. 'Don't bother me with particulars. I've too much to organise. Speak to your sister, Ludmilla. And Hulde? Well, I'll leave that bit of tricksiness up to you.'

Bang on twelve they started, the church thronged from side to side, end to end, a boat about to embark on an adventure to a place its voyagers could neither know nor anticipate.

'From early days,' Wenzel calls out, looking magnificent in a cape collared with fox fur standing proud from shoulders to ears, 'your island of Rügen has been a most important place. The largest island in all of Germany and of singular form: intersected by indentations of the sea, lending it a beauty none other can boast; as filled with hill and dale and wild-wooded ravines as the mainland over the water is flat and beset by marsh and lake.'

The panorama behind Wenzel flicking quickly through to the first new scene to demonstrate this fact.

'And a holy place, protected by sheer chalk cliffs and the ramparts built to keep it safe; owner of the Konigsberg, the King's Chair. A place from where Odoacer set forth with his army to conquer Italy and Rome.'

Another enthralling zoom-by of the panorama, pausing on Odoacer with his sword held high, great white cliffs framing him as if he were a god; gasps from the audience, who've never heard their history so declaimed and admired, knowing only the shame of being the last pagan stronghold in the west.

'Heroes all!' As if Wenzel had read their minds. 'A strong people! A courageous people! People who had principles, stuck to their old religion, would not bow down to the bullying yolk!'

And now appears Svetovid, god of the Slavs, walking before the landscape of their island like the imposing god he was. Pietro, within Svetovid's hollow core, holding up the imposing edifice with his hands as Longhella comes on, priestess divine, filling Svetovid's outstretched horn with mead that fizzles and cracks and gushes flame.

'Here is your oracle!' Wenzel declares. 'Representative of the Old Days when all men had was themselves, before the light of Christianity dawned!'

'I implore you,' Longhella sways and calls, wide dark eyes heavily lined with kohl, 'Old Master, protect our island! Make it fertile! Give us sons and daughters to carry on our line!'

Longhella's entire involvement thereby done; Longhella coming off stage, spitting on a cloth, wiping her eyes clean, none too pleased to see her sister bearing down on her.

'What do you want?' Longhella demanded. 'Come to crow about your being the princess when all I got was one shitty line? And don't think I don't know that was all your doing. Livia practically told me as much.'

Ludmilla tensed, but could get out no words as by then Eric the Memorable, along with his Danish army, were storming the ancient temple fortress of the Rani and the crowds were oohing and aahing at the great booms of weaponry and the fountains of green and red sparks gushing up from fire buckets.

'There's a reason,' Ludmilla said, leading Longhella aside as the Rani carried on with their battle. 'There's something we need you to do. It's important.'

Longhella scrunched up her nose.

'Important to who? To you and Heraldo?'

Ludmilla put a hand to her neck.

'To Philbert,' she said simply. 'We need to get a message to him, and you're the best person to do it.'

That got Longhella's attention. She'd not been much interested in Philbert's plight previous to him being landed on Rügen, although now he was here she had to admit she was intrigued. A real live murderer in their midst, a man on the run, like a character from one of their many stories. She found the prospect of meeting him titillating, not that it would do to tell Ludmilla. Ludmilla briefing her sister on her mission, before the Great Storm of 1157 began to wreck the thousand ships the Slavs were sending in defence of their great god Rani's outpost of Rügen Island; another sweep of the panorama, the tremendous sounds of thunder and crashing waves keeping their audience enthralled.

Longhella's only annoyance being that she was supposed to take Hulde with her.

'I'll not,' she said flatly. 'That little bit can stay as far away from me as possible. I don't want anything to do with her.'

Ludmilla suppressing her annoyance, getting out her explanation. 'We can't send you off alone, and Hulde's the only one not needed.'

'Not needed is right,' Longhella spat. 'Not by me, not by anyone.'

Despite her outburst she saw the point. Everyone else all hands on deck during this new play of the conversion of Rügen, all the menfolk—Lupercal and Jericho included—needed for the battle scene to come when Waldemar the First and his tame Bishop Absalon began the siege of 1168 to crush the Rani rebels once and for all beneath their Christian heel.

And no choice than to accept Ludmilla's terms, setting off into the early afternoon towards the dark forests of Jasmund with Hulde treading on her skirts; the two of them toting wicker baskets to gather their putative foraging wares, Longhella's newly sharpened knife hidden about her person, fingers itching to turn its blade not into trees—no poetiser she—but into Hulde's slender pearl-white neck.

Just give her an excuse and she'd do it without a qualm.

Valter and Mergim settled into a different kind of life now they'd been on the road a few months. Valter proving himself adept and useful, bringing with him his filthy bedroll, a length of canvas for shelter, his skillet, and his tools. With the latter he constructed a cart entirely out of wood and dowels, no need for glue or nails, on which to drag their paltry possessions. Their days spent trundling along tracks and byways, setting camp and a fire at night; Valter whittling hafts and handles to hawk in the next villages passed through. Valter teaching Mergim the rudimentaries of wood carving, a pastime both found soothing. Valter occasionally turning his hand to a lump of unpromising wood, creating hedgehogs or larger versions of the chess pieces he'd used to make back in the day. Surprised when Mergim produced a small box from his pocket and undid the crude latch, laying out a tiny chess board, its squares demarcated by scorch marks from heated lengths of wire laid into the wood, and a dozen little play pieces of acorns planed flat at one end, the opposing side created from conkers split down the middle.

'Lost a few along the way,' Mergim apologised. 'But we could play draughts, if you'd like.'

Valter drew in his eyebrows, wondering if Mergim knew about Valter's previous side-line, though if he did he didn't show it. A week or so later, Valter handed Mergim a small pouch and when Mergim undid it he spilled into his hand a perfect set of miniature chess pieces, all clearly recognisable. One side carved from light-shaded wood, the other from dark.

'These are… they're wonderful, Valter. Thank you!'

Valter stroking the sides of his mouth, a genuine smile wheedling itself upon chapped lips. Nights next spent in quiet battles; no thundering canons, cracking gunfire or cascading sparks needed for these two who took the greatest pleasure in moving the tiny pieces around their tiny board, trying not overturn their armies with a misplaced thumb.

They had their first piece of luck outside Linz, where they met a Tibetan contortionist—a small woman, lithe and sinewy as a stoat—who'd spent a few months with the Pfiffmaklers a couple of years back, leaving them not far out of Leipzig.

'That lad of theirs was falling over himself to see the new railway there,' she told them, laughing at the memory. 'I think he would have joined the navvies if Wenzel had let him. Goes all the way to Hamburg now, so I'm told.'

'That could get us on a bit, that railway,' Mergim said to Valter later that night. Valter not much interested, had found a peace in this travelling, Mergim never pressing him into conversation, never alluding to their past. No more discussed was why Mergim was bothering to take Valter with him, although they did spend an hour or so each evening with Valter tutoring Mergim in the German language Mergim had only a smattering of, and only in that way long-term citizens of Zadar had: a pinch of this language here, a pinch of another there, conversations often starting in Italian, passing through German and ending in Croatian or Hungarian.

Valter still getting blind drunk on occasion, if rarely now. More often they'd buy a couple of bottles of wine, a bag of flour, a few sausages or cuts of meat with money earned from Valter's carvings, passing the evenings companionably playing chess or whittling wood, slicing sausages into the skillet, making flat breads fried in their fat.

By late summer they were in sight of Leipzig, stumbling on a large hiring fair where crowds of labourers jostled amongst tenant farmers and landowners to offer their services for the harvests soon to come. A young clerk desperately trying to take charge.

'Fruit-pickers to the left! Potato-sorters to the right! Those with experience of grapes and vines need to get themselves to the north of the field!'

The crush tremendous, the clerk humiliated to find his orders routinely ignored. And not only were there hirelings and hirers but a tumult of fairs folk touting their wares.

Mergim and Valter setting up camp a way distant, Valter adamant he wouldn't go anywhere near the fair, didn't on any account want to risk bumping into anyone he'd met previously with Andreas or, more latterly, with the Pfiffmaklers.

Mergim not understanding Valter's underlying panic.

'We're hundreds of miles from where you were when you were on the circuit,' Mergim argued, 'and hundreds of miles, and years and years, since you left the Pfiffmaklers.'

Valter not to be moved. Valter knowing about fairs and the way they travelled, how they gossiped, how information split and moved, shifted into song and play.

Mergim going in alone; Mergim not long in finding a snippet of information on the Pfiffmaklers after assiduous asking.

'Pfiffmaklers? Pfiffmaklers! Why yes! Saw them in Wittenberge-on-the-Elbe. Ooh, must have been June or thereabouts, but don't press me on that. Hadn't seen them in years. They was all looking well. And didn't regret the loss of that Old Grandma of theirs, who used to be able to cut a piece of wood with her tongue. Heard she's in a convent now. Still going strong. Saint in the making, if you can believe it. Heavens! We laughed about that all night long we did. Old Grandma Pfiffmakler a saint! On the other hand, if she's managed to stay alive this long maybe there's summat to be said for it.'

Good information.

Mergim moving off, moving away, about to head back to camp when his eye was caught by a troop of actors leaping onto a stage. At their fore a harlequin, dizzying and diverting in his diamond-patterned costume, spooling out his opening song in high and piercing voice:

Our year of revolution was done in 1848,
But hold on workers, labourers! It's not too late.
We turned governments upon their heads,
Hurled politicians and princes from their goose-down beds;
We ousted Metternich from our shores,
And we can still do so much more.
Fire up, sisters, brothers,
Fathers and mothers.
Fire up!

On came the dancers, banging drums, clattering tambourines and, shocking for Mergim, behind them began to ripple and flutter the red, white and blue tricolour Mergim knew so well. Mergim hemmed in by the crowds. Mergim staying to watch the show.

And so, Ladies and Gents, begins our tale, Harlequin intones, his actors getting into their places.

Of heroism, brotherhood and betrayal.
Of men, bound by common faith and goal,
Who fought to free the Serbian soul...

Mergim's breath catching in his throat.

We must begin at the start, Harlequin advises;
In order to understand the beating heart
Of our cousin country who has so much to teach us,
Who doesn't preach to us
Instead gives us hope, gives us scope
To carry on our fight...

Mergim's skin crawling with dread anticipation as the actors ready themselves for battle. Sees the leader of the Serbs, his beard black and grizzled as a bison's pelt, and knows what must come.

Centuries of oppression! Harlequin will not desist;
Of foreign rule, taxes and domination!

Harlequin moves to left of stage now he's primed the scene and on come the righteous, readying themselves for battle against the Turks; next minute the stage a stramash of fighting bodies, hand-to-hand combat that seems so real with the dinning sounds of clashing metal, screams and groans, the stink of men's sweat—real or imagined—the slippery out-pouring of blood from hidden vials; the shocking sight of men twisted and broken spilling from the stage at the feet of the audience; men who stay there, prostrate and bleeding, the whole performance through, reminding everyone how battle and revolution have consequence, and all the more reason to fight on because of those already fallen.

Too much for Mergim, who knows this part of Serbia's history better than most; who has been sunk into the mire of it right up to his neck.

Vomit hot in Mergim's throat as he beats his retreat, skin pale and sweaty, dreading the songs Harlequin might soon belt out, bringing back that whole life previous to Kragujevac he's been trying so hard to forget.

Valter right.

This no place for either of them.

Stories told, stories assimilated and spat out again.

Valter's story, Mergim's story, and Hulde's too.

Mergim pushing through the crowds, Mergim putting his hand over his heart, willing it to calm, Mergim heading for the woods.

An innocent village put to the slaughter!

The only survivor a single daughter...

Harlequin's clear and sonorous voice ringing out. Hulde's name not mentioned, although might as well have been. Mergim doubling over, stitch in his side making it hard to run further. Nearby, the lilting lines of a song thrush. Mergim choosing to concentrate on it, but truly all he can hear is the mayhem perpetrated on a lonely village at the very edge of the Adriatic, a village with its fig trees and sundial and buried mounds of the dead. Proof of unending conflict right there at Mergim's feet: a blue-grey, black-speckled eggshell ousted from its nest, broken about its middle, tiny wet-downed chick with its yellow mouth agape—crunched into non-existence as Mergim's boot came down before he could stop it.

Rotten Wood, Unexpected Meetings

Warm morning, considering the time of year, Philbert feeling the need to stretch his legs. Puts Kroonk in her crate and saunters some way from their camp, alighting on a small track meandering away from the trees. It comes to a stop directly on the cliff edge and, looking down, he sees a myriad ledges on which birds must nest in spring. Looking closer at the nearby trees he sees ropes carefully coiled and coifed on the middling branches, guesses lads must use these to go down the cliffs searching for eggs.

He's been on the island for over a week, notching off the days on a twig kept by his shelter—which was no grand affair, a branch of fir partially axed through and pulled to the ground, pegged down by sticks, cleared out in the middle, the outer foliage woven through with moss, lichen, smaller branches and twigs. He's angled it to keep out the prevailing wind, able to block up the entrance should the weather turn to cold and snow. He's dug a small fire-pit inside and collected enough bracket fungus for tinder to get it going whenever he needs.

The building of his shelter has occupied him for several days, and he spends an hour or so each morning adding to it, making it watertight and windproof, until it is so unobtrusive it looks like nothing more than a fallen-down tree. It's the longest he's stayed anywhere for the past few years, and rather likes having a homestead; soon settles into a pattern of fetching water from the lake at the centre of the forest, collecting nuts and any mushrooms still extant, checking his traps for small birds or squirrels, eking out the supplies Heraldo has provided him.

For all that, he's getting restive; needs to break cover for a while. Decides to head on through the trees, see if any messages have been left for him. Communication a hit and miss affair, neither he nor Heraldo having any precise knowledge of when a message might be made, Heraldo coming with him as far as the forest edge where the firs were necklaced by a thin line of deciduous trees. Heraldo pointing out a few stout beeches with smooth expanses of grey bark and handing him a crib sheet by which they could leave short messages.

A flock of fieldfares flash and flitter above his head, followed by the harsh alarm cry of a wren, and he stops, cocks his head, listening; hears voices; hunkers down behind a conifer and an uncomfortably prickly bush of butchers' broom. Stays put.

Hulde's basket is filling with winter salad plants: bitter cress, chickweed and wild mustard, all growing well during what was so far a mild winter. She also has a good heap of rosehips and sea-buckthorn berries, and is busy picking juniper berries from a large low-lying bush. Longhella some way ahead as Hulde tarries, digging up some dandelion roots Rosa can make into a throat-warming brew. She doesn't need Longhella's advice or guidance in any of this, has been well taught over the years and is enjoying this solitary spree into the woods. And with Longhella, Hulde always felt solitary. She doesn't harbour any animosity towards her. There were plenty of Pfiffmaklers to go around so one here or there didn't matter. In the early years she'd hardly noticed, although it had puzzled her as she'd grown and become aware of how acutely and actively Longhella disliked her.

'It's just the way families are,' Ludmilla had told her. 'You should have heard Old Grandma carping on at Matthys, and him her only child. They rubbed each other wrong at every turn, and her and Lotte—that's Matthys's wife—could barely stand to be in each other's company for more than a few minutes without spitting at each other.'

Enough for Hulde to be included into a family, however it was; couldn't wish to be included in any grander family than the Pfiffmaklers. She had occasional nightmares, sad and ghostly affairs compared to how they'd been in the early days when she'd wake up screaming, sweat running down her body, sometimes having peed herself. Longhella grumbling in the background:

'Not again. Honestly, I'm going to take myself off on my own someday where I never have to hear her complaining again.'

But always Ludmilla had been here, taking Hulde into her arms, and Heraldo not long behind removing soiled bed linen without a murmur and providing her a clean shift.

'There, there, my little sweet pea,' Ludmilla would say. 'All good as new.'

And good as new was what Hulde was now. All grown up in the Pfiffmakler way, Longhella's dislike of her no more troubling than the bloom gathering on the skin of a ripe plum. Unexplained, if of no bother.

Somewhat surprised, therefore, when she heard Longhella calling out her name.

'Hulde! Where in blazes are you? Get yourself here right now!'

Hulde giving the dandelion root one last tug to pull it free, putting it in her basket alongside fork and trowel. Same trowel Peppe had made for her years before, honed from childish toy into useful thin-wedged, sharp-edged tool carried by Hulde on all her foraging trips.

She didn't bother replying, merely followed the sound of Long-hella's voice and found her standing like a slender sapling, as graceful as ever, despite the frown upon her face.

'Look at this,' Longhella demanded, as Hulde came up beside her, waving the point of her knife at a tree. 'What do you see?'

Hulde looked and answered.

'Someone's carved their name in it,' she said. 'Or maybe not a name exactly.'

'Not a name is precisely right,' Longhella replied querulously. 'I thought you were supposed to be looking out for signs. Didn't I tell you to do that?'

'You did,' Hulde agreed, neglecting to add that Longhella was in the lead so Hulde couldn't possibly have seen it.

'Means we've gone too far,' Longhella sighed. 'Heraldo told me as much. Means we'll have to back-track. How much stuff have you got anyway?'

Looking disparagingly into Hulde's basket, annoyed to see Hulde had far more than she had herself.

'Well, I suppose that will have to do,' Longhella sniffed. 'So get you back down the way. Find the first of the signs and look out for those beggaring beeches Heraldo was blathering on about.'

Hulde hid a smile, for *I suppose that will have to do* was as much of a compliment as she'd ever had from Longhella.

'I think this is one of the beeches,' Hulde called, after a few minutes. 'And yes, here's the other one, like Heraldo told us. Sentries on either side of the path.'

'Well good for you,' Longhella replied, stamping towards Hulde. 'So come on. Let's get it done.'

Hulde bringing out the creased piece of paper folded in her smock pocket, Longhella wielding her sharp knife.

'You read, I'll carve.'

Hulde unfolding the paper, about to call out the symbols Heraldo had dictated:

One triangle: *we're here, and haven't forgotten.*

One square, with three horizontal lines beside it: *we'll be moving up country in three days.*

One diagonal slash left to right: *wait for further instructions.*

Hulde suddenly stopping, Longhella turning towards the younger girl with irritation, then Longhella stopping too.

'Did you hear…' Hulde began, Longhella flashing her blade towards her.

'Shush!' Longhella hissed, motioning Hulde to come stand at her back. This the closest they'd ever been, the two moving in a slow circle as they surveyed their surroundings: the bleached blank bole of the first beech tree, the track heading off into the pine forest, several denuded maples, a hazel, the track again, the second beech tree on its other side, a bush of butcher's broom, its bright red berries scanned over, its foliage looked through.

'I see you!' Longhella shouted. 'Make yourself known!'

Longhella snaking an arm about Hulde's waist to keep her close, pushing Hulde behind and against her. A rustling then, someone standing up from the undergrowth holding up his hands, moving cautiously towards them.

'It's only me,' the young man said. 'No need for alarm, ladies.'

'Don't you lady me,' Longhella said, levelling her knife. 'Don't know who you are or why you're spying on us, but better make damn sure you tell us soon.'

Philbert moving his hands slowly towards his head, removing his olive-green hat.

'You're Longhella,' Philbert stated, remembering her well. 'Guessing Heraldo sent you? I was trying to be stealthy. Obviously not stealthy enough.'

Hulde peeping out from behind Longhella's waist, taking her first look at the Little Maus, the hero of 1848, and oh my. Everyone was right. There really was no mistaking that head. As so she said.

'They've been gone for hours,' Heraldo was fretting.

'Well, we knew they would,' Ludmilla pointed out. 'An hour or so to that place in the forest, a little time foraging, an hour and more back.'

The show at St Michael's had gone well, gone down very well, far better than Prisoner 101 might have done. The Pfiffmaklers packed up for the day, retreating back to camp, the rest of their Advent Cycle due to be carried out on the morrow.

'What if someone's got to them?' Heraldo couldn't rest. 'I should have insisted the boys went with them.'

'Because boys are so much better at protecting women than women are of men?' Ludmilla pointing out the obvious disparity, given what had happened to the Pfiffmaklers in the past, Old Grandma rising to the fore when no one had even known she was around.

Heraldo flushed.

'That's not what I meant,' he blustered.

'It's exactly what you meant,' Ludmilla retorted, putting out a hand and patting her husband's arm. 'Don't worry,' she went on. 'Longhella can skewer a moving rabbit through its neck with her knife, let alone a bigger target.'

Heraldo smiled, for Ludmilla was right. He'd seen Longhella doing exactly that; an undoubted show of brinkmanship, one all the younger Pfiffmaklers had taken part in after seeing a knife-throwing act that had practically parted a woman's hair down the middle without leaving a scratch. Longhella's concentration and application after it leaving him a little queasy: the way Longhella took aim, poised the blade between her fingertips before sending it spinning through the air. Only a few practices needed before she had her own act down pat, the pitiful squealing of rabbits proof of that. And Longhella even better with arrows and bow.

'This has to be the dreariest place we've ever been,' Diderik said. 'Have you any idea where we're going?'

Rasvlach would have skelped the lad, had he not been thinking the same thing and anyway Diderik was out of reach.

'Thing to do,' he said instead, 'is figure where someone would stash himself on an island he doesn't know.'

'We don't know it either,' Diderik complained.

'Which gives us the advantage,' Rasvlach quick to retort. 'Think back on what the boatman said.'

'The island of the damned,' Diderik sighed, remembering the words exactly.

'Filled with woods and cliffs, promontories and inlets.' Rasvlach a sanguine man, one who could pick the bones out of any corpse laid at his feet without remorse or compunction. 'So where would you go?'

Speaking more to himself than Diderik, whom he was beginning to find incredibly tiresome. Thinking about ways in which he could get rid. All fine having a partner when they were going from one place to another capturing this or that man who had a bounty on his head. But this was the big score. This the Biggest of Big Scores, needing special handling. Was going to require a stomach made of iron, a man who would be able to saw the head from off the neck of the Anatomist's Dream and deliver it whole and unencumbered, take it all the way to Metternich to reap an oh so rich reward.

Diderik wasn't cutting it; Rasvlach knowing a liability when he saw one. Kragujevac had taught him many things, as it had taught Mergim, and one of those lessons was to jettison rotten wood the moment the river was high enough to take it downstream and well away from you. Make it so that it had never been, or at least never associated with you.

Diderik rotten wood as far as Rasvlach was concerned.

Not necessarily the right time to cut him loose quite yet. Diderik coming up with an idea Rasvlach couldn't immediately dismiss, and wouldn't have thought of himself. His own ideas being speed and distance: get landed, get up country, get out.

'I'd hide in the nearest forest,' Diderik said. 'I'd hide up and wait. We know he's accomplices, someone who brought him over. We mayn't know who they are but we can be sure they're people newly arrived here. Find them, find him. And it's the island of the damned,' Diderik added. 'Can't be too hard to locate newcomers, given a name like that.'

Rasvlach impressed, not that it would do to say so, for Diderik had the right of it. Only problem being how to find out such information. Last thing he wanted was to make himself known on the island, raise any alarms, make of himself a target when things hotted up, as he surely hoped they would.

They'd been on the trail of the Little Maus for months, Rasvlach doing his usual: digging and delving in the worst kinds of places, asking questions, carrying out interrogations, finding out everything he could about Maulwerf's Fair of Wonders: where they'd been, where they were now. Figuring that wherever they were his quarry would steer well clear, and also that he'd stay close to places he knew, where he'd been before. Fairs people tight-lipped folk, close as clams when you asked about their own; not so the peddlers who roved from fair to fair and gossiped good as sparrows in a hedgerow, walking-talking broadsheets, passing news from town to town.

He'd had to bloody his knife several times before he'd the news he'd been waiting for and that someone had spied the loose nail furtively dragging his pig in a cart—and Rasvlach had a good laugh about that—across the Paulsdamn, a low-lying causeway built across Schweriner See, the largest lake outside of Schwerin and the main artery carrying traffic towards Güstrow and Wismar; and from those towns only a hop, skip and jump to Rostock that had festivals spilling down its streets all year round.

A place used as a base for many fairs people who came and went according to the time of year: attending the Spring *Warnemünder Woche*, then the *Niege Ümgang* procession in July that had bands and guilds marching through the town declaring their wares; followed by the hiring fairs at Michaelmas, various autumn celebrations including the *Warnemünder Hochzeit* hosted by the Hanseatic Brewery; the year culminating in Rostock's famous Christmas markets that started end of November and brought folk in from far and wide. Which was when Rasvlach hit his jackpot, hitting up all those peddlers for their news, chatting amiably over pints of Hanseatic Brewery beer, forking out his last few coins because Diderik was a real dunce when it came to pickpocketing, even in a place as crowded as Rostock.

Finally getting the information he needed. Some peddler's lad tasked with handing over a message to a boy with a head like a lute-case. Rasvlach's knife itching to take off one digit or another until the boy volunteered that yes, he could read; and yes, he'd glanced at the note, but all he could remember was something about a Joshua Tree and honest! That was it, and please God, I need all my fingers! The note given to him—blurted out at the last second as the knife hovered above his knuckles—by a girl with orange skirts, and that was really it! Honest, that was really it!

Every plan having its flaws.

Every plan having its Rasvlach tracking down its sources like Valter's mouse sniffing about his erstwhile hovel, taking that last piece of flatbread soaked in sausage juice down into its nest to feed its young.

'Well my, if it isn't the Nut Boy himself,' Longhella was saying, using the moniker Philbert most disliked. Longhella looking Philbert up and down: scrawnier and younger than she'd imagined, his taupe skewing one side of his face very slightly to the right though not in an unpleasant way, merely unexpected. Nothing like Livia, the Janus woman, whose face was divided right down the middle like the dark side of the moon against the light.

'We've met before,' Philbert said, bowing briefly. 'Twice in fact. Last time at the opening of the Great Magendie's viaduct.'

Longhella giving a short and bitter laugh.

'Don't remind me. You royally buggered that gig up for the rest of us. And after going up all those blasted steps.'

Another voice, softer, more hesitant.

'Do you remember me?'

Hulde nipping out from behind Longhella now danger seemed averted. Philbert looking at the girl and not remembering, which was so unusual for him that he frowned, studied her, tried to figure her into past situations.

'I don't,' he admitted.

Longhella brushing the comment aside. 'Well you wouldn't,' she said. 'Hulde's not exactly one of us. Didn't take part in any of our shows back then. Still doesn't. Not really.'

Trying to deflect Philbert's interest away; trying, as usual, to keep the limelight and conversation focussed upon herself. A fixed part of her personality never changed since she was young. Philbert, annoyingly to Longhella, dismissing her; Philbert staring at the girl, who had to be ages with himself, putting the pieces together.

'You're Hulde,' he stated, Hulde smiling back at him.

'You've got a really big head,' Hulde said, ignoring Longhella's tutting. Philbert responding by re-donning his hat.

'Don't let it disturb you, miss.' Putting out his hand and shaking hers. 'I gather you've a rather interesting history yourself—'

Longhella interrupting, as was her way, although this time with some urgency.

'Quiet. And I mean very quiet!'

Hulde and Philbert stopping short, hands clasped in warm shared histories of being misunderstood.

'There's someone else out there,' Longhella hissed. 'Philbert, get yourself gone. One triangle; one square, three horizontal lines; one diagonal left to right. Hulde, grab up that basket of yours and back down the track quick as you can.'

Hulde doing as told, moving away one yard, ten, then Longhella speeding past her, knife flashing, her arm suddenly grabbing into a bush of green alder and hauling out a small scrag-end of a boy, his arms flailing, hair catching on some old blackberry runners, blood coming up in pinpricks on hands and forearms as he squirmed in Longhella's strong grip.

Everyone Finds Out Something

Neubrandenburg: the old town surrounded by three moats and its ring-wall two miles long, twenty-five feet high, with timbered houses, towers and gates incorporated along its length.

'Looks like they wanted to keep folk out,' Valter observed.

'Or in,' Mergim said, thinking back to the filthy moat about Kragujevac.

Neubrandenburg a handy intersection for merchants on the trade routes between sea and mainland, between Stralsund and Berlin, Rostock and Szczecin; only fifty miles from the coasts of both the Baltic and the Mecklenburger Bucht.

Valter this time electing to approach the town with Mergim out of necessity if not desire, it coming up early winter and a good time for folk to replace working implements ready for the onslaught of labour needed in spring. To this end he'd loaded their barrow with hafts and shafts that could be finished off to order, peg-toothed rakes and pitchforks, shepherds' crooks, ox-yokes, carding tools and spindles for looms, this being a well-known weaving town. He'd also made some chess sets, on Mergim's encouragement, quietly proud when they sold out the first morning they set up shop in one of the markets growing like weeds outside the gates leading into the town proper; places where no one needed papers or licenses, merely set up their wares and hoped they would sell.

And Valter's did sell, as did Mergim's—once Valter had tidied them up—one satisfied customer passing the word to another and another, and by day three they'd off-loaded everything they'd brought with them and had a full purse to see them through the next leg of their journey, which was north again.

Eight months they'd been on the road, clocking up over one hundred miles a month, totalling almost nine hundred miles in all. None too shabby a journey for a man coming off the bottle and another who'd been ten years in jail where the furthest he'd walked had been from one wall to another and back again, never mind he'd repeated that distance forty or fifty times a day.

Both having the feeling they might be on the last push, being about as far north as they could go, where the Pfiffmaklers had said they would be heading—assuming they'd not changed their minds along the way. The snippets they'd picked up had been encouraging. Following the tip they'd had about the Pfiffmaklers being seen in Wittenberge as late as June, they'd since been told of sightings in Schwerin and Güstrow around the Michaelmas Hiring Fairs. Information leaving Mergim a little breathless, his chest tight with anticipation as he and Valter packed up their empty barrow outside Neubrandenburg with nothing but their bedding, tools, and the food and drink they'd purchased to see them another while through.

'What's your feeling, Valter?' Mergim asked, as they headed away from the market without knowing precisely where they were going. 'East to Rostock or north to Stralsund?'

Fifty or so miles to each, Mergim's heart jittery in his chest. Could hardly believe how far they'd come, how lucky they'd been, how close they might be to their goal. How Hulde might react if they really did catch the Pfiffmaklers up, if she would remember him. How she would remember him if she did.

Valter not so surprised they'd managed to hear of the Pfiffmaklers on their journey, fairs folk having tongues loose as old nails in old wood when they were talking to their own, or thought they were. Thinking on the many birds who took annual migrations far longer and with fewer signposts than they'd done themselves. Thinking on Andreas telling him about reed warblers, Andreas singing their little song to him when he was young: *tyri tyri cher cher; chiry chiry cher cher.*

'Always leave in August; early September at the latest,' Andreas told him. 'Head off south to places warmer than our own but come back fighting the following spring. Remember that, Valter. They always come back stronger.'

Tyri tyri cher cher; chiry chiry cher cher.

A warm sound in Valter's throat as he whispered the warblers' song like Andreas had done, and the words Andreas had said at the end:

No one needs to be in the cold forever, Valter.

A sentiment Valter had always doubted, and doubted now.

No reed warblers to be seen. Birds long gone. As he wished he was.

Dreaded meeting the Pfiffmaklers again. Wasn't sure he could go through with it. All this travelling with Mergim had seemed just that—travelling. Moving from one place to the next. Putting one foot in front of another not caring where he was going or why. This Mergim's task and Mergim's main event. Valter thinking he should do what the warblers did and call it a day. Call it winter, because it was winter, although no snow yet, and only a smattering of frost—but still.

He hated this place they'd come to, flat and filled with lakes.

Found himself longing for the mountains, for their sturdy uprising to fill his horizon, overshadow his days and nights, remind him of where he'd come from, of what he'd come from. His little hovel in Osijek a mean place that had done him well, and found himself wondering how the mice were faring; if they would see another winter through without his throwing out little titbits to them. His throat constricting, tears coming on to imagine it might not be so, that without him they would not see their way through to another spring.

This entire trip seeming suddenly vainglorious, and wishing himself back. Wishing himself back to the very start of it, before Mergim had found him. Wishing Mergim had never found him. Realising the stupidity of that wish, how he might have been if Mergim hadn't found him when he had.

Yet now the end of their travelling was in sight, that end to meet the Pfiffmaklers again, he couldn't bear the thought. Couldn't bear to see them so twined up in the happy ball of string he was never going to find the beginning of, let alone the end. Folk like them so far from his ken they might as well be a different species. Pfiffmaklers like Andreas's birds on the wing, travelling here and there according to their own instinctual purpose, picking up folk like him like birds picked up mites or ticks or inveigled worms and beetles from the ground. Him the type of worm they spat out soonest chance they got, or should have. Him the type of worm born into the same yard of detritus he was destined to stay in his whole life through.

Oh Valter.

Jesus. That was spooky. He really thought he'd heard Andreas call his name.

'Valter,' Mergim said again, Valter turning his head slowly; no ghost of Andreas, only Mergim.

'What do you think? Rostock or Stralsund?'

Valter numb to the question, numb to the outcome, yet something in his head telling him the right way on. Some memory of where the Pfiffmaklers might have gone. His head might not be as big as Philbert's but it had stored up memories nonetheless, and he recalled someone mentioning Rügen Island back in Vienna.

It'll be perfect, Wenzel had told his collective family, including Valter, no matter how peripherally. *A place so far north no one else will have been there, and they won't have seen an Advent Cycle in years!*

And so to Stralsund Valter and Mergim headed, on Valter's meagre information.

Mergim picking up the pace so they crossed the last fifty miles in four days, arriving footsore and weary, camping up outside the town, Valter unwilling to go further until they had news, positive or otherwise. Valter still intent on leaving first chance he got if he heard the Pfiffmaklers really were in the vicinity, a chance he imagined slim to non-existent.

Until Mergim put him right.

'They were here, Valter! By God they were really here, and not three weeks back!'

Someone else hidden in the undergrowth.

Philbert running back along the track through the pines and beeches, one hand holding his hat upon his head, mind working through the brief message Longhella had given him, which didn't take long.

We're here, and haven't forgotten—so much evidenced by Longhella and Hulde turning up.

We'll be moving up country in three days.

Wait for further instructions.

Longhella's meaning clear: stay where you are and we'll be in contact soon.

But who the hell had been there to rumble them? Philbert was unnerved, ran straight back to Kroonk, got her out of her crate, took the two of them deeper into the forest where light didn't fall, where nothing grew except the tall pines side by side, timber to timber.

Pulled down a new branch beneath which they could hide. Began all over again his homesteading. Became nervous and vigilant, keeping Kroonk on a rope so she didn't travel far—which he hated to do. But only three days. Only three more days to stay hidden, until help finally came.

'What the beggeration do you think you're doing?' Longhella had Ortwin on the hop once she'd hauled from his hiding place.

Ortwin's eyes prickling with pain and the humiliation that Longhella didn't even recognise him. Ortwin unable to say a word until Longhella shook him, and shook him hard.

'Better get it said, or I'm going to split you ear to ear,' Longhella brandishing her knife, placing the point of it against Ortwin's neck, drawing blood. 'I'm not playing here. Tell me why you're spying on us or you're going to bleed out like a pig.'

'Wait,' Hulde intervened. 'Surely he's one of the lads from the village?'

Putting out a hand to stay Longhella's arm, succeeding only in making Longhella's knife scratch down Ortwin's neck, making him squeal in alarm. Longhella narrowing her eyes.

'Doesn't explain a damn thing about why he's skulking around on our skirt-tails.'

'I was looking out for you,' Ortwin croaked, 'in case of…'

'In case of what?' Longhella stuck the knife tip in a little more. 'What do you know?'

Tears leaking down Ortwin's cheeks. So much for being the romantic hero. This woman so far out of his league he might as well have wished for the moon to turn into a coin and roll into his hand.

'Nothing,' he whispered. 'Just thought…well…seeing as you're strangers…'

'I think he was trying to protect us,' Hulde finished for him, and so pathetic did it sound coming from someone else's lips that Ortwin was utterly broken. More so when Longhella let out a short laugh and shook him again before releasing him. Ortwin crumpling to the ground like a dropped puppy.

'Him? Protect us? That's mighty funny!'

Hulde wincing at the cruel spite, helping Ortwin up, which act of kindness he found harder to bear than Longhella's words.

'Come on,' Hulde said, Ortwin trying surreptitiously to wipe his face and nose on his sleeve as he rose.

'He's crying like a baby, our noble swain,' Longhella laughed again, sheathing her knife. 'Grab him up, Hulde. I'm in mind to pinion him to a tree until he tells us how much he saw and heard.'

Longhella moving away, as if ascertaining which tree she would use for the deed.

Hulde hesitating, her body arrested mid-motion, trying to understand why, then getting it.

'She said my name,' Hulde whispered to Ortwin. 'I think that's the first time she's ever said it to my face.'

Ortwin not caring for the nuance, staring up instead at Longhella, wondering what new tortures were to come. He still found her magnificent, although now in a scary kind of way, like she was some avenging goddess; thinking back to the play in the church when she'd been the oracle shouting out the prophesies of Svetovid, the bloody god of the old Slav stronghold their island had once been. How he'd sneaked out afterwards and followed these two into the forest. He swallowed convulsively as Longhella swung back towards him, pointing out the scaly twisted bark of an ancient sweet chestnut.

'This one will do,' she declared. 'Let's get his arms pulled back all the way around and pull and pull until they come out of their sockets.'

'Oh please don't!' Ortwin pleaded. 'I didn't see anything. Honest I didn't! Just saw you two heading off with your baskets and thought I'd come with—'

'Not good enough, my lad,' Longhella stated with menace. 'I can see it in your eyes. Something you're not telling me.'

As quick as Old Grandma on that front, both able to detect other people's lies with as little effort as they might peel an orange, maybe because both were so good at telling them themselves.

'Best get it said,' Longhella advised, 'unless you want your arms to end up longer than your legs.'

Ortwin swallowed again, making his Adam's apple bob in his scrawny neck, wriggling his fingers, not wanting them to turn into toes.

'Heard a couple of your folk talking a couple of nights back,' he admitted quietly, hanging his head. 'Saying they was going to send you off to meet someone. And that someone else was on his trail, but not to tell your father about—'

Longhella was up in his face in a moment, grabbing his chin with strong fingers, lifting it up so he had to stare into her eyes which seemed to Ortwin extraordinarily alive, as if fireflies were flickering at their edges. Danger there, he understood, but sweet danger, one he could never deny.

'What do you mean, *someone was on his trail?* What else did they say?'

Ortwin furiously raking through his memory for the exact words.

'Some Serbian fellow,' he mumbled, his mouth constricted by Longhella's grasp. 'I think that's what they said.'

Longhella's fingers flexing involuntarily, squeezing Ortwin all the more as she calculated the odds. Ten years since they'd left Italy; ten years since they'd given their depositions about the events that had unfolded there, hers included—not that she'd been involved in the main event. Of course not. Ludmilla and Heraldo had seen to that, as always. But only one man she could think of who would be on their trail, and surely their trail, not Philbert's. Longhella smiling, realising she had an ace up her sleeve, and oh, what an ace!

She was really going to make her irritatingly self-righteous sister squirm.

Mergim had made some enquiries of several street performers, confused by what he'd learned. They'd apparently linked up with the Pfiffmaklers for several days, doing a few turns around Stralsund to entertain the meagre crowds. So much easily understood. Told also, by a young couple who specialised in acting out Pulcinella and Pierrot sketches, that one of the Pfiffmaklers, the young man who had such odd musical instruments—who had to be Heraldo—had asked about a Joshua Tree in an insignificant village a few miles along the coast.

'Is it famous then?' Mergim had asked, the man shrugging his shoulders.

'Some,' he said, not sounding convinced. 'Get a few folk calling in on it on their way to Anklam, from where they go over to the islands of Usedom and Wollin in the Stettiner Haff.'

Which meant nothing at all to Mergim.

'Wouldn't have thought twice about it,' the Pulcinella added, adjusting the tired hoops of her frilled-out skirts so clarted with dirt and detritus they'd taken on the grimy colour of an over-ripe mushroom, 'only someone else asked about it not long after.'

'I think we should take a look,' Mergim said to Valter. 'It's all a bit odd. Had to be Heraldo who was asking about it first. So who was the second person? They said it was an old man, but were a bit vague on that. Said he looked old, but maybe wasn't. What do you make of that?'

Valter could make nothing of it, and didn't care.

'Let's just go,' he said. Anything to delay the upcoming meeting with the Pfiffmaklers. 'We've been on the road for months. And if the Pfiffmaklers are on the island they'll be stopping a while and will come back the same way, so what's a few days here and there to check it out?'

Valter had put his finger on it, and Mergim didn't see the harm. It was a mystery, and it intrigued him. Not much mystery going on in Kragujevac, but two folk asking about a strange tree in a strange place? He was curious. So off they went, following the simple directions they'd been given: go out of Stralsund to the right, keep to the coast, keep going until you find the most desolate village you've ever seen made of mud and poverty, a broken-down pier, and that will be the place.

Mergim and Valter arriving not long before sundown on a desolate afternoon; seeing the broken-down pier, seeing the Joshua Tree at the edge of the forest. Getting there as the men were eking their way out of the forest with their scrawny goats and their scrawnier bodies, the women gathered at the communal quern grinding dried peas into flour. Mergim asking if there was anywhere here they could stay, provide warm food and beds.

Mergim met by stony stares and incomprehension.

'No one stops here,' he was informed by a man with a grizzled beard and a face looking like it had been ground beneath a cartwheel, yet authority in it, speaking for his own. Mergim not put off, Mergim not spending ten years behind the walls of Kragujevac without being able to stare another man down.

'Except that maybe someone did,' Mergim prompted. 'Maybe not long back?'

His interlocutor spitting out a gob of phlegm.

'That bastard! Don't remind me. Treated us like we was vermin. And if that lad with him was his son then I'm sorrier for him than I am for meself, and that's saying something.'

'Jacob!'

One of the women had quit grinding peas and come to see what was what, reprimanding the old man for his language, so maybe Jacob's wife. Jacob's-maybe-wife looking about as skinny as she could get without actually croaking.

'And what did they do while they were here?' Mergim persisted.

Jacob looking at his maybe-wife.

'Didn't stop long,' he said. 'Sat at our tree for a while, waited while us all had come out the forest and then threatened us black and blue for someone to take them over.'

'Over where?' Mergim asked.

'To the island,' Jacob replied, looking at Mergim as if he was the stupidest man in the world. 'Though the young'un didn't look no way pleased.'

One of Jacob's village men appearing, having corralled all their animals inside their evening paddock.

'Didn't half!' he commented. 'Looked like he was about to piss his pants.'

'Oh for goodness sake,' Jacob's maybe-wife said, apparently a lot stronger in mind than she looked in body. 'You lot need to scour out your mouths. We've visitors here.'

Not having missed Mergim's earlier question about warm food and beds, seeing a chance for making the odd precious coin.

'Come you on,' she jutted her chin at Mergim. 'We ain't got much, but we can surely give you a roof for the night if you don't mind bedding down in the barn. Will keep out the rain, if not the rats. And rain is surely on its way.'

Mergim smiling at the old woman, following her direction. Valter trailing on behind, dragging their small cart.

'Ain't got much,' old man Jacob grumbled at their backs. 'Ain't got bloody nothing.'

Valter looking around him and seeing it was so, seeing too how like this village was to his own way back when.

'Got a good curl of cured pork sausage in our wares, if it's any use,' he said, so completely out of character Mergim turned to look at Valter, saw his red hair beginning to spike as the rain the old woman had predicted began to fall, coming out of the sky in a sudden downpour, the women at the quern scooping all they could rescue of their hard-won flour into their aprons and running for their rundown homes.

Meagre pickings, Mergim glad for Valter's offer. Gladder still once they'd gained Jacob's own small shack when Valter took from their barrow not only the coil of good sausage but also a small sack of cracked wheat.

'Any good to you?' Valter's voice hesitant, apologetic, as he offered it to Jacob's wife. And surely she was his wife, as was made plain when they entered the dark domicile consisting of nothing more than a flat earthen floor, a single bed, a rickety table set before a small fire.

'Any good?' she exclaimed, through blackened broken teeth. 'Oh bless you! Bless you!'

The start of a feast that night in the small village on the very edge of Germany.

A place that hadn't seen a curled pork sausage enriched with blood and caul fat, peppers and spices, for years.

A place where a small sack of cracked wheat was a luxury and needed celebrating.

A place where both Mergim and Valter blushed to be so fêted and felt so ill at ease, until someone turned up with a few bottles of potato vodka. A place that welcomed strangers who brought them gifts, if not strangers who straggled through their village and looked at their Joshua Tree with contempt before passing on to better-heeled places; rough men like Rasvlach and Diderik who'd brought them nothing but threats.

The entire entourage decamping to a communal store barn desolately empty of stores.

The men crowding inside, squeezing in so tightly next to one other on mouldy bails of straw and compacted reeds their fleas could jump from one sour body to another with only a slight stretch of their legs. Jacob's wife arriving with bowls of sliced sausage and the wheat boiled in murky water flavoured with flakes of salt panned from the sea and a coarse black pepper that made Valter sneeze. No source of warmth in the barn, the fug of bodies enough, along with the burn of piss-poor tobacco plumped out with dried heather and ground-up pine needles. The alcohol soon loosening the men's tongues, once everyone had eaten.

'We can't thank you enough,' Jacob said for them all. 'That was a real fine meal. A real fine meal.'

Valter and Mergim embarrassed once again, for to call that meagre offering a fine meal spoke wretchedly of the villagers' usual fare.

'We're mighty glad to have provided it,' Mergim said politely, accepting his wooden mug of vodka and sipping with diffidence, for it was worse than what he and the other inmates had stilled up in prison. Valter taking a goodly gulp, screwing up one eye as it burned its way down his throat. To say it was pleasant would have been an overstatement, but he welcomed its warmth. Noticed the instruments of what had obviously been a poor harvest leaning in a raggled heap in one corner of the barn like skeletal ghosts of better times past.

'Could fix some of them up, if you like,' he offered, indicating the motley array with his thumb. 'Could carve you some new dibbers and mauls, a flail or two. Fashion out a few hoes and the like. Guessing you've got wood stored somewhere? Maybe already seasoned?'

The villagers hardly able to believe their luck.

'We have!' someone called out. 'We'd a load of them already turned but then the lathe belt broke. Gonna have to wait until we tan some hides before we get it fixed up again.'

Valter having no need of complicated pieces of machinery like lathes. Everything he did carved and fashioned by hand, and so he said. Folk quick to give him a challenge.

'Could you fix me up a wooden reel for me fishing?'

'Aye! And new oars too.'

'And I've need of two table legs.'

Valter smiling shyly, agreeing this would be the work of a mere few hours once he had his tools, assuming they wanted basic and not fancy. His tools quickly got, along with the wood he needed, the men in the barn awed as Valter got out chisels, vice and hammers and had the fishing reel tapped out of a block within the hour, and two fine table legs knocked up a short while later, complete with the dowels needed to fix them in place.

'That's some skill you've got,' one of the men whistled with admiration as the rain battered down on the roof of the barn and the wind skirled beneath its unsteady eaves, the background sound of the sea whipping up and around the remaining legs of their broken-down pier adding an oddly musical accompaniment to this impromptu celebration. And the villagers in no doubt this was a celebration. Good food and good workmanship top of their list when it came to having something of worth.

'Can you tell me about your Joshua Tree,' Mergim asked, as more alcohol was passed around. 'How long's it been here?'

'Long enough,' Jacob told him. 'Had a fierce bad bout of some disease ooh…gotta be seventy or eighty years back, when me own dad was a nipper. Took out two thirds of the village, it did. Got them all buried underneath where the tree is now and then it started growing on top of them, all by itself.'

'Tree of Life, is what my folks called it,' another old codger added. 'We used to burn its branches to keep the sickness from coming back and it worked, because it ain't come back since.'

'And that's how it's the shape it is,' another man added. 'We chopped down all the lower branches for the burning, and then the top just split itself into three. One straight up, one each to either side like the sign of the cross. Like it was telling us we'd done right and should keep on doing so.'

Mergim coughed as he took another sip of bad drink. He wasn't a superstitious man, but this detour to visit the Joshua Tree on a whim felt like it had significance. Couldn't have said why, only that it seemed they'd come to the right place at the right time. A question on his lips before he'd time to think it through.

'Did you ever hear of a group of entertainers called the Pfiffmaklers?' he asked, noting the shiver going through Valter at the mere mention of their name. Everyone in the barn looking at Jacob, who took a sip, ordered his thoughts, tried to remember.

'There was one lot,' he said, looking up into the darkness of the eaves, no light left to them apart from a few greasy candles set into holders on the barn walls. 'Months back, it were. Can't really mind them. Only stopped a day. Could've been their name. Did some sort of show, though it weren't for us. Couldn't really get a handle on what it were all about.'

Mergim nodding. He didn't know a huge amount about the Pfiffmaklers, despite his thinking about them for years and this tracking down of them through the months and months since his release. What he did know was that a place like this wouldn't have had the time or money to support them for anything more than a quick pass-through. And yet still, still, he knew in his bones they must have been here and that one of them had found something about this place important enough to remember it.

Look for the most desolate place you've ever seen, made of mud and poverty.

A description not far wrong. So why would any of the Pfiffmaklers remember it?

The Joshua Tree.

It had to be the Joshua Tree.

And first chance he got in the morning, Mergim meant to see it for himself.

The Second Face of Fear Those Accused, Those Accusing

The afternoon skies darkened as the rain swept over from the mainland, tiptoes of its trailing veils touching the earth before moving swiftly on as if racing for home.

Philbert and Kroonk snug in their newly made bower hidden deep in the forests of Jasmund, fat droplets plinking through their green-branched roof now and then, no inconvenience to either, nor to the embers in the fire pit on which they were roasting the cones of stone-pines until the scales opened and they could pick out the nuts like winkles from their shells.

Longhella and Hulde not so lucky, on the outskirts of Ortwin's village when the rain came down. Ortwin casting an odd glance down the empty streets from where the clutter of makeshift stalls had cleared, the first instalment of the Pfiffmaklers' Advent Cycle over, the next due the following day, anticipated to be an enthralling finale; wondering vaguely if his family had noticed they'd not seen him since yesterday morning. Supposed not. There would be no evening meal, not with all on offer during the day's entertainments. And, now that Longhella's threats in the forest glade were over, he'd regained some self-confidence and was back to enjoying his adventure, needing no coercion when Longhella demanded he accompany her and Hulde back to the Pfiffmakler camp.

The rain didn't bother him, as no more did it appear to bother his companions, the two of them merely hoisting up their skirts a few inches, re-tying their belts and heading on. Longhella's plaits glistening where the raindrops clung to their myriad intersections as she strode forwards, straight backed, head held high, as if she despised whatever the weather was throwing at her, sweeping her long fingers occasionally beneath her chin to wipe away the raindrops gathering there. An oracle on the move and much to tell, though specifically warning Ortwin not to speak until she—and only she—told him to. An order he was happy, thrilled, if he was honest, to comply with. Ortwin no longer blubbing, back to being a heart-struck swain.

The rest of the Pfiffmakler's were awaiting their return with no great anxiety. No one overly concerned about Philbert, only vaguely remembered him, if truth be told. They'd sympathy for his plight, discombobulated when Heraldo chose to involve them so directly in it. Pietro stating that unease for them all, comfily bivouacked beneath a tented tarpaulin to protect the fire from the rain corralling them in.

'I know he's a lad on the run, and a young one, and is sort of part of our own,' Pietro said, 'but the fact remains he's a bit of a liability.'

'Soonest shot is soonest done with,' Yssel agreed.

'Isn't the exact point that we don't want him shot?' Heraldo put in quickly. Yssel rubbing softly at her cheek to be so misconstrued.

'I didn't mean shot as in shot,' she said, in her defence.

'Except that's what will happen to him if he's caught,' Heraldo retorted. 'Or worse.'

'That's not what mother meant, and you know it,' Ludmilla put him right. 'All she meant was—'

'She meant what we're all thinking,' Wenzel growled, putting a swift stop to the argument. 'He's a risk, my lad. A risk for all of us. And one you chose to take on our behalf without asking. Or rather asking and being denied, and doing it anyway.'

Heraldo sniffed, but remained belligerent.

'Someone had to do something,' he fired back. 'No one else has lifted a finger to help him these last three years.'

'Maybe for good reason,' Rosa intervened, although she would have liked to take her son's side. 'Anything to do with that lad is dangerous. You know that. Especially now.'

Getting a warning glance from her husband, getting a furrowed brow from her son.

'Now? Why now?'

Wenzel sighed, dottled out his pipe and got it refilled. A ritual everyone respected, no one speaking while he got it done. Waiting for what he would say next, which he knew would set the lot of them alight. But time to say it, to spell it out, worried as he'd been by Heraldo's plan.

'Because Metternich is newly back in Germany,' Wenzel told them, holding up his hands to ward off questions. 'I didn't want to tell you. I didn't want you all to know, but this Little Maus? This Philbert you're so fond of, Heraldo? We all knew he'd a price on his head ever since Lengerrborn. But I've learned a bit more since Rostock than you ever did, and that he's a blasted bigger price on his head than he ever had before. Which means Metternich is not going to let up until he's that lad's head pickled and put on his table as a centrepiece. So, like your aunt said, sooner we get him away from us the better.'

'Perhaps all the more reason we should help him,' Peppe quietly pointed out, the debate ceasing as they heard through the rain the swishing of wet skirts and Longhella appeared, lifting up the tarpaulin and letting herself in; Hulde, bright eyed, bright cheeked, on her tail, drawing in a thin wan boy behind her.

'Meet our little spy,' Longhella announced, making as grand an entrance as she could, lent drama by a new and heavier downpour slamming onto the tarpaulin, the wind allowed by her entrance making the flames move and jink, blowing up a flight of red embers that she batted away from her drenched and muddied skirts. 'He followed us all the way from the church to the woods,' she went on, as Peppe stood up and gave her his seat by the fire, others bunching up to make way for Hulde, leaving the lad standing bereft in the darkness of the tent.

'It's Ortwin, isn't it?' Ludmilla said, studying the pathetically dripping figure. 'Come and sit down by—'

'Leave him standing,' Longhella commanded. 'He's a prisoner in our dock.' Proceeding to tap out his misdeeds on her fingers. 'Not only did he follow me and Hulde, he also skulked around in the bushes waiting to see what we would do and who we would meet, and you all know what that means and, you're going to like this, Ludmilla,' she flashed a smile at her sister, 'he did all this because he spent a night hiding out in the woods just beyond here, listening for all he was worth.'

Gratified to see Ludmilla glancing worriedly at her husband.

'You always think you're so sneaky,' Longhella went on. 'You and your blasted plans. Never think anything can go wrong. And yet here's a pimply little boy who almost scuppered the lot of it—'

'One moment,' Wenzel interrupted. 'What do you mean, he spent the night hiding out here? Why would he do that?'

Looking from Longhella to the boy, who was shivering, clutching his hat between his fingers so tightly he was squeezing out the water it had absorbed on their walk over. Longhella leaning forward, scooping up the last flat bread from the stones, folding it delicately, if not putting it to her mouth, wishing she'd thought to torture that particular detail out of Ortwin when she'd had the chance.

'Why don't you ask him?' Rosa intervened, taking pity on the lad who'd been so helpful sourcing paint for the new canvases she couldn't believe anything bad of him.

All eyes fixing on Ortwin, who hung his head, a few drips running from hair to eye to chin, Ludmilla convinced he was crying, and no wonder: stood in the middle of their tent like a starfish stranded on a beach, at the centre of an interrogation.

'What did you hear?' Ludmilla asked gently. 'And why were you where you were in the first place?'

Ortwin not lifting his head, nevertheless replying, ignoring Longhella's command that he speak only when she told him to.

'Well, you was all so exciting,' he whispered. 'We don't hardly get no change out here. And I just thought…well. I didn't mean no harm, and I didn't hear much. Honest I didn't.'

Longhella spat into the flames, took a small bite of her bread, could feel the tide turning in Ortwin's favour. Any number of youngsters over the years tagging onto them, hoping to run away from dull and ordinary lives; it never occurring to them that the Pfiffmakler life might come to seem dull and ordinary if you lived it long enough.

'How much did you hear?' Ludmilla asked. 'It's important. You have to tell us, Ortwin.'

Ortwin swallowed, glanced over at Longhella who was looking studiously into the dimming flames.

'Just that there's someone hiding in the forest, and someone else...'

A ripple of consternation passing through the Pfiffmaklers, given what Wenzel had not long told them about Metternich and his renewed rewards. The rain ceasing of a sudden, all that was left being the dripping of it through the trees surrounding them and from the tarpaulin above their heads, and from Ortwin's abject form at their centre.

'Oh but there's so much more,' Longhella announced as she stood up, shaking out her skirts with one hand, throwing the last of the flatbread into the fire with the other, jagging up a thin green flame as the oil caught and burned. Longhella always one to make a good exit, at least now the rain had ceased.

'We've to look out, Pfiffmaklers,' she warned, 'because you've not heard the best of what Ortwin here told me.' Lifting up the flap of the tarpaulin as she got out the last of the speech she'd been preparing all the way here, adapting it as necessary to changed circumstance, as was the Pfiffmakler way.

'Ortwin told me something Ludmilla and Heraldo knew but neglected to tell any of you.' And oh so sweet the moment as she saw Ludmilla and Heraldo wilting, the rest of the family leaning forward to hear what she would say, getting it out as she would any line in a play. 'Our old friend Mergim's time is up. He's done his ten years and he's out of prison. And, family of Pfiffmaklers, he's on our trail. And if I were him? Well, after what we did to him, I'd be wanting blood.'

Mergim woke in the village barn wanting nothing more than to slake out his mouth and get a good rinse. Nothing like bad alcohol to make you feel like hell in the morning. He swung his legs down, boots cracked and leaden, wriggling his toes inside dirty socks. Valter was sleeping, stretched out on a couple of the mouldy bales, his mouth curved in a slight smile, one hand protectively resting on the pile of wooden goods he'd chiselled out the previous night, going at it long after the drink had run out and the men had gone home to their beds.

A bit of a star turn, our Valter had turned out to be, his face creased in concentration as he worked on despite the paucity of the light, hands moving of their own accord, going with the grain, sure and steady. Valter more relaxed than Mergim had ever seen him. Valter working on until the last remaining candle sputtered out in exhaustion, much as Mergim had done, listening to the regular movements of Valter's paring knife, the softer sounds of him polishing the wood smooth with squares of dog-fish skin.

Mergim happy Valter had agreed to accompany him on this trip. He'd never have got this far without him and the selling of his wares; and Mergim's German passable now where before it had been poor and scratchy.

He coughed quietly to clear his throat, stood up, brushed away the small needles of straw catching at collar and cuff. Moved to the door splintered at top and sides, the base eaten away by rats, scratched thin by feral cats sharpening their claws, slivers of light coming in to him from the gaps. The wood creaking quietly as Mergim pushed the door open enough to get himself outside, pushed it closed behind him.

Let Valter sleep.

He deserved it.

Valter the undoubted hero of the hour.

Mergim stretched, arched his back, rolled his shoulders, breathed in the frosty air.

It was early, a thin mist whispering across the surface of the sea, hovering below the broken pier as if exploring its barnacle-encrusted pilings, tracing fingers along the grooves and lines left by limpets; the sun a faint halo half-pushed above the watery horizon, marram grass and creeping juniper down by the shore shivering with gossamer and the slightest touch of breeze. A few fishing yawls resting open-mouthed upon the shingle, oars neatly crossed from bow to bow; fishing nets, slung from poles to dry, threaded here and there with short streamers of weed cracked into dull browns and greens, the empty carapaces of tiny crabs.

No one else abroad. The ramshackle habitations making up the village quiet and still; their wattled walls, patched-up roofs and half-limbed shutters seeming weary, keeping quiet, unwilling to wake their wards into yet another day of hard graft.

Let them too sleep.

Mergim turned from the sea, made his way up the thin frost-cracked track leading to the Joshua Tree, towards the dark forbidding stands of forest beyond where the villagers raked for nuts and fungi, and their animals snuffled through the mast, scraped their hooves at roots, nibbled at bark to keep themselves alive.

The Joshua Tree couldn't be missed: tall and gaunt in the low-lying mist, a scatter of dropped leaves on the seat collared about it. Mergim looking up its length, noting the branches splitting to left and right at such perfect right angles it surely hadn't happened naturally, must have had help from the survivors of whatever plague had struck the village way back when. And must have been helped since: the vertical stave straight as a church steeple, its topmost end even now—well into December—still harbouring a couple of desiccated leaves. Mergim wondering if this tree acted as the villagers' church and chapel, for the place was too small, too rudimentary, to have acquired an actual one of its own.

He was unaccustomedly moved, walked quickly the few yards towards the Joshua Tree and sat down upon its bench, running his eyes over the carvings made in its bark up to where a tall man standing on the bench might reasonably put his mark. Names and dates of folk who had trothed themselves here, or marked the passing of kin. The bark healing over, becoming ridged, the memorial of a village that might not last much longer. Mergim realising all the folk he'd met the previous night had been middle-aged, if not old; all the young ones presumably getting out first chance they got.

A dying village then. Mergim knowing all about those.

Ten years for Mergim in Kragujevac because of it. Which wasn't long enough, in Mergim's opinion. No getting over that.

Jesus. What a waste. What a goddamn waste.

Tears in his eyes as he spread his hands over the seat of the Joshua Tree to left and right. Fingertips touching the wood as if it would heal him. Fingertips finding scratches, grooves newly made, splinters splitting from their sides. Fingertips moving over the scratches, weirdly recognising something in them.

Bleary morning eyes looking down upon the seat about the Joshua Tree, Mergim blinking and blinking, for how could this be? And yet there they were: the staggered lines topped with dots any inmate of Kragujevac would recognize; a mark tattooed upon their arms when they first came in, representing their age when they arrived, the length of their sentence, their optimal time left afterwards, their release date in Roman numerals—if they had a release date—alongside their initials.

Any number of variations, although most of the murderers' were similar: two or three short verticals representing the decades of life before they'd entered Kragujevac, the last vertical topped with yearly dots to bring them into what was usually their early twenties or thirties; five stacked horizontal lines, the decades of their sentence, meaning the rest of their lives. Only Mergim's differing substantially: four short lines and five dots to bring him into his middle forties, one horizontal for his ten-year stretch; another vertical line for whatever life was left to him on the outside.

'You can always add some dots if you need to,' the tattooist had told him. 'You never know. You might be lucky.'

Mergim studied the scratches in the Joshua Tree seat: two verticals topped with two dots; two horizontal dots; five verticals. Meaning a lad who'd been twenty-two when he'd been locked up in Kragujevac, sentenced to two years imprisonment, long life remaining to him afterwards. And initials next to it, not quite so clear, harder to make out. Possibly an O or a D, followed by what might have been a H or an N. And more scratches besides, Mergim leaning down to study them. They were crude, small, and probably done in a hurry for there was no great depth to them, hard to see because of the dampness of the wood, so had to have been recent. He ran his fingers over the scratches, pulled his head in on his neck several times to adjust his focus, checked and rechecked, his mouth opening in shock as he became certain what had been left on the seat of the Joshua Tree in this village of dirt and poverty.

The dots and lines.

The scratched initials.

Then XII-LI RUGN INSL.

'Well, I'll be damned,' Mergim whispered, the last notation not taking much deciphering: December 1851, Rügen Island.

Houses That Survive, Storytellers Who Do Not

Friedrichstadt: a town built plank by plank by Dutch settlers while others of their countrymen were crossing the Atlantic and founding the city of New Amsterdam. The road outside stretching towards the River Eider and, if you followed the Eider up to the coast, you'd find Tönning, seat of the Gottorf Dukes, main port for centuries exporting cattle to England. This is Eiderstedt country, where the farmhouses are loftier than anywhere else in Germany; these *Hauberge* topped with large pyramidal-shaped roofs resting on strong pilings of local stone, the trick being that when the walls are swept away by floods—not infrequent—the pilings and roofs remain intact.

The Eiderstedt to the west of Schleswig-Holstein; Philbert leaving the latter for the former in February 1849, not long after the rivers had burst their banks and scoured the land, scattered it with detritus, fields left muddy and treacherous, though all the more fertile because of it. His primary impression being devastation and loss: folk hunched over barrows piled high with paltry household goods rescued from the swirling pools of water collected in dip and dale; hastily constructed wicker cages carrying squawking chickens; men looping ropes about the necks of oxen, horses, pigs, to haul them from the mire, leaving those they could not rescue to slowly sink, shriek and bellow, starve and die.

The whole place stinking of bloated rotting carcasses, animal and human, of excrement and waste; silage fermenting in the excess water bobbed and baubled with apples and bottles of pickled pears denuded from their places of winter storage; great rafts of straw, wasted hay and seed potatoes building up by the banks of stagnating pools inhabited by coots and moorhens, ducks and grebes, who began building nests too early, triggered by the wealth of materials on offer and the unseasonable warmth melting the snow long before the norm. Which would result in their early broods being destroyed by March frosts a few weeks later; all those nests abandoned as eggs froze, thawed and softened, split themselves open to reveal downy chimera neither one thing nor the other. Bundles of bloodied feathers with stubs of beaks and feet, unopened eyes.

A depressing sight for Philbert, and more unsettling for the muteness the countryside had subsided into. No ringing of church bells, no striking of blacksmiths' hammers upon anvils, no shouts or bartering at markets. Instead, tired anxious people swearing and slogging to get cartwheels out of ruts, trundle them on aways, keep their children from running off to rescue one animal or another, getting themselves stuck in mud two feet deep sucking at their legs like it was trying to drag them down unshriven into Purgatory.

And then he'd passed into Eiderstedt proper and seen the *Hauberge* rising from the thick mist clinging to the sodden ground; folk gathering piles of scattered timber into heaps, lifting hammers and nails out of niches hidden high in the pilings; using gaff-hooks to pull down ladders from the upper floors nestled below the roofs where their most precious and useful belongings were stored. A scene not of desolation then, but of hope and resurrection; the floods expected and planned for.

Reminded of a broadsheet report he'd read a few months previously—when Maulwerf's Fair had still been wondrous, friends and acquaintances still alive when now they were dead—of the daring exploits of one Lieutenant William Lynch, who'd led America's first expedition into the Middle East, dragging two metal-hulled boats over miles and miles of camel-threaded desert for the specific purpose of finding out everything he could about the Dead Sea. Precisely why he'd fixed on the Dead Sea Philbert didn't know, although if Philbert had been William Lynch he'd maybe have done the same. The Dead Sea: a name as mysterious as it was enticing.

He remembered precisely the words written in the broadsheet by the journalist accompanying the American expedition:

The water is perfectly clear and transparent. The taste bitter and salty, acting upon tongue and mouth like alum, smarting in the eye like camphor, producing a prickling, burning sensation, and stiffening the hair of the head much like pomatum. There was a considerable breeze, yet the water lay perfectly calm and motionless. We saw no living fish nor animals in the water, only birds that flew over and above though never settled; and we all noticed an unnatural gloom, not only on the sea but over the whole plain below Jericho, like a vast funeral pall had been drawn down from heaven by this lifeless lake.

Which was what the land had looked like before he'd entered Eiderstedt, unnaturally calm with water and heaven-sent gloom.

Until he'd witnessed the *Hauberge:* high, haughty and solid, unmoved by the sweeping devastation those waters had produced in other places. Their inhabitants doggedly adhering to the expected resurgence of ordinary life, given a few planks of wood, a few nails, a determined hammer. Walls soon rebuilt between the pilings, beneath the pyramidal roofs.

Philbert lying on his back as his time in Eiderstedt spooled through his head, Kroonk snoring gently, a warm weight at his side. Philbert looking up between the needle-thin slivers of his new homestead's roof into the sky beyond, a sky become heavy and yellow as rain shifted into snow. Hope in him that Heraldo would come through, as the *Hauberge* had for the people of Eiderstedt.

One diagonal slash: *Wait for further instructions*

Three horizontal lines: *Three days.*

No *Hauberge* this, but Philbert as protected.

The snow soon settling over those tiny cracks, cutting him off, keeping him and Kroonk in darkness.

Warm and safe.

'Fuck's sake! Now it's snowing?'

Rasvlach incensed the world could move against him in this way. Almost an entire week they'd been on the island going in one blind direction after another, delayed time and again by following tracks that led nowhere. Or, more precisely, along tracks leading to one isolated farmstead after another, forcing them to retrace all those hard-won steps. Finally arriving on some main track when the snow began its onslaught, obliterated all before them so they couldn't be sure where the track ended and the snow-covered marshes to either side began. Exhausted, twilight upon them, they'd stumbled across an abandoned church and forced a way through its tumbled gravestones, paths long since covered by collapsed ragwort and tangles of bindweed all shrouded by snow, hiding the brambles that tore at their trousers, almost ripping off one of Diderik's boots.

'Better than rain,' Diderik offered, as they tucked themselves behind a sarcophagus in the vesperal gloom of a side chapel, dragging about them a tattered tapestry ripped from its wall along with a few altar cloths and surplices left behind by whoever had abandoned this church, this chapel, this graveyard.

'You've no more sense than a pile of cow cack,' Rasvlach rumbled, though he saw the point: snow fell and gathered, solidified. Unlike rain, whose sporadic falling had made their life this past two days a torment: soaking them, bringing up welts on their skin below the straps of their packs and harnesses, making it hard to think, harder to sleep, even with the rough spirits Rasvlach had brought with them, which both liberally partook of and made up the most part of their baggage. Bottles chucked out to left and right the moment they were emptied.

'Feels a bit like Kragujevac,' Diderik commented, words coming out in rags and stutters as they cowered in their freezing chapel. 'Just walls…and having… nowhere to go.'

His teeth chattering, his body frozen. Soon so cold he couldn't remember how he'd got here. Mind on hold. Keeling over stiff as a rake. Rasvlach flinging an arm about his shoulders, pulling him close, resting Diderik's head upon his chest.

'You hear that, boy?' Rasvlach asked, Diderik's ear becoming warm as he detected the steady unhurried beat of Rasvlach's heart. A self-primed pendulum seemingly undisturbed, as if nothing could harm it: not the cold, and certainly not the walls of this church, nor Kragujevac. Diderik closing his eyes, breathing coinciding with that beating heart as if it was a knelling bell keeping its own rhythm, needing no hand to move it on.

'Got to keep to the centre of yourself,' Rasvlach advised. 'Think on that and you'll not go wrong.'

Allowing Diderik to lean on him, absorb his strength for ten minutes more before pushing him upright and away, pulling the mouldy tapestry about Diderik's head and shoulders. Diderik seeing his breath coming out in soft plumes as Rasvlach lumbered to his feet and stumbled off, returning a while later with an armful of hymnals and damp bibles. Rasvlach's strong fingers ripping them into shreds, piling them up like a giant rat's nest, setting them alight with his flint and the few candles he'd managed to locate. Diderik seeing Rasvlach squatting beside the small fire, grinning over at Diderik.

'Don't look so shocked, my skinny little pile of shit,' Rasvlach said, stretching chapped lips, baring bad teeth and pale gums as he threaded thin strips of smoked pork onto sticks and held them over the flames to heat through; placing a rickety pan on the fire's edge, stirring the pea-flour paste as it thickened. 'Didn't think I'd let you freeze to death like that gasbag Gitas, did you?'

Diderik managed a weak smile, because he couldn't think of any reason why Rasvlach wouldn't, if only for the entertainment value. Rasvlach laughing like a trombone when Gitas had declared he'd had enough of prison and was off to freeze himself to death. Always an odd fellow, that Gitas; come from the island of Mani in the Greek Peloponnese, where his folk apparently lived in towers specifically designed so the men could spend their days shooting at one other because of unspecified and long-lived vendettas, while the women worked the fields.

If Gitas could be believed.

'Oh such a strange place,' Gitas had told them. 'Every time I bend my back I'm reminded of the great ridge of the Taygetos running through the peninsula like a spine; the mountains dividing the Prosiliaki in the east from the Aposkiaderi in the west: the Mani who live in sunshine and those who live in shade.'

'Which side are you from?' Diderik had asked, Rasvlach rolling his eyes and interrupting.

'Ooh, that's a hard one. Let me take a wild guess...'

'The side of shadows,' Gitas got in, without rancour, 'where the mountains rise up and stand against the sun. Where we understand the distinctions between light and dark, good and evil, life and death, all the better because of it.'

He always spoke like this: elliptical, poetic. Gitas a balladeer who'd travelled up and down the Balkan states with the laments of the Mani constantly on his lips, until he'd been convicted of beating one of his countrymen half to death for which he'd never given explanation. Gitas talking, singing, speaking, about those towers, those ancient and unlikely vendettas. Everything falling from his lips in the keening songs of his island where dying seemed the main preoccupation, whether you lived in sunshine or in shade.

'Death will make his garden,' Gitas explained one night. 'He has planned his orchard of lemon-tree maidens, cypresses of young men, rose-bushes from all the little children. Our old men the hedge to hem the rest of them in.'

'Must have a lot of gaps in that hedge,' Rasvlach had guffawed, 'seeing as how your men spend all their days shooting each other down before their time.'

A surprisingly valid point, one Gitas rebuffed by breaking into song.

The Underworld is a trick. It will deceive you.
It's nothing like the world above.
There are no coffee houses there, no shops.
No reunion with mothers, daughters or sons.
Only the white becoming black,
That which was healthy becoming pale;
Rose-blushed faces growing grey with cobwebs and dust.

'Christ's sake,' Rasvlach had muttered. 'Anyone know anything cheerier?'

Rasvlach by no means a cheery man, but it had been a dark night, filled with wind-whipped snow like this one; a wind sharpened on a strop that would stop you in your tracks if you tried to go against it; a wind having the vestiges of water in the shit-filled moat crick-cracking, breaking its ice into shards colliding and grating against one another like the inmates in their snow-bound prison. All they could hear, once Gitas ceased his singing. An eerie, lonely sound, yet not so eerie nor so lonely as what Gitas had sung next, starting on one repeat note lifting with every few words:

And I too shall go the way to Ane Pula
To see the stars in heaven,
To howl out my complaints,
Make the universe shake with my screams of grief.

In the silence left by this awful ululation Gitas had stood up, declared his intent to go out into the snow and die. Eyebrows lifting, a few mouths smirking, no one seeing fit to convince him to stay as Gitas bowed on the threshold.

'I'd be grateful if you'd follow our Mani traditions,' were his parting words. 'Chop off my hand when I'm done for, take the tattoo from my arm. Preserve them. Keep them to dip into the wine you drink at celebrations so they will bring you luck.'

'As if any of us ever have any luck,' Rasvlach muttered as Gitas took himself off into the snow-blinded night. No one really believing he'd do himself in; instead would curl up in the outhouse where the prisoners stacked their piles of winter wood.

Going out the following afternoon, the snow-clouds having spilled themselves empty, the wind stilling its screaming. Got out their wide-headed brooms and began to sweep a path to the woodshed, clear away the drifts built up against the outer walls. Someone hitting something more solid than snow, calling everyone over as he went at the pile with his hands.

Gitas: hunched like a hibernating hedgehog.

Head breaking from the circle, borne far back upon his neck.

Eyes frozen and wide open.

Fringes of frost upon eyelashes, brow and beard.

Lips drawn back from yellowed teeth.

'Looks like he really did rail against the universe,' someone said, leaning on his broom, work arrested.

'Much good it did him,' added another.

'Least he died looking at the stars, like he said,' said the first, no one pointing out that stars were the last thing anyone could have seen in the snow-clad night just passed. Everyone clinging to the strange romance of Gitas dying this way, as he'd promised. Thinking it not such a bad way to go given how old he was and wouldn't be getting out of Kragujevac except in a box. Sombre mood broken by Rasvlach's rumbling laughter as he came up between the loitering inmates and poked the frozen Gitas with the end of his broom.

'Christ! He actually did it. Who'd have thought it?'

Rasvlach lunging forward with his knife, severing Gitas's hand from his wrist with a few gristly twists and hacks to get through the frozen flesh, next slicing a neat rectangle about Gitas's tattoo with a dexterity that had several inmates nodding with admiration. Rasvlach teasing away one corner, pulling it back like a magician from the layer of yellow fat beneath. Wrapping both body parts in a dirty piece of linen he tucked away in his trouser pocket.

'What?' Rasvlach asked, as several of his fellows tutted, coughed and turned away. 'Only doing what he asked, and Jesus. In this place, we need every scrap of luck we can get.'

A scrap of luck he'd been asked to perform on several inmates who wanted their own tattoos removed before they left Kragujevac, subjecting themselves willingly to Rasvlach's knife.

Diderik ambivalent about what kind of luck he'd been given, for several weeks later Rasvlach had cornered Diderik as he was cleaning out the latrines and put to Diderik his plan of escape, which had brought Diderik to this freezing chapel on the island of the damned.

Diderik swallowing down the hot pork strips and peas-pie.

'I wonder where Ane Pula is,' Diderik murmured.

'Ane whosit?' Rasvlach asked, distracted, scraping out the pot with his fingers.

'The place Gitas said he needed to go to see the stars.'

Rasvlach belched, Rasvlach retorted.

'Don't see how you'd need to go anywhere specific. You can spot the buggers from about anywhere.'

Rasvlach always so literal. Diderik having to admit Rasvlach was right. Yet still the words pulled at him. So mysterious, so without explanation: Ane Pula. Maybe the horizon between life and death Gitas had been so fond of talking about. Maybe the gateway to his orchard hemmed about by a hedge of old men, Gitas presumably by now plugging one of the gaps Rasvlach had pointed out must be there.

Diderik casting his eyes up to the window of the lady chapel they were encamped in, seeing its grime-encrusted glass and all the points of light refracted through its colours here and there made more intense by the snow. Stars shining brightly out there in the night. He'd no names for them, no songs to sing about them, but liked the idea of them being up there in the black night, steady and certain—like Rasvlach's heart—with their own fixed paths and ways to go, nothing and no one to steer them wrong.

Diderik having no such fixed path, shivering his night through, murmuring and moaning once or twice as he incorporated into his dreams the long drawn-out screams and wails of a young badger lost in the woods.

Another morning, and Wenzel wasn't happy.

One thing to tell the Pfiffmaklers about Metternich, quite another to get them all panicked, which had been the effect of Longhella's pronouncement before she'd departed from them the previous night. Longhella might be a thorn in all their sides yet, as thorns tended to be, she was sharp and astute, making an obvious leap neither Ludmilla nor Heraldo had despite it staring them in their faces. Namely that the Serbian Philbert had spoken about on his boat ride to Rügen had to be the newly released Mergim tracking them down to take his revenge. And they all knew he had cause.

No one more disturbed than Pietro, who'd been so instrumental in his capture. The last thing Livia needed was a shock of any kind, late in her pregnancy as she was, and late in her life to be bearing at all.

Not to mention they were about to give their last performances at St Michael's before moving on and putting the most dangerous part of Heraldo's scheme into play. Wenzel tugging his beard in the darkness as he fought to get the frayed pieces of those plans in order. Disturbed by Heraldo peeping into the tent before Rosa and Wenzel had even raised themselves from their bedrolls. Wenzel gritting his teeth at the interruption.

'I need to speak to you, Papa,' Heraldo whispered fiercely. Plainly he too had spent the night mulling over what Longhella had said and needed to have his say, but for God's sake, Wenzel hadn't even had time put on his socks.

'Shush lad,' he whispered back, not wanting to wake Rosa, rolling himself carefully from her side and getting up, following Heraldo out. The night had brought snow settling all about them, dropping furtively onto the lake which took it to its own, swallowed it whole and, come dawn, its waters dark and smooth as slate. No wind. No more snow falling. Wenzel finding the calmness of the lake troubling as he stumbled out of his tent, seeing in it a perfect reflection of the reeds and trees about its edges and the clouds above, melding the barriers between two alternate worlds.

Both worlds disturbed as Heraldo dipped in a jug to bring out water for boiling, his hurried footprints making looping patterns in the soft snow, Wenzel watching the ripples on the water spread and settle. Such fine lines to negotiate for folk like the Pfiffmaklers, ones Wenzel was beginning to find blurry and out of his control. Especially this Little Maus business.

Always a possibility someone was still after him, given Metternich's renewed reward, but a Serbian? Why a Serbian? Surely not likely this far north so far out of his ken. Mergim, on the other hand, well, he could see how that might have gone. Mergim had appeared truly repentant. Then again, ten years in some godforsaken prison could easily switch a man from penitence to revenge. And Mergim had proved himself a man capable of doing the worst.

Wenzel thinking mostly about Hulde.

That long wide street the Pfiffmaklers had happened upon years back with its fig trees and wasps, the barely dried lime-wash mixed with oxblood on the houses. All coming out at Mergim's trial. The Pfiffmaklers hadn't been there in person, had supplied sworn statements properly witnessed. Testaments condemning Mergim to penal servitude in Kragujevac.

Perfect sense for Mergim to come after them once he'd got out.

Perfect sense that Mergim would want to slaughter the Pfiffmaklers in their beds.

Perfect sense for Longhella's interpretation of events to be correct, and that Heraldo—by bringing Philbert over to the island—had opened up some god-awful crack and let the devil in.

Let Mergim in.

And what better way to set himself up for the rest of his life than by claiming Metternich's reward? No doubt he thought he'd earned it. And what better justice if he scythed down the Pfiffmaklers who were helping him?

Wenzel sitting heavily, coughing into his handkerchief, blowing his nose to clear his pipes while Heraldo poked at the fire to bring it back to life. All the usual morning rituals, except this didn't feel like a usual morning. And not merely because of the crisp smell of the snow, Wenzel's nose twitching with the cold; Wenzel's nose detecting something else entirely.

Something coming.

Bad things coming.

And only Wenzel to stop them in their tracks.

Peppe and Heraldo having the right of it, he was realising.

Philbert a lost child as Hulde had been, and his responsibility. Pfiffmaklers inadvertently the ones to set Mergim on his trail, and Pfiffmaklers' duty therefore to get him out of his way.

All those old stories about Philbert coming back to him: the Westphal Club, Metternich's soldiers so unexpectedly storming in; Von Ebner, long time fighter for the downtrodden and the common labourer, being cut down; all those men of Lengerrborn about to be put up against the prison walls and shot for doing nothing more than being in the wrong place at the wrong time. Philbert, the Little Maus of legend, the Anatomist's Dream, the one to rescue them when none else would have dared.

And now Philbert himself in need of rescue.

Wenzel shook his head, took a puff at his pipe, took the cup of coffee Heraldo was holding out to him.

'All right then, son,' he said to Heraldo, before Heraldo had the chance to speak. 'I understand, and I apologise. You were right. Philbert is ours to take care of, so let's sort out what needs doing. Go about it the safest way we can.'

Mergim And The Mathematician

Mergim returned to the village from the Joshua Tree, his mind in a tangle.

Immediately before him was the sea. The mist had lifted, hovering a few yards above its surface as if unsure whether to stay or go. And, now he was looking, he could see beyond the mist the outline of an island: white cliffs, dark tight woods.

Rügen.

How has this happened? he murmured, as he went back towards the barn. For how could it be that someone else from Kragujevac was here, in this most isolated of places, right on the edge of nowhere and right at this time? About as credible as meeting someone with the same birth date as yourself in a pool of twenty-three murderers in

Kragujevac. The weird coincidence discovered when a new inmate was having his tattoo inked into his arm. The same question posed to their resident professor of mathematics, highly thought of in academic circles, until he'd drowned his wife in a bucket of piss for spilling coffee on the paper he'd been working on. Mergim remembering how boggling the answer had been.

'It's around a fifty-fifty chance,' he'd informed them breezily, to general and overwhelming disbelief.

The professor holding up his hands to stem the shouts of derision.

'Your immediate deductions as to the probability,' he'd asked, 'would be what?'

A bit of head-scratching, until someone offered an answer.

'Three hundred and sixty-five days of the year multiplied by the twenty-three of us?'

The professor nodding slowly.

'So you might think,' he'd answered calmly. 'An enormous number. Eight thousand, three hundred and ninety-five.' Trotting out the total sum, as he'd done many times before to all the first-year students taking his course on statistical analysis.

'I don't get it,' Mergim had stated. 'How does a chance of one in over eight thousand become a chance of one in not very many?'

'Ah, my friend. You've put your finger on it. How indeed?' The professor smiling, leading his students into pastures new and green. 'The reason being that your initial intuition of the probabilities involved is deeply flawed. You've to tip the conundrum on its head. You've to think instead how extraordinary it would be if we all had completely different birth dates. Think in exponents, not linear lines.'

'What the hell are you on about?'

Here came the grumbles.

Same reaction he always got.

'Think of someone tossing a coin,' the ex-professor went on. 'Each time a coin is tossed there's a fifty-fifty chance it will come down heads or tails. It doesn't matter how many times it has already come down heads or tails. It might have come down tails thirty-five times in a row, or heads sixty-six, which doesn't alter the probability of it coming down heads or tails the next time.'

'Unless you've a trick coin,' someone guffawed, everyone agreeing. Except Mergim, who was trying to follow this logic of probability, or improbability, because it so exactly summed up what had happened to him once he'd been thrown into the mix of someone else's concerns.

'It's like this,' the professor explained. 'Coincidence seems like coincidence merely because you don't have a grasp of what might *not* have happened. You have a dream in which a favourite dog or horse or girlfriend has died.' A few knowing smirks, a few digs at those who'd had plenty of girlfriends, who might have been a little over fond of either horse or dog. The professor going on, once the jibes had quietened.

'You have your dream, and several days later your dog or horse or girlfriend dies.'

'Because you've stuck her with a pitchfork!' Mergim's nearest neighbour laughed a little manically, being how he'd dispatched his own girlfriend and her dog; dog first, obviously, to get the weight and heft of the pitchfork and because it had been barking and nipping at his heels ever since he'd first met the girl he professed to love; might not have moved on to the girl had she not gone down on her knees and picked the hairy mutt up and looked at her supposed lover with such blind hatred he had been compelled to act. Him closing his eyes now. Cut off from his fellows. Tears leaking down his cheeks into his beard. Inmates either side moving a few inches away. Too much emotion. Too much grief.

'Leaving that possibility aside.' The professor cleared his throat. 'The object of your dream dies suddenly and unexpectedly and, because of your dream, you believe you've had a premonition, have somehow foreseen the future. But,' he held up a finger, 'what you never consider is how many times previously you've had variations of that dream and no one and nothing has died. You take one event from the many and make it significant. Your mind makes connections that aren't there.'

No one convinced, least of all Mergim. He could follow how the dream part might be true, if not how it related to the problem at hand, namely how two of the murderers in this prison—two of only twenty-three—really did have the same birth date.

'I don't follow,' he said, the mathematician's eyes sparkling. He loved this part. His sleight of hand about to be revealed. He picked up a lump of chalk, tipped up the packing crate he'd been using as a seat, jotted a scatter of letters and numbers upon its wood.

'This is how we write it mathematically,' he explained. 'Here's P1—that's Person One—and his birth date is X, which leaves the other 364 days of the year unaccounted for. Then P2 comes along, his birth date is Y, his one day of the year, leaving 363 days. Then P3, Z, and 362 and so on. They're all part of a larger equation.'

'Heads and tails,' Mergim murmured, inching towards the light.

'Heads and tails,' the mathematical genius agreed. 'To you this looks like gobbledegook. To me it says that the larger the sample group—in our case twenty-three— then exponentially greater is the chance of any two of us having the same birth date, but the likelihood of all of us having different birth dates is even greater. It makes randomness seem studied, organised, which is the opposite of what randomness truly is. It's like telling us that if we toss a coin twenty-three times in a row it will first come down heads and then come down tails, then heads again, then tails, which is far too ordered, and incredibly unlikely to happen.'

'I'm getting a headache,' someone complained.

'I need a bloody drink.' Another was more pragmatic, getting out a bottle, pouring everyone a tipple, the professor included.

'Can you tell it us again?' Mergim asked, his mind tipping towards the edge of understanding, enjoying the challenge, not quite getting to the core. The mathematician smiling over at him, recognising a willing student, tapping at Mergim's knee.

'You're Number One,' he said. 'Let's say you're the first person to arrive here. You're Number One, and your birth date is the first of January. And then I come along, Person Number Two, and I tell you my birth date is the second of January. What would you make of that?'

Mergim frowned.

'A huge coincidence?' he asked.

'For why?' the mathematician prompted. 'Why should it be any more coincidental than me having a birth date on the sixth of August or the tenth of October, or the nineteenth of May?'

Mergim faltered, beginning to detect solid edges in the shadows. Took a sip of his drink, remembering the lines of holes he'd used to make in the lasts back when he'd been a cobbler; remembered the shepherd lad in the hills pointing out one sheep after another amongst what seemed to Mergim a crowd of shit-clarted woollen blobs from which he couldn't have identified an individual if his life depended on it.

Shepherd lad the first of many to be dispatched on someone else's say so.

'Because numbers are just numbers?' he offered. 'Because they could be in any order and it's us who give them sequence and meaning?'

'Bravo!' the mathematician replied. 'You've finally got it!'

Maybe Mergim, but no one else. The rest harrumphing, losing interest, moving away, pulling themselves into their usual cliques and groups, pouring out more drink.

Only Mergim and the mathematician left.

'I need to understand this,' Mergim said.

'Everyone does,' the mathematician replied, 'though not everyone has the capacity to do so. Not everyone can grasp that randomness is just that: it's random. It has no care whatsoever about humans and our obsession with making connections, seeing meaning where there is none. True randomness means the notion of intention is without meaning, in the truest sense.'

Mergim thinking on Hulde left alive in a heap of dead bodies.

Mergim Number One.

The start of it all.

Mergim compelled to tell the mathematician his story; no real need, everyone here knowing the bones. Mergim famous, infamous, because of it. Nevertheless Mergim spilling out the nuances to the mathematician he'd never spoken about before; about the shepherd boy; about Hulde; the infighting between religions and within religions, all swirled up during Serbia's fights for independence. How the Pfiffmaklers had been caught up in it unawares.

The first and only time he would ever talk about it in Kragujevac.

The mathematician sighing when Mergim reached the end of his tale, Mergim hoping for explication, for excuse.

The mathematician giving him none.

'That's how it goes,' the mathematician had sighed, shrugging his shoulders. 'That's randomness for you. It rules the universe. We might have been born here or there, or not at all. Every life is like a tree growing in a vast forest; every decision made throws out a branch here, a twig or leaf there. Wind comes and wind goes. Rain falls or it does not. Lightning strikes and cleaves the bole right down its middle or burns out its core. Or it does not. The totality is out of our control, Mergim.'

Mergim finding the whole conversation unsatisfactory, had been hoping for something profound and exculpatory and found it wanting, found himself angry.

'You're telling me nothing!' he'd argued, banging a fist down on the mathematically-inscribed crate that had become a table, making both their drinks jump on the jittery wood. 'You're telling me I'm just what I thought I was. A blasted idiot! Which is what I am.'

The mathematician understanding Mergim's anger, the stupidity of decisions made; the mathematician remembering how he'd been in such a rage at practically nothing he'd held his wife's head down in his piss-bucket for the seven minutes it had taken her to drown. Seven minutes during which she'd managed to force his hand up only once and taken an awful gasp drenched with accusation, agony and fear.

Putting his hand to the flames of the meagre fire and keeping it there so he could feel that same agony and fear, until Mergim pulled it free.

'God's sake, man,' Mergim whispered. 'What are you doing?'

Although it was no mystery.

Every man here suffering the same terrible guilt swooping down on dark black wings when you least expected it, clutched you in its claws, forced you to carry out whatever recompense was available: banging your head against a wall, going out into the snow to die, holding your hand to the flame until it scorched and burned. The mathematician no different from the rest. Nothing all that random about why any of them were here. Nothing and no one to blame but themselves. Mergim bathing the mathematician's hand in alcohol— yet another use—before bandaging it up with strips of ripped-up cloth.

'Apologies,' the mathematician muttered, giving in to Mergim's ministrations.

'It's no bother,' Mergim replied. 'Sorry for being so angry. I did understand what you said. About randomness, I mean. And it's given me some comfort.'

Which it had, now his ire had ebbed and he'd time to think on what the mathematician had actually been telling him. The mathematician, flexing his newly cocooned hand, giving Mergim a grim smile as he lifted his drink with the other.

'You're a good thinker, Mergim,' he said. 'Wish I'd had more like you in my classes.'

'Me? At classes?' Mergim smiled too, for Mergim had no schooling, not since he was ten and his village got ripped stitch from seam about his ears. And yet oddly here he was, a student at the lectures of a renowned mathematician, drinking in all he could of what the man could teach him. The teacher tapping once more at Mergim's knee.

'It's odd, your name,' the mathematician said. 'Does it have a meaning? A derivation?'

'Exile, in Albanian,' Mergim told him.

The mathematician quiet for a moment as Mergim rolled him a paltry cigarette from their reserves, the mathematician waiting until Mergim got it lit before saying more.

'It has another meaning in the English. Or almost. Megrim means a headache, a god-awful headache. Had a fellow in the department suffer from it terribly. Couldn't stand the light. Had to close himself off from everyone for days at a time. Told me it could get so bad it's like a dejection of the spirit, like your soul is rolling out of you. Like when a horse refuses to work, lays itself down and dies for no obvious reason.'

First Mergim had heard on it and Mergim had no reply, although had an old mule do the same. Fine one day, the next on its side refusing to get up, refusing food and drink, like it knew its end was nigh and seeing it through stoically until it expired.

'But you'll not do that, Mergim, will you?' the mathematician implored. 'We've all in here got our hopes on you.'

The mathematician waving his bandaged hand at Mergim, getting out his letter with the other.

'For my son,' he wept. 'Can't get it to him but by you.'

Another letter Mergim was expected to deliver once he got out. Another letter Mergim had taken and added to the pile he'd already got. Letters Mergim had gone to great lengths to deliver and which had, by good grace, brought him to Osijek and Valter.

'Got to tell you something else.' The mathematician become drowsy, head lolling, bandaged hand resting on his knee. 'Told you about the woods, the trees, all that randomness. But there's times you can choose which leaf to let fall, which seed to release. You'll never know what will become of them but, when you get that opportunity, if you get that opportunity, don't ignore it, Mergim. You're the only one of us might get such an opportunity again.'

The professor's head nodding forward, weighed down by the enormity of his sins.

Just another murderer in Kragujevac who knew there was no way out. That all the randomness in the world could not save him.

Unlike Mergim.

Only murderer in Kragujevac ever to be set free.

Suspicions, Surmises, Possible Salvation

'You really believe it's Mergim?' Heraldo asked his father as they sat side by side on their seating log, looking out on the calm face of the lake, an otter sliding into the water a few hundred yards away up the bank catching their attention for a moment.

Wenzel coughed, took a sip of coffee, his left shoulder twitching at the mention of Mergim's name, his scar tightening with the cold. Godammit. It all seemed a lifetime ago, but there were still reminders. His scar, Hulde, and now maybe Mergim.

'Got to be,' he spoke gruffly, throat still rough from the morning. 'Aged about fifty. Come from Serbia. Timing's right. Ten years in prison a long time to hone a grudge, get it sharp as a whip.'

Heraldo said nothing for a few moments, watching the otter make a straight line through the lake.

'How can we be certain he knows about Philbert?' Heraldo asked, Wenzel shaking his head. Always questions with this boy. Always had to dig deeper than most.

What kind of butterfly will this caterpillar turn into?

What makes this pebble glint while that one's dull?
Where do all the birds go in winter, and how do they know how to get back again in spring?
How would you go about building a bridge?
How do the tides turn and shift?
How do all the leaves on a tree know to fall at the same time?
What makes the rain turn into snow?

Wenzel thinking on the snow falling silently outside his tent during the night, noting its weight on the canvas, the slight luminosity it seemed to hold on the other side. The thoughts he'd been having about Mergim, Wenzel inside his snow-covered tent as Mergim had been within his prison. Nothing much to do there, he presumed, once their labour was done, except talk and drink. No great leap to believe news of Metternich's renewed and very handsome bounty had percolated so far abroad, considering the kinds of men incarcerated there. Only one of them needing to know about it. Stuff men full of the idea of an easy mark, an easy retirement plan. Not hard to see how Mergim might have learned about it; tracked one of their ex-members down and a specific ex-member at that.

'I think because maybe he found Valter,' Wenzel said quietly, 'and he's maybe trying to kill two birds with one stone.'

Or maybe kill all of us, Wenzel was thinking.

Perfect sense.

Mergim finds Valter, Valter having fallen to pieces after Andreas died which had been obvious to all. Valter heading back to the places he knew. Maybe Zagreb or Osijek. Mergim released from prison, going back to those same places, finding Valter, Valter telling Mergim the Pfiffmaklers were heading north, as far north as they could go. Wenzel maybe having mentioned Rügen once or twice long ago. He couldn't be sure, yet Rügen not so far from Schleswig-Holstein, the last place Philbert was known to have been.

Good Lord.

The plot was practically writing itself out before him

'So it's my fault,' Heraldo murmured. Wenzel taking a deep breath, tipping out the last of his coffee, seeing its dregs stain the newly fallen snow.

'No, son. What's done is done. We were all responsible for what happened to Mergim.' Wenzel putting his large hand over Heraldo's.

'If he's set on coming after us, we couldn't have stopped him. Thing to do now is figure how to go from here.'

The otter re-emerged on the bank outside its den, a small red-scaled fish clamped in its jaws. It stood for five, ten seconds, head held high, whiskers twitching, scenting the dawn, maybe scenting them, before disappearing, its day done. Bright flash of wet fur iridescent through the reeds.

'What, then, do we do?' Heraldo asked, wishing they could vanish into the undergrowth like the otter.

Wenzel weighing all this up since his revelation about Philbert, the duty they were due him.

'We've our last performances to give at St Michael's,' he decided, 'then we're off. We fetch up Philbert and get off the island. Your plan was to get him over to Denmark?'

Heraldo nodded.

'There's a large port, Sassnitz,' he said, 'not far from here. Lots of trade boats going over, so that's what we do.'

'Very well then,' his father added. 'That's what we'll do, except we'll all go. Get ourselves entirely away.'

Heraldo enlivened, Heraldo leaping up, Heraldo missing the regret in his father's voice.

'Are you sure?' Heraldo asked. 'It means going where we've never been before!'

Good God, excitement in every sinew, brightening up his face. Heraldo envisioning strange new places and people, a million discoveries to be made.

'New places to go!' Heraldo sang loudly. 'New places to see!'

'New people to entertain,' Wenzel finished the clan mantra for him without enthusiasm, seeing headaches abounding: lands and people who might not accept them or their letters of recommendations, and yet another language to familiarise themselves with. A hard road ahead, one he'd rather not take.

Wenzel heaving himself up. It wasn't going to be easy, but there it was. They were Pfiffmaklers and, as was the Pfiffmakler way, they would learn to adapt like they'd always done.

Just got to keep one step ahead.

Diderik and Rasvlach stayed another day in their chapel. They'd ventured out in the morning to find snow still falling sporadically. Nothing to be seen but the flat white brightness of the marshes to one side, snow-laden forests to the other. No houses, no points of reference, no nearby footprints of mules, carts or men; only a few splayed patterns in the snow where black grouse had desisted poking at birch buds on branches lowered by the snow almost to the ground and, at the sound of their approach, pushed their wings against its surface to gain flight, flee into the forest. No sounds but the unhurried gurgling from a nearby unseen stream; the thick-throated craws of rooks wheeling high on the wing.

'Might as well hole up,' Rasvlach decided, directing Diderik to find more firewood, Rasvlach having done his bit the previous evening with the prayer books. Diderik complying; returning with several armloads to find Rasvlach already having cracked open a bottle and slugging it down, casually flicking a few owl pellets across the paving of the floor with thumb and forefinger.

'How about a game of Blind Man's Fancy?' he asked, as Diderik came in and laid down the first of his wood. Diderik taking a few skinny twigs and setting them in a tepee over the embers of the fire so the draught caught them, licked and embraced the wet pine needles that soon went to warmth and flame, spitting out a few fine colours as the resin inside them bubbled, resisted, and gave in.

Blind Man's Fancy.

Well, why not.

Nothing else to be done this day, glared as it was with white light and filled-up tracks, making further direction or progress impossible.

'Best make damn sure you don't lose your coat,' Rasvlach added. 'Might have coddled you last night; won't be so forgiving now we've to spend another one out here.'

Diderik nodding, saying nothing, knowing how this went: Rasvlach hitting the bottle early; Rasvlach seeing nothing of the day ahead; Rasvlach wanting nothing more than to get through the next twenty-four hours in alcoholic oblivion in the hope that when he woke up again the following morning it might better serve him.

Blind Man's Fancy.

A gambling game learned in Kragujevac. Diderik fleeced the first few times he'd played, lost his bedding, his clay pipe, his boots, until he'd learned the rules. Which were simple: don't gamble anything you're not prepared to lose; don't gamble anything of value until the person you're playing has drunk a lot more than you have and, most importantly, don't gamble with Georg Rasvlach. Not until he's absolutely stocious, because Rasvlach was a fine cheat and it didn't matter a jot to him if he had to flip a card, a marble or an owl pellet. One way or another he'd get it done in his favour. The aim of his game not to play but to win. Always the same with Rasvlach.

Diderik knew it, and played along with it on this day of fine bright snow, ice-covered burns, birds that had taken off and hidden in the forest. Diderik believing, as he brought in the last of his firewood and heard Rasvlach prattling on about Blind Man's Fancy, that he might yet be saved. That if he could get Rasvlach drunk enough, he might yet be saved.

Ortwin woke early in his cellar, alerted by the altered dawn light seemingly full and luminous, taking on a glow that fell brightly into the corners of his room. Flinging aside his blankets, his thin features threaded with a smile. Quickly breaking the ice on his wash pail, sluicing his face and armpits, lips drawn back over his teeth with the sudden shock of the cold. He dressed more carefully than usual: put on his best shirt. It might be damp but had the merit of being clean, not too frayed at cuff and collar; pulled on long johns; selected the braces kept for Sundays, weddings and funerals, clipped them to his trousers. He could do nothing about the trousers themselves, for he only had the one pair. Brushed them down and took out his sewing kit, added a small patch where a tear had developed over the left knee following his mistreatment by Longhella in the forest. His humiliation by the Pfiffmaklers the previous night ameliorated by Peppe leading him out of the tent after Longhella's announcement, the rest falling straight into talk.

'Sorry you had a hard time of it, lad.' Peppe sounding truly apologetic. 'I know you were only trying to look after our girls, do the right thing. And I'm proud of you for that, as is Wenzel, though he didn't say it.'

Ortwin sniffing, then smiling, standing taller.

'It's all I meant, honest it was.'

'I know. Want me to walk you home to Sagard? Would be my pleasure to do so.'

'No sir, thank you. I know the way.'

Looking up the dark track, shivering with trepidation to go alone into the black night but unwilling to abnegate the compliment Peppe had given him by reverting to being a scared child.

'Tell you what, let's compromise.' Peppe understanding, Peppe fetching a lantern. 'Here. This'll see you right, and you can give it back to us at the church tomorrow. You will be coming, won't you?'

'Wouldn't miss it!'

Ortwin's enthusiasm fervent as ever. Ortwin marching up the track. Ortwin getting back to Sagard too late for the evening meal, if not for the latest news.

Important news he could impart to the Pfiffmaklers in the morning.

Ortwin feeling a lightness to his being.

Ortwin loving the winter.

Loving the cold that kept him away from the hand-blistering work in the fields.

Loving the ice glazing over muddy puddles, making them clean and new.

Loving the short days, the long dark nights he could spend alone in his cellar with his rush candles and his mice-nibbled creased-paged books. Reading those books over and again. His library small, comprising only four volumes:

A book of collected German verse;

An anthology of folk tales collected by one Thomas Winther;

A history of Rügen Island;

The last more obscure: the *Versuch Metamorphose Pflanzen Erklären*—Experiments on the Metamorphosis of Plants Explained—its foreword telling the reader that its author, Goethe, had not only been a great writer but a great scientist too, who'd discovered the anatomically important intermaxillary bone and founded a vertebral theory of the skull; his latest thesis, Homology, expounded in this book. Goethe positing that the leaf was the base-mark of all plants, other parts mere variations of that single unit of growth.

Ortwin hardly understood this last, but the foreword had been written by the person he most admired in the world, before he'd met Longhella, the person who'd also written the history of Rügen: Ortwin's grandfather.

He'd only met the man once, on a return visit to Rügen following the death of the wife he'd abandoned forty odd years previously after she'd refused to leave with him, unable to contemplate living anywhere but Rügen, preferring to live her life and bring up her four extant children with whatever Rügen had to offer. A man, to Ortwin, as mysterious as he'd been fascinating; a man who'd begun a new life in Denmark, become a famous Professor there, started a new family but always sent money back home to the one he'd left behind. A man short and crooked when Ortwin had met him, with round spectacles, the eyes behind them keen and inquisitive; the man who had singled Ortwin out—in a good way—when he'd come down to his cellar.

'So, young Ortwin,' the Professor had said. 'You don't seem quite like the rest of the family.'

Ortwin blushing, no acne back then but face as sallow as a half-baked pudding and back already curved with the scoliosis that hollowed out his chest, making him look like a chicken ready for the pot.

'Not quite, sir,' Ortwin got out, as his grandfather sat himself on Ortwin's pallet, splaying out his legs, rubbing at his knees. 'Always wanted to do what you did. Get out, like. Make something of myself.'

'You ever hear of Jacob and Wilhelm Grimm?' his grandfather asked, Ortwin admitting he hadn't. 'Well, look you that you do. They're gathering folktales from all around, making great leaps in linguistic theory. And I'm helping them, Ortwin. Think on that. Got introduced to them by my friends, Franz Xaver von Schönwerth and Thomas Winther, who've collected tales from Denmark and Germany, almost five hundred from this region alone.'

Ortwin unable to make a proper reply.

'Never let it be said,' his grandfather went on, 'that people from around here can't amount to anything and if they do say so, well. Just think on me, your grandfather from Rügen, and von Schönwerth from Regensburg, both contributing to what might turn out to be the greatest linguistic and historical project in all of Germany for years to come.'

A heat in Ortwin's chest simply to be in the same room as this great man.

'But what's this?' the great man asked, picking up the book from Ortwin's night-crate. 'A book of German verse?'

Ortwin blushing, confessing he'd not given it back to the school when he'd left. A crime going unchided by his grandfather who instead opened the book to where Ortwin had marked it with a single stem of grass, dried and brittle, reading out loud:

'Im Nebelgeriesel, in teifen Schnee, Im wilden Wald, in der Winternacht... So a bit of Goethe takes your fancy, does it? Well done! He was a real genius. I met him once. Twenty odd years ago that was, a couple of years before he died.'

Ortwin couldn't answer, couldn't quite comprehend how the man sat here on his bed down in his cellar on Rügen Island was taking part in a hugely important study and now was telling him he'd met an actual poet, a really famous one, whose work he'd been reading in his school book.

Im Nebelgeriesel...

The story of a boy who lived alone in the deep dark woods through the worst of winters, surviving on his own despite the odds. A boy Ortwin sympathised with, drew solace from. A boy who'd killed the vile cat plaguing his days and night and had been torn to pieces because of it, set upon by wolves sent by the witch Anna, whose familiar the cat had been. A punishment far outweighing the crime, as Ortwin saw it, as Goethe's telling confirmed.

Ortwin glancing at the grandfather no one in the family ever talked about; Ortwin seeing in this small crooked man something of himself. Same hollowed out chest beneath that smart waistcoat and cravat; same slight curvature to his spine making him sit on Ortwin's pallet exactly as Ortwin would have done: slight shift to the hips to make himself more comfortable.

'Know what we discussed, me and Goethe?' his grandfather asked, which of course Ortwin did not. 'Puppet shows!' his grandfather laughed. 'All he could talk about. How they'd fascinated him as a boy, as a young man. The reason he went into theatre in the first place, and from theatre into poetry. But never lost his interest in how things worked. How we worked, we humans. Never lost it.'

'I suppose we are like puppets,' Ortwin commented. 'The way folk move us around like we've no say in the matter.'

His grandfather looking startled, then nodding in agreement.

'You've the right of it there, my lad. But it doesn't have to be that way.'

Take me, for example, being the clear implication.

'So you've left your schooling?' he went on, as he fingered the pilfered book. Ortwin nodding too. Same slow, contemplative movements as his grandfather.

'Had to. Needed on the farm.'

Grandfather understanding, knowing how it was to scrape a living from this land, how every hand was needed if those hands were to have food to put into their mouths.

'Always room for change,' he commented. 'You can start as one thing and turn into another. Always room for metamorphosis.'

Ortwin's mother calling them up for dinner and no more time for talk, and later that day the funeral was done and his grandfather away. Ortwin going down to his cellar, more bereft by his grandfather's leaving than the grandmother put into the ground who he'd never liked, finding her like Anna's cat: sharp and prickly, unaffectionate, always griping, never thanking.

And there on his bed lay three books, neat within their gold-embossed leather covers, spines bright and straight, unlike his. Gifts from his grandfather: the *History of Rügen Island* penned by himself and brought to such life by the Pfiffmaklers; a collection of Danish tales by his grandfather's friend Thomas Winther; and the monograph by Goethe who had shaken his grandfather's hand, and to which his grandfather had written such a glowing preface.

'Metamorphosis,' Ortwin whispered, not exactly understanding the word but putting to it his grandfather's meaning: always room for change, always room for hope.

Hope bolstered by Ortwin finding tucked in the back of Rügen's *History* a slip of paper on which was written, in neat and tiny writing, his grandfather's name and address in Denmark.

A hope sparked anew by the arrival of the Pfiffmaklers, for if anyone knew as much about puppet theatres as Goethe and his grandfather it had to be them.

Ortwin, that morning, deciding to act. Ortwin having news to impart. Ortwin fixing his gaze on the track, waiting for the Pfiffmaklers, waiting and waiting for the Pfiffmaklers.

And for change.

And for hope.

And for metamorphosis.

All of which would come to Ortwin, in ways he could never in a hundred years have foreseen.

Ragged Cats, Ragged Causes

Philbert was thinking of Lengerrborn, of those battered old cats lined up against the windows of Doctor Ullendorf's laboratory windows; of Helge, Ullendorf's sister, in her kitchen cooking up enticing meals of pancakes, fried potatoes, schnitzels and plum cakes. Hearing himself and Helge singing, as they often did back when Philbert had been a mere boy and not a murderer and a fugitive.

All brought on by the snow, reminding him of that song Helge had taught him about the boy living alone in the wild woods. The resonance eerie, for here was Philbert now: a wild boy in the snow-bound woods, wolves on his tail. Not literal ones, at least he assumed not. He'd certainly seen no sign of them on Rügen, not like there'd been in other forests he'd sojourned in.

He didn't fear them for himself, wolves appearing to have learned that humans were more dangerous creatures than they. Feared only for Kroonk. She might smell more human than normal pigs, but was an easy target when away from him, snuffling about in leaf mould, scoffing up mast. Philbert checking for scat whenever they entered a new forest, looking for high spots in the flat terrain, places where earth had been scraped up by paws and claws, large fur-filled dropping deposited on top. Wolf spraint very different to those left by fox or badger, Philbert getting down on hands and knees to sniff them to be sure.

An odd occupation, it would seem to other people. Not to Philbert, who'd been three years on the run, who'd kept his large head close to the ground for much of that time, become accustomed to the sounds and signs of the animals around them, become one of them. All carrying different scents in scat and urine, easy for him to distinguish boundary marks left by fox, badger or wolf at several yards and, on closer inspection, learning to detect the differences between individuals.

All of a whole, this olfactory map of a forest, common to both himself and Kroonk; only time the two of them took real fright was when they scented bear, when they saw dark excreta the thickness of Philbert's wrist, or the large splayed footprints in wet mud, an anthill torn apart and destroyed, a disembowelled elk or deer partially covered over with bracken. Which was when they ran, Kroonk's bristles bristling, Philbert's breath coming fast. Hightailing it out of there quick as they could, moving many miles away, out of a bear's compass of predation, for both would be prey, as far as bears were concerned. No fear on its part, not like the wolves. Human and pig equally regarded as ready sources of food.

Wille wau wau wau.

Wille wo wo wo.

Helge's singing in Philbert's head. Old echoes from an old life.

The snow shivering down from the pine needles when they moved through the wood to fetch their water, Philbert checking his traps set up in the tree branches; found a skinny pine marten and one flying squirrel, fat as a dormouse, with wide square flaps of skin between its limbs serving as wings. Regretting this last catch, for the squirrels were a joy to watch, gliding from tree to tree way up in the canopy, descending like acrobats from high to low, which had been this particular one's last flight, the weight of its landing releasing the sharpened stick of Philbert's deadfall trap, skewering it neatly through its neck. A quick death, which was good in several ways, not least of which being the meat tasting better.

There wasn't much of either animal once skinned and cleaned, though nothing went to waste: main portion going to Philbert, offal cooked up with mast and pine needles and served to Kroonk. Not her favourite meal, but she took what she got. As did they both. The skins, small as they were, Philbert used to bait another trap he'd set across a fox path. Not much hope of success: foxes wily, mistrustful of the slightest whiff of human, and tending to steer clear. The single exception he'd ever come across being a Siberian fox exhibited by a Siberian couple who always drew a big crowd. Folk fascinated by a wild animal no longer seeming wild, snow-white fur mottled with black spots, snout less sharp than the usual. An animal who rolled over and bared its belly on command, allowing itself to be petted and fondled by numerous human hands.

'Our families have been breeding them for fur for fifty years,' came the showman's spiel. 'They breed quickly and successfully, and we learned to take the calmest pups from the calmest parents, mated them with other calm pups from other calm litters, and now—only fifteen generations down the line, ladies and gentlemen—we have Sashenka here, who is more like a dog than a fox.'

Sashenka obediently acting on cue, wagging a bushy tail, taking the offered titbits. Onlookers enchanted, pushing fingers through soft white fur that should have been roaming the tundra instead of performing tricks. Philbert in no position to argue the point, given how Kroonk—a walking source of bacon, smoked ham, salami and schnitzel—had been his companion since she'd been a piglet. And how was it different to people pairing to bolster a family's weak line, introduce beauty, intelligence or connections? All a gamble, and rarely for love, although it worked differently on the fairs' circuit than for the main population. Philbert seeing true pairings brought about by choice instead of necessity: Hermann and Hannah, Lita and her bowman, Alarico and La Chucha Lanuga. So much more freedom for them, being on the edges of society.

Fifteen generations for a Siberian fox to changes its stripes, its fur, its snout, its behaviour. How many more to change the basic essentials of a man?

Philbert knew many things, this not one of them; guessed the answer being a damn sight more than fifteen generations. Men seeming to have behaved more or less consistently since they'd first plastered their handprints on the walls of caves, placed themselves at the pinnacle of creation. Self-involved, predicating their superiority on brains and greed, blood and murder. Numerous creation legends bearing such an ethos out.

Hulde's round face popping into his mind, and her story as related to him by Heraldo on the journey to Rügen, giving a quick precis of who made up the Pfiffmaklers these days. All those crossed religions and rival factions, debates between Heaven and Earth having no solutions, and no sympathy for whoever got caught and skewered in the deadfall traps of their endless arguments.

Philbert's mind wandering.

Reciting to himself the early history of Islam as given him by a Sufi scholar.

Quraysh clan starting a war with Mohammed in 622;

Betrayal of the Bani Quraiza;

Abu Bakr's men setting out to conquer Syria;

Mohammed's widow leading her forces against Abu Bakr's son;

Caliph after caliph murdered by their own;

Othman's bloodied shirt—the hacked-off fingers of his wife still clutching it—hung in place of honour at the mosque in Damascus.

On and on, murder after murder.

Sufi scholar Harun fleeing to Europe in despair, despairing further to discover Christianity equally faction-ridden and soaked in blood.

'Should have gone to India,' Philbert told him. 'Sect there called the Jains who value all forms of life equally; won't crack a flea or squash aphids threatening to ruin crops.'

Facts learned from a Tibetan contortionist back in the day.

Harun laughing, and then not laughing. Harun packing his single bag, informing Philbert he was off to India to discover it for himself.

What he found when he got there Philbert didn't know.

Hoped for the best, expected the worst; feared for a man like Harun in a world that had people like him, the Huldes and Philberts, chased into corners, both wanting the same: both wanting a place where pretence was unnecessary, where differences held no sway, where they could lay down their heads—however big they were—and wake up with them still attached in the morning.

Times and places not yet come.

A time and a place, Mergim was thinking, *to let fall a leaf.*

Wondering if that time might be now, the place Rügen Island.

Mergim, having left the Joshua Tree, standing, looking out to sea.

Mergim blessing the mathematician for his learning; a man who'd been grizzled and hollow-faced when Mergim left Kragujevac a few years later with his lessons learned.

He'd never quite understood the mechanics of what the mathematician had called his Birthday Paradox, the statistics of it, but had gleaned enough to realise that randomness could not be dismissed, that it might not be so extraordinary therefore that someone else from Kragujevac had wound up here, given all the gossip swilling around Kragujevac like floodwater down a drain.

Mergim had never spoken about the Pfiffmaklers, about Hulde, to anyone but the mathematician, yet much of his life story was nonetheless known. The old turmoil in Serbia, Croatia and Albania never dying down for long, not for hundreds of years, so no reason to assume his part in it would be forgotten or forgiven. Some folk as much prisoners of their past as the inmates were in Kragujevac. And not such a stretch therefore that someone in Kragujevac had been outraged Mergim had only got a mere ten years for his part in the struggles. And if someone wanted to find him, he'd not exactly hidden his tracks.

Less an impossibility then, those marks on the Joshua Tree seat, XII-LI RUGN INSL, more a probability waiting to happen. Someone from Kragujevac seeking him out, someone who'd guessed where Mergim was going and why.

White cliffs, tight black forests.

Hulde over there, waiting to be found.

Alarm prickling at the back of his neck as he had a sudden thought: Hulde maybe the ultimate goal instead of himself because of their shared history. How bitter a revenge that would be, to finally finish her off just as Mergim was about to find her, or maybe at the exact moment he found her.

He couldn't shrug the thought, found himself moving away from the Joshua Tree with great speed, the pain of contemplating such a revenge raw and urgent.

Remembering a few times in Kragujevac when the rations had been particularly short, the men spending twenty-four hours straining at their stools in the latrines in agonising constipation. Mergim lucky not to develop the anal fissures and haemorrhoids most already suffered that made grown men bleat and howl like women in childbirth. Mergim swallowing down the rudimentary medication of dried rhubarb mixed with solute of buckthorn bark and liquorice, and never such relief in all his life when it took effect.

Diarrhoea never more welcomed.

Something as simple as a bowel movement not to be underestimated.

A miracle the human body could stand so much pain and frustration, and then forget it the moment all has—quite literally—passed.

Pain at the heart of so much, Mergim thought, as he moved swiftly towards the village. If only it could be wiped out in a moment. If only he could wipe his slate clean and start again. If only he could wipe Valter's slate clean and let Valter start again.

Seeing Valter emerging from the barn as the villagers began to yawn their way out of their meagre houses, the men rubbing at the backs of their aching heads, the women mopping at the stone about the quern to get it dry, ready to pour in the last sacks of dried peas, get them pulverised into flour to see them through the next few months of winter.

Celebrations over. Back to grind and toil and bad meals.

Only Valter alleviating the situation as he dragged behind him the sack of implements he'd fashioned during the course of the night. Jacob flashing a smile as Valter revealed his handiwork, ready for inspection. Valter lifting up one of the newly made oars and holding it out against the low grey light of the sky to gauge how well—or how poorly—he'd honed it in the diminished conditions of the barn. Valter taking out a fine-toothed plane and running it about the edges of the blade to rid it of the tiny splinters of imperfection only he could see. Placing it down, taking up the second one, repeating his careful task, sanding both with studious attention before handing them over to Jacob as Mergim drew level.

'Can you take us to Rügen Island?' Mergim asked Jacob, Jacob holding up the oar Valter had passed him, casting a curious eye over first the oar and then Mergim.

Some years back the great Prusso-German statesman Bismark had said of Mecklenburg—and in particular of villages like Jacob's— that when the end of the world came that's where he would choose to be: *because everything happens there a hundred years later than anywhere else.* A good joke, most thought, although that was pretty much Jacob's opinion of Rügen. Island of the Damned, still living in its own pagan past.

'Now why would you be wanting over to a godforsaken place like that?' he asked.

Mergim stood his ground.

'Think there's folk over there we might know.'

Jacob narrowed his eyes. Hard to forget the couple other men they'd taken over not long back, harder to believe Mergim and Valter would have truck with the likes of them. Mergim seeing his hesitation and offering explanation.

'Remember those fairs folk I mentioned last night? Well, we've acquaintance with them. Valter travelled with them for a while.'

'Is that a fact?' Jacob asked, looking at Valter. Valter studiously refusing to meet his eye, running his finger down the side of the second oar's blade before handing it on to Jacob.

'Well, well, then,' Jacob said quietly. 'Why not? Every babe needs its baptism,' meaning the oars. 'And can't think of anyone we'd rather help than you.'

Mergim wondering if Valter would demur, if Valter would choose to stay, though he did not. Away two hours later, Mergim and Valter perched in the bows of a boat, a village man plying the oars; Mergim and Valter's barrow and possessions piled up in the space between. The smooth water the boat divided keeping its own counsel, allowing them easy passage; the bow waves behind them slick and sure, opening up like an arrow head as they went towards their goal.

'Snow's on its way,' their oarsman informed them. 'Any notion where you're going once you get there? Any particular place you want me to land you?'

'We don't know the place at all,' Mergim admitted, his hand gripping the side of the boat. 'Nearest you can get us to a township would be best.'

'Very well, then,' the boat man said. 'After I've landed you, head yourselves north and if you're quick you'll get to Bergen before the snow.'

Smiling as he plied his new and efficient oars, admiring their lightness, their easy and equal weight, the way the blades cut through the water, the depth of draught making their pulling a delight and not a chore.

'But gotta tell you,' he added, glancing over his shoulder, adjusting his course, looking askance at his passengers. 'That place ain't never been easy, so if you want back again, say in the next two weeks?' As if such a course of action was inevitable. 'Then we'll be waiting. Set yourselves a fire on the beach I'll land you on and we'll be out for you, quick as we can.'

Shaking his head.

'Jacob's orders,' he added. 'Though in truth we'd have you both back in a trice.'

Because of Valter, Mergim knew. Not because of him.

The man quiet for a while, during which time Mergim fixed his eyes on the white cliffs, the dark forests, over there on the island, wondering if Hulde was really there. Wondering what he would say if he found her. Wondering about forests and trees and the ability to let fall one leaf or seed and the consequences of doing so. Wondering about the men he'd left behind in Kragujevac; if one or more was coming on behind him, if he was maybe leading them directly to Hulde, or if—as the marks on the Joshua Tree suggested—they were already there.

A skitter of foreboding running beneath his skin, knowing there was more to Kragujevac than murderers who'd acted in the heat of the moment, in the torment of drink and despair. Who carried on living in that torment of drink and despair.

Others in there, he knew, who'd done deeds as despicable—with deliberation and forethought—which they would do again in a heartbeat if they believed they could get away with it, turn a profit or serve a cause, never mind the law saw fit to judge theirs as the lesser crimes. Feuds from the old lands persisting, deep as any well tapping into far-below aquifers, surfacing and re-pooling far from the source of their originating springs.

The Third Face of Fear
Betrayed And Betrayers

Rasvlach was out cold, snoring in a heap of blankets, Diderik's boots and coat lying casually beside him: spoils from Blind Man's Fancy which, as predicted, Rasvlach had won. Diderik unconcerned. Diderik banking up the fire, thin grey smoke spooling and gathering in the eaves of the deserted chapel, spreading across the ceiling, winding between the darkened wooden struts, one umbrosity sinking into another until they could not be distinguished. He padded quietly in stockinged feet as he gathered a few necessaries into his back-pack: a small sack of coarse-ground rye flour, a little dried pork, one bottle of spirits—let Rasvlach keep the rest—an empty flagon he could use to melt snow into water if he couldn't find one of those under-ice burns. This backpack he took to the door of the Lady Chapel and placed it outside before returning, retrieving coat and boots. Putting the latter on quietly as he could, slinging his coat over his shoulders, checking for his tinder box—which was there—and his pouch of tobacco, which was not. A loss he could live with.

Rasvlach stirring as Diderik stood, let go a half-formed curse from his lips, turned in his tattered heap.

'Just going for more firewood, boss, while it's light enough,' Diderik spoke quietly, waited for any reply, though none came. Diderik blinking, pulling his woollen cap over his ears, heart thumping, then took his way to the door of the Lady Chapel, picked up his backpack, heading out of the church, treading as lightly as he could into the early afternoon.

It was eerily calm and quiet, the snow unbroken, the footprints from his morning foray for firewood buried and gone. He made a bee-line for the edge of the forest and ducked beneath the branches, went in ten, fifteen yards—as far as he thought Rasvlach might follow once he woke to find his companion gone. Less snow on the ground in here, most of it gathered on the outspread arms of the ancient firs towering above him which seemed to wilfully draw together at their tops, blocking out the sky.

Dark in this undercroft; Diderik scrambling about, getting together a pile of fallen branches, making them into an identifiably intentionally gathered heap, then scuffling up a load of snow just beyond, threw himself into it a few times and flailed around as if he'd been attacked. After this, he headed into the forest another few yards before winding his way off to the left, tripping over hidden roots and stumps and the mounds made by wood ants, stumbling through tangled growths of briars, coming out a long half hour later onto the ragged edge of the forest and doggedly following its edge along, his boots going in six inches with every step, sinking further on occasion when he wandered into a hidden ditch. Cursing then, hauling himself back out, setting off again; daring to move further onto what he supposed was the track they'd been following, before the snow had come down, once he'd rounded a curve and could no longer see the top of the abandoned chapel when he looked back. The going progressively easier, snow more compact as the track progressed; forest one side, some kind of fencing or hedging on the other against which the night-before wind had driven the snow up in drifts, left the track more visible.

No clear idea what time it was; anxiously keeping a weather-eye out for glimpses of the pale blank sun through the occasionally shifting banks of clouds that were heavy above, glimpses he marked with concern. Diderik—never a bright spark by anyone's standards—understanding the sun was sinking more swiftly than he'd anticipated. Diderik never having grasped throughout his travelling with Rasvlach how the further north they went the shorter were the winter days. Diderik ploughing on regardless, and more urgently as the snow began again to fall soft and gentle. A pretty sight in other circumstances, though not for Diderik who went at it with the desperation of a man who, no matter how cloth-headed he might be, knew this at least: if he didn't find habitation, help or somewhere to hole up within the next hour or so, when the sun went down, he was done for.

Might as well have stayed in the Lady Chapel of the abandoned chapel, waited for Rasvlach to play out his last game of Blind Man's Fancy, for the moment when Rasvlach deemed him of no more use and would take out his butcher's knife, chop Diderik limb from limb, chuck him piece by piece into the snow-blinded forest for the wolves and foxes to pick at and take as they chose.

'Mind you ignore all tracks going to left and right,' the boatman advised Mergim and Valter as they got themselves ashore, the man solicitous, dragging his vessel in as far as he was able so they could retrieve baggage and barrow without getting their boots wet. 'Keep heading north. If you've a choice then go straight ahead. And if you see anyone, ask for Bergen. If your Fairs folk really came here that's likely where they went. Good luck!'

He waved a cheery hand as he pushed his boat back out into the water. 'And remember what I said about the fire. Load it with fresh brushwood so we can see the smoke.'

Mergim raising an echoing hand in farewell as Valter piled their gear onto their barrow.

'Thought you mightn't come over,' Mergim said, as he turned to help. Valter shrugging.

'Wouldn't be nothing but a burden to a place like that, no matter how much wood I can turn.'

Mergim conceding the point.

'Still, the Pfiffmaklers. Wasn't sure you'd want to meet them again.'

Valter spat.

'I don't. Then again, I don't have to. You're the one has all the stuff to say. No need for you to tell them I'm around.'

Mergim nodded.

'If that's what you want.'

'Christ yes, that's what I want!'

Valter vehement, Valter adamant. Mergim taking a deep breath.

'Well, all right then. We're agreed.'

'Better bloody well be agreed,' Valter muttered. 'Don't want to see hide nor hair of any single one of them again, especially not that la-di-da Ludmilla.'

Who treated me like I was one of her special causes, like I was a puppy about to be drowned, like I was something broken only she could fix. Her and her blasted sympathy. Never want the humiliation of that ever again.

Valter still smarting from the degradation Ludmilla had caused him with her simpering smiles, her attempts to engage him in deep conversations about his past.

God forbid.

Only one of that crew who'd ever vaguely understood him being the Janus Woman, which fact caused him yet more pain—if that was possible—unable to think on her without the concomitant guilt coming from remorse and despair for what he'd once attempted to do to her. Stopped by Andreas. The only person who could have stopped him once he was on the march.

'Keep your distance,' he'd overheard Livia, the Janus Woman, chiding Ludmilla. 'Valter's to find his own way, and it can't be yours. He's not some puppet to be fixed by you giving him new strings and a quick lick of paint. He's to find his own way.'

The Janus Woman telling Ludmilla the one thing that made sense to Valter since Andreas had died, namely that he could never be a part of this life called the Pfiffmaklers. No belonging there. Any wisp of it ceasing the moment Andreas had died.

Valter belonging nowhere. Never had, never would.

Unlike the Janus Woman, who'd somehow sewn herself into the Pfiffmaklers stitch and weft.

And good luck to her, for if anyone deserved a bit of luck it was she.

Valter quietly surprised by this revelation of compassion, him truly hoping she'd found her own belonging and wishing her well.

Valter shivering with that oh so brief ray of unaccustomed warmth and light to be thinking of someone other than himself.

A small chink chiselling itself into the carapace he'd spent a lifetime building about himself to keep the wild world at bay, stave off his past and, most especially, the hummy-chummy life of the Pfiffmaklers that could never be his own. Valter leaving them a few days after overhearing that conversation. Valter set on finding his own way as Livia had directed. Not that it had proved a good one.

One step forward, two steps back.

Steps taking him ever further away from the Pfiffmaklers.

Back to where everything had begun.

Until Mergim had found him.

And now here he was, years later; maybe only a few days, a few miles, from bumping into the whole blasted lot of them again.

Well, not if he could help it.

He'd helped Mergim. He'd done his part. He'd tried to be a better man.

But that, as far as Valter Poppelmann was concerned, was as far as it went.

Like the old Christmas carol, Philbert felt the night for what it was: silent, clear and calm. Kroonk asleep beneath their fallen-fir bivouac. Not so Philbert, who pushed his way out into darkness, felt his way to the edge of the cliff a half a mile north. Philbert sitting below the osprey nest, moon full and bright in a sky holding snow in the clouds to left and right, a broad strip of moonlight laying a path across a sea smooth as silk, sleeping safe and secure as Kroonk. Philbert not fooled by this lull. The sea, like life, most likely biding its time; calm one day, vicious the next. Water in all its forms unpredictable, shifting guise in a blink: mizzle to downpour, sleet to snow to boot-dragging drift. Water taking its own way. No predicting whether it would help or hinder.

Philbert not alone in his misgivings, for Rasvlach, in his Lady Chapel—the owl pellets from Blind Man's Fancy a-crumble between his fingers—had woken up.

Ortwin's early morning vigil paying off.

Ortwin spying the Pfiffmaklers the moment they appeared on the outskirts of Sagard, Ortwin running towards them, eager with his news.

'A stranger's been found!' he informed them. 'Couple of hours after sunset last night. Stiff as a pikestaff, lying face-down in the middle of the track, all the snow piling over him. Almost ran him over they did. Took him for a dead elk at first, but he's got to be your man.'

'Hold up, lad,' Wenzel said, as Ortwin opened his mouth to speak again. 'Who is this person? Did he give a name?'

'And isn't he just as likely to be someone from another township, right here on Rügen? Maybe come to see our show?' Heraldo added.

'Hardly,' Ortwin scoffed. 'The Huber brothers what found him go all over the place year in, year out. They're travelling butchers and know just about everyone all over, and they didn't recognise one bit of him.'

'Did you actually see him yourself?' Wenzel asked, Ortwin flashing a smile.

"Course I did! They took him direct to St Michael's, right in the middle of choir practice.'

'You're in a choir?' Heraldo surprised, for a boy with a chest as hollowed out as Ortwin's didn't seem a likely candidate, his suspicions confirmed when thin lines of red blossomed over the angular lines of Ortwin's pinched cheekbones.

'No,' the boy admitted. 'But I'm allowed to sit and listen, and I went there last night after leaving you.'

'Ah,' Heraldo said. *And why wouldn't you, after the grilling Longhella gave you?*

No better place to be.

'What did he look like?' Wenzel not thinking of Ortwin at all, nor what suffering Longhella had perpetrated upon the lad. 'How old was he? Stocky? Thin? Hair colour?

Wenzel realising how much of this might no longer apply. The Mergim they'd known might have wasted away in prison, be half the weight, bowed at the shoulders where he'd previously borne down on them like an ox; might be grey at the temples, or grey all over, or have no hair left at all.

'What's all the commotion?' Rosa asked, catching up husband and son.

'Ortwin thinks Mergim might be at St Michael's,' Heraldo piped up quickly, Rosa raising her eyebrows in quick alarm.

'Is that so? Wenzel?' Rosa turning to her husband.

'We're about to find out,' he said grimly, leading them on. Wenzel falling into step with Ortwin, thanking him for telling them about the stranger, for no reason anyone else might have mentioned it. Having a quick stab of guilt about their last encounter.

'I apologise for last night. I'm sorry it was Peppe and not myself who thought to see you home. Can you forgive me?'

Ortwin nodding vigorously.

'I'd prefer you keep that visit to us a secret. Are good at keeping secrets, Ortwin?'

'Lordy yes,' Ortwin replied.

'Tell me one,' Wenzel said, putting Ortwin to the test. 'Tell me something you've never told anyone else.'

Ortwin not having to think too hard.

'My grandfather once met the poet Goethe, shook his hand, talked with him about puppet theatres.'

Wenzel raised his bushy eyebrows. Had not expected anything so dramatic.

'Is that so? Puppet theatres, eh? How come your grandfather only told you?'

Ortwin blushed, fearing he was not believed.

'He's a very famous man in Denmark,' Ortwin countered. 'He writes books. I can show you. He gave me some when he came back for grandma's funeral, and that's when he told me about Goethe.'

And so much more. Ortwin really was good at keeping secrets, telling no one about their conversation, and no one about the books.

'Well, well,' Wenzel gave the lad a smile. 'That's very impressive. And you've told no one about your little visit to the woods?'

'No one, sir,' Ortwin said earnestly. 'Cross my heart and—'

'I believe you,' Wenzel interrupted, hating that particular oath. Had seen too much death to have anyone wish it voluntarily upon themselves, even in the small capacity of a childhood rhyme. Thought flashing through him of Andreas, of the small vial Rosa had discovered once Valter had been taken away and she and Yssel got on with preparing Andreas for burial. A task for women wherever they'd travelled; maybe having stronger stomachs for such things than men, who never liked hanging around the dead, happy to go out and dig a grave in a forest glade but on no account wanting to undress a corpse, get it washed, push stiffening limbs back into clothes they'd tidied and pressed. The dead needing to look their best before being put into the ground.

Remembering something Andreas had told him about rabbits, how they always gave birth at night in the claustrophobic darkness of their burrows; how they were almost always pregnant again within a month; how if food was scarce, or there were ructions in the burrow, then the does absorbed the embryos right back into their bodies as if they'd never been.

'I suspect some women wish they could do the same,' Andreas had said at the time, Wenzel shocked and then reflecting that yes, he was probably right. Vision of Ludmilla and Longhella singing *The Sisters Seven* with great vehemence:

Oh we were sisters seven, now five are dead with child,
And there's only you and I, love, and we'll stay maidens mild.
But scarcely had Maidre spoken, and turned her round about,
When the bonny Earl of Livingstone came calling Maidre out.

Rosa telling him of Ludmilla's regret she'd not yet had a child of her own with Heraldo. But they had Hulde, and now there was Livia.

And now there was Livia…

Livia and Hulde alone at the camp, electing to stay on to prepare the day's meals. Livia not wanting to risk slipping on the snow on the walk to Sagard, Hulde not wanting to leave Livia on her own. Decision made that once their Hildegard section was done, once the day was warmer, the snow softer, they'd send someone down to fetch them up with a trap for the rest of the set. Wenzel worrying about that decision. Wenzel taking steps to put it right.

'I need you to do something for me, Ortwin,' he said, putting a hand on Ortwin's shoulder, Ortwin looking up at Wenzel with the same awe and respect he'd looked at his grandfather. Two strong men from different worlds to the one he lived in, Ortwin wanting desperately to pass from his world into theirs.

'Anything,' Ortwin got out.

Wenzel nodding slowly.

'Right then, this is what I need you to do.'

'Where the fuck is that no good lad?' Rasvlach mumbled, pushing off the moth-eaten tapestry, the greasy blankets that had accompanied him all the way from Serbia to Rügen, spreading out his arms, grasping at whatever he could find, which wasn't much: fingers bumping into the diminished pile of last night's firewood, the vodka bottle Rasvlach had all but emptied, the piss pail he'd availed himself of during the night despite not remembering doing so, splashing himself inadvertently with its contents.

'Hells bloody bells,' he cursed, getting himself up on his elbows, head thick with yesterday's drink and not-remembering. Felt the crush of owl pellets between his fingertips: thin shards of bones, scraps of fur, of devoured mice. The game of Blind Man's Fancy. Remembered that much at least. Giving the idiot Diderik a run for his money. The lad never learning. Had his coat and boots here somewhere about, not that Rasvlach was actually going to keep them. Barely any light, hands feeling around the dusty floor. No sign of either coat nor boots. Diderik maybe not such a bonehead after all. Had to admire the lad on that point, doing as anyone in Kragujevac would have done: taking back what had been won the moment the winner was out for the count.

'Ha!' Rasvlach managed through crusty throat and crusted tongue. His notion of conceding. Looking for a flagon of water to slake his thirst, finding it at the edge of the still burning fire, recognising Diderik's handiwork, the way he'd built the wood into a kind of triangle so it would collapse onto the embers under its own steam, keep the fire burning if left unattended. Which it had. But where the hell was Diderik? Faint memory of Diderik telling him he was going for more firewood; so faint a memory it seemed an echo of the mismatched dreams he occasionally had immediately before waking.

Rasvlach grimaced. Grabbed at the nearest bottle, a slick of alcohol left in its base. Got it down him, then got down the several inches of water in the flagon by the fireside. Not enough. Rasvlach needing more. Cursed again under his breath that Diderik was not here to provide for him on command. Pushed himself further up on his elbows. Noticed something not quite right: Diderik's back-pack gone, as too was one of the small sacks of flour they'd deliberately left away from the fire so they wouldn't start to bloom with all that shouldn't bloom on flour if it was still to be edible.

'Fuck's sake,' Rasvlach got himself up to sitting, mind tumbling with various scenarios he couldn't exactly form. Managed to get himself standing, staggered over to the door of the Lady Chapel and from there to the main door of the church and looked out. Nothing but flat white snow lit by a large bright moon. No idea what time it was; maybe twilight, maybe dawn. Rasvlach looking and looking, finally seeing an anomaly in the forest directly beyond him. Rasvlach stumbling down the path towards the collapsed lych gate and staggering over the snowy track, pushing into the trees, the moon aiding his way.

Rasvlach finding a pile of brushwood and a load of scumbled up earth and snow directly behind it.

As if Diderik had been in some kind of fight.

As if Diderik had been attacked by brigands or wolves.

As if, Rasvlach thought, Diderik had salted the scene, for there was one essential missing. There was no blood, and no way anything of wolves or brigands had gone down without it.

'You treacherous little bastard,' Rasvlach muttered through his beard. 'You conniving little shit.'

Rasvlach returning to the chapel, packing up his gear. Getting the harness of his trap upon his shoulders and heading out. It might be almost night; it might be late or it might be early. No doubt that it was freezing and he was a little drunk. None of which was going to stop the likes of Rasvlach. He'd suffered worse, and knew the way Diderik would have gone: carrying on down the track they'd started on before they'd reached the chapel. And Rasvlach had the means to stick out the night if he had to. He'd the cart, he'd the blankets and the most of their supplies, and he piled on the brushwood Diderik had so helpfully left for him.

Rasvlach on the move, and God help anyone who got in his way.

Rasvlach starting off at a furious pace and then slowing, because what the hell was Diderik going to do? Track down Metternich's little Monster of Nature on his own?

Hardly.

Diderik didn't have it in him, not to track, nor to capture, and certainly not to hack off the Little Maus's giant head. Rasvlach's thinking becoming clearer as dawn began to lighten, luck on his side, it not being night after all. Diderik of no more use to him anyway. Diderik always deadwood waiting to be discarded. Diderik dead as the deadest wood if and when Rasvlach found him. Rasvlach emboldened by the freedom of being solitary. Liked a good carouse with his fellows every now and then but being with another person night and day got very wearing.

Prison polarising people that way; a place where you were constantly together, always someone watching, so when you got out you either couldn't stand being on your own or else preferred it. Diderik of the first kind, Rasvlach the second. Rasvlach knowing Diderik would stick to the first people he met until he found another group to shift to. Main danger, Rasvlach thought, being Diderik spilling his guts out about what he was doing on Rügen, which could really bugger things up for Rasvlach. Not that Diderik knew everything, Rasvlach holding back one very pertinent piece of information. Diderik right when he'd supposed The Anatomist's Dream had to have accomplices. Diderik knowing nothing about them. Unlike Rasvlach, who was no slouch when it came to information-gathering. And what he'd gathered was that most of the Fair's folk in Mecklenburg stuck to their own, moved around the province from town to town, city to city, rarely further. Only one peripatetic group he'd heard of shifting from that pattern, moving in and out of Mecklenburg for the previous few months; latterly hovering around Regensburg and Rostock until immediately before Advent, when they'd pulled up sticks and vanished into thin air.

Or vanished over the water to Rügen.

A crew called the Pfiffmaklers.

He stumped along the track, day and mind lightening the further he went. Rasvlach periodically forcing snow into his flagon, shaking it until it became liquid enough to swallow, diluting the residual alcohol in his blood. Memory beginning to clarify, Rasvlach pausing several times as he searched its dusty corners because he'd an inkling he'd heard on these Pfiffmaklers before.

Rasvlach tramping on.

Rasvlach regarding the few pointers around him.

White snow, dark forests, he murmured, start of one of the old songs his father and uncles used to sing not long before Serbia had been liberated.

Brought to mind something more.

Ancient history tumbling through his head like all those jagged dreams he had when all the pieces were there but never quite fitted. Dreams centring on Rasvlach being in some unnamed town, a town that shifted with every dream yet was nevertheless the same; Rasvlach desperately searching for the place he'd left all his important belongings; Rasvlach wandering aimlessly about the unrecognisable streets trying to find them.

Not that he ever did.

Always woke in a cold sweat, confused and frightened by a loss he couldn't name or specify.

Rasvlach, on this cold and snowy road, nevertheless finding a link between two particular names: the Pfiffmaklers, and Mergim.

Settling on the last.

The murderer he'd tried to cosy up to because, like Diderik, Mergim was soon due for release. Not that Mergim had been as pliable as Diderik. Mergim about as pliable as a piece of rock.

Rasvlach stopped in his tracks, raised his head to the sky.

How the hell could he have forgotten?

Follow a crow long enough and you'll find carrion.

Rasvlach remembering how the last time they'd talked—or rather he'd talked and Mergim had not listened—he'd spat at Mergim on the other side of the wire, disgusted by the man, and more so when he'd got back to his bunk and railed on about Mergim being an uncommunicative son-of-a-bitch and been blanked by several of his fellow prisoners.

'You don't want to be talking about him like that,' some old lag had warned.

'Why the piss not?' Rasvlach's usual retort, whenever challenged.

'Because Mergim's a bit of a hero in these parts,' he was told. 'Delivered a war criminal to the Serbian authorities.'

'And why the buggeration should that bother me?' Rasvlach had asked after a blink, because bothered he was, not that he was going to let on, concentrating on squishing a few lice scuttling out the hem of his bedding blanket. 'Fucking little bastards,' he murmured, as he did so.

'Fucking little bastard is exactly right,' the old lag explained. 'That's what most folk here think of the man Mergim brought back. So watch your mouth, Rasvlach. The weight of opinion in here is that Mergim did right.'

Rasvlach sniffing, needing argument, needing his own side heard, because in his own circles Mergim was entirely in the wrong. Mergim a traitor as far as Rasvlach was concerned. Rasvlach saying so to his fellow inmate, his fellow inmate responding to the opposite.

'Think you're wrong there, friend.' Old lags never knowing when to shut up. 'Has to be a time when we leave the past behind us, now we've our Independence. And Mergim helped with that.'

Rasvlach holding his tongue for once: a Croatian in the middle of a Serbian prison a vulnerable target. Quick flash of a knife in the night and no more Rasvlach.

Rasvlach lowering his head, ploughing on up the track, rage in every step as dawn became morning, and morning became full-blown day, and birds began to come out of the trees in their perpetual search for food: rooks swirling in krawking crowds above his head, jays screaming at each other over uncracked acorns, woodpeckers hammering their heads against dead wood deep inside the forest, poking their barbed tongues into crevices to pull out insects and pupae who'd believed themselves safe.

Rasvlach hammering at his own deadwood, picking at the prattle he'd gleaned about Mergim in Kragujevac; Rasvlach hauling at his cart, tramping through the snow; Rasvlach finally getting at what had been niggling him about that name Pfiffmakler.

Where he'd heard it before.

Old lags talking about that bastard Mergim like he was a bloody saint, and how it had been a group of Fairs folk who'd seen fit to help him return to Serbia the criminal Rasvlach believed was no criminal.

Old lags cackling in approval, unaware of the diehard Croatian in their midst.

And diehard Croatian Rasvlach was. Only thing Rasvlach cared about—apart from Rasvlach himself—being the dire humiliation suffered by his family following Serbia's Declaration of Independence. His own folk sent packing back home to Croatia with their tails between their legs, no sign the revolution would continue now Serbia held the keys to their kingdom. Treachery threaded into Serbia's soul, no caring how much Croatian blood had been spilled for their cause.

Jesus. No wonder his father had hung himself from the nearest beam after returning to their armpit of a village. All those years of fighting and hardship undergone for their neighbour proving futile: Serbians living like lords; Croatians left to scrabble about like beetles between the stones scattering their land from top to bottom.

Nothing ever going to change.

Rasvlach swearing beneath his breath at the enormity of betrayal he'd only just grasped.

Rasvlach on his last mission.

The Anatomist's Dream his goal.

But if he could take down others while he was doing so then all the better.

Mergim might be out of Rasvlach's reach. Pfiffmaklers another matter. He'd lay odds, bet his last game of Blind Man's Fancy, they were here on Rügen.

Island of the Damned, indeed.

And damn them he would, first chance he got.

If Only We Could All Roll Up Like Hedgehogs

'I hope this morning's Hildegard will go well,' Livia worried, kneading dough in her bowl.

'Of course it will,' Hulde encouraged, mixing up the meat of the several small animals Longhella had skewered earlier that morning, rolling it into small balls to be folded into Livia's dough to make the dumplings they would eat later that night when all was done, before they moved on up the island and solved the puzzle of what to do with Philbert. Hulde hoping she would meet him again before Wenzel and Heraldo spirited him off the island. She'd been rather taken by him, despite their meeting being so brief, lasting mere minutes.

And you must be Hulde. I gather you've a rather interesting history yourself.

No one had ever said that of her before. Hulde's past, as she saw it, being past and gone. It never occurring to her anyone would find it of interest, certainly not this real live participant in the revolutions that had so recently shaken the whole of Europe by the scruff of its neck and let it be known all might not go on as it always had. Someone who'd murdered Schupos, had songs written about him and theatre troupes playing out his life story. How he knew about her—Hulde of all people—let alone found her history interesting intrigued her. And the way he'd looked at her, as if fixing her in that giant head of his, she'd found obscurely thrilling.

'What do you think will happen to Philbert?' she asked Livia as Livia patted out the first piece of her dough, taking the pinch of filling Hulde handed her, the two working efficiently and well together as they always had, always getting along, these two disparate folk adopted into the Pfiffmakler clan. Livia not answering immediately, concentrating on getting the dumplings filled, amassing a small pile before she answered.

'My guess is they'll try to get him over to Denmark,' she said, looking at Hulde's serious face. 'Are you worried about him?'

Livia always on the mark when it came to Hulde; Ludmilla and Heraldo, Hulde's adoptive parents, always so kind and caring, and no one gladder than Hulde when they'd finally tied the knot after years of skating about each other, yet only Livia seeming to completely understand her. The younger Hulde asking Livia to step out with her on the third of May the year after they'd left Italy. Livia frowning, consenting, grasping Hulde's hand and taking Hulde into a wood bursting with bluebells.

'How good they smell!' Livia had exclaimed. 'I think a green-leafed wood filled with bluebells is one of the best things a person can ever see.'

'What will come after the bluebells?' Hulde had asked, Livia squeezing the small hand within her own.

'Summer, Hulde, is what will come. And your summer, my little chickpea, when it comes, is going to be the best summer this earth has ever seen.'

The two still standing hand in hand when Ludmilla, always nervous in those early days when Hulde was out of sight, came to find them.

'What are you two up to?' Ludmilla asked, neither answering, although Livia let go Hulde's hand, recognising Ludmilla's right to it.

But never forgotten, that time at the edge of the bluebell wood.

The best summer this earth has ever seen.

Livia so certain Hulde had no choice than to believe her.

Livia right: Summer a long time to a child as young as Hulde had been back then, her past not exactly forgotten, bricked over and buried by all that post-bluebell summer had afforded her: the Pfiffmaklers adopting her as they shuffled slowly upcountry in the vague direction of Vienna. Heraldo teaching her to play both lute and lyre, Hulde's fingers eager and flexible as she learned to pluck and strum; helping Heraldo rebuild a curtal—*a forerunner of the bassoon,* he'd told her, not that Hulde knew what a bassoon was. Hulde giggling when she'd first tried blowing through the reed, producing the sound of a rabbit being murdered by a weasel. Heraldo laughing, sitting down on the ground behind her, legs stretched to either side of her, her back against his chest as he held her fingers over the various holes in the base and showed her how to blow properly, how to purse her lips, draw air up from her lungs and hold it in her cheeks before expelling it in a quick short blast, when out came a pure, mournful wail from the curtal's horn that had Hulde entranced. Hulde practising for weeks on end until she'd presented the Pfiffmaklers with a short performance, a tune of her own composing, that had Ludmilla in tears.

'It's like...I don't know, like wind blowing through rushes,' Ludmilla finally said.

'More like a fart from a cow's backside.' Longhella dismissing Hulde's efforts, the effect of which was everyone else encouraging Hulde to do it all over again.

And singing. Ludmilla teaching her the rudimentaries that summer. An odd experience for Hulde, Ludmilla starting with the one song Ludmilla knew Hulde was familiar with.

Jesus Saviour, on thy breast I would lay me down to rest.
Forgive my wayward heart, teach me to be my best.
And when the day of my life is past, and twilight comes at last,
When my eyes finally close and I take my last repose,
May your angels vigil keep
As I lay me down for my last sleep.

Ludmilla revealing to Hulde so much more than that single mournful dirge, bestowing on Hulde a whole new world of songs about a myriad topics. Hulde had loved the singing, not as good at is as she was with Heraldo's instruments. But she'd persisted, stuck at it, caterwauled her way through walks and woods when she was alone; practised and practised until she could eventually hold her own. Nowhere near as talented as Longhella and Ludmilla, taking an age to conquer the next level, which was the descant. Eventually daring to sing in public, mostly due to Livia's discreet encouragement.

'Have you actually heard her?' Longhella had carped. 'She's obviously the progeny of screech owls.'

Hulde privately agreeing with Longhella, but Livia had faith in her and Hulde had not let her down. Would never want to let Livia down, nor any of the Pfiffmaklers come to that.

That best summer Livia had predicted rolling on into a best winter. Hulde's world opening up as Ludmilla taught her how to read, and she progressed with her music and her singing. A few blips of course, like when Uncle Andreas had died, for she'd liked him immensely. He'd been such fun, always with his Igel-Iritch patter Hulde found mighty amusing, never having heard of hedgehogs before and finding the whole idea of them ridiculous.

'They're like moles or rats, only covered head to tail with spines,' Andreas had explained. 'When they're frightened they roll themselves up into a ball. And they can squeak like the burst bladders those boys are always playing with.'

Meaning Lupercal and Jericho, who sometimes allowed Hulde to play with them. Blowing up a pig's bladder, giving her a stick, the three of them spending the next few hours batting the slowly deflating bladder around a flattened square of grass with one or other of them, usually Hulde, put to guard a goal; the boys bawling in delight when they managed to shoot it past her head, or even into it; the feel of it against her skin at first disgusting and then elating, once she'd figured out she could bite through the bladder and end the game decisively in her favour with that oddly alluring squeal—as of Andreas's hedgehogs—as all the air went out of it.

Hulde thinking of Andreas as she and Livia carried on with their dumplings, as they'd been doing the night Andreas had died. Such a shock to lose him so suddenly it brought the old nightmares back, nightmares she couldn't explain either to herself or others, although others seemed to know more about them than she did herself.

Ludmilla and Heraldo solicitous as always, yet Livia the most comfort at that time. Livia coming to her, explaining how death was not always the worst option.

'Andreas loved you, loved us all, but he was very sick, and occasionally there comes a time in a person's life,' Livia saying what no one else would, 'when they weigh up their options, choose whether to go or stay. And Andreas chose to go. It doesn't mean he thought less of us, merely that going on was harder than not. Do you understand?'

Hulde snuffling against Livia's shoulder because yes, Hulde understood.

'He'd awful difficulty with his fingers,' Hulde said.

'He did,' Livia agreed, 'and so much more.'

Hulde suddenly aware of it since it had been spoken out loud.

How Andreas had been unable to use a knife to eat his food for the past while; how Valter had to cut up his meat and hold it to Andreas's mouth for him to take. How Andreas could no longer undo the sack in which he kept all his hedgehoggery; all those little wooden artifacts Hulde had found so curious and turned around and around in her hands.

How he could no longer walk on his own.

How Valter had to curl Andreas's fingers about his sticks before Andreas could take a single step.

'Will we bury him?' Hulde had asked.

'We will,' Livia assured. 'And in a good place. Valter will see to that.'

And a good place it had been, and a ceremony solemnly carried out. Hulde wanting to sing for Andreas. Not daring to do so. Her voice nowhere near good enough, nor her confidence. Instead reciting the words in her head.

When my eyes finally close and I take my last repose,
May your angels vigil keep
As I lay me down for my last sleep.

Ludmilla standing to one side of her, Livia the other.

'It seems sad now, my little chickpea,' Livia had whispered, 'but it really isn't. We've to celebrate folk when they go, not mourn them.'

Livia's wise whisper felt once more on Hulde's neck as she remembered, when Livia suddenly dropped her dumpling pastry and pulled Hulde towards her along the length of the log.

'Don't speak. Don't murmur. Don't move.'

Hulde letting go the last of the meat-mix from her hands into the snow as Livia pointed and Hulde saw: a shadow emerging from the woods, a man coming down the hill towards the lake; a man with the late morning sun behind him so they couldn't see his features but by Andreas's angels, there was something about the way he walked that Hulde found familiar and frightening. Threat there, she knew, as apparently did Livia.

'Do you have your knife with you?' Livia asked, Hulde patting herself about her waist but no. No knife. She'd left it in her tent. No Longhella she.

'No,' Hulde admitted, 'but we've fire and sticks.'

Women, Pfiffmakler or otherwise, well versed in the treachery of men, Livia more attuned than most; and if fire and sticks were all they had, then fire and sticks would have to do. Livia and Hulde getting slowly to their feet, shading their eyes, watching the alien shadow gain heft and height as he moved from the tree line towards the end of the lake where the eel traps were laid.

'Maybe he's a traveller looking to fill his water canister,' Hulde posited, 'or to ask for a bite of food.'

Speaking fast, heart racing, hair horripilating all over her body.

'Maybe,' Livia agreed. 'Or maybe not.'

The titles of Ludmilla's songs rippling through Livia's mind: *Reynard the Fox, The Lady in the May, Lily of the Greenmantle*; men coming across pretty women going about their daily tasks and taking the worst advantage. Livia fixing her eyes on the man as he reached the lake's edge, stooped, scooped water from hand to mouth, straightened up, turned slowly and deliberately in their direction, held his stance as if scanning their camp, seeing who was about, seeing what he might be able to make or take.

Maybe a simple traveller; so many travellers about these days spawned by the failed revolutions: men on the run with high tempers and fixed ideas, parted from comrades, left to forage for their livelihoods as they pillaged the lands they'd previously been fighting for. Men who couldn't or wouldn't go back home because of what they'd done, or men who simply didn't care. Men who'd done and become the worst, who looked and saw, took and departed, not giving a damn about what they left behind.

Livia not worried for herself, for she was old by their standards, obviously disfigured and undeniably pregnant. Not so Hulde, who was young and personable, and no one here except Livia to defend her. Livia wishing they'd ducked themselves down behind the seating log and stayed there the moment they'd spotted him moving out of the trees. Not an option now. She'd made a terrible strategic error by standing up and looking, making of themselves targets as visible to the man at the end of the lake as he was to them.

Still hope for Livia while that man stayed where he was.

Still hope while she saw him standing stock still.

Still hope, until that man glanced back up to the tree line and gave a nod, and then oh God, she knew there were more of them. That he was not alone. That it was she and Hulde against all that was about to come. She felt a wriggle in her belly, her child moving, brandishing its tiny fists against her skin as if it too was getting ready for the fight. And by Christ, Livia was going to fight. She'd no idea what was about to befall her and Hulde, but was damn certain she wasn't going to go down without giving it everything she'd got.

'Get behind the log, Hulde,' Livia ordered.

Hulde complying.

Hulde doing more, Hulde reaching out behind her towards the fire, finding the end of a burning stick, pulling it free, feeling the heat of it racing up the sap, holding on. Fingertips blistering, and having to let go.

Livia her only thought now; Livia and her belly needing to be protected.

If only they could roll themselves up like hedgehogs.

Hulde spying something that might be of use: Longhella's bow and flitch of arrows, used to dispatch more small furry animals than Hulde cared to think about. Longhella absolutely refusing to teach Hulde how to use them. Not so Lupercal and Jericho, who'd been more inclined than Longhella to introduce Hulde into the Pfiffmakler ways.

Hulde taking them up, Hulde getting an arrow into the bow.

'I can take him,' she whispered to Livia, 'if he gets close enough. Or at least slow him down.'

Oh Longhella, Your Bow And Arrows

Mergim had stuck rigidly to the instructions given him by the villager who'd landed them on Rügen: keep straight on; don't go to either left or right; ask the first person you see for the track to Bergen.

Good advice; meeting a pair of travelling butchers a few hours in, whose directions had been clear and concise. Once at Bergen, they'd gone straightaway to the church. Informed there that the Pfiffmaklers had moved on to a place called Sagard.

'Can't miss it,' the Pastor said. 'Keep going on up the road that way.' Pointing their direction. 'You'll cross a causeway, and then it's only a few more miles. But snow's coming, so keep a watch out.'

'I will, sir. A thousand thanks.' Mergim would have recited every one of those thousand thanks if he'd the time, but they were so close he could feel the future bearing down on him.

'And be sure to tell them,' the Pastor said, as Mergim and Valter departed, 'they've really breathed life into the Christmas Season for us. I wish they could come every year.'

Shaking his head sadly, knowing this probably would not be so, that next Advent would be a dull repast comparative to the pageant put on by the Pfiffmaklers.

It hadn't occurred to Mergim that Christmas here was just around the corner; Serbians sticking to the old calendar, eleven days behind: January 7th their big day. A solemn time in Kragujevac as the inmates contemplated what they'd lost and would never have again. The festivities all about family in Serbia, the keeping up of old pagan habits that would have had the Joshua Tree villagers' heads bobbing in consternation fit to break their necks. Forget the Island of the Damned, they would have cast the whole of Serbia into the pit. Mergim smiling as he conjured up the scene in his head:

On the three Sundays preceding Christmas, he could have told them, *the parents tie up first the children, then the children tie up their mothers, and then their fathers. No one released until they can produce an acceptable gift.*

Old Jacob might have had a heart attack there and then.

And there's more, Mergim could have confided. *Gangs of young men frolic and dance in the streets, dressed up in costumes and masks, parading and singing, thrashing the walls of houses with sticks to beat out the demons.*

Probably not enough tuts in the world for Jacob and his villagers to express what they thought of that.

And worst of all, Mergim might have finished, in suitably hushed tones, *huge bonfires are set up outside the churches, at their centres enormous boles of golden oak. And, after their Christmas meal, the Serbs bring their own boughs of oak to throw into the conflagration, aim being to send up showers of sparks to bring them luck.*

Mergim laughing gently to himself as he imagined all the villagers rushing to their Joshua Tree and genuflecting madly to rid themselves of pagan taint. Mergim thinking he'd maybe stop by there when all was done, tell them of Serbian Christmases as he had already told them in his head, hope Jacob wouldn't have a heart attack after all.

Christmas a time for forgiving.

Hoping, hoping, he would find Hulde, and thereby find his own.

Ortwin was thrilled with his mission to take the Pfiffmakler's trap back to the camp to fetch up Livia and Hulde; the cart usually hand-hauled, but Wenzel inveigling a mule to which he quickly had it secured. Ortwin really rescuing maidens this time around, like he'd fallen into the pages of one of his books, become a part of them—maybe Schiller's poem on forging bells. A strange topic for a poem Ortwin had thought, until he'd read how the bell, once made, rings out its own tune, becomes independent of the maker it will long outlive. The stirring verses as the bell is hoisted aloft, high above village and villagers, to take its rightful place:

Pull, pull!
Lift, lift!
Let it move, let it swing!
Let it sing!

Ortwin lifted like that bell out of his normal life as he got atop the trap and drove it down the lane, the mule making quick headway pushed on by Ortwin's exuberant cries of encouragement. Ortwin's paltry chest puffed out; Ortwin standing up on the boards like a charioteer, delighting in the bite of wind against his face. Ortwin's heart singing like Schiller's bell… until he topped the short rise beyond the bend and got a clear view of the camp, when he saw all was not quite right; a man who shouldn't have been there striding with slow measured steps along the edge of the lake, already past the otter's new hide, and only a few hundred yards from the two women. Wenzel obviously right to be worried, sweat prickling in Ortwin's armpits as he contemplated the fact that there really might be maidens needing rescue, and no one to do it but himself.

Valter stayed in the trees. As close as he wanted to get to the Pfiffmaklers, although there didn't seem to be many of them around; assumed most had departed for the village Mergim had said the name of, which Valter couldn't remember, setting up for their latest Advent Cycle. Christ, he'd forgotten how much he'd hated those Advent Cycles. Pfiffmaklers dazzling their audiences with pyrotechnics and clever words, pretending a religion they'd no real truck with. Pfiffmaklers looking after Pfiffmaklers being about the only religion they ever had. Even Andreas had taken a step back at this time of year, Andreas never a man for God or the godly, finding their strictures too cloying, too narrow.

Too much talk, not enough action, had been Andreas's view. *Yap, yap, yap about doing the right thing unless it could— for a single second, God forbid—put them out.*

And yet Andreas doing the godliest thing Valter had ever known: Andreas taking up the damaged scraps of Valter from the side of the road and looking after him until the day Andreas had died.

And still hard, that dying, for Valter.

He couldn't understand how it could hurt so much, how it still hurt.

How it hurt so much more since Mergim had come to his door.

Like it had come right back at him and happened only yesterday.

And kept happening again and again.

I'm such a fucking mess.

Looking down on Mergim by the lake, Mergim nodding up at him just the once to let him know he was about to have the single best day of his life if all went how Mergim hoped it might go.

Valter not caring to nod back.

Valter looking down with dispassion upon the scene.

Two days they'd been on the island.

Only two days for Mergim to zero in on the one person he'd been wanting to find since he'd walked out of his prison in Kragujevac.

Mergim so certain.

Mergim so solid throughout all these months of walking and walking, of talking and talking to find out what people knew.

Valter tagging along because he had nothing better to do.

Valter never really believing Mergim would be able to reach his goal.

Valter never really believing they could catch up the Pfiffmaklers.

Until they had.

Mergim's heart is tolling like a bell. He can feel it in his throat, has to concentrate on taking deep breaths to stop himself from falling, his knees apparently of a sudden unable to bear his weight. And yet he moves on, taking steady steps towards the two figures he can make out standing by a fallen log. He doesn't register their disquiet, his eyes flitting from one to the other, a thunderous roaring threatening to overwhelm him as he fixes on the younger one who is maybe fifteen: pale round face, delicate contours delineated by hair pulled back into a loose ponytail, the tip of it resting on her shoulder, soft and felted as the ear of a summer hare. Mergim blinking, taking an involuntary gasp.

It's her! I really think it might be her.

Mergim feeling the world closing in around him like he's in a tunnel, Hulde's small face the light at the other end; hearing only his breathing, the slight crunch of snow beneath his boots.

And then, what the hell was happening?

Noise erupting: shouting and yelling, wood screeching and jamming, his eye line splintered by a cart appearing from nowhere skewing wildly down the lane towards the camp, a froth-mouthed hinny in the lead, hooves skittering on the snow, a dark figure above her waving skinny arms; the girl who might be Hulde still as a spindle for just one moment and then flexing, pulling back a hand; next second a shaft of wood flying by Mergim's ear, nicking the outer helix, forcing him off balance.

Mergim losing his footing, slipping down the bank.

Mergim in the water, the shock of the cold stripping him of sensation, of conscious thought.

Eyes wide open, gazing in vague wonder as a school of minnows scatters about the body fallen in their midst.

Scatter and reform, flitting off into the darkness.

Flashes of green and silver as they depart.

Maybe the last of the world Mergim will ever see.

'I hear you've found someone in the snow,' Wenzel said to the Pastor of St Michael's.

'Strange news travels fast,' Pastor Hulm replied brightly. 'And yes, you're right. I've got him bundled up in the crypt.'

Wenzel frowned.

'Isn't that the last place he'd need to be?'

Crypts being cold, dank places where you stowed the dead, not someone you were presumably trying to keep alive.

Pastor Hulm smiled broadly.

'Ordinarily yes, that would be the case,' he confided. 'But not here, not at Advent. We don't spread it around much, but down there we've got one of the oldest depictions of Svetovid on the island. Pagan, of course, built into the very foundations of this church.'

Svetovid.

Same as they'd depicted in their earlier play. Ancient god of the Rujani people from whom these islanders were descended.

'He's a sun god, in the old religion,' the Pastor explained, 'and old beliefs die hard. So every year, approaching the winter solstice, we light a fire that burns for seven days to remind us winter will always be succeeded by spring. And, of course,' he added quickly, 'that the light of Christ has vanquished our pagan past.'

The Pastor had the grace to look embarrassed, although Wenzel understood.

Old beliefs not to be dismissed, people in places as poor as this taking help and hope wherever they could find it. Lighting a fire in a church's crypt by the depiction of their island's ancient god not seeming to him so unusual.

Until he got down there, when the sight was strange indeed: fire burning in a pit whose sides were smooth and dark, sandy soil transformed into a glassy substance by the hundreds and hundreds of fires over hundreds and hundreds of years burned within it over the seven darkest days of winter. The pit dug at the base of a stone sculpture carved into the foundations of the church or, more likely, the church having been built around it; the flicker of flames leaping at its darkened feet casting its features into deep and shadowy relief. Hard to find anything less Christian-looking than this; a few old folk perched on the side of the pit poking the fire every now and then with long sticks, feeding it from a great bundle of brushwood piled in a far corner. Adding to the oddity was the body prostrate on the stone sarcophagus to one side, covered in blankets, white tip of his nose poking out from beneath a gently steaming compress over forehead and eyes; only sign of life being the smallest quiver of pale lips as the man beneath drew breath.

'Doesn't hardly seem alive,' Wenzel murmured.

'Probably shouldn't be,' the Pastor agreed. 'Yet best place for him if he's to have a fighting chance. Fire's tended night and day, so always folk by him. Heat him up gently was the advice. Feed him and water him the moment he can swallow.'

Wenzel edged his way around the fire pit, feeling the need to cross himself as he looked into the blank stone eyes of Svetovid, who seemed more alive than the man on the sarcophagus.

'Well, it's not who I was expecting,' he said quietly, almost reverently, as he looked at the casualty, saw how young he was. Surely not Mergim. Just some lad lost in the snow who'd the good fortune to be pulled up and out by a couple of travelling butchers.

'Who were you expecting?' asked Pastor Hulm, curious at Wenzel's interest.

Wenzel shaking his head.

'No one,' he answered. 'Or rather someone we bumped into years back. Foolish really, to think it might have been him.'

Offering nothing more, Wenzel glad to ascend the steps from the crypt and get back into the church, emerging into the proper world as the Pastor closed the hatch behind him. Wenzel understanding those misgivings Pietro had tried to express about how cut off he'd felt this island to be, how Other the people who inhabited it. Slavs, Pietro had said, though not pejoratively. Merely Other. Which was exactly what Wenzel felt now, only it was he who was Other, intruding on other people's belief systems, people sitting in the crypt below him feeding a fire at the feet of their ancient god trying to give life back to someone who—by all accounts—should already be dead.

Valter burst out of the tree line when he saw Mergim slip and fall. He didn't know what had occurred to cause it, but certain he was that Mergim had not resurfaced and Valter had an urgent need for that not to be so, Mergim become the line pulling Valter back into the world as Andreas had wanted. Valter having the awful premonition that if

Mergim died then so would Valter, and this new Valter bursting out of the tree line did not want that at all. He vaulted down the snow, scrambling and slipping, yelling and calling.

'Get him out! You've got to get him out!'

Valter tripping on a snow-buried boulder, going arse over tit, bashing his nose, sending a fine spray of blood over the snow.

He couldn't get up fast enough, so much in a frenzy he fell again, slid several yards down the slope on his backside, arms pushing at the snow with all his strength to get down faster.

I have to get there. I have to get there.

Seeing the dark water of the lake, Mergim's body floating face down, arms out-splayed, feet sinking with the weight of his boots; sharp flashes of white and green as a school of minnows split themselves about Mergim's body and rejoined once again at his head as if here was a meal here not to be missed.

'Hie! Hie!' Valter called as he went, needing someone, anyone, to do what he was going to be too late to do.

Hulde dropped her bow. Couldn't believe she'd actually hit the stranger who'd been bearing down on her and Livia like a dark black night.

'Go!' Livia implored, Livia having doubled up, some great and hideous pain gnawing at her belly. Hulde not wanting to leave her, Livia adamant. 'You've to see to him. We can't just let him drown! We don't even know who he is or why he's here.'

Hulde's resolve divided as Ortwin's mule came snorting and skidding into their camp, disentangled from its cart; no sign of Ortwin, whose shouting and distractions had given Hulde the time to aim and fire her arrow. And now a new distraction: someone yelling as loud as Ortwin had been doing; someone plummeting down the slope from the trees, heading directly for where their unknown putative assailant had gone into the water.

Hulde began to move; memories skittering and colliding, shaken loose by her running, sparks of them flying like a bough of golden oak thrown into a Serbian's Christmas fire. Hulde recognising it was Valter sliding down the slope, orange hair bright as sunlit fox. Hulde seeing his mouth opening and closing, Hulde hearing no words. Everything about her hushed as she saw again the man striding slowly down the lakeside, gait as calm and assured as it had been once before. Snatches battering through the barrier she'd built against her past. Disjointed, jumbled, yet vivid and viscerally real.

A cloud of snowy white egrets, Hulde wishing for their wings so she could rise up and be saved.

Stars shooting across a night sky, soft voice in her ear:

That's your family up there, looking down on you, so you're not to be afraid.

Afraid Hulde had been all the same, and afraid she was now.

Feet stopping of their own accord. Couldn't take another step.

Too feared to see what she would see if she reached the man in the water and turned him over. Couldn't bear to see his face again.

God damn him! God damn him!

Hulde closing down.

Nothing she could do to save Mergim, even if she wanted to.

Which she did not.

Valter still sliding. Everything seeming to have slowed down. He'd seen the mule skidding into the camp of Pfiffmakler tents; seen the woman cramping over the fallen log; seen the girl setting off on a run towards Mergim and thanked God.

Until she'd stopped.

Standing there like she'd been turned to stone.

'God's sake, girl! Get yourself shifted!' Valter wailed. 'Get yourself to the water!'

Valter abruptly halted as he collided with a juniper bush hidden by the snow.

Valter pushing and fighting, getting himself up, setting off again towards the lake and the girl who was standing by doing nothing.

Valter seeing her in profile and understanding: Hulde. Years older than when he'd last seen her, but in no doubt.

'God's sake!' he said again as he pushed past her, knocking her over, Valter hearing the soft sound of her falling into the snow, not caring. Valter leaping straight into the water, grabbing at Mergim's legs, twisting them, trying to turn him over. Valter crying as he pulled and hauled.

'Help me!' he yelled with awful desperation, tears pouring down his cheeks. 'Hulde, help me!'

Hulde, shaken by him shouting her name, regaining herself. Hulde splashing into the lake, taking Mergim's head roughly in her hands and pulling him out, hearing him sucking in air.

And then pushing his face back under.

'Give me one reason why I shouldn't kill him,' she hissed, looking over at Valter who looked like an old man and a wreck, still straining and pulling at Mergim's legs, Valter's eyes wild and mad as she'd ever seen.

'Because he only came here for you,' Valter pleaded. 'It's all he's ever wanted. To see you! Make sure you—'

All the breath going out of Valter as Mergim's left leg spasmed, his boot catching Valter in the throat; Valter releasing his burden, falling backwards, grasping at the reeds growing in the shallows, hauling himself back towards the bank.

'It's all…been…about you, Hulde,' Valter stuttered, the cold creeping up him like a cat into a cradle and he let go of the reeds, closed his eyes, hoping for an end.

Any end.

He didn't care what kind of end it would be anymore, only that it would come.

That the fuck-up who'd been Valter Poppelmann would cease to exist.

Ortwin woke spread-eagled in the snow, flat on his back. Above him a wide blank expanse of sky from which, he soon gathered, snow was gently falling, eyes blinking as several flakes fell directly upon them. Ortwin moving his fingers, touching several splintered planks of wood, trying to put back together what had happened. He'd been kicking the mule on, he'd been yelling and screaming and they'd been going so fast, so erratically down the small slope towards the Pfiffmakler encampment the trap had come adrift, broken free, skewed off into the trees and smashed itself to bits, depositing Ortwin amongst the wreckage like a starfish in a tangle of tide-stranded kelp.

He moved first one arm and then the other; one leg and then the next. Hoped he'd not broken anything, couldn't properly move, then again could feel no pain. Took a few deep breaths, dizzy and disoriented, couldn't figure out which way to go; started crawling anyway; crawling out of ditch and detritus and going on, the impetus to carry out his mission his only focus.

'Valter!' Hulde's turn to do the yelling and imploring as she got Mergim's head out of the water. Not sure she'd ever meant to kill him; her skirts waterlogged, wrapping themselves about her legs; all she could do to keep her footing. Turning her body anyway, pulling Mergim with her, his head cradled against her belly, mouth and nose a whisper above the surface. Hulde desperate, Hulde shouting at the top of her voice.

'Valter! Come and help me, you little piss-ant piece of shit!'

One of Longhella's favourite invectives spat from Hulde's lips before she'd thought it through, shocked by the thrill of saying such awful words, but they had effect: Valter stirring, Valter slapping his arms in the water, opening his eyes as he registered what she'd said, his face pale and vacant, his body moving, grabbing once more at Mergim's legs, taking his half of the weight, the two manoeuvering their burden back to shore.

'It isn't him,' Wenzel informed Rosa, once he'd regained the church, shivered off the warmth of ancient fires burned to placate or invoke an ancient god.

'Well, that should be a relief,' Rosa quick to reply. 'And yet you're worried.'

Wenzel wondering how his wife could interpret him with such ease. Rosa enlightening him.

'You're pulling at your beard, my dear,' Rosa smiled, stopped fiddling with the scenery rolls and put her hands upon his shoulders, looked directly into his face. 'Fine now, my love. But let me tell you this: when we retire, that beard-pulling habit has to stop. I'm not stepping out with any man who has a chin looks like a half-plucked duck.'

Wenzel smiled too, put an arm about Rosa's waist.

'It'll stop,' he said, 'when we've no more worries.'

Rosa pulling him a little closer.

'And when will that be? Because I have to tell you, Wenzel, I'm tired. We've been on the trail too long and it's enough for me.'

Wenzel leaning himself away, holding his hands to Rosa's shoulders so he could see her face. See her properly. See if she was joking.

She was not.

'Why have you never said?' he whispered.

'I've said it many times,' Rosa whispered back. 'You just haven't been listening.'

'But Heraldo, Ludmilla…'

'Can take care of themselves,' Rosa finished for him. What she'd been meaning to say for a long time, terribly afraid of how Wenzel would take it. 'Why can't we do what your mother and father did? Why can't we retire and leave the youngsters to it?'

Wenzel pulled his wife close, putting his arms about her.

'I've been thinking the same recently.' Words muffled by his beard, not yet plucked, and by Rosa's hair, still luxuriant, if grey-threaded, within its perfect plait.

'I've been thinking,' Wenzel said, 'of that homestead outside of Termoli, what we could make of it, you and me.'

'I loved that place,' Rosa laid her head on her husband's shoulder. 'So what's stopping us?'

Wenzel weighing up Rosa's question with his usual logic, his fors and againsts. Wenzel knowing this was not the time to haver or pretend. Rosa to him the beacon sailors see when they've been shipwrecked, clinging onto every piece of wreckage that comes to hand, heading towards that light, the one place salvation might be found.

And no time to be lying to Rosa.

'I've no idea who that lad in the crypt is,' Wenzel therefore said, 'but I think the net is closing. I can feel it, Rosa. Something not right. And if we're ever going to get this lad Philbert away then we need to do it now. I had a word with Heraldo about it this morning, made the suggestion that when we send Philbert over to Denmark we all go with him.'

Rosa's dismay as evident on her face as a white swan on deep dark water.

'No,' she whispered. 'Please no.'

Wenzel smelling the rosewater she'd sprinkled in her hair, stroking a hand across her forehead, love strong in him for every wrinkle about her eyes and mouth, every curve of her body, no matter the skin of breasts and belly were slack now with child-bearing and age.

'But maybe not us,' he said, as he pulled her to him. 'Maybe this is our time, my dear. Maybe we send them on and we head back to Italy, like you've always wanted.'

'And Mergim? What are we to do about him?' Rosa asked, Wenzel spreading his hand about the base of her neck, resting his chin on the top of her head, Rosa feeling the movement of her husband's jaw as he spoke, reassured. Wenzel so strong since Old Grandma had left them, Wenzel slipping into the role of Leader of the Pfiffmaklers as if he'd been born to it—which he had—Rosa nevertheless impressed how swift and decisive he'd been ever since.

'We'll worry about that when it happens,' he said, as if to prove her analysis.

Neither aware that day had already come.

Svetovid Arises

Rasvlach hauled his cart onwards. He'd not the speed of two butcher brothers on their trap pulled by two strong steeds, and was already hours and hours behind Diderik. Rasvlach having to make frequent stops to get his breath back, take a swig of melted snow or something stronger. Rasvlach making it half way to Sagard, not that he knew where he was, only how the track had become more demarcated the further he went, several smaller paths sneaking out of the forest on one side and the bogland on the other to join it, so surely heading somewhere more substantial than another dead-end farm.

Throughout the day he'd been looking for signs of Diderik. None forthcoming. The snow seeing to that. More irritating was that he'd seen no one else either. A fact he cursed, thinking it no doubt to do with Christmas; folk here maybe fasting during the day as they did back home, which always kept them tight within their own circle.

A lull in social activity until the festivities commenced: no market days, no trading, no unnecessary travelling. Finding it irksome he'd passed not a cottage, nor a farm nor a barn, and was going to have to spend the night out in the open, the brief afternoon soon crushed out by the sinking of the sun and another heavy pall of snow clouds coming in from the north-east which looked at any moment about to spill their load right on top of him, as if in spite.

He pulled his cart off the track, unloaded it, turned it on its side, used his billhook to slash through pine branches, pulling them over to make a rudimentary shelter; dug a small pit with his spade and got a fire going. No chance of running out of firewood here, where all behind him was trees upon trees upon more trees; bleak dark conifers brooking no undergrowth except sprawling masses of recumbent brambles out here on the forest's edge.

Dark quickly down upon him. No fear in Rasvlach for it, with his single pinprick of fire. Felt the forest a great heavy cloak at his back, shielding him from the worst of the snow that soon began to fall. No sense of beauty in that falling, not for Rasvlach; no love for the silent holy night soon to come; no joyous awe to hear the calling of owls emerging from the forest or seeing them swoop across the track heading for the boglands and possible prey. No appreciation of their swift and steady flight. No kinship for Rasvlach with other forest denizens snuffling and snorting for roots and the tender bark of striplings that would never make the winter through.

Rasvlach not a man to dwell on such things. Rasvlach blind to the efficient economies and glorious excesses of the natural world about him, had no more emotion looking on the iridescent breathtaking blue of a hairstreak butterfly than when he stamped snails or ants beneath his boots. An empty vacuum at the heart of Rasvlach, never understanding folk who simpered on about such things, and despised them for it. Rasvlach viewing everything about him that was not Rasvlach as of malevolent intent until it proved otherwise.

A sad world to inhabit, you might think, where you suspect enemies at every turn; a world in which the sea inspired no joy or wonder, conjured instead a hydra's head of all the bad things that could come because of it. Rasvlach not perceiving it that way. His disregard for the aesthetic, for the softer side of life, giving him power, allowing him to dominate people weaker than himself. Cruelty as easy come to him as taking breath.

Trust no one and nothing, being Rasvlach's philosophy, one he should have stuck to. Should have cut Diderik loose the moment he'd sprung Rasvlach from Kragujevac. Instead he'd given the lad a chance, a way of life earning good crust and wouldn't take him anywhere near Kragujevac ever again. Took him further from its walls with every month that passed.

Bitterness in Rasvlach's craw to think on that. Diderik should have been grateful, but oh no. Diderik just had to go and prove the point: Rasvlach right all along.

Trust no one and nothing.

This night in the cold, in the dark, on the edge of a forest, making Rasvlach an even harder man than he'd been before.

God damn Diderik.

God damn the Pfiffmaklers.

God damn anyone who stopped him from reaching the goal of a lifetime and getting that shitty little Philbert's head pickled and presented to Metternich.

Rasvlach could almost taste the gold he would be given when that happened and, in his mind, had already begun to spend. He didn't want much, was at core a man of simple pleasures.

A small house on the edge of the Rhine.

As much drink as he could get down his gullet.

Someone to clean up and do a bit of cooking, service him when needed.

A tavern close by where he could play the occasional game of Blind Man's Fancy, or whatever type of gambling they did in those parts, certain he'd be able to rig it after a bit of practice. Make the locals grumble at his expertise. Make them curse, call him a liar and a cheat, at which point Rasvlach would growl and bring out his knife, make them cower and confess they were bad losers.

Given all that, Rasvlach's life—such as it was—would be complete.

But first things first.

Rasvlach needed to find Diderik and shut him up, make certain he didn't blab to anyone about what he and Diderik had come to do on the island.

Secondly, to find those godforsaken fairs folk who were hiding Philbert.

Thirdly, to get to Philbert before they spirited him away.

Rasvlach contemplating his plan of action as he sat the dark night through, cursing the falling snow that was going to hamper him the following day.

Rasvlach staring into his fire.

Rasvlach keeping completely still when a winter-hungry fox came out of the forest a yard to his left, head hanging low, nose to its accustomed trail across which Rasvlach had inadvertently camped.

Rasvlach slowly and quietly pulling his knife from his belt.

No chance at all for that skinny-haunched fox who'd trodden so somnolently out of the trees expecting nothing more than another long night of emptiness, so weak in mind and body it hadn't even registered Rasvlach, nor his fire, nor the knife that tore so unexpectedly through its throat. The fox laying down obediently upon its flank as its lifeblood dripped away and Rasvlach wasted no time, got it skinned and gralloched almost before it was dead, got it portioned and on the fire.

Feasting that night for Rasvlach, fox meat never tasting so good. For most it was too stringy, too gamey, too tough. Not so for Rasvlach, who'd always enjoyed a challenge, and for him the best kind of meat.

No hope, then, for the fox, and maybe no more hope for Diderik who, at that very moment, was opening his eyes in the crypt below St Michael's, a face above his he'd never seen before. A face as ravishing as it was filled with rage, not that Diderik cared either way. Merely glad he was able to open his eyes and see anything. Jolted by the words coming from the ravishing angel's mouth.

'So you're awake, you little piss-ant piece of shit. Time to start blabbing.'

Longhella never much one with small talk, and oh so much less was she tolerant of it now. Longhella—Longhella, of all people—so shocked by what she'd seen an hour since, she was boiling over with rage and sorrow and needed answers, and who better to ask than the stranger who'd blown in from the cold. Someone had to pay and it might as well be him. Longhella moments back from the camp by the lake; Longhella—and of course it was she, spare bloody wheel as she always was—sent by Wenzel to see what was taking Ortwin so long.

Longhella getting down the track to find a smashed-up cart, and Ortwin struggling through the snow on hands and knees going in the wrong direction, his pale face streaked with mud and blood. Ortwin, obviously confused, looking up at Longhella without understanding who she was or why she was there. Longhella about to lean down and pull him up when she heard a strange snorting, moved the few yards around the bend and saw the camp laid out before her: a mule struggling with the weight of a canvas tent it had somehow become entangled in; saw too—God knew how or why—the awful Valter Poppelmann and the more awful Hulde dragging some man inch by inch along the lakeside path, the three of them dripping wet.

Longhella muttering beneath her breath, abandoning Ortwin and striding quickly on down the track, about to put hands on hips and start haranguing Hulde and Valter about what the blazes was going on when she was arrested by a heart-wrenching mewling, as if a kitten was being torn limb from limb. Longhella moving slowly forward, afraid of what she might find. Longhella finding it so much worse than she'd anticipated as she reached the fallen log to see Livia—the Janus Woman she'd always despised—on the other side, curled over in a dreadful mess on the snow, skirts all bloodied, her bad face contorted. Livia sucking in air between her teeth, Livia heaving, Livia whimpering, hands stretched out over the dreadful mucous spreading about her legs as if trying to pull it all back in again. Longhella, usually so unmoved by other people's suffering, bringing her hands to her mouth, shocked into immobility as she realised what she was witnessing, which was Livia and Pietro's child being expelled prematurely, its life ended before it had properly begun.

'You need to get back down the crypt,' Pastor Hulm caught at Wenzel's arm, pulling him urgently to one side. 'One of your girls is beating merry hell out of our survivor from the snow.'

Wenzel and Rosa too busy organizing props and troops to have noticed Longhella's return. Wenzel and Rosa casting anxious glances at one another as Wenzel went off with Pastor Hulm, descended back down the steps to find Longhella lambasting the recumbent man with her increasingly impressive powers of invective.

'Why are you here?' she was asking him, her face inches from his, her fingers twisting in his hair, pulling him towards her. 'If you don't tell me right here and now I'm going to take out my knife and slit your belly side to side, let you see how you like it.'

Wenzel coming down the steps like he was walking into hell. All the old folk who'd been tending the fire now standing, havering at Longhella's back, uncertain whether to intervene or no, the flames casting a ghastly orange luminosity of shifting shadows about the cellar, Svetovid's sculptured face gazing down on Longhella as if he approved.

'If you don't spit it out now, my little man, I'm going to slice that tongue right out of your mouth and let it do the talking all by itself.'

'Longhella!' Wenzel said. 'What's going on? What are you doing?'

Longhella banged the man's head down on the stone of the sarcophagus with an audible thud, and brought it up again.

'He's going to tell me what he's doing here or I'm going to gut him like a fish,' came Longhella's response.

'Stop it! Stop it now,' Wenzel ordered. 'You're going to kill him if you go on like this.'

Longhella turning slowly towards her uncle, pulling Diderik's pale face with her.

'It's nothing less than he deserves. You don't know what's happened,' Longhella stated. Wenzel alarmed, for never in his life had he seen such an expression on Longhella's face. Rage, certainly; anger, yes, on an almost daily basis. But not this. Not this anguish, for that was what it was. An anguish apoplectic. He held up his hands.

'Tell me,' he said. 'Let the man go. Tell me what's been going on.'

Longhella releasing Diderik, whose head went back to the stone with a horrid thump.

'He's a murderer!' Longhella got out, then of a sudden Longhella was all weep and weakness, a child again. Wenzel stepping across the floor towards her, wrapping her in his arms. And oh so strange it felt as Longhella turned her head into his shoulder and wept.

Rosebushes for all the little babies.

Longhella would have spat at that Mani songster in Kragujevac had she been there.

She didn't understand why she felt such pain for Livia and Pietro's loss and yet it was in her like a weevil that couldn't stop it's chewing.

The awful mess of Livia; Longhella trying to get Livia back to her tent, Livia pushing her away, fighting against her, unwilling to leave the log, leave behind what remained of her dead child.

And the awful mess Pietro had become when Longhella tore back to Sagard and told him what had happened. Pietro—a man Longhella loved and cared about, and who loved and cared about Longhella—setting off on a run, slipping and sliding on the snow, wailing like he would never stop.

Completely rational therefore, to Longhella, to fixate upon the man in the crypt: a stranger appearing on the island at the exact same moment. Longhella needing to blame, needing to make someone—anyone—pay.

'It's Livia,' she would have wailed, had not Wenzel been holding her so close. 'It's Livia,' she snottered against his shoulder. 'It's Livia…'

A quiet time that night for the Pfiffmaklers, who'd put on their last half-hearted shows for the congregation of St Michael's, Wenzel unwilling to go back on his word. Pastor Hulm telling him all would understand but Wenzel adamant. No telling anyone of their affairs. Shift and shuffle of actors for Hildegard and the Creation of the World now Livia and Pietro were unavailable. All grand, as far as the congregation of St Michael's were concerned, having nothing to compare them to. Only Pastor Hulm comprehending the terrible irony of the Pfiffmaklers performing on stage the Joyous Birth of Christ while they were grieving for a life not brought to term. Pastor Hulm returning with them back to the lake-side after all was done, offering his services.

A small hole dug into which Livia and Pietro's miscarried child was laid. Pfiffmaklers mumbling politely as Pastor Hulm gave out his prayers at the paltry grave and then departed, feeling his attendance depletory. Small worry for the fellow in the crypt Wenzel had insisted be brought along with them, given Longhella's earlier treatment of the man. Only Wenzel's word they weren't going to flay him alive for reasons unknown to Pastor Hulm.

Diderik himself surprisingly calm and compliant, going without complaint, thanking the old folks for their care before getting up and staggering from the crypt on shaky legs, head thumping, maybe believing he was leaving the den of the devil incarnate.

Svetovid taking some folk like that, especially when the fires were burning.

Pastor Hulm not knowing the half of it, nor the real devil Diderik hoped to leave behind.

The lake was smooth, like polished glass, as the sun sank and took with it the slight wind, tugging down the temperature so the snow—heavy in the clouds above them—had not the chance to fall.

No one saw the beauty in it. Pfiffmaklers sitting in gloomy silence about their fire, all thoughts of Christmas vanquished; glancing with downcast eyes every now and then at the Benedettas' tent where Livia and Pietro were trying to reconcile themselves to their loss. Rosa had been by several times with herbal concoctions and offers of food, all rejected. Rosa heartbroken for the two of them. She'd suffered several miscarriages before Heraldo and would have liked to have offered hope because of it, but could not. She'd been young back then, far younger than Livia was now.

When Livia discovered herself pregnant it had seemed a miracle; they'd all clapped and danced and drank, including Ludmilla whose own hopes of having a child had so far come to nought; Ludmilla, in consequence, over-investing in Livia's condition and taking the tragedy harder than the rest. Rosa looking over at her niece's blank face, Ludmilla's hands spread listlessly over her knees as she contemplated the disaster that had overtaken them. Hulde sitting in silent solidarity at her side.

At least she has Hulde, Rosa thought, and thanked God for it.

And, thinking of Hulde, Rosa thought too on Mergim—comatosed by the cold water of the lake.

What a shock that had been, and how much more of a shock for Hulde, poor child.

Maybe the same shock that had led to Livia's calamity.

It was all such a mess.

Not to mention the wretched Valter Poppelmann turning up with Mergim. Valter trying to mollify his appearance with the trite excuse that the two of them had tracked the Pfiffmaklers a thousand miles across country for months and months for the sole purpose of Mergim wanting to see how Hulde had turned out. As if anyone was going to believe anything that came out of Valter's mouth. She'd always thought him a waste of space, both before and after Andreas had died. She'd sympathised with Valter's plight and put up with him for Andreas's sake. Andreas might have been a scoundrel, but he was one of their own when push came to shove, and he'd been fun. Valter different, seemingly incapable of change; a man dispensable, shuggly and unreliable. Wenzel as relieved as she when he'd finally chosen to leave them.

And now here he was again, all these years later, apparently Mergim's new best friend.

Nothing good will come of it.

At least Wenzel had the foresight to have Mergim bound hand and foot, insensible as he was from apparently nearly drowning after Ortwin crashed in on the scene, smashing their cart to pieces in the trees, allowing Hulde's attempt to stop Mergim's advance with Longhella's bow and arrow.

And, oh lord, she'd not checked on the child in a while. No bones broken, yet Ortwin too concussed to take back to his home, word sent there with Pastor Hulm how he was being well looked after. Time to get to it. Rosa replenishing her medicaments and compresses and heading to the tent in which Ortwin had been laid. Rosa looking over at her husband sitting stalwart on the log, saw him dottling out his pipe, refilling his cup; saw the twitch of his mouth within his beard and knew he was about to speak to the family. About to set the last in motion. Hoped to God he knew what he was doing, though had no real doubts.

If anyone could sort out this mess, it was Wenzel.

Rosa never so lucky as the day she'd found him. Rosa smiling to remember Old Grandma Pfiffmakler's bitter words when they'd announced they would wed:

The hole suffers as much as the nail.

Grandma meaning herself, with Wenzel forcing Rosa into the Pfiffmakler family—not that it had been hard for Rosa. Nor for Yssel and Peppe, come to that. All nails put into their right places once they'd met, making something far greater than they would have been on their own. Grandma admitting as much at the end, despite grumbling to the last.

You've made fine children. You've made the Pfiffmaklers what they are. Make sure you keep it that way. I don't never want to hear you've botched the whole lot up.

Old Grandma always one for the showstopper, for the last moralistic words before she brought the curtain down and went into the convent at Nocera.

Rosa wondering what Old Grandma would have done in this situation, if it would have crossed her mind, as it had crossed Rosa's, to tie up Valter, Mergim and the boy they'd picked up from the church, weighed them down with stones and chucked the lot of them into the lake to drown.

A speedy resolution to an ongoing problem.

But no, she reflected, that was not the Pfiffmakler way.

And no more hers.

If that had been the case they would never have found Hulde, would never have encountered Andreas—a man so irritating at first, but in time a companion of such great worth she still missed him all these years later.

'You won't believe it,' he'd once told her, 'but all those sticklebacks in the ponds your children are so fond of finding? Well, they're one of the few animals in the world where the males make the nest, look after the young, bring them up. Imagine what a furore the world would be in if that happened in humankind!'

Rosa had laughed out loud at the thought, and Rosa rarely laughed out loud. He'd had such a way with him, had Andreas. No wonder folk bought all his hedgehoggery stuff, nonsense as it was. Such a kind man, and no wonder he'd taken on the irascible Valter when no one else would have lifted a finger to help him.

As Heraldo had done for Philbert.

It seeming now to Rosa, as it had for the rest of the Pfiffmaklers, despite their earlier misgivings, that Heraldo had done right. Kindness the most precious of virtues. One never to be ignored. And kindness, given what had befallen Livia and Pietro, all the more to be valued. Andreas pointing the way with his adoption and protection of Valter; Pfiffmaklers carrying on his legacy with Philbert. Small mercies needing to be celebrated and replicated.

Rosa walking towards the tent in which Ortwin was sleeping, needing to be doing, needing to be useful, glancing back at Wenzel, hoping he'd a better solution to all their problems than drowning all the newcomers in the lake.

Wenzel did.

Wenzel slotting into his head all the various pieces of information coming in at him from every side. He was terribly anxious for Pietro and Livia, of course. But more worrying, at the moment, was the re-emergence of Mergim and Valter, and that lad Pastor Hulm had so helpfully stowed in his crypt, and how their multiple appearances might impact their shaky plans of wrapping things up with Philbert. Last thing he wanted being himself and Rosa having to disappear over to Denmark with the rest. Heraldo might be jubilant at such a prospect, not so himself nor Rosa.

First things first.

Time to question the lad who'd been rescued from the snow and put into the crypts of St Michael's. He'd no direct link to Valter or Mergim, as far as Wenzel knew, but his turning up at this time, exactly at this place—as Longhella had so brutally pointed out—too much of a coincidence to ignore.

The family was suffering. The survival of the Pfiffmaklers at the fore.

'Bring me the lad,' he ordered. 'The one from the church.'

Longhella needing no further instruction, having Diderik in a headlock the second Wenzel gave his order, dragging him forward into their circle of fire.

No Svetovid this time, for which Diderik was thankful; that whole place had given him the creeps.

The man on the log ordering everyone else away, saying he needed quiet and no interruptions to his interrogation. The young woman who'd brought him here sighing dramatically, fingers twitching as if eager to get back about his neck, but Longhella subsiding, as did the rest. All removing themselves to a respectful distance, standing like clumps of reeds at the water's edge, or retreating back to their tents.

'What's your name?' Wenzel demanded.

'Diderik,' Diderik supplied.

'Why are you here on this island?'

Diderik never the sharpest knife in the box, and not quick enough of mind to lie, even if he'd chosen to.

'We came to find the boy,' he therefore answered.

'The boy? What boy?' Wenzel asked, leaning forward.

'The one with the bounty on his head,' Diderik maddeningly vague as he pushed feet and hands out towards the fire, Diderik still really cold and not entirely certain what was going on.

Wenzel frowning, worst fears confirmed, pushing on regardless.

'And by we, who'd you mean? You, Valter and Mergim?'

Seeing blank confusion on Diderik's face.

'Well no,' Diderik got out. 'Me and Rasvlach. Why would Mergim be here?'

Assuming it was the same Mergim, which seemed about as likely as the moon falling from the sky. Wenzel's fingers tapping on the log at this new introduction.

'And who is he, this Rasvlach?'

Diderik pausing, not knowing how to answer. For who indeed was Georg Rasvlach? A man he'd met in prison; a man whose epic escape he'd helped engineer; a man who'd promised much and delivered little.

A man Diderik was scared to death of.

Someone other than Diderik supplying the answer.

'He's a real mean son-of-a-bitch, and if you've run from him, lad, then you did right.'

Unnoticed by anyone Mergim, on the other side of the fire, had begun to thaw, had recognised Diderik immediately and was listening intently, propped up against a barrel of flour, bound hand and foot. As was quite right. No reason for anyone here to trust him. Mention of Rasvlach stuttering up a chord in him for, as far as he knew, Rasvlach should still have been locked up inside Kragujevac, though patently was not. The scratching on the Joshua Tree seat making sudden and bad sense.

XII-LI RUGN INSL.

Mergim thinking out loud.

'December 1851; Rügen Island,' he said. 'It was you.' Looking over at Diderik. 'You left a message at the Joshua Tree, and you helped that bastard escape when I would not.'

Diderik feeling the life squashed out of him at the accusation, because it was true. Wenzel standing up suddenly, like a bear scenting a hunter on the wind, mostly because Mergim had come back to life unexpectedly and might need to be contained. More so because

Mergim appeared to know more about what was going on than he did.

'Pfiffmaklers!' Wenzel yelled, needing to corral the troops, get them back, get everything sorted once and for all. The younger cohort of Pfiffmaklers not so far away they couldn't hear his command, Heraldo and Ludmilla first back on the scene, followed swiftly by Longhella, Lupercal and Jericho. No sign of Yssel and Peppe, who'd gone to the Benedettas' tent and were sitting vigil outside in case they were needed. And they were.

The sounds inside seeming at first soft and cracked and then visceral, like someone breaking eggs into a skillet; and next Pietro emerging, head hanging, arms useless at his sides.

'She needs help,' was all Pietro could get out, his pallid face mad and scared, eyes jittery and wet. 'There's more blood. There's so much more blood.'

Yssel pushing him gently to one side and going in, calling immediately for her husband to go fetch Rosa. Yssel's normal calm jagged into pieces as she mopped at the purperae coming from between Livia's legs, at the blood that didn't seem able to stop its flow, like a fountain had found its calling. Blood still following its vocation a few minutes later when Rosa arrived, Yssel looking up at Rosa, her hands running with all she'd tried to blot and staunch. Livia unconscious, head lying back upon her pillow, riven face pale and rigid as the camel-bone carving of the Madonna, Hulde's anniversary gift from the previous year, clutched in one hand, perhaps for comfort, perhaps merely the nearest prop to hang onto while her body continued to betray her, obeying some internal command to contract and expel until there was nothing left.

Livia emptied out like a treasure chest broken into by a thief in the night who'd never had compassion, and certainly wasn't going to start now. Rosa and Yssel on their knees beside her, skirts soaking up Livia's blood, shaking fingers laying aside swabs and clouts having no more use. Rosa closing Livia's eyes, seeing and hearing the end of the Hildegard of Bingen play Livia and Pietro had worked so hard upon: Pietro laying his hand upon Livia's swollen belly with the gentleness of a hen-bird fluffing out her feathers as she sat upon her eggs, and Longhella singing out the finale's song:

In that hall there stands a bed,

And the bells of Paradise, I heard them ring,
Covered all over with scarlet so red,
And I love my Lord Jesus above everything.
And under that bed there runs a flood,
And the bells of Paradise I heard them ring,
One half runs water, *the other runs blood,*
And I love my Lord Jesus above everything.

But no love, nor Paradise, in this running of blood and water.

Rosa grinding her teeth, swallowing repeatedly to keep back the tears as she stood, went to the tent door to tell the waiting family the worst of news, couldn't get out any words, merely shook her head.

And oh lord, Pietro's face collapsed as he howled out at the cloud-ridden sky that no, it could not be so.

But it was.

Livia gone after her child, and nothing anyone could do about it but dig another grave, lower another body down.

And so much vitriol then from Longhella for Mergim, whose unwarranted and sudden reappearance she held responsible for the loss of both mother and child. Longhella wanting to beat him into his own early grave, her invective as loud as it was futile.

'You bastard pile of absolute crap! You've no more worth than a beetle or an ant!'

She couldn't stop. She went at Mergim hand and fist.

'I should strike you through the heart! Shred your beggaring throat from ear to ear for what you've done! Pull out your blasted innards and have the foxes pick through them so you'd know what real pain is…'

Longhella having to be forcibly pulled off Mergim by Heraldo and Wenzel; Longhella ranting and punching her fists into the air; Longhella more bereft than anyone believed possible. Pietro the only one able to calm her, seeming to find his own calm in calming her.

'Hush little sister, hush,' he said, pulling in her flailing arms, restraining her, hugging her to himself. 'It's done, my dear. It's done.'

And done it was.

Livia as dead as was her child.

Pfiffmaklers subdued; Pfiffmaklers trying to figure out where to go from here.

Pfiffmaklers having no idea, retiring to their tents in sadness and despair.

Only Wenzel, Father of the Fair, staying on the fallen log late into the night.

Wenzel raising his head to the heavens because oh, how wondrous was this night despite all that had gone on beneath it.

Departed were the clouds, a broad swathe of bright stars covering the world in a nimbus from horizon to horizon, and the moon full bright; all reflected in the stillness of the lake like both were made of diamonds; and a single bat, more swift-swooping than a swallow, going down and about the camp and then over the trees to the water and back again, over and over, its life on a loop as it repeated its passage again and again while Wenzel watched, fascinated by that easy flight, the way it swerved and jinked, the mastery of dip and swerve only a few feet above his head.

And then a voice from the darkness, from the shadows by the fire.

'Was it my fault?' Mergim asked softly. 'Because if it was, and if I could, I'd swap my life for hers in a moment. I truly only came here because of Hulde, to see she was well. Nothing more, nothing less. She was all I could think of when I was in Kragujevac. Whether she came out right. Whether what I'd done to her would make her like me and mine. Whether you'd managed to… heal her.'

Mergim appalled by the tragedy of Livia and her child, and more so that he might have been responsible; bruises rising up on chin, cheek and temples from Longhella's remonstrations the least of what he deserved if it was so.

No immediate recrimination from Wenzel, no anger in his blood as in Longhella's. Wenzel knowing miscarriages occurred for any number of reasons, only glad that Rosa had never died from any of hers, and a strengthening of resolve in him to do what was needed, get away in the shortest time possible, leave this blasted island for good. Wenzel turning his head towards Mergim, who hadn't budged his back from the barrel in all this while. Wenzel suddenly aware how many long hours that had been.

'Do you need to relieve yourself?' he asked, the question so unexpected Mergim let out a short laugh.

'Well, I wouldn't say no, now you mention it. But what about the… mechanics… of it, so to speak?'

Raising his bound hands, the scenario going through his head so cumbersome and humiliating for both parties he had to fight to keep down a manic burst of inappropriate laughter. God, but it had been a long, hard day. Elation and dread at reaching his goal after all these months; being shot at, nearly drowning, being tied up like a hog for market; beaten by a young woman who'd gone at him with the ferocity of a vixen whose cubs had been clubbed to death before her eyes. Mergim maybe causing the death of not one human being, but two.

Mergim overwhelmed, his head falling to his chest as two tears rolled from the corners of his eyes. Christ, he'd been a fool. A goddamned fool. What had he been thinking, barging in like that? He should have had the wit to send Valter in first, smooth the waters, let the Pfiffmaklers prepare. He started as Wenzel stood, saw the gleam of a knife swooping through the air like that goddamned bat, closed his eyes, got ready for the end. It had been a long time coming and he let out a long sigh, hoping it would be quick.

And quick it was, Wenzel slashing through the ropes about his hands and wrists and standing back, lips twitching within his beard.

'No mechanics for me,' Wenzel said in explanation. 'Not for you, not any man. Do your business and get back here soonest. I need you to tell me all you know about this fellow Rasvlach.'

Hands Unbound, Eyes Closed

Rasvlach was weighing up his options. Had fed well on fox meat and several handfuls of wheat-flour mixed with snow formed into patties cooked on the hot stones of his fire. The fire had died down, the embers covering the rest of the fox joints so they'd cook slow and thorough throughout the night.

Rasvlach wasn't sleeping. Rasvlach hadn't properly slept since he was a nipper. If he didn't drink his daily quota and pass out into oblivion he spent his nights wide-eyed and awake, or closed-eyed and grumbling, head jumbling through a load of incoherent thoughts that hardly ever amounted to dreams, except those horribly disturbing ones about the unnamed town, seeing as he wasn't exactly asleep.

Tonight different. He'd drunk enough to dull himself to the cold, and eaten enough to feel pleasantly over-full. Needed now to think, sort out his next moves. Diderik legging it complicating everything. Rasvlach doubting Diderik would have the guts to either carry out Rasvlach's plans, even if he had the means to, or scupper them if he did not. Most likely he would worm himself into the first town or hamlet he stumbled across, give out some sob story about being stranded, beg for supplies, get himself off the island soonest. Start his long trek back home to find the bleating mama he'd always been going on about. All his joys of monies received—once they'd delivered the Anatomist's Dream to Metternich—being about freeing her from drudgery and them living a happy carefree life where she didn't have to sew dresses or empty swill buckets, or whatever it was she did on a daily basis. Rasvlach couldn't remember the details. And had no care either that she would most likely never see her son again. Which had certainly been Rasvlach's intention, who'd never for a moment considered sharing Metternich's reward with Diderik. As presumably Diderik, maybe not so dull-headed as Rasvlach had taken him, had finally figured out for himself.

Still, it was a worry. Rasvlach having no idea where he was on this blasted island.

Knew it wasn't large. Only a few townships worthy of the attention of folk like the Pfiffmaklers so shouldn't be hard to track them down, not once he got anywhere substantial. And he couldn't be far off. This track getting wider with every mile taken. Tomorrow would bring him to a place, a town. The same place or town Diderik would have landed, if he hadn't frozen to death during the night. And he also had Diderik's insightful comment that the Little Maus would most likely choose to hide out in a forest where there was cover, easily hidden, not easily tracked. Unless you were Rasvlach, who'd been brought up in forests and knew them whiff and breath, could tell you what had passed along its paths and when. Rasvlach alive to scent and scat, break and bower, the cut and crush of leaf or branch.

The sum of knowledge gleaned throughout his adult life brief and brutal: take or be taken. Childhood lessons not unlearned, could be put to good use. And if a man—or a boy with a giant head and a pig—was hiding in the forest he had the tools to find them. Just needed to find the relevant forest.

Rasvlach making his schemes during that night of wondrous stars Rasvlach had no care of. Rasvlach focused on his goals.

Get to a town, any town.

Ask about the Pfiffmaklers.

Ask about nearby forests.

Ask about Diderik.

Rasvlach ready for the last push.

Rasvlach taking out his many knives, getting them sharpened, getting them to gleam and shine with the pleasure others might have taken in the stars and moon high above his head.

For oh, so wondrous was that night.

Not that Rasvlach noticed.

Wenzel hadn't really been concerned Mergim would make a break for it but if he had, well, what the hell. He wouldn't have cared. Old Grandma's overriding principle had been that folk were folk. Wherever you found them they fell into basic categories essentially the same at core: cruel or kind, welcoming or not; self-serving, self-assured or self-ignorant. No point trying to change them any more than trying to shift the position of all those stars above his head. So black and white in her thinking, Old Grandma, so blinkered. Right until the very end, when she'd disproved her own theories by transforming herself into someone completely different. And if Old Grandma could be changed then surely anyone could. Including Mergim, and it seemed it was so: Mergim returning to the fire, buttoning up his trousers, taking the seat Wenzel motioned to him. The two sitting side by side upon the log by the fire.

'Thank you,' Mergim said, rubbing at his wrists where the ropes had burned and chafed. Wenzel taking a moment, lighting up his pipe.

'You've no need to worry about Hulde,' he told Mergim. 'She's grown up well and loved, and will be a fine woman when her day comes.'

A soft sigh coming out of Mergim.

'Can't tell you how glad I am to hear it. I hated to think I'd damaged her. I mean really damaged her.'

Wenzel puffed on his pipe.

'Truth be told,' he said, 'I suspect you did her a favour in the long run.'

Words he'd thought before, never said out loud; finding Mergim's presence oddly companionable.

'They were on the run, her folk. Well, you know. Years and years in the mountains, all her young life. Even if they'd settled in that village it wouldn't have been long before someone other than you came to roust them out, got them on the move again. But now, well. She's one of us. She's a part of us, loved and safe.'

Wenzel pinching the tip of his nose between his fingers. Only him and Mergim awake during this strangest of nights, apart from the bat that continued its swoop and flight along its self-demarcated highways and byways. So sure. So easy. So unlike them.

'What happened to Valter?' Wenzel asked, aware he'd not seen him for hours.

'He won't have gone far,' Mergim assured. 'He'll have gone back to our camp up top of the tree line.'

Mergim thinking again on those questions he'd tortured himself with: how he shouldn't have come striding in without forewarning, how he should have sent Valter in first. Realising now the futility of it, how Valter would never have gone to the Pfiffmaklers voluntarily. Valter revealing himself only because he'd thought Mergim was drowning in the lake, which in itself had come as something of a surprise when he'd learned of it.

'He's not a bad man,' Mergim said. 'He's just lost his way. Lost it a long time ago. And was terrified at meeting you lot again.'

Wenzel puffed at his pipe, Wenzel not understanding why that would be so. All the Pfiffmaklers had ever given to Valter being a place to belong. Certainly Valter had never let up being a pain in the arse, a bleeding hemorrhoid in constant need of care and attention instead of making himself useful and pitching in, which he never did.

Everyone relieved when he'd left except Ludmilla who, inexplicably, felt they'd failed him. Mergim making that less inexplicable with what he said next.

'He found you too... together,' he said, which was putting it mildly. 'Men like Valter, and me, come to that, don't rub along too well like that. It's like we're water droplets in oil. The oil is all happy sticking together, but we, well. No matter how good the oil, we're always desperate to come up for air.'

Mergim taking a sidelong look at Wenzel fearing he hadn't said it right, had given offence. Wenzel merely nodded.

'Never heard it put like that,' was his only comment, 'although I understand it. Fairs folk are close-knit. It's the only way we can survive.'

Unconsciously adopting Hulde's way of looking at life, how it went in bursts and generations. Uncomfortably aware it had been Livia who'd brought up this new aspect of Hulde and her world view.

'See this bracelet she made me?' Livia had said, holding out her wrist. 'One bead for every year she's been with you, for how long we've both been with you. And can I tell you what she said about the church we're going to, the one on this island?'

'Of course.' Wenzel had been indulgent, pleased to be included in the small ritual he'd known Livia and Hulde had forged since they'd joined the Pfiffmaklers and tried to keep secret, even from Ludmilla.

'She was talking about how old that church was,' Livia had said, 'and can you guess what Hulde said?'

Which of course he could not, had looked at Livia long and hard because the good side of her face, the half able to express emotion, had been so utterly serious.

'She said, *it's as old as long as I've been alive times forty*. Which somehow makes it not seem that old at all. Don't you think that's odd?'

Wenzel hadn't. To him it made perfect sense. Pietro viewing the six or seven centuries since churches had been built here as a huge lacunae separating that time from this; Hulde seeing the same time as Fairs folk often did: a baton handed down from one generation to the next, a continuous thread going from past to present. The Pfiffmaklers five generations strong, starting with Old Grandma, and set to go on for who knew how much longer. Hulde only the latest link following down the line along with however many children she, Ludmilla and Longhella would eventually bear. If not Livia. Trying to shake that particular thought from his head, regarding the ropes he'd cut loose from Mergim lying like snakes balled up in winter to protect themselves from the cold. Folk like the Pfiffmaklers exactly like those ropes, those snakes, intertwining with others who came their way, strengthened and extended by their additions. By Livia, Pietro and Hulde and, for a time, Andreas and Valter.

Wenzel thinking back on that conversation with Livia, it seeming to Wenzel now that Livia had been trying to tell him something deep about differently woven strands. Ridiculous, of course. Making messages up where there were none, trying to find meanings where none were to be had, but there were those strands again: Hulde, Valter and Mergim, all brought so tangentially into his ken.

Mergim ten years in prison, coming out with the express intention of seeing how Hulde was doing, trying to vindicate the wrong he'd done.

Hulde needing to find connection with a past she couldn't rightly remember, span time out to make it comprehensible, include herself in it however she could.

Valter a man who, in the maelstrom and aftermath of Serbian Independence, had chosen to disappear like mist on an April morning. Who'd tried to find his way with the Pfiffmaklers and failed.

Wenzel leaning forward, pulling the pot of coffee from the edge of the fire, pouring out two beakers, one for himself, another for Mergim.

'So what about this Rasvlach?' he asked, handing Mergim his cup. The coffee lukewarm and bitter, partway filled with dregs. Mergim thirsty, glugging it down in one before answering.

'Now there's a man no one could say was good,' Mergim answered shortly.

'Not one for the oil, then?' Wenzel asked, Mergim lifting the corner of his lip in a scowl.

'Nor one for the water. That man is vitriol through and through.'

That man soon covering his tracks, covering over his fire, loading the rest of the cooked fox meat onto his barrow and forging onwards.

That man soon enough only a few hours from Sagard and learning from a couple of charcoal burners he met on the track he wasn't so far from Jasmund and that yes, there were entertainers in the area and they'd just put on the last of their performances the previous evening. And right grand they'd been… and yes! How did he know? Pfiffmaklers! That was their name, and they could put on a right good turn. Camping out, oh where was it the village children had told them? Down by the lake, not far from the causeway. Couldn't miss it. Any other strangers? Well obviously the one the butcher boys had hauled in from the snow, near dead as alive.

That man pulling his cart onwards, going like old Svetovid with the fire burning at his heels.

Wenzel had many more questions to ask of Mergim, fighting to get them into comprehensible order. The darkness beginning to lift, the bat swooping home to its roost, the up above glory fading into an ordinary backdrop of a grey cloud-covered dawn. So much to get sorted before the rest of the camp arose in muted silence to lower Livia into her grave.

'The Joshua Tree,' Wenzel asked first. 'How did you come to know of it? And what exactly was it you found there to bring you here?'

'We were in Neubrandenburg,' Mergim told him. 'We'd followed you up north, starting from the Danube.' Mergim pausing, still astonished they'd actually achieved the feat of finding the Pfiffmaklers. 'Anyways, was asking around about you of a few street performers, and some of them remembered you being at Stralsund. A Pierrot and Pulcinella, though were a bit ragged.'

Wenzel let out a short laugh.

'I remember them,' he said. 'Young couple just starting out. The two of them looking like they'd lived in hedgerows all their life.'

'That's them,' Mergim agreed, recalling how sad and grimy had been the Pulcinella's skirts. 'It was them that said Heraldo had been asking about a Joshua Tree, had been there once though couldn't rightly remember exactly where it was.' Mergim hesitating as Wenzel shifted in his seat, narrowed his eyes at the mention of Heraldo. 'Not that they said his name,' Mergim went swiftly on, 'only how he had a load of odd musical instruments, and if there was one thing Valter told me about your son then that was it. And so we went to check it out. Found the Joshua Tree village. One of the sorriest places I've ever been.'

Wenzel nodding.

'You've got that right. Place was on its knees, as I remember. Our stuff didn't go down too well. Only stopped for a couple of hours before moving on.'

Wenzel's memory for places good and strong, as behoved Fairs folk who needed to map out where to go again and where to avoid. And that place, a squalid village with no name as far as he'd learned, had been squarely of the latter. Not two coins to rub together in the entire place had been his estimation, and no appreciation at all for their entertainments.

The perfect place for Heraldo to pick Philbert up.

'Well it was there, at the Joshua Tree itself,' Mergim continued, 'where I found something I could hardly believe. Evidence that someone else from Kragujevac had been there not long since and left his mark.'

'And that's what you were saying to Diderik, just before… well. Just before we found out about Livia.'

Wenzel struggling to say her name, seeing Pietro standing outside his tent hanging his head, heard the soft-edged calls of alarm coming from within, Rosa's blood-boltered hands loose and useless at her sides as she gave a slow shake of her head and closed her eyes.

No uncertainty in that moment, as there was in this.

'It is,' Mergim agreed. 'He'd left notification of himself, his sentence, his initials, time and place: Rügen, where he was going.' *Leaving his paw print on the world in case Rasvlach did him in,* Mergim added in his head. Saying out loud: 'What I can't figure for the life of me is why Diderik and Rasvlach would come all the way here.'

Not so Wenzel, who could see all laid out before him: that story he'd previously envisioned writing out its plot, except it hadn't been Mergim at its centre but this unknown variable who was Rasvlach who, according to Mergim, was about the worst of men anyone would want to meet.

'He's here for Philbert,' he told Mergim. 'He's going after an escapee from the revolutions a few years back. He wants his head. And I mean that quite literally. Your Rasvlach want's our Philbert's head.'

Quite when Philbert had become 'ours' was a moot point. However it had come about, Philbert was now under his care and the noose was closing fast.

'I need your help,' Wenzel said to Mergim. 'Will you offer it?'

Mergim didn't hesitate.

'Anything. You only have to ask.'

Ortwin Takes To The Boards

Philbert's head was ensconced snuggly on Kroonk's shoulder. He'd put his arms about her, pulled her close during the night to keep the two of them warm for it was fierce cold, a wind having whipped up from the sea with the dawn that felt about ready to slice a tree in two at the waist. Outside their bivouac the pine trees were bending and soughing as their needles dropped with the ice formed on them overnight, weighed them heavy, made them clink with the wind gusting in from every side.

Philbert opened his eyes, woken by the urgent sighing of the trees about him, the cracks of bark as boughs were bent further than they were used to; a new and unsettling feeling falling upon Philbert that whatever was about to unfold with the Pfiffmaklers was not far off.

He was scratchy mouthed, and his armpits stank. All he could do to put his nose to one and then the other before pulling away in disgust. Kroonk never seemed to have this problem. Kroonk always smelled like Kroonk. Slander, those rumours about pigs being filthy beasts. Kroonk the primmest, cleanest person Philbert had ever met. Person maybe too strong a word for most, if not for Philbert. Kroonk for him a companion since childhood, a stalwart who'd never let him down, who'd stuck with him through thick and thin. And thin it had been at times, and this particular time most of all. Philbert, usually the most stoic of people, fearing, for no reason he could pinpoint, all was about to be up.

He stuck his head out of his shelter, sniffed the wind as a badger might have done, knew all was not right. For starters it was later than he'd initially believed. At least a few hours after dawn. And there was movement, out there in the morning. Something, or someone, shifting themselves through the undergrowth, not sticking to paths but coming directly at him through the trees. He tipped his head this way and that, listening for more clues, obfuscated by the wind that was maddening, kept whipping itself up and then dropping again, making it difficult to tell what sound was coming from which direction.

But he'd heard enough.

He needed to get out and get out fast.

'Come on,' he said to Kroonk, gathering his belongings. Tough call whether to put her in her crate and pull her, or leave the crate empty and let her roam. Philbert deciding on speed, Philbert running from their shelter towards the edge of the cliff until they hit the path; Kroonk, sensing alarm, jogging along obediently on his heels

Wenzel was ready to mobilize his troops.

Everyone raw and stricken after lowering Livia into her grave, no one willing to argue.

'We've to move, and move quickly,' he announced. 'I believe Diderik's companion—name of Rasvlach—is close on Philbert's tail.'

Diderik, white as a cobnut, feeling all those Pfiffmakler eyes nailing into him, having told Wenzel all he knew, which was that Rasvlach had figured Philbert was being helped and probably by now figured they were doing the helping.

'Don't know how he got on to that,' he'd said to Wenzel, 'but he's good at getting information.' No mention of knives or hacked-off hands. 'Thought you'd hide him somewhere, maybe in the forests you can see from the mainland.' No mention either that it had been Diderik himself who'd worked that out, not that Rasvlach had thanked him for it, although Diderik had seen the gleam in Rasvlach's eyes and knew he thought him right.

Wenzel not reacting to Diderik's information overtly, though internally he'd been thinking: *So this is it. Pretty much our entire plan uncovered, our movements predicted down to the last dot.* A chilling thought. One that had him talking a few things out with Mergim in private before he gathered the clan.

'So here's what we do,' he told them that morning. 'Heraldo, take Longhella and Mergim and get to Philbert.' Ignoring the muffled objections that Mergim be anywhere near any of this. Fact remained that Mergim knew Rasvlach, knew his ways, could handle himself, and Wenzel was not to be dissuaded.

'Peppe and Ortwin, get yourself up to the coast quick as you can and get some kind of vessel to take us over to Denmark.' Swift glance at Rosa, slight shake of his head. No need to let anyone know they would not be going with the rest.

'Everyone else, get packed up and on the road following Peppe and Ortwin. Ortwin, what was the name of that place you told me about?'

'Glowe,' the recovered Ortwin supplied, cheeks going red to be included at the heart of the action. 'Easy reach from here and Jasmund, and right at the end of the Causeway that goes—'

'One moment,' Ludmilla holding up her hand. 'Why are we going that way?' Younger Pfiffmaklers having done their own digging, seeing as this had chiefly been their plan. 'What about Sassnitz? It's equally as close.'

'That's why we chose it,' Heraldo went on for her. 'It's the obvious place. It's already got established trade routes directly to Denmark, not to mention...'

Drying up as Wenzel bored into him.

'And what's the wrong word in that sentence?' he asked. Heraldo frowning, Ortwin piping up in his stead.

'*Obvious.* It's the obvious place to go. Which is why we shouldn't.'

Wenzel dipped his chin in agreement.

'The lad's right. No discussion. North is going to be better than east, and my best guess is that Rasvlach will try to snatch Philbert in the forest.'

'Surely that's impossible,' Heraldo argued. 'The place is enormous!'

Wenzel looking over at Mergim, who cleared his throat and spoke.

'Not to a hunter like Rasvlach.' *Mine not the only story to do the rounds in Kragujevac, everyone having a tale to tattle about someone else.* 'He grew up in forests and knows tracking like you know theatrics.'

Sounds of disturbance as everyone thought about that, and the veracity of its source, everyone now knowing about Kragujevac's role in all this.

Wenzel held up his hands.

'Listen to me, Pfiffmaklers. Diderik here was with Rasvlach until he chose to leave him. Which means Rasvlach is close. Likely he's already reached Sagard and knows we're about to pack up and move on.'

'So let's just go grab the son-of-a-bitch there!' Longhella shouted, eyes red-rimmed, hardened by tears, hand moving to her knife, about ready to set off on her own and strike the man dead, not that she had any idea what he looked like.

'He's too canny for that,' Mergim supplied softly. 'Whatever he's going to do he'll come at it sideways. He's a tracker, so we've to lay false tracks.'

'And how do we do that, Mr Mergim Murderer?' Longhella hissed, Mergim standing his ground, if not looking comfortable.

'I know what you all think of me,' he said, not that Longhella was going to let that lie.

'You don't know the—'

'Longhella!' Wenzel cut her down before she got started on another tirade. 'We don't have time for this. We've only two advantages this Rasvlach doesn't know about: Diderik is one and the other—like it or not—is Mergim. So we do as he suggests. We head into Sagard. We let it be known we're heading on to Sassnitz to perform some more Advent Cycles before returning to the mainland. We try to catch Rasvlach in the forest before Rasvlach catches Philbert. And here's another advantage we have over Rasvlach: we know approximately where Philbert is and we know how to communicate with him. Any more questions?'

Only one.

'What about Valter?' Ludmilla asked.

'What about him?' Wenzel couldn't hide his irritation. 'Valter can do what the blasted hell he likes.'

Everyone in agreement, turning away, one small voice rustling in the wilderness.

'I'll go get him,' said Hulde, 'if Mergim will tell me where he is.'

Canny Rasvlach, for Mergim had pinned him well, had not gone far into Sagard, in fact hadn't gone into Sagard at all, stopping instead at a farmstead on the outskirts, one picked particularly because it had Advent candles on a window ledge and an apple bough wrapped in mistletoe slung above its front door. Rasvlach knocking, slipping into well-worn character-acting the Pfiffmaklers might have appreciated under normal circumstances, as an elderly woman opened the door to him.

'I'm so sorry to intrude,' Rasvlach began, 'especially at this time of year, but I'm afraid I'm hopelessly lost.'

I'm a peddler, was supposed to have hooked up with some fair's crew called the Pfiffmaklers, but lost my way. And oh my! Those shows they put on. They really reminded me of my youth, last time I saw them. Doesn't seem like people stick to the old ways any more.

'Oh but come in, sir. This is a time for giving, after all. Can I get you some milk? Some bread and cheese? I've not much, but you'd be very welcome to it.'

Rasvlach sidling in, looking sorrowfully back at his cart.

I'm a wood turner by trade, but my good-for-nothing apprentice robbed me of all my equipment and goods while we were snow-bound several miles up track, if you can believe it. Left me with a pile of sticks only good for burning. And at Advent. Shaking his head sadly. *I don't understand the young these days. What they've come to.*

The old woman tutting as she brought him food and drink, glanced at his cart and saw that it was so, that all this poor man had was a couple of sacks of flour and a pile of rotten wood.

You'd be welcome to the wood for your fire, for all your kindness.

Oh Rasvlach! Have you no shame? But no. Rasvlach did not, and never had.

If you could direct me to another forest, maybe one big enough that I can go right inside it, cut down some good boughs, but not on the outside, so I don't offend any folk already using it. I know it's not right, but well. He's left me with nothing.

'Oh you poor man!' No one more eager to help than the old homesteader. 'You're in luck, though. You're only a few miles from Jasmund Forest and there's grand good growing there, but,' she advised, 'like you said, best go right into the middle and take only what you need. Go up behind Sagard and beyond the beeches.'

You're a saint! Kissing her hand. *Blessings of the Season upon you! And are there tracks? Places I should start? Ones I should avoid?*

No stopping the Christmas spirit pouring from the woman's lips as she gave him detailed instructions on the layouts of the paths cutting through Jasmund, of the Black Lake at its centre, the places young boys went to the cliff side to gather eggs in Spring. Not often a stranger came out of an Advent Night and asked for her blessing—never, as it happened—and after what she'd seen at St Michael's, with the Pfiffmaklers' shows, she was primed and ready for it.

And where are they going next, these Pfiffmaklers? Does anyone know? I really need to find them. I fear my sorry old life depends upon it.

The woman biting her lip, her face suddenly brightening.

'I do! Of course I do! I heard it from the baker when I was in to fetch my bread earlier this morning. Young Ortwin reckoned they'd be heading off to Sassnitz, heard it from them direct so he said. Oh my.' Shaking her head. 'I'll be sorry to see them go. They really brightened up the season. Like you said, the old ways. Brought them all back.'

Don't suppose there was any news of my apprentice? Ah but no. Why would there be? He'll be long gone. What's an old codger like me going to do about a lad like that? No. Spirit of the Season like you said. The young will always be the young. No point grieving about them or being angry. They're simply trying to find their way like we did, way back when.

The old woman moved by his forgiveness, his humility. This truly the most emotive Christmas she'd ever had.

'There was a lad,' she told him, 'though don't think he can be yours because he was dragged up out of the snow with nothing but the skin on his bones, and there weren't much of that, so I heard.'

Well, Praise the Lord, one lost soul found. What could be more fitting at this time of the year?

'I think the baker said he left with the travellers.' The old woman helpful to the last.

Rasvlach not breaking character, although was having trouble not to grind his teeth at Diderik's betrayal, or beating this bleating woman's head into a pulp onto the floor beneath his boots.

It's the season to be helpful.

All he could manage, and then he couldn't get out of the door quick enough.

Thank you! Thank you so much! You're my Christmas light!

'God's speed,' the old woman called after him, holding up her hand, feeling miracles abound until, as she was closing her door, she saw through the gap her erstwhile visitor reaching his cart, taking out a knife fit to butcher an ox and savagely cutting through the cord holding the firewood to it, his boots kicking at the wood as it spilled all to the ground so she would have to spend a long hour on hands and knees to gather it all together again.

Thinking back on him sitting at her table, and that maybe he'd not been as old as he'd made himself out to be, nor so humble. She'd never really held with Svetovid and his fire as her husband and father had done. Now she was havering. Crossed herself again and again as she peeped from her window, watched Rasvlach heaving and swearing and hoisting his cart straps onto his shoulders as he lumbered off and away, her regarding all the broken wood he'd left her as a putative Christmas gift scattered like so much detritus in the snow. And so no gift, and no visiting saint. Her taken as a fool, and by her Christ, and by her husband's and father's old ways, she wasn't going to put up with it.

On went the skis and into her hands went the sticks, her believing the devil himself was heading to Sagard. She might be an old woman, as creaky as her ancient skis, but she knew the back way into Sagard that would, on skis, get her there at least a half hour before him.

The Pfiffmaklers packed up camp, kicked over their fire, set off to Sagard to salt their tracks, glancing back over their shoulders at the two graves by the lakeside with their wooden crosses and Pietro kneeling beside them, unable, unwilling, yet to leave.

'It's good he's got some time alone,' Rosa sighed, 'at least until Hulde gets back.'

With or without Valter Poppelmann, she was thinking, *preferably without.*

Wenzel didn't reply. Nothing he could say was going to make any difference. And when Hulde returned, *preferably without Valter Poppelmann,* he was thinking, it would give her and Pietro some time to mourn privately together and God knew, they needed it. Of all of them it was going to be hardest for Pietro and Hulde; Pietro most of all, which went without saying. Longhella's anger had been shocking, if not entirely out of character: taking on their collective grief and spilling it out in wild tears and invective as the rest of them had been unable to articulate. A purging of sorts, a fierce burning that in Longhella would die down within a few days, smouldering far longer in the rest.

Wenzel concentrating on pulling his cart up the track, trepidation squatting like a dark black toad within his chest. He should have been pleased to learn the spoke jammed into their wheel was not Mergim; Mergim turning up without the express intent of retribution, instead was proving himself an ally. And pleased he had been the previous night talking with Mergim, for ostensibly they were many against the one and if it came down to an even fight they'd outnumber Rasvlach with ease. Mergim not of the same mind.

'You don't know him,' Mergim disagreed. 'He's been on the margins his whole life.'

'Haven't we all,' Wenzel had stated, which was true enough. Mergim shaking his head.

'You're nothing like him, as neither am I. Not any more. You've to listen to me, Wenzel, because I'm telling you he's a different kind of man.' Remembering being told of Rasvlach's casual cruelty, the story of him merrily cutting off a fellow prisoner's hand when they'd found him frozen in the snow, tucking it away for luck. 'He'll have spent all this time figuring out the odds, and won't give a pin that there's more of you than him. He's seeing the big pay-off here, and to him that's all this is about. And there's nothing he won't do to see it through. And I mean nothing. Don't matter how many we are, he's going to find a way in, and probably before we even know he's here.'

'You make him sound like the devil himself,' Wenzel had scoffed, had not been worried. Not then.

'Don't underestimate him,' Mergim argued. 'Of course he's not the devil, and of course he's just one man. But he's a man who doesn't think like you and me. It's like he's his own universe and doesn't think outside it. You've no idea what he's capable of doing to get what he's reaching for.'

Wenzel's mind stumbling then, the unknown always more frightening than the known. And all he knew of Rasvlach was that Diderik had been so scared of the man he'd chosen to depart into a snowy night, risking—and nearly achieving—being frozen to death rather than staying another minute with him. A man even Mergim was wary of. Wenzel unable to ignore the fact that Rasvlach might already be in the forest tracking Philbert, and Philbert having no idea he was there.

Wenzel thinking of the old blackthorn stick his father had been so proud of, lines scoured and corkscrewed up its length from a strangulation of honeysuckle; the younger Wenzel finding it disturbing how a plant smelling so sweet could cause such indelible and deep scars, as if it had deliberately laid and made them; like life sometimes does with men—and women come to that. Livia springing to mind. How it could twist and turn about a person for no given reason, tightening its hold, laying down its lines, changing people from one thing into another. *A wondrous stick*, his father had proclaimed as he'd chopped the branch from its tree and spent many hours removing the honeysuckle stems and buffing the wood, capping it with a ram's horn for a handle. A tortured stick all Wenzel saw, whose tender bark had fought and hardened against its strictures, tried to outgrow its bounds and failed; become something it was never meant to be. Useful, if dead; cut away from kith and kin. And hard as an iron bar the few times his father had chosen to lay it against Wenzel's backside and thighs when he'd got himself seriously out of line. Seeing Rasvlach as that stick: cold, dead and hard.

'And he's no love for me,' Mergim had added, furthering Wenzel's consternation, 'nor you neither.'

Wenzel frowning, for how could that be? He'd never even heard of Rasvlach until Diderik had given them his name.

'I only found it out once I started asking,' Mergim went on. *All those tales running through Kragujevac like rats down tunnels, winding and weaving, gnawing at old bones.* 'Mad sore, he was, when he learned the man we brought back to Serbia had been executed.'

Thank you, old lags, for the snippets you passed on.

Wenzel had let out a long breath.

It seemed impossible Hulde's past could still be having ramifications. Eleven years. Eleven years of having Hulde with them, and Livia and Pietro. Eleven drilled beads on Livia's bracelet, and the consequences still coming.

He'd not replied, instead had ticked off his plan in his head: Ortwin and Peppe to go north early doors after Ortwin had spread the idea in Sagard that the Pfiffmaklers were next off to Sassnitz; the two reaching Glowe and the coast in a few hours. Peppe given almost all the money they had, Peppe the right person for the job because Peppe had been born to bargain, could cajole a donkey out of its ears if he needed to. Securing a boat not a hard job, not for Peppe.

The rest of them heading to St Michael's to bolster the belief they were going to Sassnitz. Setting off from Sagard in that direction before swerving off a few miles on, as Ortwin had directed them, once they'd hit the broad path going about the forest's edge.

Riskiest part of the plan being Longhella, Heraldo and Mergim heading direct from Sagard into the forest to fetch up Philbert.

A worry worsened once Wenzel and the slow-moving carts reached St Michael's to be ambushed by the Pastor and a group of townsfolk pressing all about them, begging them to stay, put on more plays, making their leaving difficult.

'I'm so sorry,' Pastor Hulm apologised. 'You've given such life to their Advent. They've never seen the like.'

'We've just buried two of our own,' Wenzel reminded the man, 'and cannot stop...'

But stopped nonetheless by an ancient woman swerving herself out of the trees, pushing herself forward by means of sticks clutched in hands so liverworted they were almost brown.

'Pastor Hulm! Pastor Hulm!'

Pastor Hulm taking a breath as Frau Gottstied hove into view. Pastor Hulm astonished at her agility, old as she was, coming to a perfect stop on her battered skis right in front of him.

'Frau Gottstied, whatever brings you...'

Frau Gottstied ignoring him. Frau Gottstied bringing up one of her sticks and poking it at Wenzel's chest.

'You Pfiffmaklers,' she wheezed, for pushing so fast through the back-tracks had her a little out of breath. 'You've to get yourselves to the forest. Dunno why he wants there, but he does. Devil's been at my place and is about to be at yours.'

Wenzel shivering at her use of the word *devil* he'd so casually dismissed the night before. No doubt in his mind to whom she was referring. The jumbled ball of winter snakes in his head swiftly untangling themselves, separating into individual strands nevertheless connected: successful revolution in Serbia, in which both Pfiffmaklers and Mergim had taken a tangential part; failed revolutions in Europe, with both Philbert's part in it and Metternich's disgrace and subsequent reappearance and renewed reward.

Throw a diehard Croatian into the mix and what you got was bitter water, bitter oil, putrid bile. Someone who saw treachery around every corner and would not stop until he'd had his dues.

Top of his list for people to hate being the Pfiffmaklers and Mergim.

Top of his list for getting out on top being Philbert.

Wenzel looking over at Mergim, Longhella and Heraldo, giving them a slight nod, telling them to be off and to be damn quick about it.

Wenzel knowing the Pfiffmaklers were suffering, needed goals and restitution.

Needing Philbert to be rescued, removed from Rügen.

Needing to prove themselves capable of spitting into the eye of the devil before he could make their lives any more unbearable than they already were.

And the devil, at this moment, was Georg Rasvlach.

Of whom Philbert would know nothing. Nor could know of the losses the Pfiffmaklers had so recently undergone, nor the renewed resolve come from those losses to see him right.

Not so Wenzel.

Wenzel coming to the conclusion that Metternich himself was responsible for this entire situation; a man—as Wenzel and a great many with him—believed to be as morally bankrupt as it seemed was Georg Rasvlach. Livia and her child might or might not have died without external intervention. Wenzel would never know for sure. What he did know was that Philbert must not go the same way. The Pfiffmaklers valued honour, were well known for the worth of their word, their loyalty to those who had been loyal to them. And therefore the Pfiffmaklers needed Philbert to survive if they were to survive themselves.

Rasvlach, and Metternich with him, be damned.

Little Mice Have Their Day

Philbert reached the track at the edge of the cliff, was at the place where the lads in spring let down their uncoiled ropes to fetch the seabirds' eggs, Kroonk battling along at his heels.

'Which way, friend?' Philbert asked of her, although Kroonk, of course, had no answer. All left up to him. They could push on along the cliff path which went he had no idea where, or skirt the forest, head back in the hope Heraldo had left a message for him, telling him where to go and when. Had to be the latter, despite the several days indicated by Longhella's previous shouted instructions not yet up. He and Kroonk clattering down along the track as if their lives depended on it, which they did, more so than they knew; Rasvlach by then having made quick progress through the trees.

Rasvlach coming in from the left side, high above Sagard as old blabbermouth had advised. Rasvlach mapping out the forest in his head as the old woman had given it him: Black Lake at its centre, reached by numerous pathways from numerous starting points; one long and fairly straight path going from Sagard to the cliffs, marked not long in by a small grove of beech trees planted to provide mast for Sagard's pigs. Several main arterial paths: the first going from Sagard to Sassnitz, the second snaking up the edge of the forest to the habitations in the north; a third reaching those same habitations by means of a path running along the top of the cliffs; and from those habitations went a wide causeway through the sea to the outer peninsula of Rügen which effectively formed a separate island.

Get beyond the beech trees and take your wood from there, old blabbermouth had advised. *No one to see you, not if you're canny.*

And canny, as we know, is Rasvlach, and for him Black Lake the place to start: *obvious source of water, especially now all is snow and ice.*

Rasvlach trudging along pathways, going first here and there before homing in, sniffing the air, noting animal tracks, their droppings and directions, the kinds of plants he was passing, all of which led him to Black Lake. Spending a while poking along its edges until he found scuffled footprints in the snow leading directly to Philbert's second camp hidden in the heart of Jasmund. Rasvlach discovering a pig-sized crate abandoned in the trees beside what was obviously a bivouac newly abandoned.

What's the wrong word in that sentence? Wenzel had asked of Heraldo. *Obvious.* And obvious enough the situation was to Rasvlach: this being where his man had latterly holed up, probably moved in closer to the lake when the snow began to fall. And not difficult for Rasvlach to find another track leading to the forest's edge, and another camp there beneath an unwieldy osprey nest built up with snow whose crenellations had frozen into ice along the outlying branches, making it shimmer and glisten in the weak-kneed early afternoon sun.

Once there, Rasvlach took a while to sit and get his breath, recalibrate his thoughts.

Tear his teeth through some fox meat, swallow some flour and salt mixed into a raw gruel with melted snow.

Rasvlach leaning against the base of the osprey tree, looking out over the sea.

Rasvlach not hurrying.

Black Lake, black forests, white snow, many tracks to think about.

The old woman had said the Pfiffmaklers were headed on to Sassnitz but, now he was here beneath the osprey nest, he was not sure that was the case. It certainly wouldn't be what he would do if he knew someone was on his mark and closing in. And that boy she said had been dragged out of the snow, the one who'd left with them, had to be Diderik and, knowing Diderik, he'd have flapped his lips first chance he got.

Pfiffmaklers a tricky and treacherous lot, directly responsible for the execution of a man who, for Croatians like Rasvlach, had been a hero. That deep boiling anger at them still in his bones. Not much in Rasvlach except violence, steeped in it all his days, as coloured with it as any piece of sheepskin tanned and beaten, soaked in dye, sold to the nearest bidder. Not a complicated man, as both Diderik and Mergim—and that winter-skinny fox—had discovered.

Rasvlach a man who wanted what he wanted, and would chop off hands, dead or alive, to get to where he needed to go. And truly not much more to him than that, except history and family and the great begrudgement he'd inherited from both that had brought him to this specific place at this specific time, and the greatest need—not felt before, not really, not as deeply as he felt it now—to annihilate those he felt had done him and his family wrong.

Namely the Pfiffmaklers who, on top of everything else they'd been responsible for, were now were aiding Metternich's fugitive.

Goddamn them. Goddamn them all.

And damn them he would, one by one if necessary, if he got even a whiff of a chance.

So was Rasvlach thinking as he sat beneath the osprey nest on the very edge of Jasmund.

Take it slow, boy, his father's voice in his head. *Take it slow when you're on the hunt. You're the boss. You're the one knows more than they do. Think it through. Think about the land. Think what you would do if you were in their shoes. Think what your quarry wants, where it will go, how it will get there.*

And so Rasvlach thought, imagined his feet inside the undoubtedly sweaty and stinky shoes of both Pfiffmaklers and The Anatomist's Dream. Found nothing in those shoes to redeem them.

Bastards through and through.

New idea forming in his head, and no part of it was Sassnitz.

Time to take a gamble. Throw the dice. One last game of Blind Man's Fancy.

Winner takes all.

Hulde went along the lakeside and up the slope from which Mergim had descended before he'd ended face down in the water. Hard for her to grasp she'd been so close to drowning him. Hard to believe she'd had such rage in her after so many years. Hard for her to pass by Pietro, his head hanging, his knees buried in the cold wet snow, lips moving in some private prayer or lamentation. Hard to not stop with him, for her to pass the graves of Livia and her dead son. And it had been a son. Livia long enough along for that to have been obvious. Hulde's throat closing up as she heard a robin singing, saw it perched—red breast straggled, feathers puffed out by the cold—on the topmost branch of a of nearby bush, unconcerned by all that had gone on. Eyes prickling with tears as she made her way upwards.

She'd not cared much for Valter Poppelmann, from what she remembered of him, but she remembered right enough how he'd been when Andreas had died, which had been distraught. About as distraught as she was now... oh but no. She mustn't think about that. Like Wenzel said, bigger fish to fry, namely getting Philbert out of the forest and them all away before Rasvlach tore them to pieces like a rabid dog. Big picture, not little ones. Not that Livia's dying had been little. Hulde would have given anything for it not to have happened. She'd loved Livia right down to the core, and right from the off, because Livia got everything about Hulde like the rest of the Pfiffmaklers never quite did.

See you and me? We're like seeds scattered so far and wide from our parent plants we never quite know what we're going to grow into. So gives us a choice and you, my darling girl, are going to grow into someone wondrous. Don't matter where we came from. World is ours. We've been given a second chance, and don't you never forget it.

And Hulde never had.

Hulde living through the last eleven years as if her earlier life had never happened. Until Livia had miscarried, until Livia had died. Ludmilla had tried to hold her back; Hulde hadn't allowed it. She'd needed to see Livia to truly believe she'd gone, the injustice too enormous to accept until she'd witnessed it herself. Holding her hand over her mouth and nose as the heavy smell of blood rose to greet her as it had greeted her before; fingertips moving of their own accord as she felt the red slip of it wash over her, the weight of all those bodies closing her in.

And all that blood still hammering in her heart as she made her way up to Valter Poppelmann, because he was not blameless in all this. Hulde scrambling up the slope, ripping her skirts on stones and snow-blown shrubs, careful only of the bracelet Pietro had handed her as she'd sobbed outside the tent and retched and then sobbed again, Pietro lifting her off her knees and slipping it onto her wrist.

She loved it, and she loved you, Hulde. Be glad we had her as long as we did.

Pietro more stoic and forgiving of his undoing than the Pfiffmaklers believed possible, calm water smoothing itself about the jagged boulder heaved right into his centre and emptied half of him out. Only Hulde comprehending the nature of Pietro's calm, even if she did not share it, for it had been Livia who'd pointed out to both the extraordinary rarity of second chances, the unlikely and capricious unfolding of events bringing them all together in the first place. Livia, and now Pietro, of the belief that eleven years of second chances was a miracle, and maybe more than any of them deserved.

She reached the top of the slope and stopped, looked back down towards the lake; saw its calm unblinking eye looking right back at her unconcerned, unmoved by the fish nibbling in the reeds about its flanks, several herons standing sentry at the end where the eel traps were laid. Saw Pietro pushing himself up from his knees, trousers soaked right to the middle of his thighs. Saw him stand and touch his fingers to his lips and then to the tops of the two crosses one by one with slow deliberation, resting longer on the last, on Livia's; saw him take something from his jacket pocket and laying it on the wood. The carved piece of camel bone she'd given Livia a few years back, the one depicting a mother and her child.

Eyes filling with tears again, brushing at them with her knuckles, pressing hard, not wanting to start weeping again. Turning back from the lake and looking into the trees, catching the bright orange flash of Valter's hair like a dying sun between the branches, and moving on.

He was sitting on the stump of a long ago chopped-down elm sprouting branches all about its base; elbows on knees, head in his hands. He didn't move as she advanced, although surely he must have heard her. Hulde finding his immobility disturbing, wondering if he was asleep as he sat, theory disproved as she came into the small glade in which he and Mergim had set up their camp and he raised his head.

'I'm sorry about Livia,' he mumbled. Hulde shocked by the sincerity and sadness in those few words and by how old Valter looked, how wretched. He'd been a handsome man once, but no more: nose broken a couple of times in drunken brawls and not properly set: lopsided, flattened at its apex and skewed to the left, out of whack with the rest of his face, which had fared no better. Hulde hardly recognised him: skin slack and sickly, deep lines gouged either side of his mouth, two days of greying ginger bristle sprouting on cheeks and chin.

'You look awful,' she said, without thinking. 'What happened to you?'

Valter let his head rest back onto his hands, closing himself off from her.

'What happened to any of us?' he murmured vaguely. 'We got swept up, chewed up and spat out again.'

Hulde stamping her foot in irritation.

'God's sake, Valter. Snap out of it. Livia's dead and the rest of us in trouble and all you can do is feel sorry for yourself!'

Sounding more like Longhella than herself. Valter looking up, eyes bleary and blank, puzzlement evident in the grimy creases forming across his brow.

'Have you no idea what's going on?' Hulde therefore asked, brushing snow off a nearby rock and sitting down. It was wet, soaked straight through her skirts though they were so bedraggled and sodden by her journey up the slope it made no difference.

Valter shrugged.

'Mergim found you. The Janus Woman died. What more is there?'

The Janus Woman. Good God. No one had called Livia that for years, not unless they wanted a lecture from Pietro on how the nature of a person is not dictated by appearance, that the sweetest fruits can be the most misshapen, that everyone has a good side and a bad and they should thank the Lord their badness was not made flesh because, if that happened, Livia would look in comparison the most beautiful person in the world. And Livia was the most beautiful person in the world to Pietro, and anyone who tried to say different could go hang.

Hulde studied Valter. Could he really not know? Hulde trying to remember when she'd last seen him at the lakeside, which had been when they'd dragged Mergim out of the water. So much going on after that—the miscarriage, Diderik being introduced into the mix, the revelation about the man Rasvlach, Livia dying....

No one giving a second thought to Valter, nor noticing he'd vacated himself from the action as soon as Mergim had been retrieved; dissolved himself into the background like one of those poplar moths who take rest on a tree trunk and can't be distinguished from the bark, unless you're looking for it.

And no one had been looking.

And Valter didn't know the half of it.

Not until Hulde laid it out for him. Valter leaning in towards Hulde as she told her tale, Valter scratching at his ear once she'd finished.

'When you say Rasvlach, you don't mean Georg Rasvlach?' he asked. Hulde shrugging her shoulders. She didn't know. The name Rasvlach all Diderik and Mergim had given them. Valter skewing up a lip in a half-mast smile because he'd lay odds it was the same man. Valter, who'd spent so many years hanging about in Serbian bars, puking on their floors and tables, getting into fights; Valter, who'd mixed with the worst of the worst; Valter, the most of his memories minced up and coming to him in dribs and drabs the following morning, if he had any memories at all. If not that night, for that night had been spectacular. For once not himself at the centre of trouble but a stocky, bush-bearded man who seemed bigger than he was through sheer bluster and bravado and having shoulders like a yoke-bearing ox, a man who'd struck all the drinks off his table and brought out a knife any executioner would have been proud of.

'I'm Georg Rasvlach!' he'd shouted, 'and all you buggering Serbs should be down on your knees begging us Croatians forgiveness for what you've done!'

Loud enough to halt all other conversations, loud enough to divert all eyes to what was going on, which was Georg Rasvlach pushing the emptied table to one side with one hand whilst shoving his knife into another man's chest, and not once but several times. Valter, sitting two tables over, fascinated by the ferocity with which that knife had gone in the first time, the way Georg Rasvlach had twisted its blade to inflict maximum harm, then pulled it out with such ease and stabbed it in again. The place by then erupting, everyone shoving back their chairs; stools, drinks and glasses flying everywhere.

Valter remembering that night mostly because he'd left, not wanting to be anywhere near when soldiers or police turned up. One of the few nights in years he'd got back to his shack able to remember doing so. The first night he'd seen the mice scuttling about his home as if it belonged to them as much as it did him. Which it did. Probably only noticed them at all because the man two tables over—before Rasvlach had attacked him—had been talking about little mice, although in what context Valter didn't know. First night he'd been sober enough to go to sleep and have an actual dream, a dream oddly enough—given present circumstances—about the Janus Woman all those years back in Zadar, before Andreas had interrupted his attempted violation of her, and that look on the good half of her face of absolute resignation, mutely telling him *you're not the first, and you won't be the last.*

Dear Christ. What had been in him to do such things?

The recollection bringing to mind another: of when he'd spied on Ludmilla and this same Hulde—who'd been a child back then, and Ludmilla not much more—splashing about in the waters of the Adriatic; how he'd seen the small pile of their clothing and thought to hide it. No notion at the time why he'd had such an idea, self-aware enough now to realise it was to make them as vulnerable as he'd been himself. Wanting to spike that little scene of happy diversion right through the heart. Ashamed of it now, as he was ashamed of almost everything about his life.

Valter looking at the present-day Hulde sat upon her boulder; a Hulde who'd grown and rounded, seemingly as innocent and defenseless as an apple ripening upon its tree. A Hulde who couldn't possibly have really meant to have drowned Mergim.

'I don't see what you want me to do about any of it,' he said. 'There's loads of you lot and only one Rasvlach.'

Hulde ground her teeth.

'Us lot,' she repeated quietly. 'Is that really what you think of us? Have you completely forgotten you'd have died like a dog in the dust if Livia hadn't had the wit to save your blasted leg?'

Valter winced, drawing in his injured limb without conscious thought because it had been a real close thing, and his scars still pulled and tautened, especially in cold weather like it was now. Anger surfacing. Same old Valter bristling whenever anyone stood up against him and seemed like they were going for the jugular. Valter getting suddenly to his feet, taking a step forward and shouting in Hulde's face.

'And have you forgotten, little Miss High and Mighty, that it was your precious Ludmilla who was the one who almost did for me in the first place?'

Immediately regretting his outburst as Hulde launched herself sideways off her rock and scrambled on her knees to get away from him.

'You're nothing but a bully, Valter Poppelmann!' she yelled, getting to her feet. 'And a lily-arsed one at that, and I hope you rot in—'

Hulde tangling up in her skirts and tripping over, landing flat on her back, pushing herself by her elbows across the snow as Valter bore down on her. Hulde banging her head on a spruce tree that had seen better days, toppled at its waist but still growing, barring her backwards escape.

'Oh for God's sake,' Valter muttered, striding forward, pulling Hulde roughly up and setting her on her feet. 'I'm not going to hurt you, child. I might not give a cuss about the Pfiffmaklers but you're a different kettle of fish. I've tramped the most way across Europe so Mergim could settle himself about you, and I'm not about to let all that go to waste.'

Hulde breathing hard, heart racing, bruises blooming on her arms where Valter had pulled her up.

'So what are you going to do about it?' Hulde retorted, as coldly as she could, as coldly as Longhella might have done. Longhella suddenly a hero, strong and fearless. Hulde wishing she was more like Longhella than herself. Brushing at her skirts, pushing back the plaits come free with the tussling. Hulde feeling ridiculous, and relieved, as Valter Poppelmann removed himself back a few paces and sat back on his log.

'And why am I Miss High and Mighty anyway?' Hulde asked, emboldened. 'That's not me at all.'

Valter shaking his head, laughter bubbling up in his throat with the ease and joy a cuckoo must have come springtime for the scene and the question was too much for him to take seriously.

'Because the Pfiffmaklers changed their whole lives for you,' he said, fighting those unaccustomed bubbles in his throat, trying to keep them down. 'All of them. Every last one of them. All because of you.'

Hulde caught on the hop, for she'd never thought about it that way. She'd been found, she'd been taken this way and that; she'd been kidnapped, thought she might die, had been rescued once more by the Pfiffmaklers, been a part of them ever since. She knew what had happened to her, had been told the story of it, yet mostly the story was to her a blur, like she was two people, a before and after. Flashes of her old self here and there: smells of mud and sweat making her jangle like she was in the inside of a bell; being hoisted up, as Valter had just done, forcing her to recall other times: egrets flying, a dark night sky, a dark man pointing out the stars to her, telling her there was her family and there her kin, as the lights and stars flashed about the skies.

'But they took you in, like they took me. You and Andreas,' Hulde ventured. 'Doesn't that count for anything?'

Oh and so much Valter could have said in rebuttal, in ire, in utter exhaustion, but the plain fact was she had the truth of it. The Pfiffmaklers had taken them in, cared for himself and Andreas like they were of their own, despite everything, and only Valter to blame for not being able to fit. For not being able to fit anywhere, except maybe that village with the Joshua Tree. Thought in him that maybe he would go back there after all, light a fire on the beach of Rügen where they'd been landed, be fetched away, be somewhere he could be useful and appreciated. Maybe even help them as Mergim had helped him. Sudden epiphany that Mergim *had* helped him, that he was not the same drink-washed sot he'd been eight or nine months before. He'd always be on the brink, always ready to fall back into old ways, but he was not falling yet. Maybe time to pay Mergim back for that small mercy.

'Tell me again about this Philbert,' he said, 'and why Rasvlach is so eager to get his hands on him.'

Hulde noting a small change in Valter, a softening of tone, a straightening of his back and maybe of resolve. Hulde retaking her boulder and trying to explain, speaking quickly, trying to hide her impatience, for she was keen to be gone, to collect Pietro and join back up with the rest of the Pfiffmaklers.

'He's been on the run for a few years. Originally part of a crew called the Fair of Wonders before they got cut to pieces. Managed to save a load of men from getting executed by Metternich's militia, and Metternich looking for him ever since. New fat reward for his capture, which is what Rasvlach means to collect. Philbert's famous in these parts,' she added. 'Had songs and stuff made up about him. The Little Maus is what they called him back then because he'd….'

Hulde stopping as Valter jerked up his head and stared at her, his eyes sparking and alive as if the sun had suddenly risen within them.

'Little Maus? Is that what you said?'

'Well of course. That's—'

'Oh for the love of God,' Valter couldn't stop the bubbling this time, Valter laughing so hard Hulde feared he might have a paroxysm and die on the spot if he didn't stop.

'I don't see what's so—'

'The Little Mouse!' Valter interrupted, slapping his leg, memories colliding and expanding exponentially as all became clear: the filthy tavern, drinks and tables flying, Serbians arguing with Croatians. Valter quelling his laughter, seeing in his head the bright flash of the knife twisted and bloodied in a man's chest, the boiling blood of the knife-wielder who'd had shoulders wider than his waist. Hadn't thought on the aftermath of that tavern brawl in the few years since it had happened, had never returned there. Had supposed the man had been imprisoned, but plainly not. Not if he was here.

Little Mice indeed.

Always someone on their tail.

And no one worse than the likes of Georg Rasvlach, he'd lay odds on that.

The many against the one.

Many Pfiffmaklers, one Rasvlach, and God help them if or when they crossed paths.

Valter coming to a decision and standing up.

'I think, Little Miss High and Mighty, we'd best get moving and moving fast.'

Hulde annoyed by the soubriquet, confused by Valter's *volte face*, standing up anyway.

'So you'll help us?' she asked. 'You'll come with us?'

Valter, already on his way down the slope towards the vacated Pfiffmakler camp, didn't take the time to answer.

Paths Taken, Maybe Not Good Ones

Philbert stopped, caught his breath. He'd arrived at the beech trees: no new messages.

Didn't know what to do, which way to turn. Certain someone was out there in the forest tracking him and Kroonk and therefore couldn't go back the way he'd come. Was at a crossroads, quite literally, bringing to mind what Heraldo had told him as they'd stood here together on his first day on Rügen.

Sagard's that way, pointing straight forward, *where we'll be in maybe a week, I'll make sure of that. And that way goes to Sassnitz. Big port there, where we can surely get you passage.*

And the other? Philbert had asked, Heraldo shaking his head.

Not really sure. Probably hits the road going to the topmost villages of the peninsula.

Obvious option for Philbert being to go to the left, but the more he looked and thought on it the worse he liked that option. The track to Sassnitz wide and straight, well-travelled, not much cover, lots of visibility. From where he stood he could see at least three tracks joining it from the forest side and two more from the other. The opposite way quite different, snaking back into the trees, lost to sight within twenty yards. So there he would go, no matter he didn't know where it led. Last task being to leave a message telling Heraldo where he was heading, consulting the crib he'd been given, slashing a few marks into the nearest beech.

'Running again, friend,' he said to Kroonk, stroking her back, shivers of pleasure horripilating along her skin. Kroonk happy as long as she was with Philbert, wherever he chose to go.

'Come on,' Heraldo urged, taking the lead, setting a swift pace out of Sagard. 'We're almost there.'

Longhella a couple of steps behind her cousin, feeling Mergim a heavy black shadow at her back.

God, that man can move quick and quiet for one so big.

Reminding herself he'd brought himself all the way across Europe, poking and prying, to find them, to find Hulde.

Always knew she was trouble. Tried to tell them, but who would listen? No one, is the answer to that. Even Old Grandma changed her tune. Old Grandma, of all people!

Thoughts beating along in Longhella's head in time with the steady trudging of her boots.

Should have left the little rat to rot in that pile of bodies back in Albania.

Longhella taking a sudden trip and lurch, for even she recognised how cruel was such a sentiment, given how they'd found the girl. But by God, she was sick of all this havering over Hulde, everyone treating her as special, like she was a precious piece of glass that might shatter at any moment.

'All right, miss?'

Longhella incensed when the hated Mergim pulled her swiftly up, shaking him off in an instant.

'Fine,' she retorted, couldn't bear his hands on her. Couldn't bear that if he hadn't come along then Livia and her child might still be alive. Couldn't bear how deeply the loss of both had seared into her, nor reconcile the grief she felt for a woman she'd for years and years been active in disliking, as she had done Hulde.

Stop bloody sniveling, she told herself as she marched onwards.

And stop bloody thinking, but she could not.

She'd never been one to put herself in anyone else's shoes, found herself doing so now.

Hulde's going to think this is all her fault.

Hulde's going to bring all the blame down on herself.

Longhella back to her normal self as she spied the beeches at the crossroads, saw straightaway there were marks on one that had to have been put there not long since, sap still bleeding about their edges. Livia and Hulde forgotten as the thrill of the chase rode riot through her veins. Longhella at heart a warrior born in the wrong place at the wrong time; Longhella putting her hand to her knife, Longhella all in the moment, wondering if she'd have the guts to slice her knife across Philbert's throat if she got the chance, beat this Rasvlach at his own game and put all to rest.

One cross in the wood, one single horizontal line with a point gouged out beside it. Heraldo looking puzzled.

'Danger. Gone right,' he interpreted. 'So if he's coming out of the forest he means the opposite way to Sassnitz. Why would he do that?'

'Does it matter?' Longhella asked, impatient to be moving again. 'Surely that's all to the good. Means he's going the way the rest of us are going.'

'It also means he's knows someone's not long behind him,' Mergim added, so close behind Longhella it made her skin crawl. Took a quick pace away.

'Got to admire the lad on that front,' Mergim went on regardless. 'Means he's cautious and astute, which is surely why he went on the smaller track instead of the larger.'

'Who cares?' Longhella said loudly, outraged when Mergim clamped his large hand across her mouth and chided her.

'God's sake, girl. Keep your voice down. Last thing we need is Rasvlach knowing we're here and where we are.'

But too late, that clamping hand.

Rasvlach, a couple of hours behind Philbert, close enough to the beech grove to hear Longhella's voice, if not what she'd said. Rasvlach more cautious and astute when he was on the hunt than Mergim and his cronies in Kragujevac would ever have given him credit for. Rasvlach smiling, for now was his time. He couldn't be sure whose voice he'd heard, nor the reason that person was in the forest; but he was a gambling man and weighed the odds, made deductions, came to the conclusion best fitted to the circumstances: Diderik had found the Pfiffmaklers, Diderik had talked, Pfiffmaklers had got wind of Rasvlach's big plan and played right into his hands.

Pfiffmaklers doing what herds should never do: they'd split up.

Only task left to him now being to pick them off.

And by Christ, he was going to enjoy every second of doing exactly that.

Exit Pfiffmaklers, one by one.

Next step, sawing off Philbert's head and setting himself up for life. His only problem, as he saw it, being how to get on fast enough. He'd enough alcohol in his cart to keep Philbert's head in a perfect state of preservation. Diderik wrong to assume he'd kept all that vodka topped up for no other reason than to drink it, yet right now he needed speed and stealth. And speed and stealth meant ditching the cart. And if that was what it took then so be it. He made a pinpoint observation, took careful heed of his surroundings, covered over his cart with slashed-off branches and mud made malleable by the snow, scooped over it a load of dead leaves.

All Rasvlach needed from here on in was himself and the soapstone on which he sharpened his many knives. And he'd sharpened those knives. Sharpened them until they had edges like surgeons' scalpels.

Look out, Pfiffmaklers. Here I come.

Pietro started pulling his cart up the lane after saying a final goodbye to Livia and their son. Hulde would soon enough catch him up on her young legs, and for the moment wanted to be alone. He knew everyone was finding his reaction to their deaths unnatural, that after a few hours of wailing grief he'd become too accepting, too stoic.

For Pietro himself it was not like that at all.

It was as if he'd been thrown off a dimensionless cliff and was free-falling into darkness, waiting to hit the ground. Had an absurd and shameful sense of exhilarating freedom to be so unencumbered, no longer tethered by a love of such intensity it had filled him up and spilled out of him every second of every day. Extinguished at a stroke were all the worries he'd been harboring: whether Livia would survive the birth of their child; whether the child would be perfect, or burdened by some malformation or disability; whether he would make a good father or resent the love that would be divided from him by Livia's overwhelming care of their child. Potential names already selected to reflect the glory of this entirely unexpected gravidity: Euforia, had it been a girl, or maybe Eurydice, they hadn't decided. Livia favouring the former, Pietro the latter.

'It's perfect! Brought from darkness into light,' he'd argued.

Livia frowning, reminding him that in the tale Eurydice never escaped the underworld.

'And all because Orpheus had to turn around to take his look,' Livia had tutted. 'What an idiot. How selfish can you get? Heraldo would never have done such a thing.' Picking Heraldo because, like Orpheus, he was a musician and played his lyre like a god. 'No wonder the women of Thracia tore the blasted man to pieces with their bare hands.'

'So we put it to rights with our daughter,' Pietro had countered, laughing, adoring the way Livia's mind worked, smoothing his hand over her swollen belly. 'Eurydice. I love the sound of that name.'

And still did. Still did, as he dragged his cart—his and Livia's cart—up the track towards Sagard. He'd never said to anyone, not even Livia, that he'd hoped for a girl. Grandma Pfiffmakler his inspiration on that front, for what a woman she'd been! Thrawn and courageous. Teaching him what it was to be alive, to be more—so much more—than others expected of you. And she the sole reason he'd met Livia in the first place.

A boy, by contrast, in Pietro's opinion, might assume he had a right to be alive and do whatever took his fancy, especially with the name Livia had chosen.

'Meraviglio Pietro Benedetta. You, me and him all rolled up into one.'

Pietro capitulating, Pietro burying the child under that name to please Livia. A small consolation given the magnitude of her loss. No notion then that he would be burying her next to their lost child twenty-four hours later, his life further ripped from its mast with such deliberate precision he might have had his own Thracian women condemning him for some unknown act. Orpheus had surely earned his end, a life for a life. Pietro's undoing so unpredictable, so cruel, it appeared to him to have been engineered for the sole purpose of seeing how he would react.

And so he would not react. He would not fall fool to whoever, whatever, had chosen to subject him to a life without Livia and their child. He would carry on as if Livia were by him, talk to her in his head as he fought for explication. Would go on calm, sure and placid as long as he was able, looking forward to the moment when his free-fall came to an abrupt end as he smashed onto the waiting rocks below.

He would not be Orpheus.

He would not look back.

He would not condemn Livia and their latent child to the darkness by publicly falling to pieces.

He's all of us; you, me and him all rolled into one.

The only one left standing being Pietro. Pietro pulling at his cart with a ferocity that had his shoulders burning, his boots skidding on ice and stones, his heart beating out the tattoo of his new calling: Drummer Boy for those who had gone. For Livia, for the Euforia or Eurydice who had never been and for the Meraviglio who had almost made it. Only a month or so to go. And only a month or so Pietro gave himself. If he hadn't hit the rocks by then by outside intervention then he would do it himself, by one means or another.

Like a pool closing in about the rock that has divided it.

Until the pool decides it's had enough, empties itself back into the sea from whence it came.

Rasvlach, once he'd concealed his cart, chose not to carry on the downward path towards Sagard. Instead pushed himself off through the trees towards the initial track he'd come in by that the old besom had so eagerly described.

'Not hard to find, when you know it's there,' she'd said. 'You'll hit the main track going from Sagard up to the northern villages that skirts the forest, and if you go across it and push through the trees you'll find a parallel path about a quarter mile in. And that's the one to take to stay hidden.'

Rasvlach therefore walking along the echo of that outer path, sketching out the forest's geography in his head, listening all the while for the sounds of folk moving along one path or another and soon rewarded.

Two people chatting idly. A young boy and an older man.

Rasvlach moving stealthily along his chosen path before diverging so he could more clearly hear what their chat was all about and who it was who had strayed into his purview.

'Do you think your plan will work?' the young boy asked.

'Of course!' the man replied breezily. 'We're Pfiffmaklers! Our plans always work.'

Rasvlach smiling, inching towards his quarry.

'How long do you think they are behind us?' Ortwin enquired eagerly, gripped by his adventure. Peppe amused by the lad's excitement and Peppe always a man who liked to be amused, especially since Wenzel had spelled out how dangerous were their circumstances. Wenzel always confiding in Peppe, as in Rosa. Rosa undone by

Livia's loss, Rosa telling Peppe this was it. That whatever happened with Philbert, she and Wenzel were going to quit the wandering life, meaning Peppe might have to come up to the pass and take over. A terrifying thought.

'You can't leave!' he'd remonstrated. 'You absolutely can't. And I can't take over. Surely it will fall to Heraldo to—'

'Yes, it will,' Rosa agreed. 'It's got to be Heraldo and Ludmilla's show, but they're so young, Peppe. And we've been doing this since long before they were born. Someone's got to see them through, and by that I mean you. And you're not to tell anyone. And I mean anyone about me and Wenzel.'

The news of Rosa's and Wenzel's decision to depart had unnerved if not derailed him. Peppe made of sterner stuff. Peppe looking on young Ortwin as he'd looked on many lads since he'd been with the Pfiffmaklers, lads who saw the Pfiffmakler life as their way out of the mundane. Understood that yearning; the Pfiffmaklers rolling into his village like a cartwheel that could not be stopped. Peppe caught beneath its heel and hauled up to its apex; Peppe as enchanted by Ysell as Rosa had been with Wenzel. That wheel rolling out of their little village taking the two of them with it. Neither of them ever regretting it. Both happy in their marriages, in the way their lives had gone because of it. Children given to both: healthy happy children, two of whom—Heraldo on Rosa's side and Ludmilla on his and Ysell's—eventually hooking up to carry on the dynasty when their parents finally bit the dust.

Peppe couldn't have imagined for himself a better life.

Peppe answering Ortwin's question without a care in the world.

'Maybe half an—'

Peppe halfway through his answer when he fell.

Peppe on the ground by Ortwin's feet, and so much blood pooling out from Peppe's neck that Ortwin, by sheer unacknowledged instinct, threw himself to one side, crawled away, got himself into the undergrowth, watching helplessly as a man strode from the trees onto the path, twisting his knife viciously in Peppe's neck to make certain the job was done before pulling it free.

Folk who didn't know Rasvlach might have considered it a lucky shot; those folk not knowing how long and hard Rasvlach had practised this particular skill, and very few better at it than he.

'One down,' Rasvlach said quietly, 'plenty more to go.'

Ortwin pissing his pants, not daring to move or breathe.

Ortwin more afraid than he'd ever been in his life.

Ortwin thinking on his grandfather and Goethe to keep himself still.

Im Nebelgeriesel, in teifen Schnee, Im wilden Wald, in der Winternacht.

In the snow, in the wild woods, on winter nights…

I must not lose my nerve.

And so he stayed, did not move, watched as Rasvlach came out of the wild woods to check on his handiwork and retrieve his trusty knife. Ortwin listening intently as Rasvlach melted himself back into the woods from where he'd come, apparently not wanting to waste time seeking out small fry like Ortwin, or maybe realising Ortwin was not one of the Pfiffmaklers and therefore of no concern. Ortwin noting which direction the man was going, Ortwin moving the opposite way, crawling on all fours through the undergrowth. Ortwin finishing Peppe's answer for him:

They'll be maybe half an hour behind.

Meaning the rest of the Pfiffmaklers, and only Ortwin to warn them that one of their own had just been killed and they might be next. He'd not been fully briefed on what was going on with the Pfiffmaklers, but knew from his grandfather's book on the history of Rügen that never yet had bandits laid themselves up in the forests with the specific intention of murdering passers-by for no reason. After all the stramashing of Danish incursions and forced conversion back in the Middle Ages—so vigorously depicted by the Pfiffmaklers' Advent theatrics—very little had happened except on paper. Rügen occupied occasionally, swapping hands from Danish rule to Swedish to German and back again. Napoleon claiming it for a couple of years before it returned home to Prussia and became what it was now: part of German Pomerania, like the rest of Mecklenburg.

No bandits in all that time.

No marauding soldiers left on the hop after various wars had swallowed them up and spat them out again to fare for themselves as best they could, as had happened in other parts of Europe.

And so, went Ortwin's thinking, this had to have something to do with the Pfiffmaklers and whatever was their great plan.

His young heart beating hard as he battled through bushes, reeds and long grasses bent low by winter snow on his hands and knees, dampness seeping up from foot to knee to groin, which was a blessing, hiding as it did his little accident if not the acrid stench of it. Ortwin moving back down the path leading to Sagard, hoping to God he would reach the Pfiffmaklers before the wolf in the forest found them out and cut them down, one by one, piece by piece.

As Pietro had predicted, Hulde soon caught him up; Valter, a few yards before her, grabbing at the yoke Pietro was pulling with all his strength, Valter taking half the strain unbidden, easing himself in beside Pietro as if he'd been invited.

Valter had been toying with what conciliatory condolences he would say but, on seeing Pietro hauling at that cart as if he was trying to cleave his heart in two, Valter thought better of it. More than most Valter knew about death and dying and the grief that came with it, and knew when to button his lip. And more than most it had been this same Pietro who'd been a small comfort to Valter when Andreas had died. Had come to him the evening they'd buried Andreas on the outskirts of the little glade of trees, Pietro appearing silently and picking up first one stone and then another and another and another, laying them over the grave. Pietro carrying on with the task until Valter finally understood what he was doing and joined in. An hour later they'd built a sizeable cairn; Peppe giving over his whittled tribute of hedgehoggery, placing it at the cairn's apex, the carving remaining in the vicinity for Valter to rediscover when he'd arrived there with Mergim.

'Doesn't help they always seem so happy,' Pietro had said back then. 'Can't hardly believe I'm one of them.'

Valter hadn't replied. Hadn't been able to get out a single word.

'Just remember this, Valter,' Pietro had gone on. 'Everyone knows death is hard, if not always the hardest option. Andreas told me that, and he told me because I was his back-up plan.'

Pietro bringing out from his jacket an exact replica of the vial Andreas had forced Valter to administer to Andreas. Valter uncomfortably aware, as he pulled the cart along in silence, that Pietro had not smashed his own vial right then and there by the cairn, nor had he given it over. Instead had put it discreetly back into his pocket and very likely still had it now.

'No building of cairns this time?' Valter therefore asked, as they pulled into the main street of Sagard, which question would have seemed to anyone other than Pietro insensitive and brash. Pietro getting his meaning, for that little vial was on Pietro's person and not far from his thoughts. Pietro taking his time answering. Valter one thing, Hulde quite another, and he didn't want Hulde anywhere near this and so he quickened his pace, Valter getting the hint and doing the same.

'Not this time,' Pietro said, as they spied Pastor Hulm standing with evident agitation upon the steps of his church as if he was on the lookout for them, which indeed he was. 'But you know as well as I that I've the means to take my own way out, when and if I choose to do so.'

Any answer deflected by Pastor Hulm hurrying to meet them.

'You're all in trouble!' Pastor Hulm informed them, as if they didn't already know.

Valter and Pietro coming to a stop in front of the Pastor as Hulde too arrived, gasping to catch her breath.

'I've nearly burst a lung keeping up with you two!' Hulde chided. 'You've been going like the clappers.'

Pietro looking at Valter and Valter looking back at Pietro; only Valter to know what Pietro was thinking. The puddle reckoning it might soon be better off in the sea.

'There's always another way,' Valter said quietly, entirely out of character, or entirely out of the character he'd once been.

'What other way?' Hulde asked. 'Are we changing our plans?'

'I think you might best be doing so,' Pastor Hulm chipped in, not that he was privy to those plans, only the details Frau Gottstied had volunteered to her Christmas visitor about the outlay of Jasmund Forest and spelling them out once more to these straggling Pfiffmaklers and their ginger-haired addition who Pastor Hulm had never seen before. Pietro glad to brush aside his own dark thoughts and concentrate on something new.

'So according to your Frau Gottstied he knows what? He knows every single path running through Jasmund?'

Pastor Hulm nodding glumly, for that about summed it up.

Pietro thanking the man, heaving off his harness, Valter doing likewise.

'Look after this stuff for us, Pastor,' Pietro said. 'We'll send someone back for it, depending on how all goes.'

Pietro off, Valter and Hulde on his heels.

'What's happening?' Hulde asked, as Pietro flung himself forward, going straight for the track leading north.

'I don't know,' he said, in honest answer, 'but I've a feeling we need to get where we're going quick as we can.'

Totting up in his head where everyone had already gone: the people, the places, most vulnerable. Haring up the lane Ortwin and Peppe had taken that would, of necessity, be cut through by the fine lines Frau Gottstied had told Rasvlach to take into the inner forest. Maybe he would still be in there, vague possibility Frau Gottstied's Christmas miracle was merely a man intent only on cutting wood. But no one, Pietro least of all, was going to rely on it. He couldn't know Mergim had agreed her description of her visitor sounded more like Rasvlach than not—particularly the part about the spilling of the wood—but Pietro knew a chink in a plan when he saw it, and so he ran.

Pietro's and Livia's cart of wonders abandoned at Pastor Hulm's feet; nominal Pfiffmaklers somewhat amused by the look on Pastor Hulm's face as they left him. Nominal Pfiffmaklers speeding along the track, soon seeing the unmistakable outlines of Longhella, Heraldo and Mergim who were just turning onto the north-going path, all arrested in their tracks a few minutes later by the waif Ortwin leaking himself out of the undergrowth on hands and knees and getting to his feet, waving his arms, shouting out this and that, mostly for them to go no further.

The herd no longer divided into four, three merging back into the one; but one of their cast missing, presumed dead, according to Ortwin. Pfiffmaklers ignoring his warnings and running like a torrent up the track to learn the worst.

To stand in shock

To find Peppe cooling in white snow and congealing red blood.

Pietro holding Hulde's shaking shoulders as Ludmilla went down on her knees beside her father and began to keen, a sound so distressing it sent the hairs up on everyone's necks and put the world out of kilter; her sister unnaturally immobile, Longhella a mute instrument that might soon clash and roar but for the moment had forgotten all her tunes, histrionic or otherwise, unable to take in the fact of her father lying dead a few yards from her feet. Mergim and Valter hovering like ghosts; Heraldo stern and silent, fists clenching and unclenching until his knuckles began to crack.

Only Pietro able to say what needed saying.

'This cannot, will not, be allowed to pass,' he muttered. And if anyone had previously believed he'd accepted the deaths of his wife and son with the stoicism of an ancient Greek philosopher they would know now, with certitude, it was not the case; for there was a death knell in his words and a dark fury in his eyes that said *here is hell on earth*, and every last one of God's ministering angels had better watch their backs because Pietro was going to twist off their wings with his bare hands for allowing such terrible things to happen.

'What do we do?' Mergim asked.

'What do we do?' Pietro repeated, the fury of a disturbed hornets' nest beating a thousand angry wings inside his head, heating him up until he felt he might splinter out into the universe like St Elmo's fire. 'We change plans,' he said, then raised his voice and shouted out his bile into the forest.

'We're coming for you, Georg Rasvlach! Get down on your knees and pray, you vile piece of humanity, for you will pay! You will damn well pay for what you've done!'

'I'm not sure—' Mergim started to say, Pietro cutting him off with such vehemence Mergim shut himself quickly up.

'He's out there,' Pietro spat. 'And he'll not be far. He'll not want to miss the show.'

Mergim having to agree on this point, for that would be just like Rasvlach, but he needed to add in the obvious.

'Or this is maybe a simple diversion. What he needs to slow us up so he can go on after the boy.'

'And it's going to help him that you split up,' Valter added, would have said more except Longhella suddenly shook herself back to life and started shouting over and over.

'He's killed my father! Your bastard man has killed my father! He's killed my father! Your bastard man has...'

Stopped by Heraldo stepping up to her and wrapping his arms about her.

'I know, I know,' he murmured, and then up stood his wife, roused by Longhella's screaming; up stood Ludmilla, her grief raddled upon her face, eyes swollen, cheeks pale, tortured by her loss. No happy clappy Pfiffmaklers now.

'I don't know where this Rasvlach is,' said she, Old Grandma high and mighty in her veins, anger and vengeance trumping softer emotions. 'But I know he's not near us now else he'd have sent another knife flying into one or another of our necks. So this is the new plan, Pfiffmaklers. Some of us must go back and warn the family, the rest of us go after Philbert exactly like Rasvlach will be doing and, by so doing, we find this Rasvlach. And when we find him we tear him into pieces. Like Pietro said, he's got to pay, and by Christ so he will.'

Everyone stilled by Ludmilla's ghastly pronouncement.

No one willing to defy it. Mergim and Valter lifting the dead Peppe to the side of the track, covering him over with broken reeds and fallen branches. The Pfiffmaklers' to bury, not wanting anyone else discovering him until they were ready. Ortwin and Valter sent back to find Wenzel because they weren't Pfiffmaklers and shouldn't be a target for Rasvlach if he was still hanging around.

The rest heading north.

The sorriest group of minstrels and troubadours you've ever seen.

Hearts tolling, boots tramping, eyes fierce and wet, watching out for Rasvlach or God's snivelling turncoat angels; folk like Pastor Hulm holding that such angels were all around them in this world, particularly in this joyful season. But of such careless, lazy angels the Pfiffmaklers had neither want nor need.

You or I might have baulked at the task that lay ahead.

You or I would most likely have turned tail, returned to Sagard and the safety to be gained in crowds and light; gathered our own to our own, buried the last of our dead by the side of the others, by the edge of the lake that shone up into the afternoon as careless and unruffled as Pastor Hulm's angels.

We'd maybe have taken what remained of the Christmas Season and wrapped ourselves up in it like a parcel that doesn't want to be opened.

We'd have tried to gladden our hearts, looked forward and not back.

We'd have closed our minds to the fate that might befall Philbert, retreated in wilful blindness because really, who was he to us?

He was no one.

He might have had verses scribbled about his doings, and songs sung.

He might be regarded as a hero of the 1848 revolutions, yet what are those revolutions to us?

They're nothing. And he's nothing. We've not even met him, so why should we care?

We'd be like those shiftless angels who wouldn't lift a finger to help anyone but themselves.

Luckily for Philbert that was not the Pfiffmakler way.

And the Pfiffmaklers' way right now was heading north, gritting their teeth against what might come. Philbert one of their own, more so now than ever. One who needed their help and protection when no one else would give it. Pfiffmaklers ready and willing to do whatever needed doing to see the task through. Ready to throw Rasvlach, and any angels they came across, into the flames of hell.

Philbert was a good way up the track, halfway to Glowe, had he known it. He was regretting leaving Kroonk's cart in the forest for Kroonk was old, having difficulty keeping up. Snow kept collecting and balling into ice between her toes, making her going far more difficult than for a strong young man in boots.

'Come on, old girl,' Philbert whispered and cajoled, stroking Kroonk behind her ears, breaking away yet another clump of ice from her feet. Philbert thinking maybe he'd been a fool to leave the forest so soon before the Pfiffmaklers were due to fetch him, that maybe no one had been after them at all. And yet the feeling, despite his doubts, was stronger in him than before. And it felt good to be on the move, and no point anyway in going back. Too much distance put between himself and the beech tree scripts. Maybe the Pfiffmaklers would find him, maybe they would not. Either way he and Kroonk were on the go with more urgency than ever, Philbert's hat drawn down to hide his large head, if not the large thoughts racing exponentially the further along this unknown track he went.

Wherever we end up, we'll end up by the sea. And where there's sea there's boats. And has to be some way we can get passage to somewhere—anywhere. I can work oars or fishing nets. I can be of use.

Swift look back at Kroonk, trotting and coughing along behind him, attached to his belt by a piece of rope because godammit, whatever happened, if she went down then so would he. Still had hope in Heraldo, who had struck Philbert as a man who stuck to his word like ants get trapped in the resin bleeding from the pine trees standing sentry to his left all the way along this track, this path going to who knew where.

'He'll come looking,' he assured both Kroonk and himself. 'He'll not abandon us.'

Though in truth, and in the art of self-preservation, Philbert had to imagine it might be the case, everything having become too troublesome. Heraldo's family putting a hard black cross against Heraldo's idea of rescuing him. Lord knew he wouldn't blame them for it. Fairs folk peripatetic by nature, suspicious of anything outside of themselves that might rock their boat. And Philbert could feel the boat rocking as he hurried along, put one boot in front of the other, urging Kroonk along with him, tugging occasionally at the rope connecting him to her, needing to impart the urgency of their passage. Philbert stopping anyway when it got too much for her. Philbert chipping away the ice between her toes.

Going on without her was unthinkable. Philbert and Kroonk, like the shepherd with his trusty dog, the mahout with the elephant he'd once seen many years before who'd declared he was more in love with his elephant than his wife.

'She's feelings,' the mahout had said. 'She's a living breathing person to me and always will be.'

Philbert understanding, for Kroonk, to Philbert, was family. The one constant in a world that had turned itself inside out several times during the course of his short life. He might be only seventeen or eighteen years old or thereabouts, he would never be quite certain, and every moment of it etched inside his giant head. A curse and a blessing all at once, all that memory he'd never been able to properly explain to anyone. All those recollections stacked up the one upon the other, like they were happening at the same moment and yet not. Like he was caught up in a river of remembrance, where every rock at the bottom of that river and every root going down into the water from its banks, and every fish that passed him by with a flash of scale and tail, and every frond of every weed he sailed by, were each of them waving out their stories, begging to be heard.

All of them heard, by him if no one else. All their beginnings and endings confided to him, finding a home inside his head which was a trove of stories, some told, many not. Such a huge spilling out Philbert had yet to do, and yearned for the day when he could do it rightly. When he could do it without fear of having his head lopped from his shoulders for what other folk had made of him, for what others had tried to forge him into.

Didn't know an awful lot about history, or of the wider implications of the 1848 revolutions. Didn't know much about Metternich, other than how folk in the Westphal Club had disparaged and blamed him, pinned on him a great many wrongs being perpetrated all across the country.

Knew, though, how one event could connect to and cause another and another; how no matter how well knit and intricately patterned a jumper might be it could be undone by the pulling of a single judiciously isolated thread.

Said thread at the moment being himself.

The Anatomist's Dream heading on up the track towards Glowe, oblivious to what was behind him; oblivious to Peppe's body slowly freezing beneath its coverage of reeds and branches, iced over with Rügen snow that had begun again to fall.

Philbert oblivious to what lay beyond.

And what lay beyond was Rasvlach, who'd spied and identified fresh pig scat on the main path not far beyond where Peppe had been despatched.

Rasvlach returning to the echo path fifty odd yards yonder.

Rasvlach's instincts having a bit of a fight once he'd noted there were more Pfiffmaklers coming out from the Sagard trail, emerging onto the northern track where soon enough they'd find their fallen Pfiffmakler. Rasvlach thinking he should maybe have finished off the halfwit boy who, surprisingly for a halfwit, had nonetheless shifted himself away quick as lightning where it was almost impossible for Rasvlach to find him with any efficiency.

Rasvlach once more weighing up the odds. Rasvlach thinking *to hell with him. The boy with the head I need to sever is within reach and, when I find him, I'm going to bring out my sharpest knife, let him see what's going to come.*

Rasvlach never a man for subtlety.

Rasvlach believing his time had come; no one and nothing to stop him.

Rasvlach speeding up that echo path until that echo path petered out and he was obliged back onto the main trail.

Philbert in front of him, Pfiffmaklers behind.

Time to be doing, Rasvlach decided.

Time to be done, one way or the other.

Look out Philbert, for here I come.

Two Bottles Of Wine And A Watermelon

Valter and Ortwin made swift headway back along the track to intercept Wenzel.

Valter not looking forward to that meeting one jot; not meeting Wenzel again, when Wenzel so plainly despised him, and absolutely not the news he was going to have to give him. Feeling like he'd swallowed a ball of ice. Ortwin chittering like a linnet alongside him, which ordinarily would have irritated him; seemed now the only part of the day that hadn't taken a somersault off a cliff.

'It's terrible what's happened. I was thinking of running away with them, with the Pfiffmaklers. Going to find my grandfather in Denmark. He's a real learned man. Has written books and everything. 'Course he's got a new family there, but I'm sure he'll take me in. Wasn't thinking any of it would involve dead bodies. He went down right beside me. Not that I knew him much, just from that bit walk out of the village. Don't think there's ever been a murder on Rügen before, least not for years. Last one was that man in Sassnitz who threw his brother off a boat for…you know… *doing it* with his wife.'

Ortwin blushing to say the words out loud. You didn't grow up on a farm without knowing what that meant, where rutting was a commonality.

'Who are you anyway?' Ortwin asked. Ortwin insensible when Mergim had been brought out of the lake and Valter squirrelling his way back up to his camp afterwards.

'Valter,' said Valter.

'That it?' Ortwin asked back. 'Who are you related to? Who's your folk? I might know them.'

Rügen all Ortwin's world, where everyone was connected in some manner, defined by a complex intertwining between families, by roots laid down centuries before. Same roots that were dragging at Ortwin's feet, same roots he'd been thinking to escape by running off with the Pfiffmaklers. Or had been. Like you or I might have done, he was reconsidering his options; wondering if the quotidian might not be better than risking being skewered through the neck and left to die by the side of the road.

'You'll not know my folk,' Valter replied shortly. 'I don't even know my folk.'

Ortwin puckering his brows, not understanding.

'How not? How can you not know your folk? You must have come from somewhere.'

Valter taking a deep breath, for how to explain to a lad like this all that had happened to a lad like Valter way back when.

'I came out of Albania,' Valter decided on, 'and never went back. No one left alive to go see. And that was a very, very long time ago.'

Ortwin silenced, having a hard time figuring how someone could be all alone without any kind of family. He mayn't like his own particularly much, but knew—right down to the thin soles of his third times hand-me-down boots—that anyone on Rügen, maybe everyone on Rügen, would always take in one of their own. Island folk not unlike Fairs' folk in that regard. It cast his heading out alone into Denmark in a whole new light. And not a good one. Would have asked more of Valter except they'd just turned onto the track going along the bottom of the forest and there, in front of them, not far from the path leading up to the beeches, were the rest of the Pfiffmaklers dragging at their carts, obviously finding the going hard now their numbers were depleted, despite the addition of Diderik.

Ortwin and Valter wilting at the sight, at what they were going to have to say.

Ortwin and Valter silenced, the enormity of that saying weighing on them like a newly fallen tree upon their shoulders.

'Stick close. Keep quiet,' Valter advised Ortwin. 'God knows how they're going to take it. You still want to run away with the circus?'

And then Ortwin did the oddest thing, at least the oddest thing Valter had experienced for a long time: Ortwin put out his thin fingers and laced them through Valter's own, grasped him tightly and would not let go.

'I don't want to tell them,' Ortwin whispered. 'How can we tell them?'

That ball of ice in Valter's stomach resurfacing, pushing up into his throat. So many bad things he'd done, yet this seemed the worst. His only comfort, his only confidence, being this unknown child's skinny fingers gripping at his own.

'You don't got to,' Valter croaked. 'Leave me to do the telling.'

Gripping tightly back. Glancing up into the sky. Hoping for that great blue sail that might yet carry him away.

But no.

The sky had closed over.

Clouds massing up to west and north: heavy, yellow-bellied, promising snow would soon be all about them, and soon was. Only a pinch, a few sporadic flakes large as moths and as feathery. One fluttering against Valter's cheek, another on his shoulder, another onto Ortwin's dirt-brown hair. And then there was Wenzel taking off his harness, striding forward, demanding crossly what was what and what the hell were plans for if they were so easily broken. Wenzel frowning up into the sky as if it were defying him, as if he'd assumed mastery, as if he believed all of nature was at his beck and call. Valter getting all that boiling back in his head. These bloody Pfiffmaklers, who'd seen him as a louse tolerated only because of Andreas despite itching to crush him underfoot first chance they got.

By Christ, man, you don't change.

Valter incensed at Wenzel, wanting no part of this. Had never wanted any part of this. Valter about to blurt everything out in the crudest possible way for maximum hurt, until Ortwin's hand squeezed against his own and gave him mercy, reminded him of the other side of life, the one that had family at its core, the one Valter would never be a part of and hankered after all the same.

Tried to say it gently. Tried to say it right. In the end was reduced to saying it as it was, as Wenzel creased his brows and stared him down.

'It's Peppe, sir,' Valter said quietly, that deferential 'sir' popping out of nowhere. 'He's dead, by Rasvlach's hand we assume. The others have gone directly on, sent us back to…'

Wenzel no longer listening, Valter petering out. Wenzel standing stock still for ten seconds, eyelids flickering, mouth working. Nothing coming out. Then Wenzel back to his crew, shoulders hunched like the harness was still upon them and thunder crashing all about. Valter and Ortwin watching silently as he imparted the blow that had Rosa clapping her hands to her cheeks and Yssel dissolving to the ground, face as wet and white as the snow onto which she sank; Lupercal and Jericho jittering and twitching like aspen leaves in the wind. Ortwin's young heart tearing for them; Ortwin detaching himself from Valter, approaching on shaking legs, going where he was needed most, where others feared to tread. Ortwin sitting beside Yssel, who lowered her head onto his young shoulder and wept.

Jesus, Valter thought, as the scene scrolled out slowly before him like a Pfiffmakler panorama. *How much more does this family have to take?*

Valter, so unaccustomed to empathy, feeling a twisting in his gut and a choke in his throat as he watched the tatters of the Pfiffmaklers shake and collapse through the shifting screens of snow no one else had noticed falling.

Valter closing wet and thankful eyes as the inappropriately beautiful and gentle dance played upon him and all around him, cutting him off from the Pfiffmaklers and their woe-filled, wailing grief.

Valter knowing he was forgotten.

Valter turning on his heel.

Valter thinking at first to go back to his camp in the tree glade above the lake and being done with it; Valter changing his mind.

Valter heading on up after the other rags of the Pfiffmaklers. Valter pausing only once, to take from his pack the snub of hedgehoggery Peppe had carved for Andreas's cairn, placing it on the heap of Peppe as he passed for no other reason than it seeming right and fitting. Valter such a stranger to what was right and fitting he shocked himself by choking up once more, had to physically shake himself out of it before heading off after Mergim and the others. He didn't know what lay ahead any more than did the Pfiffmaklers. Had an urgent need, like them, for direction and it seemed the only direction was to go on.

The younger Pfiffmaklers, towards whom Valter was aiming, were mute as they processed towards the top end of Rügen Island, until the snow began to fall.

'That's all we need,' Pietro muttered although Heraldo, who had fallen into step beside him, did not agree.

'It's to the good,' Heraldo said. 'It'll mask Philbert's trail. Make it harder for Rasvlach to find him.'

It took all Pietro had to not to throw a fist into Heraldo's handsome face for making their going all to do with Philbert. The mere mention of his name made Pietro flinch.

Don't you speak to me about him, went Pietro's internal monologue. *If it wasn't for him, and your caring about him, then my wife and child might have stood a chance of being alive. And what about Peppe? Have you forgotten about him?*

Aware he was being unjust, Heraldo merely trying to give everyone aim, take the good out of the bad, but Pietro couldn't stop himself. He didn't give a curse about Philbert any more. Didn't give a curse about what had brought them to this island. All Pietro cared about was the son-of-a-bitch he held responsible for all that had happened since they'd come here. Wanted to look Georg Rasvlach in the eye and ask him: *Why? Why have you done all this?*

I ain't done nothing, came the reply in Pietro's head. *Nothing to do with me how your lady died. Not my fault Mergim and Valter turned up on your doorstep and she took a fright and went the way she did. Only thing I'm after is the Anatomist's Dream, and I'm surely not the only one looking for him. It ever occur to you that's what Mergim and Valter are really after? Trying to pip me to the post? And they're the ones to blame for your lady's passing, if anyone is. Nothing to do with me.*

Pietro pushing forward, trying not to believe his internal Rasvlach, although how was it less preposterous for Mergim and Valter seeking them out in order to see how Hulde was doing than it was for them to be tracking Philbert, who had such a huge reward on his huge head? Maybe they'd started as one thing, ended as another. Valter never a trustworthy man, and who knew anything about Mergim other than that years ago he'd been a murderer and a kidnapper who'd backed the wrong horse and swiftly changed sides when he'd little option to do otherwise. Maybe the Rasvlach in his head was right, and Pietro putting blame in the wrong place.

Or maybe, came the voice again, *there's no one to blame at all. Maybe Livia would have miscarried and died without any outside intervention.*

Pietro's head battering him, hammering out the worst.

And ever thought on this, Pietro? That you're the one to blame? Remember Rosa saying to you and Livia, when you first told her your joyous news, how dangerous such a pregnancy could be so late in a woman's life? How she offered you an out, offered to get rid? How you both said no, wouldn't consider such an option.

Late spring back then, ditches dancing with Queen of the May and Milk Parsley, swallowtails the size of your hand flittering and settling on that white-as-weddings flower froth; luminous green of the beech leaves, air sweet-laden beneath the limes. Livia blooming with them, Livia carrying their own new life of Euforia, Eurydice or Meraviglio Pietro Benedetta. Life so perfect it seemed nothing could go wrong.

It's all gone wrong. The words forming and reforming in Wenzel's head and on his lips like starlings gathering at dusk before the roost. Words blackening his sight, blocking out the light, crowding out everything bar themselves.

Livia and her child are dead, and now Peppe too. And the children are hot-footing it through an unknown land on the trail of a fugitive and a murderer.

Wenzel thinking back to the morning when he'd learned Heraldo had disobeyed him and decided unilaterally to bring Philbert in.

We don't need this kind of trouble. It's madness.

We can't just turn our backs on him. He's one of our own. Think on what would have happened to Hulde if we'd done the same to her.

Perhaps all the more reason we should help him.

Those last words being Peppe's. Peppe the only Pfiffmakler to share Heraldo's and Ludmilla's concerns for Philbert, the only one who'd agreed it was the right thing to do.

He's a boy got himself into a bad situation, too young to even understand why, Peppe had said. *If we don't help him then who will? It's our duty, Wenzel, whether we like it or no.*

Our duty.

Peppe always so grateful to the Pfiffmaklers for taking him and Rosa in, and always so caring of others; Peppe the first to welcome Livia and Pietro into their ranks with open arms; Peppe the one who'd thought to whittle out that little hedgehog to honour Andreas; he and Pietro the only ones to bother comforting the wretch Valter after the rest of them had buried Andreas and believed their duty done.

Their duty.

Wenzel getting stuck on that word for, despite all that had happened, the Pfiffmaklers still had their code of honour to uphold, their word as honest Fairs' folk at stake. Lose that honour, that belief in it, and they would lose everything.

All or nothing in their world.

The pouch of letters and passes amassed so painstakingly over the previous fifty years by Old Grandma, which had done them so well since her leaving, would mean nothing if word got around the Pfiffmaklers had bowed down and betrayed one of their own. Philbert not unknown; Philbert a hero to all fairs folk from here to who knew where, and it wouldn't take long for folk to know if and when the Pfiffmaklers had thrown him to the dogs.

Result being the Pfiffmaklers abjured by anyone who might have previously fought for a few minutes at their table. Pfiffmaklers reviled, elbowed out of the main fairs by any means necessary. Pfiffmaklers shoved into the margins like that sorry Pulcinella in her grimy skirts. Everything they'd done, everything Old Grandma had fought for at so much cost to herself, of no more worth.

All that would become of their legacy being: *The Pfiffmaklers? The Pfiffmaklers! I'll not sully my lips with their name. They're the ones delivered Philbert, the Anatomist's Dream, our hero of the revolutions—a Fair's Person no less—to that megalomaniac Metternich.*

Wenzel swallowed, steeled himself, made a decision.

'Rosa, Yssel,' he spoke quietly, not the time or place to shout out orders. 'Go back to Sagard with the boys. Ortwin will go with you. Ortwin, get some men organised to come and bring Peppe in. And our carts.'

Carts abandoned by the side of the track; snow-covered misshapen parcels below the fir trees like demonic Christmas gifts.

No remonstrations from either of the women. No *but what about you? What will you do?* For they already knew what Wenzel would do. He would go directly after Rasvlach and the remaining family and would not stop until he had them found. Neither did Lupercal nor Jericho argue as they might usually have done.

'Look after your mother and your aunt,' Wenzel asked of them. 'Keep them safe. Find lodgings. Pastor Hulm will help. And you, with me,' he added, pointing at Diderik, who'd shuffled off to one side during the proceedings. Diderik drooped and forlorn, partaking to himself his own share of the guilt.

It's all gone wrong, he was thinking. *If only I'd never agreed to help Rasvlach escape Kragujevac. I should instead have gone home to Mama, begged work in uncle's shop, learned how to measure out linens and lace like she always wanted.*

But like an idiot he had not. He'd served his time, and couldn't contemplate going back to the tedium of everyday life in the village where everyone would laugh and sneer at him for the stupidity of his crimes; saw in Rasvlach an exit strategy, a brother-in-arms, a man who would lead him into exciting adventures and brave deeds. All come to this: to Diderik standing in the falling snow, watching yet more lives collapse and implode because of Rasvlach. Horrid vision in him of Rasvlach severing the hand off that man with the tattooed head and throwing it to the dogs while its owner watched and howled.

Rasvlach throwing everything to the dogs, Diderik's life included, for what came after this he didn't know. Stranded in a strange country with strange people and no way to get home again, probably ever. Eyes welling up to think of his mother, how disappointed she must be in him. Hard enough for her when he'd been caught thieving, bringing such shame on the family; recalled seeing her sitting at the back of the court house when he'd been sentenced, his trial lasting less than ten minutes.

Did you see this young man take the aforementioned bottles of wine and the watermelon?

A watermelon! What had he been thinking? About the last thing you could hide about your person; but he'd been drunk, and very thirsty, and anyway he'd been dared, and you couldn't go back on a dare.

I did, your Honour.

And you, Madam. I believe you witnessed this same young man fleeing from the scene?

I did, your Honour. Almost did myself a damage tripping over that watermelon when he dropped it.

And that was that. Two witnesses to his crime and two years in Kragujevac because of it. Ten minutes to change the course of his life; ten short minutes, two bottles of cheap Serbian wine and that blasted watermelon. And Rasvlach. No getting away from the latter. He'd tried to escape him. Wenzel Pfiffmakler undoing all that.

'You. With me.'

Diderik unfolding himself and obeying, regarding Wenzel's hard face, knowing he had no choice.

What would come would come, as it always did. And who was watermelon-and-two-cheap-bottles-of-wine Diderik to stand in its way?

How To Point A Pig

'I can hear the sea,' Ludmilla murmured after an hour or so of tramping up the track, snow obfuscating their view if not immediately soaking into their clothes, instead alit and was brushed off with ease and gave more light than the lowering afternoon might otherwise have afforded.

'Me too,' Heraldo agreed. 'What do you think we should do when we get to Glowe?'

Heraldo walking beside his wife all this while, seeing the strain of her father's death in every step she took, feeling it with her. Peppe a constant throughout his life, a second father, who had facilitated the greatest joy in his life—apart from Ludmilla—by bringing abandoned instruments back to life. Peppe patiently teaching him the skills he needed in choosing the right kind of wood for the purpose, how to cure, carve and hone it.

Without wood there would be so much less music, Heraldo. Think on that! Only flutes made of bones, organs of mud and reeds. And no almond oil. Your mother and aunt would have skin rough as dogfish without rubbing it in every night. Ha! Tell me I'm wrong.

Heraldo could not. Peppe right, as so often. Heraldo as grieved by his death as Ludmilla was. And all the more reason to go on, do what Peppe had wanted, which was to see Philbert right. Peppe the only one to stand up against Wenzel and come out in favour of Heraldo's and Ludmilla's schemes to help the boy. Heraldo nevertheless wishing he'd never set eyes on Philbert and put all this in motion.

Heraldo remembering a night by the fire a few months previously, somewhere outside Leipzig when they'd been happy enough, the Pfiffmaklers. The older ones, Livia and Peppe amongst them, sitting off by themselves repainting puppets, preparing scripts and the evening meal; Longhella away with her bow and arrows to murder small animals for the pot; Heraldo tweaking at several instruments to get them in tune with each other for their next day's performance; Hulde sitting by Ludmilla as they darned several pairs of well-worn socks; Lupercal and Jericho as restless as ever when they weren't turning somersaults and leap-frogging over one another as they practised their routines.

A wind-rustling autumn evening opening the door into winter, the first frost yet to come.

'We should play a game while dinner's getting ready,' Ludmilla had said, as Lupercal darted past her, jogging her elbow, making her stab her needle into her finger.

'Which one?' he immediately asked, tarrying a while as he watched the back of Hulde's head, the smooth skin of her neck, admiring her deft needlework so much better than Ludmilla's, despite it being Ludmilla who had taught her the skill.

'The one Pietro invented,' Ludmilla answered, rethreading her needle.

Lupercal screwing up his eyes, pretending to forget.

'Can't recall,' he said, getting a punch in his side from Hulde.

'You know fine well which one,' Hulde remonstrated. 'The one where you get as many words in the sentence to start with the same letter.'

A game devised by Pietro especially for her so she could improve her vocabulary which back then had been pitiful, trying out new languages she'd not been born to, soaking up the basics soon enough if not the details.

Ludmilla dipping her head in agreement.

'Hulde, do you want to choose the start word?'

Hulde pausing her needlework.

'Eurydice,' she announced, thinking on Pietro and Livia. Hulde the only one to whom they'd confided their choice of names and sworn her to secrecy, but this was hardly breaking a confidence. Eurydice part of the fables and fairy tales that were the lifeblood of the Pfiffmaklers, and all well versed.

'So it's a doubler,' Jericho sighed, as he joined them, meaning extra points to whomever could get in part of the actual myth from which Eurydice came; Jericho nevertheless getting down cross-legged beside them preparing to do battle.

'Ooh, I love a doubler!' Lupercal exclaimed, sitting beside Jericho, mind already working, always better at this game than his brother, getting out a pouchful of marbles for the scoring. 'Can I start?'

'Start away,' Ludmilla said, smiling over at Heraldo who lifted his head from his work and smiled back.

Such easy times, no trouble in them. Months to go before they got to Rostock and Heraldo had sifted Philbert from the crowds.

'Excellent Eurydice,' Lupercal began, exclaiming loudly, 'expired essentially from excess enamour and ended in Elysia. And… I name Jericho!'

Lupercal notching up to himself eight Es and an extra one for being relevant to the tale. A tidy pile of marbles to mark his success.

Jericho grinding his teeth, nominated to carry on the story using the next letter of Eurydice's name without having time to properly think. Staggering like a grouchy bear through his sentence.

'Until…unfortunately…she upfound herself in the underworld…'

His brother laughing.

'Upfound! No such word, though we'll take it. Nothing like a bit of invention. So that's four to Jericho, and another for relevance. Who do you name?'

Jericho a little annoyed, but a game was a game, and he'd time to catch up.

'I name Heraldo.' Looking over a little sheepishly at Heraldo, who was almost as bad at this game as he. Heraldo plucking a few strings as if to remind them all that where Eurydice was concerned Heraldo was Orpheus with his lyre. Heraldo smiling broadly because, unwittingly, Jericho had given him a plum of adverbs to use as he wished.

'Reckless, recondite, remorseful, repentant, his reciprocations returned and requited,' good Lord, Heraldo was on a roll, 'our Romeo Orpheus returns to redress and right the wrong…and I know that wrong is spelled with a W, but I offer it as an honorary R.'

'Oh well done!' Hulde clapping, beaming over at Heraldo, needle abandoned in her half-darned sock.

'That's eleven!' Lupercal counting out the marbles without rancour. 'One more again for relevance and another if we add the honorary. Do we agree to the honorary?'

All agreed. Fourteen a damn good score.

And now came the reason Heraldo recalled this particular scene at this particular time as they tramped towards Glowe through the snow, having just at that moment become aware of the sea and therefore were almost at the coast and maybe their goal.

Hulde named next; Hulde taking a minute or two before beginning, as was acceptable within the parameters of the game.

'Why,' she began, 'if I too can invoke the honorary Y. Why, Orpheus, did you yaw your way into hell, yell and yowl and yarely get your yeo-woman, yet yield to your yearnings, yaw back your sight so you'd to leave your loving yeo-woman behind?'

Exclamations of appreciation for her dexterity with the Ys, although in truth if you knew your Ys, which Hulde did, then there weren't that many of them to remember and make use of once you'd got their meanings sorted.

'That's sixteen,' Lupercal quickly clacking out his marbles, 'one more for the honorary and an extra point for relevance—so eighteen altogether. Highest score so far! Highest score ever!'

Game passing to Ludmilla, who'd been spectacularly bad with the D's, and next back to Jericho who'd redeemed himself with the I's.

Heraldo not pushing the memory further, for Hulde's part was what seemed so relevant to him now. Orpheus and Eurydice: Orpheus's urgent quest to bring his loved one back from the underworld and reintroduce her to life; about to succeed until, by stupidity, hubris or bad judgement—a triumvirate of flaws no one should admire singly, and certainly not together—he'd done precisely what he'd been told not to do: he'd looked back. Eurydice thereby dragged kicking and howling from the promise of light back into the darkness of the underworld, condemned to gnash her teeth in its perpetual night and curse the idiot Orpheus for offering hope before snatching it back again. Heraldo measuring himself against Orpheus: both musicians, both setting themselves tasks of redemption, both failing spectacularly and with dismal predictability, given their shared flaws.

Stupidity, hubris and bad judgement.

Doing what they'd been warned repeatedly not to do.

Heraldo thinking back to that quiet village on the edge of the quiet forest, the fog breathing in off the sea; a sea as smooth and untroubled as a pool of quicksilver, its surface broken only by Heraldo drawing his boat in by the broken-down pier, the two swans paddling beneath its blackened boards lifting their wings into baskets and soon away into the dense mist.

'Is it you?'

'It's I.'

Heraldo believing himself a noble saviour, the only person prepared to do the deed that needed doing.

Hubris.

Heraldo believing he'd devised a fool proof plan that could not be thwarted.

Bad judgement.

Heraldo believing nothing could go wrong.

Stupidity.

And because of his triumvirate of flaws he'd condemned his family to a darkness they would never escape; his family hollowed out at the core like a deer hung up by its heels and gralloched, paunch disembowelled, left to lie steaming in the snow.

Like Peppe.

Heraldo would never forgive himself.

Stark dread in him that neither would his family—for how could they?—the Pfiffmaklers, as they'd been a few days before, at an end.

'Look!' Ludmilla's hand upon his arm as she pointed onwards, Heraldo unable to lift his eyes from his feet, unable to comply, black dog gripping at heart and head with his all-consuming guilt.

'Just look, will you,' Ludmilla came again, shaking his arm. 'There's something on that tree. It's a message. It has to be from Philbert.'

Heraldo closing his eyes, taking a deep breath before coming back into the world as the unfortunate, unrescued, unrejoicing Eurydice would never do.

Squarish circle in the holly bark: *I hope you're seeing this.*

Triangle on the next ash: *I'm here and haven't forgotten.*

X on the young maple a few yards on: *Danger still abounding.*

Below, a horizontal line, a rough square with a dot inside: *Looking for a place to hide.*

And, below that, two more scratchy circles Philbert hoped the Pfiffmaklers would interpret as: *Keep looking for more of these and nearby will I be.*

Philbert reaching the chalk cliffs at the other end of Jasmund Forest that fell down sheer into the sea; Philbert seeing Glowe village below him on a small isthmus pushing out into the Baltic and, beyond Glowe, a wide causeway linking the peninsula of Jasmund to that of Wittow. Rügen not so much one island as an archipelago connected by a network of lagoons fed at their seaward side by the Greifwalder Bodden pushing its way in a ragged circle from Stralsund up channels into lakes and lagoons that would have ended back where they'd started, had not that small land bridge going from Lietzow to Sagard and Sassnitz stood in their way. The same place by the lake the Pfiffmaklers had made camp.

For Philbert, a few hours ahead of the Pfiffmaklers, the snow had not yet begun to fall. He could smell it in the air, knew it was not far off; the day beginning to tire and falter beneath the heavy clouds seemingly intent on bringing afternoon into evening before its time. And so, at the very neck of Jasmund, he left more marks in the trees for the Pfiffmaklers, moved back not into the forest but down the track and off into the scrubland on the other side as he sought somewhere he could make a rudimentary hide for himself and Kroonk.

Battering his way through coppice and undergrowth, through gorse and juniper; finding a small glade of willow and alder by a stream running into the vast lagoon below separating him from Glowe. Couched himself up, got Kroonk settled, slashed at a few branches to give themselves shelter, which was when the snow began to fall. Philbert sitting on a square of tarpaulin to keep himself dry, learning early doors, in the first months of exile without protection of tents and carts, how to avoid what was essentially trench-foot of the buttocks.

Philbert putting his arm about Kroonk's neck, keeping her close, when he was troubled by a shout resounding through the still air, words unarticulated to Philbert's ear though no mistaking the challenge, the anger, or maybe anguish, within them. And more shouts, not long after.

Clear as the water running by his feet that his earlier suspicions had been correct and someone other than the Pfiffmaklers was on Rügen and on his trail, most likely that son-of-a-bitch from Serbia the hummingbird lady in Rostock had warned him of.

Philbert deducing that he could surely only have got so close by following the Pfiffmaklers who, unlike Philbert, had made no secret of their movements; meaning, therefore, that he knew of their attempts to aid him. Philbert putting interpretation to that shouting. It could have been anyone. Children gathering wood, nuts or fungi, pausing in their work to pelt each other with snowballs, rioting in the late afternoon before heading home to farmyard duties, fireside or church. Then again it could have been one of the Pfiffmaklers, interfered with in some unspecified way by Philbert's unknown assailant.

Being cautious, Philbert chose to believe the latter. Which belief in turn led him to another: Heraldo's attempts to help him gone badly awry and no rescue for Philbert, no matter how many signs he'd carved into trees.

Philbert having to consider he was as he had always been since Schleswig-Holstein, which was alone.

Himself and Kroonk left to look out for themselves.

Pfiffmaklers no longer to be relied upon.

Time to help himself.

He'd one advantage: he'd Kroonk. She was no night owl, could see no better in the dark than he could. But point a hungry pig in the right direction and she will always find the quickest way to food, meaning the quickest way to Glowe. Her nose would take him efficiently from the high places to the low, from this side of the lagoon to the other. And, once there, they could cross the causeway into Wittow beneath the banner of the fast-approaching night.

Kroonk Lives Up To Her Calling

Wenzel was raging. No tempering of that rage by grief, grief instead making his anger all the sharper, all the more vicious. Livia's dying had been one thing; tragic, yet a death that may or may not have happened all on its own. Peppe's murder quite another, Peppe Wenzel's closest friend and confidante, apart from Rosa herself. More frightening was the notion that it mightn't have been Peppe at all, for any one of them would have done as far as Rasvlach was concerned: Longhella or Ludmilla, Heraldo or Hulde. Assassination of the Pfiffmaklers a perk on Rasvlach's path to Philbert, Peppe presumably merely the closest and easiest target.

Wenzel barging up the track leading first to Heraldo's hopeful beech trees, ignoring them and ignoring Diderik who was hopping and running to keep up with his fast pace. Only thought in Wenzel being to hem in the bastard who'd done for Peppe before he got to any more of them. One part of the family already going up the leftward side of Jasmund Forest, Wenzel's idea being to close in from the other side, get to the path going along the top of the cliffs, cut off any escape. Plainly Philbert had shifted himself out from the depths of the forest and drawn Rasvlach with him, and Rasvlach had taken advantage when the Pfiffmaklers had come looking for him. Wenzel unsure at that point whom he despised the most: Philbert, for not having the courage to wait in the forest for Heraldo, or Rasvlach, who had looked through the whole lot of them like they were made of glass.

Either way he wanted blood.

Simmering over with the need for it.

No caring for the luminosity of the afternoon, nor the snow silently bestowing beauty from its arms, layering the gaunt trees, softening the ground beneath his feet.

Had it swept over Rügen in an avalanche it wouldn't have stopped him, and never would there be enough of it to wash clean Rasvlach's slate.

'It's getting dark,' Mergim observed. 'We should either go back or get ourselves prepared for the night.'

'We're not going back,' Ludmilla stated, giving Longhella's hand a quick squeeze, the two sisters marching side by side since they'd caught the vague murmurings of the sea, hand in hand, the closest they'd been to each other in years, a joining of siblings in the face of inexpressible loss. Hulde, pale and trembling, behind them with Heraldo, Mergim in the lead, Pietro at their backs.

'There's nothing we can do,' Heraldo offered. 'We've to go back.'

Heraldo seeing the stiffening of Ludmilla's and Longhella's collective shoulders. The two back to being one, the twins folk had taken them to be when they were younger.

'We've to find Philbert,' Ludmilla replied for them both, 'else all this is meaningless.'

'I agree,' Pietro said, for he had no intention of returning, even if he went on alone.

Everyone's eyes until then forward to the track, glancing from side to side in case of possible attack; only Hulde entranced by the snow, keeping her face upturned, feeling the chill of it to be warranted if not the gentle thrill it gave her to watch the snowflakes waltz, drift and settle. A raw wonder in her there was beauty in a world as terrible as it had recently become.

And every single flake different, if the men who study them can be believed, Heraldo had once told her. Hulde taken aback, not so much that it might be true but that people studied snowflakes. *They capture them and put them between glass slides, look at them under their microscopes. And so far no one has ever found two the same. Just like you. Only one Hulde in this world.*

And only one Heraldo! she'd been quick enough back, the two of them laughing like mules having thrown their packs. Hulde thinking the world would a better place if there were more than one Heraldo in it. And more than one Livia, and more than one Peppe. Hulde squeezing shut her eyes to think on it, tears leaking down her cheeks. Pietro's two short words, *I agree,* immediately at her back, startling her; opening her eyes, hit straight on by a snowflake, blurring her sight, making her blink, made her head twist on her neck to aid its dissipation.

'Oh wait!' Hulde called out. 'Look! Look over there!'

The cortege had dribbled to a stop with the brief argument about whether to go on or retreat, everyone following her pointing finger.

'It's another circle,' Hulde exclaimed. 'Right there, oh and see that? There's another mark just beyond.'

Gouged point, horizontal line— *Going to the left.*

Philbert's scouring marks catching a few snowflakes where the rest had been unable to settle and drifted off beyond, these smaller trees not having the protection of the many in the forest.

'He's near, then,' Ludmilla stated grimly. 'Anyone for going back now?'

No one.

Mergim, at the forefront of their party, better accustomed to moving about in near darkness than most—Kragujevac never a fun-filled, light-humming place—heading to the left as Philbert had directed, scrambling down a short slope through copse and shrub, holding up a hand as the others slipped and slid, skimbleshanked, behind him.

'Water,' he whispered. 'I hear running water.'

Eyes peeled.

Memory coming back to him, his father telling him: *If you're up in the mountains and short on water, always look out for alders or willows. Especially willows. They're bound to water like babes to milk.*

He was far from the mountains now, but the adage held true: willows still bound to water, and there were willows a hundred yards away from him to his right. Crack willows he'd guess, the reddish hue of their branches barely visible in the failing light; willows, and green alder alongside them, and water running by their feet.

The perfect place to hide had you been sifted out of the forest by a man like Rasvlach. Shelter and water your most basic needs. Rasvlach would know that too, then again he didn't have the advantage of carvings left in trees, only tracks through the forest surely by now covered by the falling snow. Other signs to follow of course and, although this group of Pfiffmaklers had been silent in their moving since they'd covered over Peppe, Mergim knew there was no guarantee. They'd gone straight up the track and had not tarried, except to send Valter and Ortwin back; they'd not deviated from their path, had not sent scouts out to left or right, nor had he made them do so. They'd looked out all that while for another attack, although none had come.

And, horrible thought in Mergim, why would it?

What would it profit Rasvlach?

Rasvlach in the raw would be like Mergim's father: men who lived by hunting. Rasvlach doing as Mergim's father would have done when trailing a wary target—a mountain lion or a wolf—animals who were also hunters and knew all the tricks. Rasvlach had gone for a weakness, had riled the Pfiffmaklers by killing one of their own, poked the bear out of its den. Guessing, correctly, that such an action would not deter them, instead hasten them, harden their resolve, push them onwards. A group easier to track than a singleton, no matter how quiet they'd believed themselves to be. All he had to do was remain in the trees, match them pace for pace as they went up their path. Pfiffmaklers doing the hard work for him, leading him to his goal.

Mergim suddenly aware how vulnerable they'd made themselves: out in the open, at the bottom of a slope, nowhere immediate to hide. Mergim scanning the top of the bank looking for humps and bumps, anything that might be Rasvlach lowering himself down onto his stomach preparing to throw out another knife. And no doubt he had a stock of them for just such a situation as this. Mergim grabbing at Ludmilla, commanding her, *sotto voce*, to run for the willow copse, telling each in turn as they arrived at the bottom of the slope. Hulde the last, Hulde pulled off her feet as Mergim's large hand went over her mouth and another about her waist, curling himself over her, drawing her with him as he saw a flash of silver up above.

Could have been a sliver of the newly risen moon glimpsed between the falling snow, could have been a white-winged barn owl swooping low and moving on. Or could have been Rasvlach lifting his knife, preparing to strike.

Philbert heard noises out there in the near night and pulled Kroonk towards him, pulled their shared blanket a little closer about her for she was shivering, as was he, not so much with cold as with dread anticipation.

'Bad stars, bad nights,' Philbert whispered. 'But it won't be our last, old girl, I can promise you that.'

An empty promise, though Kroonk making a noise in her throat that in a cat would have been a purr; Kroonk happy beside her master, her partner, her friend. Both tired and oh so long in the running; both prepared to run a little further if needs be. Philbert unfolding the topography of the land in his head, this place not chosen lightly: the stream by their feet clearly seen earlier in the afternoon to make its meandering way slowly down towards a crick of the lagoon below, and the sparse lights of the village beyond. Unfolding too his plan for his and Kroonk's survival, getting ready to move: follow the stream, head towards the village, turn left as they reached its outskirts and away they'd be across the thickly wooded causeway and into Wittow. Evening swift and wild with snow which would aid them, just needed to wait until there was darkness enough to cloak them.

Philbert holding his breath.

Sounds coming closer, footsteps quick and hurried; surely more than one person, surely several. He cocked his head, he stood, back bowed beneath their makeshift bivouac of bent willow and green alder. Philbert swiftly lifting their tarpaulin, getting it rolled and stowed into his pack, checking the rope about his waist attaching him to Kroonk, preparing to move and move quickly.

Then a voice, low-rolled and soft as the snow but recognisable; if not the caller then the words:

'Is it you?'

Phrase repeated, urgent, insistent.

'Is it you?'

And then another voice, a young woman's.

'Are you sure he's here? I can't see a blasted thing and all these blasted branches are catching at my hair.'

'God's sake, Longhella. Keep your voice down! Ever thought of becoming an auctioneer at a goose market?'

Philbert arrested in his flight, Philbert smiling, for oh so good it was to hear that bickering again. Years since he'd last met the Pfiffmaklers at the opening of the Great Magendie's aqueduct, but lord, he remembered that bickering well. The two sisters in their orange skirts, the long plaits of hair sleeked down their backs like snakes that had abjured their winter hiding. The two of them so alike they might have been twins, except for one being marginally older than the other.

'You're not telling me I've just come up all these steps for nothing,' the younger one had grumbled.

'I'm not telling you anything,' the older had retorted. 'I'm simply letting you know what I've been told and that the fool they call the Great Magendie has shut his doors on us and everyone else, never to know the glories of the Pfiffmaklers.'

'For why?' Longhella had retorted. 'He invited us up. What's he doing changing his mind, goddamn it? And now look. I've only gone and ripped my blasted skirt.'

No hesitation in Philbert then, Philbert responding as he'd done before in the silent village on the outskirts of the forest. Philbert not abandoned by the Pfiffmaklers after all, and couldn't have been more glad for it. Philbert crawling out of his shelter and leaning towards the voices.

'It's I,' he said quietly. 'It's Philbert. I'm over here.'

First time he'd spoken his name or heard it since he'd left Maulwerf's Fair of Wonders on the edge of the ice, apart from at Professor Ullendorf's Anchorage, which for him had been no Anchorage at all.

Pietro hadn't followed Mergim and the Pfiffmaklers down the slope. Pietro had stayed up top, taken out his knife and prepared for Rasvlach bearing down on them. Small flash of silver in the falling night. He could hear the others scuffling through the snow and then into a thicket of green alder and willow not easy to navigate; a stramash of creaking branches and the rustling of year-end leaves as they pushed their way through. Pietro holding his post until all were in, and still did not follow.

Rasvlach had to be out here somewhere, biding his time.

Pietro under no illusion that they'd managed to slip up the snowy track unnoticed.

Pietro on the alert, detecting a shadow lumbering up the track they'd recently left.

Pietro checking his blade.

An everyday knife, used for eating meals, slicing sausages, meat and bread; nothing like as sharp as those the Pfiffmakler women kept for personal protection and for gutting and skinning animals for the pot. But plunge it in deep, with enough force behind it, and it would do the job. And nothing Pietro wanted more than to plunge it in deep and hard.

Pietro getting into a crouch as the shadow got nearer; no knowing who it was, snow dancing like a million mayflies over spring waters.

Pietro waiting and waiting, heart steady as an old grandfather clock tick-tocking in some ancient hallway, its calm pendulum determined by a vengeance insistent on having its day. And then he was up on his heels and springing into the line of fire, knife held high, ready to thrust it in and in, again and again.

Wenzel noted the falling light with grim stoicism. He'd gained the topmost path and was following it along the edge of the cliff and was almost at its end. He'd been marching like a fiend, Diderik's ragged panting behind him a constant reminder he was not alone. For a young man, Diderik didn't seem to be keeping up all that well. Being nearly frozen to death a couple of nights since being the most likely cause. Wenzel regretting bringing the lad with him but he was needed, sure and certain recognition of Rasvlach Wenzel's primary reason.

'We're at the top, lad,' he therefore said, to encourage Diderik on. 'Keep close. Keep to my back and stick to the path.'

As if Diderik needed telling. This mad dash through the snowy forest not anything he wanted to repeat, but more than that he didn't want to be left behind, be left alone, not while Rasvlach might be prowling somewhere nearby. Diderik knowing he'd be top of Rasvlach's list for getting rid once he'd secured his primary goal, which was the Anatomist's Dream. Everything in such a fangle, and Diderik having no idea how to get out of it. Yet there seemed to be loads of Pfiffmaklers and only one Rasvlach, so hope had to be on their side.

'Stop,' Wenzel commanded. Diderik obeying, taking the few yards separating them with uncertain strides, wanting to be as near to Wenzel as possible, pulling up a few inches behind Wenzel's back.

'What do you hear?' Wenzel asked. Diderik havering, Diderik listening, though mostly what he could hear was his own heart beating too loudly. Pushed it down. Tried to listen as commanded.

'The sea, I think,' he answered, uncertainly.

'Anything else?' Wenzel asked, Diderik trying to put a pause on his heart, trying to listen past it.

'A burn, maybe,' he said. 'And…something else. Something moving. Just away to our right.'

Diderik hoping he answered correctly. Remembering Kragujevac, the times he'd been asked some apparently simple question and replied wrongly. No understanding, not at first, how such questions were designed to elicit wrong answers. All part of the Kragujevac game. Those at the top beating down those at the bottom. Men meting out their punishments on others weaker, and Diderik weaker than most. Everyone knowing about the wine and the watermelon before he'd even passed through the gates. Hilarity their main reaction, and no answers ever good or right enough where Diderik was concerned.

How the lifers coped with it he didn't know.

Maybe they were a different breed.

Maybe they had different rules.

All Diderik knew was if he didn't stick to Wenzel he'd not a hope in hell of leaving Rügen alive.

'It's me! It's me!' Valter whispered loudly, as Pietro levelled his knife at Valter's throat, Pietro having sprung up out of nowhere and clamped himself about Valter, the point of his knife pushing hard against Valter's neck, too blunt to immediately draw blood.

Pietro's heart deflating as he realised his error.

'What are you doing here?' Pietro's voice sad and flat as he pulled away his knife. 'I thought you went with Ortwin to the others.'

'I did,' Valter said. 'And then I thought, well, what the hell. Might be better needed here.'

Pietro scratched his forehead, weighed up his options. Pietro looking at Valter.

If there was treachery here, he couldn't see it.

'Where did Wenzel go?' he asked. 'After you told him about Peppe?'

'He went up top of the island,' Valter gave the information without a beat. 'Took Diderik with him.'

'The idea being?' Pietro asked, Valter taking a few moments to answer as he thought it through, for Wenzel hadn't actually said.

'Pincer movement,' he replied slowly. 'Trying to hem Rasvlach in, would be my guess. You lot coming from one direction, him and Diderik from the other.' Valter looking about him. 'What happened to the others?'

Pietro motioning with his head, not wanting to be too precise. Valter still an unknown quantity.

'They've gone after the boy,' he said vaguely. 'But you and me, we're going on up. See if we can't do as Wenzel wants.'

Valter nodding. The afternoon had stepped into night but the pellucid path of the snowy track along the tree line enough to lead them to the coast. And they couldn't be far; the gloaming eerily calm and quiet, snow inhibiting bats and night-birds from leaving their varied nests. No flutterings from the forest, no cracking branches, no lift of leaves. The wind non-existent. Only the gentle flurrying of snow in this most silent of nights, the murmurs of the sea lapping the base of the chalk-white cliffs.

Rasvlach had to be out there somewhere, a slinking wolf, waiting to attack.

The hairs going up on the back of Valter's neck as he caught a scent on the air: the faintest whiff of smoke maybe, or no. More like fox-must, like they were near a den, the scent deep and disturbing: wet wool, damp leather, maybe a man's sweat. Valter staring into the darkness between the trees, seeing nothing. No flicker of movement, no ominously shifting shadows, no foxes, no Rasvlach. Not that he could see. Valter pulling his collar up about his bristly chin, panicked when he glimpsed the slightest movement up ahead.

Do me proud, Valter. Be the best man you can be

Valter catching at Pietro's arm, holding a finger to his lips, jutting his chin towards the forest. Pietro's sense of smell not so acute as Valter's.

'There's something up ahead, in the trees,' Valter whispered direct into Pietro's ear, for the softest sounds could carry far on still nights such as this. Valter directing Pietro across the track and into the ditch, Pietro obeying. Pietro going down on his knees once there, peering over the short embankment as Valter, shoulders hunched and tense, inched forward, wincing every time his boots made soft squeaks in the snow. Pietro's sense of smell might be intermittent, not so his eyesight; all the Pfiffmaklers, including the adopted Benedettas, spending a good part of their lives in semi-darkness, gathering firewood or erecting tents and canvases in the dimmest starlight when others, not so used to it, would be hard-pushed to make out their hand held up in front of their face. And, as Valter made his excruciatingly slow crawl onwards, Pietro saw a dark shape beyond him, not in the trees at all—which were almost at their end—but on the path clinging to the top of the chalk cliff like ermine stitched to the bottom of the cape he'd given Lydia last Christmas.

He crept along the ditch, keeping pace with Valter.

Got out his blunt-edged knife again and, when he judged the moment right, up he went in long-legged strides across the track as Valter too came to life, both slamming into Rasvlach—for who else could it be?—and bringing him down.

'We've actually found you!' Heraldo whispered, the first of the Pfiffmaklers to emerge crook-backed from the copse into a small clearing, seeing Philbert's pallid face peeking between branches which, momentarily, appeared like prison bars until he stood away from them, revealed himself fully. Kroonk bustling out on her rope, snuffling joyfully at Heraldo's legs.

'She remembers you,' Philbert observed. Heraldo absurdly joyful this should be so.

'She's one smart pig! I can't tell you how glad I am to see you. Are you well? Any sign of Rasvlach?'

Philbert raised his eyebrows.

'I don't know who that is,' he said, any further questions arrested by Ludmilla pushing into the clearing behind her husband, and next Longhella swearing bountifully beneath her breath.

'This skirt is going to take a month of buggering Sundays to sew back together. Look at all these rips! I might as well have hung it out on briars and let a pack of wild dogs have at it.'

'Hello to you too,' Philbert said brightly, amused by her truculence, until she turned her face towards him. No place for brightness there; hatred and hardness in every pretty line. No time to ask why, for on her heels came Hulde pushing through the tangles; Hulde wide-eyed and panicked; Mergim having no idea that by putting his hand across her face and another about her waist and pulling her with him he'd awoken every nightmare she'd ever had. Hulde stumbling towards them, grabbing frantically at Ludmilla's hand, Hulde breathing so quickly she feared she might faint as Mergim came on behind her and stood like a giant at her back.

'Saw something,' Mergim rasped. 'Movement up on the bank. We've to go.'

Philbert grabbing his pack and putting it on his back, no one arguing as he gave command.

'Down the burn,' he whispered quickly. 'It'll take us to the lagoon. Kroonk will lead the way.'

And so Kroonk did, as if she were a dog leading sheep; faint memory in Philbert's head of the farmer who'd had to move his flock because the larks trilling above his meadows were imitating his whistles so precisely they were confusing his dogs. Precisely what they needed now: confusion and misdirection, Philbert leaning in towards Heraldo and speaking softly; Heraldo nodding, taking the burn in one swift stride, moving back up the slope a little way, picking up stones as he went and shoving them into his pockets.

The rest going down and down behind Kroonk, whose snout snuffled unerringly along the water course, Kroonk picking her path careful and quick; everyone following, everyone's eyes accustoming to the darkness—forty-five minutes for the human eye to adjust from day to dusk to night, when the iris is at its most dilated and begins to interpret the world in shades of grey, aided this night by the reflectivity of the snow. Everyone tensing as they heard arrhythmic noises not too far distant, calmed by Philbert's whispers that it was Heraldo laying a false track.

Heraldo doing his job well. Nothing too obvious: a small sound here and there as he plinked his stones off into the undergrowth and up the slope, gathered together a few snowballs for good measure, lobbing them as far away as he could. Kept up the charade for ten more minutes before returning to the burn, following the mess of footprints; direction eased as he spied the glassy eye of the lagoon a half mile down below winking up at him through the snow. Heraldo cheered, Heraldo soon catching up the rest as they spilled out about the mouth of the burn where it joined the lagoon.

Everyone relaxing, breathing easier.

Believing themselves safe.

Vengeance, Like A Raging Wind

Oh Georg, my son. What have you done with your years?

I've learned, Father. I've tracked and hunted like you taught me to do.

And what have you learned, my brave treasured boy who was so quick to strike, who couldn't wait to release the arrow from its bow?

To trust my instincts, and no one but myself. I admit I slipped up there for a while with Diderik, but that's long gone.

Hard lessons, my boy, always hard learned, but you got there. So where are you going now?

I'm going alone into the dark, Father. But you taught me well, and I'm almost there.

And almost there was Rasvlach, almost down to the lagoon.

No hard thinking required about what his quarry might do or where they might go, not once Peppe had been despatched and

Rasvlach had headed quickly on up the track, got to its end, looked down on what lay below. Seeing a small farming and fishing village, people dotted about its edges in the late afternoon calling in their cattle to be milked, bringing in sheep and goats; heaving-to their boats, dragging in their catches, women coming out to dress the fish, put them on the griddle for their tea or salting them down for sale or the smoke-house.

Rasvlach no idiot when it came to people, studying them like he studied any animal he and his father had ever hunted, the lodestar being to understand their ways. And no way was Philbert going to rely on the Pfiffmaklers or put them in danger once he realised someone—Rasvlach—was in the forest with him. He would run the easiest path for escape. He would head to the coast instead of back into the forest. He would see this village, as Rasvlach had done, and see the causeway and try to get himself over. People as predictable as any other animal. Nothing special about the human race. They liked to think it so, but when bargained down to being the hunted they always reacted the same way as any animal.

Study the land, son. Be aware of the wider circles. Plan your attacks well and your defences better, for you will need defences when going after larger game.

In the early days, after escape from Kragujevac, he'd been content to wander wherever his latest commissions took him, moving from place to place without conscious plan. All changing once he'd got wind of the Philbert-Metternich situation. Time to be aware of those wider circles, to plan his attacks well and his defences better. And no better defence than to be going where no one will look for you. Rasvlach stitching together the topography of Germany as he passed through it, buying up piecemeal maps here and there, lists of waterways, railways, cities leading to other cities. Wiesbaden—where Metternich had resurfaced after years of exile in England—a long journey on Shanks's pony, and a track easily ambushed if you had angry Pfiffmaklers on your tail.

More fool you, Pfiffmaklers. By bringing Philbert to Rügen you've done me a service.

Rasvlach sorting through the maps in head and hand.

Never forget that once you've downed your prey you need to get it shifted. You can kill the largest elk in the forest, but you might as well have downed a mouse if you can't get it away.

Getting away from Rügen to Lubecker Bucht would be easy, islands always chockfull of boats garnered licitly or otherwise.

Water is your friend, son. It will hide your tracks, mask your scent and take you faster than your own two feet can carry you.

From Lubeck to Hamburg; from Hamburg on a vessel down the coast to Rotterdam with the head of the Anatomist's Dream soused in vodka.

Learn to lash a raft and you'll not go wrong. Use what you have about you. Make every second count.

And from Rotterdam up the Rhine to Wiesbaden, to the castle of Johannisberg.

To Metternich.

To Rasvlach's great reward.

All he needed do now was secure his prey, bring it down, get it shifted.

And, after an hour or so of patient waiting, he'd spied his prey slithering down the snow scree by the burn, movement easy to pick out in this white-filled, snow-reflecting night.

Thank you, Father. You've taught your Georg well.

Still a way to go, for Philbert was not alone. How he'd caught up with the Pfiffmaklers, or the Pfiffmaklers with him, was a mystery. But mysteries didn't interest Rasvlach. Rasvlach all about the doing: lashing his raft together with whatever he found about him, making every second count. Making every knife count. And, as Pietro had surmised, he had plenty.

Rasvlach long ago off the cliff path and down the slope a few hundred yards beyond his quarry, picking his hidey-hole with care. Good views of the lagoon. Good views all around. Easy escape routes marked and mapped, along with another couple other hidey-holes. Then creeping through the undergrowth, finding his place, Rasvlach pulling one knife out, getting it aimed at the nearest mark, the stillest: one of those orange-skirted girls, skirts now faded grey in the darkness. Rasvlach used to hunting in the dark, when so much game was abroad.

Best time for it, son, when they're least expecting it. Wary of the day, as is quite right. Nothing like a hunt through the forest at night to bring you alive, once you've got your eye in.

And Rasvlach had his eye in.

Rasvlach calculating distance, speed, strength of impact.

No wind to deflect him.

Some disturbance on the slope above. Not enough to put him off.

The perfect shot about to let fly.

'God's sake!' Wenzel cried out in alarm, bowled into simultaneously from two sides, words snuffed out as his head was pushed into a heap of snow, his shoulders cracking in their sockets as his arms were pulled behind him and a boot landed heavily on his back.

'We've got him!' The cry of victory muffled by the snow in Wenzel's ears as he was roughly turned about, hands and feet grabbed at, ready to be trussed and bound; and then, as suddenly as they'd been grasped, his ankles were released.

'Stop! Stop!' one of his assailants cried, Wenzel looking up to see Pietro's face a couple of hand-spans from his own and such a look there: a feral ferocity as frightening as it was unexpected.

'It's Wenzel. It's only Wenzel.'

It's only Wenzel.

And oh Lord, the heartbreak in those words, the disappointment. Wenzel would never forget either.

He couldn't know that twice Pietro had believed himself to have cornered Rasvlach and twice had been thwarted. Wenzel now understanding the puzzle of Pietro, how all the stoic fatalism following the death of wife and child had been an illusion. Here was the real Pietro, as unforgiving as a river in spate, and as unforgiving as any of them would have been in the same circumstances.

The mask cracked and broken.

And some comfort in Wenzel to realise Pietro was as human, as fallible, as raging and reckless in the face of grief as he.

'Where's the family?' he asked, standing up, brushing snow from his clothes, shaking his head to get the last of it from his ears.

'They went down the slope towards the burn. Got a message from Philbert,' Pietro told him without apology.

'No sign of Rasvlach?'

No sign of him at all, not by any of them. Not by Wenzel coming in along the cliff path, nor by Pietro and Valter coming up the side of the forest. No sign, no sound, no indication at all he was anywhere near.

'Which means chances are he's onto them,' Wenzel surmised grimly, neither Pietro nor Valter disagreeing, all three having to take the worst-case scenario as the most probable. 'And he's a head start on us all, given when he got to Peppe.'

No point going into the specifics: Valter returning to tell Wenzel, Wenzel and Diderik forging upwards through the forest and along its topmost end. And speaking of Diderik, where the hell was he? Wenzel regretting all over again bringing Diderik with him, Diderik proving to be as much of a stone about his neck as he he'd been to Rasvlach before him.

'Where's that bloody Diderik?' he said, looking behind him, Valter following his gaze, both making out a forlorn slump in the shadows by the edge of the pines.

God's sake, Wenzel thought unkindly, *don't tell me he's gone and almost frozen himself to death for a second time.*

'Someone go get him,' Wenzel commanded, and that someone was never going to be him or Pietro, the two already heading down the slope towards the burn they could hear gurgling below. The task of retrieving Diderik left to Valter.

Valter not demurring. He didn't know who Diderik was, had no idea how he fitted into this picture but Valter glad to get away from Pietro and Wenzel and that simmer he recognised in them both: a simmer surface thin, vengeance like a raging wind beneath it waiting to rise up, to roar and roar, and to destroy. Valter going to Diderik, a sodden mess too weak to keep up with Wenzel's furious passage, who'd sunk down the second he'd seen Wenzel's attackers coming in upon him and hadn't moved since.

'Come on, lad,' Valter encouraged, lifting Diderik up, guiding his steps, hauling the lad along with him, whomever he might be.

'What's your name?' he asked the lad, who had got to his feet without conviction or strength, and would have fallen had Valter's arm not been keeping him upright.

'Diderik,' said Diderik, words slurred by the cold that hadn't properly left him since he'd abandoned Rasvlach. 'And I think I've done a terrible thing.'

Valter pulling him onwards, pulling him down the path towards the burn, the backs of Wenzel and Pietro already disappeared into the dark.

'Tell me,' Valter said. 'There's nothing you can say will be worse than what I could tell you.'

Valter meaning every word. Valter feeling an echo of himself in this young body he'd dragged up from the snow.

Best man you can be. Promise me.

'Tell me,' he said again, Diderik leaning against him, Valter feeling Diderik's mouth moving against his shoulder; Diderik weak, Diderik weeping freely now, despite their steep descent down the slope.

'I let loose a man,' Diderik blubbered, 'who I shouldn't have.'

'Fellow named Rasvlach?' Valter asked, given all Hulde had told him, Hulde not as tight-lipped as Pfiffmaklers usually were. Despising them for it and for what they'd caused in this boy, which was the same self-loathing he'd felt so viscerally himself for the most part of his life.

'Your marvellous pig has got us down here, just like you said. So now what do we do?'

Heraldo as upbeat as his innate character demanded, exhilarated by what had appeared to be a close call, wanting to find a good ending. Heraldo closing in on Philbert who was pushing his hat down upon his head, thinking Heraldo more cheerful than he had a right to be.

'You're such a bonehead,' Longhella complained, not of the same mind. 'I've no idea what my sister sees in you. We're stuck in a place no one knows and, hello Pfiffmaklers? Did anyone think to take the money from my father's pocket that was supposed to pay Philbert's passage over?'

Silence then, and a sinking in all their stomachs for no one had.

Certainly not Mergim who, with Pietro, had moved Peppe's body into the ditch and covered him over for later recovery.

'I've a couple of southern thalers,' Mergim offered, thanks to Valter's carving.

No one convinced it would be enough, if anything at all; all thirty-five German states issuing their own currency and coins, only accepted benchmark in these northern parts being the Vereinsthaler no one liked, them being too heavy with silver, too valuable, so far above what a normal person might earn it might as well have existed in another universe.

All stopping, wondering what to do, how to proceed.

All standing aimlessly at the water's edge.

Philbert about to mention his plan of going over the causeway under cover of night, save the Pfiffmaklers from doing anything more for him, when everyone suddenly turned and ducked as they heard a scrambling to their right in that dark snow-falling night.

Hulde's eyes catching a bright line flashing towards them, thin as fishing wire.

Hulde thrusting out her hands and shoving Longhella face-flat in the snow.

Hulde about to yell warning when Rasvlach's knife caught her, sent her reeling with the force of it, the blade so hard flung it went into her upper arm, grated between the bones and came out the other side.

And another sent forth a few seconds later as they all flapped in confusion, this one slicing into the flank of Kroonk who screamed like a screech owl in her torment, took up a wild trotting circle bowling over first Heraldo and then Mergim; Kroonk the unknowing saviour of the former from a third knife wheeling into the space where Heraldo's chest had been, landing uselessly in the snow a few yards beyond where he fell.

Rasvlach quick from his hidey-hole as the Pfiffmaklers scattered like seeds thrown out to hens.

Rasvlach sending a loop of rope around the nearest neck, Ludmilla's fingers going to it, Ludmilla's fingers trapped within its circle as it quickly tightened, a gasp leaving her lungs, heels kicking as she was dragged unseen from the family, pulled on by Rasvlach into the shallows, the splashing going unnoticed as Kroonk continued to scream and Philbert called out for her and Mergim swore loudly as he saw the knife in Hulde's arm and scrambled towards her. Confusion multiplied as Wenzel and Pietro, the source of that scrambling noise that had alarmed the Pfiffmaklers in the first place and caused Rasvlach's aim to miss, crashing onto the scene. Wenzel unaware what was going on, nevertheless calling for order. A few more minutes of panic and pandemonium before he established some kind of calm as he reassembled the crew, assessed the damage.

Hulde not too bad, Mergim having tightened a tourniquet about her upper arm and pulled free the knife, bandaged her up with a long strip of his shirt, held her close to his chest beneath his coat to keep her warm. Hulde in no state to argue.

Kroonk's screams dying away as she found Philbert and Philbert found her, and he staunched her bleeding, the knife already gone, shaken free by her panic; Philbert crumbling into her wound—short and not too deep—some bracket fungus kept in his pack for kindling.

No fatalities, no one else injured, the three Rasvlach knives retrieved—no point leaving them behind. Slight disturbance when Valter and Diderik slid with ungainly strides down the slope to join them. Wenzel clearly telling everyone who they were and were no threat.

'Everyone simmer down!' Wenzel commanded, once the several minutes of chaos had run its course. 'We're all safe, and we're all together. Time to—'

'Ludmilla, where's Ludmilla?' Heraldo shouted, Heraldo searching, Heraldo failing to find.

Heraldo calling her name again and again, unanswered emissaries sent out into this blackest of black nights.

Plan your attacks well and your defences better.
And so had Rasvlach done, had in fact married the two.
No better bargaining chip than to have one of the Pfiffmaklers' own.

He dragged Ludmilla a hundred odd yards up the side of the lagoon before pulling her out of the water, assessed what was left of her, which wasn't much. Limp as kelp thrown up by a storm, face blue as whelk ink but, as he loosened the rope from her throat and pulled her fingers free, he knew she was still alive. Only just, but only just was enough and still needed tying up to be on the safe side.

'God's sake,' Rasvlach muttered, pulling his waterlogged boots from the lagoon, sitting on the bank, taking a bit of a breather. Disgusted with himself that of three knives thrown only two had hit targets, neither intended. Trust those blasted Pfiffmaklers to move exactly when he would have had them still. Yet a win, nonetheless: another Pfiffmakler down, one beloved pig skewered. Nevertheless, he prided himself on being accurate and deadly and had been neither on this occasion, which really stuck in his craw. He was, in his defence, the one against the many and how many bloody Pfiffmaklers were there, by the way? They seemed to be multiplying by the minute.

Fairs' folk always an untrustworthy breed. Cunning as foxes, loyal as fools.

And fools he'd proved them to be, having nabbed one of them right from beneath their noses—and what a catch she was. A beautiful creature, long-haired, as long-necked as the doe he'd caught not long before his father chose to string himself up and be done with a disappointing life. One more Croatian forced into desperation by the Serbians Rasvlach had hated with every breath ever since.

'Drag marks!' Pietro shouted as he searched about him.

'And more,' Wenzel said, following them to the water's edge, spied a stick standing vertical in the snow and Rasvlach's hastily drawn hieroglyphics beside it.

Him for her.

A simple bargain.

Philbert for Ludmilla.

'Goddamn it, goddamn it,' Wenzel repeated over and over, his world shrivelling, unable to lift his eyes from those stick-marks in the snow.

Dark black water.

Ink black night.

White, white snow.

And Wenzel thinking, thinking, thinking—*how the hell are we going to get out of this?*

Mergim Offers A Solution

'How the hell are we going to get out of this?' Pietro asked of Wenzel, the Pfiffmaklers desolate as they took in the enormity of their situation. To give up Ludmilla was unthinkable; to deliver Philbert to Rasvlach a terrible violation of their code, knowing what would happen to him, and what would happen to what was left of the Pfiffmaklers once word got out about them doing it. Not to mention their own personal need for vengeance.

Pfiffmaklers attacked, Pfiffmaklers dead. Someone needing to be brought to account.

Rasvlach could not be allowed to win.

The snow had ceased its falling, the air become brittle and bright with incipient frost, stars pricking the heavens as the lazy snow-bearing clouds slowly shifted off along their way.

If only the Pfiffmaklers could do the same with such unapologetic ease.

Heraldo had strode and searched up and down the edge of the lagoon, calling out Ludmilla's name; no care for himself, or if another Rasvlach knife hurtled towards him and his noise in the darkness. Looking for where Rasvlach must have landed her and found nothing. Last of the snow cancelling out their tracks had he been looking in the right place, and he couldn't be certain of that. Maybe the man had had a boat waiting and was sitting, oars-drawn, in the middle of the lagoon laughing softly as the moon gave an occasional wink from up above.

Heraldo sat down on a rock and stayed there, head in hands.

Wenzel approaching, and then retreating. His son too bowed, too broken. Nothing anyone could say or do to stitch him back together while Ludmilla was unaccounted for.

The rest of the Pfiffmaklers cut down reeds, laid them out as a mat on which to sit; used the few surviving bulrush heads as kindling for a fire. Plenty of brushwood around, they'd not run out, would stay warmish throughout the long night, and the reed piths peeled and dipped into bottles of oil for rough-made lamps. Lamps weak and tremulous, vulnerable to the least puff of wind, lagoon jittering back their lights' reflections as silent as the Pfiffmaklers were themselves.

Pietro humming with regret, sorting through all the possible scenarios that might follow, none of which were good.

Longhella mute, numbed by the loss of first her father and now her sister too.

Valter and Diderik keeping to the edges, not wanting to intrude.

Mergim holding Hulde to his chest, his coat flung over her.

Hulde sleeping from either shock or blood loss, her legs lying gently between his own which Mergim found so moving he daren't twitch a muscle in case he broke the spell.

Philbert sat similarly with Kroonk, her warm weight beside him, head on his lap, muzzle nuzzling inside his coat, Kroonk shivering with every breath passing through her. His Kroonk. For so long his Kroonk. The gift from his father to his mother that had caused his family to sunder irrevocably and led directly from that time to this.

Such a long life it seemed to Philbert from then to now, filled with happenings and amazements. Philbert's head a carnival of memories, a jamboree playing out sights unseen, sounds unheard, by anyone but himself: Maulwerf's Fair of Wonders; Kwert, his marvellous mentor; Herr Himbeere with his tattooed head; La Chucha Lanuga and her White Jester. And the Pfiffmaklers: Heraldo and all his instruments, his fingers quick and sleight; Peppe and his wife, Peppe who'd stood up for him with Heraldo, his daughters as similar in looks as orange-pips, as different in temperament as the sun is from the moon.

The girls with their long, braided hair and their orange skirts.

No shaking the old image of them passing him by up Magendie's steps and then down again.

Another family wrecked because of him and his blasted head.

A French taupe, he'd been told, *a growth so unusual a scientific man is lucky to see one in a lifetime.* Doctor Ullendorf rationalising its beginnings for him: a renegade band of cells growing with gay abandon, not caring to stop; churls hurling through a wood with cudgels and happy *halloos* as they beat their own paths and drums, ignoring the rest of him which carried on as usual: sedate, rule-obeying cells sticking to normal schedule. Such a strange notion, for his taupe to be the cause of so much strife. So much loss of life.

The massacre on the ice of Maulwerf's Fair of Wonders—maybe his fault, maybe not.

The slaughter at the Westphal Club—his fault by proxy; he the reason all those intellectuals had gathered there, allowing the chink in their careful armour Metternich had been waiting for.

And now Rügen, Rasvlach and his knives. No Philbert, no Rasvlach; no getting away from that.

The anarchic band of churls in his head leading him to this stark choice: him for her.

Philbert for Ludmilla.

No slipping away for him this time around. Time for that band of churls to step up, take responsibility for their actions, accept Metternich's revenge. But oh man, how he was going to miss this earth, this world, this life; what might have become of him if allowed to carry on in it. Lump in his throat as he stroked his Kroonk. Would beg the Pfiffmaklers to look after her in her final years, which couldn't be many more. Years spent without Philbert. He couldn't bear to think on it.

Yet what other option did he have? It had to be this way, delivering up his churls to save someone far more loved and valued than him, except by Kroonk.

He could see no other option.

Philbert, breathless with anticipation as he got ready the words, looked up into the sky, saw the stars, cast his eyes over the white expanse of snow all about him, the black water of the lagoon sucking at its muddy banks, water winding through the waterways of Rügen like a serpent; wondered about the toads buried about its edges, the caddis fly larvae who would survive the winter and come out again in spring as new and different beings, as he would not.

Taking it all in, holding the scene within him alongside so many others. Always room for more within his giant head, until his giant head was lopped off his shoulders. He supposed he'd always known it might come to this but, now the moment was upon him, Philbert found he couldn't go with grace. Was sweating badly, kept rubbing at his mouth, didn't want any of it. Tapped at Kwert's *Philocalia* in his pocket, words from St Ephrem's *Hymn to the Pearl* seeping from its pages, moving to his lips, puppet masters to the puppet:

Revenge is owed, as is justice,
And from these depths will you gain height.
It befits the wheat to carry the grain,
Likewise the head of the king to create the cortege
Needed to steer the righteous chariot onwards.

He didn't want to be the head of the king nor the cortege.

He didn't believe there was any height to this depth, only a going downwards he didn't want to be a part of. He didn't give a damn about steering any chariot, righteous or not but, more than any of it, more than anything, he didn't want to be held responsible in perpetuity for the death of Ludmilla Pfiffmakler. Beautiful, blameless Ludmilla, who'd looked after the orphaned Hulde. Hulde in the forest saying, with apparent approval: *I can't believe your head is really as big as they said.*

He'd have liked the time to get to know this Hulde, whose life in many ways paralleled his own—one big event, not of her own making, dictating the course of her life, as had been the same for him. But no. That would never happen, not when he'd seen Heraldo so bereft. Normal head that would shake and stumble for the rest of his days if he didn't get back his wife. Heraldo excluding himself from the family as he had probably never done before in his life. Heraldo hunched upon his boulder as if he'd become a part of it.

No. Philbert could not allow it.

He stood, Kroonk murmuring as he pushed her gently from him, whispered in her ear, gave her one last stroke.

'Got to go, old friend. Wish it could have been otherwise.'

Taking a few strides towards Wenzel, towards the other Pfiffmaklers on their reed-based beds, all apparently asleep except Wenzel himself who was sat upright, taking the first watch of the night. A night long past its centre. Mergim due to take over a while back, but what the hell. Let him have his rest, and Hulde with him. Long hours from evening darkling to first murks of morning light and dawn glimmer. Wenzel unlikely to sleep through any of it, as he'd not slept through the night before.

Philbert approaching on silent feet.

Philbert sitting down next to Wenzel as the fire flickered and Wenzel threw on a few more branches. Wenzel guessing what might come, dreading it and wanting it in equal measure.

'You've to make the bargain,' Philbert said, hot hard lump in his throat as Kroonk waddled over and sat herself beside him, unwilling to be parted.

Wenzel swallowing, pulling stupidly at his beard, putting out a hand and grasping it about the base of Philbert's neck.

'Thank you,' he croaked. 'Thank you.'

Face contorting, eyes closing, warm wet tears falling down both their cheeks.

Uneasy came the morning to the remaining Pfiffmaklers, awoken from unrestful sleep into the ethereal: mist lying low on the lagoon, drifting over their makeshift camp and up the brook to the lip of the slope from where they'd descended the night before. All shuggling their shoulders, all having cramped limbs, cricked necks, damp clothes. All moving silently as they washed faces and armpits, sluiced mouths in the salty water of the lagoon that had dropped a couple of inches and come back in again, the rhythms of the world going on regardless of what this day would bring for them.

A little way off Mergim unwrapped Hulde's wound, washed it clean, dusted it with Philbert's proffered bracket fungus crumbled between Mergim's large fingers, before tying it up tight again.

'How does it feel?' Mergim asked her as she blinked open her eyes. 'Any burning or itching?'

Hulde shaking her head.

'It's fine,' she said. 'Thank you for looking after me. I'm sorry I almost drowned you the other day.'

Mergim having to supress an inappropriate laugh at this candid apology.

'I deserved it,' he said. 'Anyone less magnanimous than you would have seen it through.'

Small smiles exchanged, Mergim wondering where such a complicated word as magnanimous had come from and how Hulde could be so graceful to take it as it was meant. Such a fine girl she'd become, and such relief to know Valter's words, *you did her a favour in the long run,* might really have been true. A curious intimacy grown between the two during their shared night: linked pasts acknowledged, linked futures not to be dismissed. Mergim clearing his throat. Something else he had to tell Hulde, and he dreaded it. Hulde's smile faltering as he began, and failing altogether when he got to its end.

'I'm real sorry to say it,' Mergim said, 'but in all the stramash after you got hurt…well. I'll just say it. Rasvlach has Ludmilla.'

Hulde on her feet immediately, pushing away from Mergim, leaping towards the rest of the family who were cowering by the fire. Pietro and Wenzel talking quietly if animatedly; Longhella leaning into Pietro's side, her usually expressive and mobile face blank as unscribed beech bark as she stared into the flicker of the flames. No one else to be seen, the shifting mist dividing them off one from another. Diderik and Valter who knew where, likewise Philbert and his pig. Hulde scanning through the mist until she discerned Heraldo sitting on his boulder with useless head held in useless hands. And it was to him she went, sinking down on her knees before him in the snow, taking his hands in hers, forcing him to lift his face which was swollen and wan and utterly without hope.

Mergim watching Hulde watching Heraldo.

Mergim's heart constricting within his chest to witness so much unhappiness befall such good people. And they were good people, these Pfiffmaklers. He'd understood it the moment they'd apprehended him eleven years previously and given him the chance to redeem himself. And he had redeemed himself: Kragujevac the means, Hulde the proof. That the Pfiffmaklers now found themselves in the precarious situation they were seemed both wildly unjust and unable to be borne.

Desperate to uncover a way to lessen their loss, give future hope.

Mergim not so good at thinking, not until he'd met that old mathematician in Kragujevac who'd taught him how supposed certainties were not always as they seemed. Certainly Rasvlach had Ludmilla, and certainly there seemed only one way out of it: to hand over Philbert and get her back in return. But here was the trick: the Birthday Paradox telling him that what seemed so clad-fast unbreakably certain might not be so.

Always an out. All Mergim had to do was to find it.

The Pfiffmaklers coalesced about their fire, as they always did, once everyone was washed and ready to face the day, though a bad day it was going to be. Diderik and Valter brought into their circle, as were Philbert and Kroonk. Hulde bringing a shivering stiff-limbed Heraldo in too.

Wenzel readied himself to announce their next, their only move.

'Philbert's going to give himself up,' Wenzel told them, having discussed it all with Pietro, neither seeing an alternative as no more had Philbert. Heraldo the first to argue, despite Ludmilla being on the line.

'He can't. He mustn't. If we give this Rasvlach what he wants then everything that's happened up to now is without worth.'

Exactly as Ludmilla had said the night before.

'It's the only way,' Longhella countered, dull-voiced, listless, no arguments burning on her lips for the mere sake of arguing; a change everyone found disturbing.

'I don't see any other way,' Wenzel said quietly.

'And he won't get away with it,' Pietro added. 'He'll never collect his reward. We'll track him down. I will track him down, right to my last breath.'

No one doubting it.

'You can't do it,' Heraldo implored. 'Ludmilla would never forgive me. There must be something…'

'Ludmilla would forgive you anything,' Hulde said, Heraldo shaking his head.

'Not this. She would never forgive me this. I started it and I must finish…'

Quite what he could finish was beyond him. He couldn't even finish the sentence.

Too much for Mergim, who'd been thinking this whole situation through hard and fast.

Too much in Mergim to let it go. Too much for Mergim to see Hulde and Heraldo and the whole of the Pfiffmaklers struggling with a dilemma not of their own making, and one that wasn't going to end well. Time for Mergim to stand up, as the pig boy Philbert had already done. Time to see if he, Mergim, had truly been redeemed, if he couldn't garner all he'd learned in Kragujevac and put it to use.

Randomness not to be dismissed.

Paradoxes to be put to proper purpose.

Mathematics not so esoteric it had no bearing on real life.

He cleared his throat, aware he was the outsider here, that no one might care to hear him contribute, but he had to speak.

'Can I suggest something?' he asked, the words catching in his throat. He coughed, Pfiffmakler eyes swivelling towards him. 'I have an idea,' he tried again. 'You might not like it, and it might not work, but it might give you a fighting chance.'

The Solution Plays Itself Out

Rasvlach hadn't slept the whole night through—not unusual for him.

No vodka, no sleep. How his body worked, both before Kragujevac and after. Rasvlach regretting leaving everything on his cart behind. Should have stowed a bottle into his backpack to see him through. A decision made back in the forest that it would be better if he didn't sleep, kept his wits about him. The Pfiffmaklers a tricky lot.

At the first faint light, a while before proper dawn, he rubbed itchy bloodshot eyes and removed his gloves, blew into his hands to warm them. Checked the Pfiffmakler woman was still breathing, which she was, him having taken precautions to ensure this would be so: pulling her away from the lagoon, dragging her partway up the bank towards the forest track, tying and gagging her. Hidden them both in a tidy bivouac pushed into a stand of green alders, making as good use of the plentiful reeds as had the Pfiffmaklers. Covering over his tracks, masking his hide with reeds and snow, making a small fire pit to keep them warm and snug. Meagre smoke dissipated by the makeshift roof above their heads so it would filter out in small wisps undetectable unless you were right on top of them.

Riskiest part of his new plan about to be enacted. A plan he'd not wanted, had no choice now but to play: him for her. Any amount of ways that could go wrong. The hunter in him cursing he'd not been able to take Philbert cleanly, make the kill in the forest and get away before anyone knew he was there. But nothing easy in this world.

He took from his pack a small bottle and gave it a shake. Nothing more than hot peppers, cloves and mustard seeds ground up in oil, but it would do the trick. He pulled the Pfiffmakler woman's arm towards him and pushed up her sleeve, spread the mixture over the section of skin above her elbow, noting how smooth it was, like silk beneath his fingers as he rubbed the oil in, waited five minutes as he heated the point of his knife in the last of the fire before kicking the fire over.

His favourite knife.

The one used to skin and gut that doe back when he was seventeen.

'You've done me proud, Georg,' his father had said as he'd admired the felled doe. 'You've done me real proud. Now let's see if you've learned all I've taught you about skinning and paunching. On your own this time, lad. Don't think you need me any longer to guide your hand.'

Last words spoken directly to Rasvlach by his father once they'd got the doe to their home.

Last of his last words given that night at dinner to his wife.

Just got to nip out to the barn, love, check on the animals. Check our Georg here has hung his deer right.

A hard night for Georg Rasvlach when his mother sent him to the barn to check what was taking so long. Georg finding his father hanging from the beam: face engorged, eyes pushed from their sockets, tongue spilling from his mouth like a black phallus, kick marks on the wood a full four feet from his boots. Plainly his father's dying not going as smoothly as planned but, once started, could not be stopped. Rasvlach and his mother idly eating curds and sugar-soaked raspberries as father and husband choked his agonising passage into the next life, if one was to be had.

And how easy would it be for Georg Rasvlach, now a man, to skin alive a woman he didn't know to get what he'd come for?

Well, easy would that be for him.

He would skin Ludmilla limb by limb until he got what he wanted.

The point of his favourite knife thinned and honed by years of being stropped and soap-stoned.

With sharp and practiced precision he drew its tip in a rectangle through Ludmilla's skin, peeled and scraped it back until he had a square of it. Not a murmur from her. Pepper oil doing its job, numbing her, making it hard for her brain to understand what was going on and, for good measure and to stop any annoying bleeding, he doused her with the oil again, tied a strip of cloth about her arm. Her excised skin so thin he could see the light through it as he stretched and wrapped it neatly about the rock he had chosen as messenger.

Him for her.

Had to underline the pact.

Rasvlach then away, pulling Ludmilla with him up the short incline and back into the pines. Selected one deep inside the forest, secured the gag, tied Ludmilla to the tree.

Only a short time now to wait.

Only one job left to do for the moment.

Rasvlach snaking back through the trees, once more brushing away his tracks as he went, until he stood on the edge of the slope above the lagoon. A mist drifting off the water, a soft and creeping creature, belly down, like a hunting dog sniffing out tracks and hidden byways. Still dark, but he could hear bodies stirring, water being splashed, faint murmurings like large birds shifting on their nests. He positioned himself above the glimmerings of fire glimpsed through the mist. Kept straight and steady. Anyone looking upwards would see him as only another black line amongst the many, blended into the tall pines lined behind him like ranking soldiers.

He waited.

No need to hurry.

Chose his moment.

Took careful aim, then lobbed his reminder, his threat, his gift, right into their midst.

'He's clever, not book-learning clever but real wily,' Mergim was saying, 'and by now he's almost certainly taken to upper ground.'

'And he'll have thought all this through,' Diderik added, Diderik brought in specifically to comment on Mergim's suggestion, the only other person who knew Rasvlach and how he worked, how he thought. 'He's like…well I don't what he's like. It's like he studies you and looks right through you and sees you for what use you'll be. And he doesn't care about anything, and I mean anything.'

'He has to care about something,' Wenzel was perplexed.

'Not that he ever told me,' Diderik said, 'although hardly ever told me anything. Not about himself. Except how he enjoyed nearly killing that Serbian bloke for bad-mouthing Croatia, which was what got him into prison in the first place.'

'I can vouch for that,' Valter put in, not looking up. Not wanting to see any more Pfiffmakler faces in mourning. 'I was there. Saw what he did after he heard about the Little Maus.'

Philbert blinking in surprise.

Wenzel glancing over at Mergim, this new avenue about to be explored when a rounded stone landed and rolled at Wenzel's feet. Wenzel leaning down to retrieve it, picking it up, looking at it with a frown and then releasing it from shaking fingers, face as white as the mist beginning to pull itself away from the water.

'He's gone too far,' Wenzel got out through gritted teeth, shooting out a hand to stop Heraldo picking up what he'd dropped. 'Don't do it, son.'

Too late.

Heraldo had seen and touched, and puked green bile into the snow.

Wenzel unable to comfort, Wenzel trying to keep down the retching coming from his stomach making his Adam's apple bob like a razorbill on rough and choppy seas. Mergim left to take charge after his own brief look.

'It's only a sliver,' he said: a neat translucent square of human skin secured about the stone with cotton thread. Far thinner than the neat squares of human skin he'd heard Rasvlach had taken several times before to remove Kragujevac tattoos. 'It's nothing more.'

Heraldo disconsolate.

'What if this is just a warning? What if he goes deeper next time? What if he skins her alive? Oh my God, my God!'

Mergim frowned, impatient with Heraldo.

'Of course it's a warning,' he said. 'This is what Rasvlach does. He's no reason to do anything else, now he has our attention.'

And by God, he had their attention. Mergim getting support from an unexpected quarter. Hulde getting to her feet with determination, if also a little on the wobble. Hulde speaking for them both.

'It changes nothing,' she said. 'It means we have to go with what Mergim said because that's all we've got.'

Wenzel steadied himself, looked up at her. Brave little Hulde, who was not so little anymore. Hulde, who'd brought the ancient history of this island right up to the present by laying down length by length, end to end, her own life-span forty times over. Brought it alive to Livia and Pietro, and now to him.

'Are you sure?' he asked her, taking a deep breath; and *oh please,* he was thinking, *don't let this be the last length you will ever lay down of your life.* But where else could they go? What else could they do? Ludmilla's skin excised and stretched across a piece of stone, with the promise of more to come if they didn't comply.

'I've never been more sure of anything,' Hulde replied, taking a step towards Mergim, gripping his hand within her own. And oh how proud he was when she did so and oh, so much prouder when she went on to raise the battle cry for them all.

'Come on Pfiffmaklers,' Hulde rallied her troops. 'We're made of strong stuff. I know it, as does Ludmilla. She'd not want us to go down without a fight. And Heraldo,' Hulde added, releasing Mergim—much to Mergim's loss—Hulde now magnificent in his eyes, as in everyone's. 'You've to stop all this snivelling if we're going to get Ludmilla back in one piece.'

Chidden, Heraldo lifted his stricken face, looking at his ersatz child, wondering when it was she'd become so wise.

'Rasvlach! It's me. It's Mergim!' Mergim boomed into the early morning, like he'd a bittern in his chest. 'We agree to your bargain! Philbert for Ludmilla.'

He'd climbed up the incline from the lagoon to the edges of the forest and looked about him.

Saw nothing.

No movement, no sign Rasvlach was near.

Heart going fast, knowing how much Rasvlach hated Serbians for betraying Croatians and Mergim likely top of his list for those to account for it.

Nevertheless he stamped up and down the track, repeating his announcement every twenty or so paces. Rasvlach had to be here somewhere. Not a chance he'd have stopped by the lakeside where, come morning, he might be more easily tracked or seen. So up and down that track he went, one foot after another, a hawker shouting out his wares.

'Rasvlach, it's me. It's Mergim. We agree to your bargain. Him for her.'

Rasvlach heard it all. Rasvlach skirting his way through the trees a few yards beyond the track. Rasvlach seeing Mergim the moment he pulled himself over the lip of the incline. Rasvlach thinking how sweet it would be to do Mergim in right here, right now. Fucking Mergim, hero of Kragujevac for bringing a war criminal in from exile, directly responsible—along with these pissing Pfiffmaklers—for that man's execution and the final straw on the camel's back leading to Rasvlach's father's suicide.

But needs must. More pressing problems. Namely setting himself up for life with the Anatomist's Dream.

So once more he waited.

No need to hurry.

Had the time to choose his moment.

He watched Mergim move himself up and down the track.

He'd no doubt Pfiffmaklers were in the vicinity. He'd not heard them, but he knew packs and how they circled, how they moved, how they looked for the weakest spot.

Pfiffmaklers making their piffling plans.

The many against the one.

No change there, as far as Rasvlach was concerned; and no reason he couldn't out-think the many, out-guess them, figure what they would do before they did it. He'd had all night to shuffle possibilities, had reckoned—once they'd agreed to make the bargain, and how would they not?—that most likely they'd spread themselves out wide, close in on him from all points of the compass. He'd been a little surprised Mergim had been chosen as the go-between, but hell, he was apparently one of the Pfiffmakler pack now, same shitting traitor he'd always been, jumping sides the moment it suited.

Rasvlach ready for the lot of them.

Rasvlach primed.

Rasvlach ready for the off.

'Bring out the boy,' he yelled. 'And bring him out with his wretched pig.'

Mergim's shoulders twitching as he heard Rasvlach's voice, motioning Philbert to poke up his head up from the incline, Kroonk struggling up beside him tethered by the rope about his waist.

'He's here!' Mergim called, shielding them with his body as much as he could. 'I have them both. Tell us where Ludmilla is.'

Rasvlach smiled. Oh so predictable, these packs of prey.

'I don't think so,' he called back. 'Not until I'm away. Take the boy to the village below, to the pier. And only you, Mergim. You, him and the pig. And if I don't make it, if you shoot me down before I meet you there, you'll never find your fine little lady and she'll freeze to death all alone in the forest.'

So up Philbert came, pale morning light keeping his face in shadow as Kroonk trotted along beside him and they joined Mergim; Mergim taking long strides—incredibly relieved he'd not been cut down as he'd made the bargain—the three of them heading for the cliff path and down the track leading directly to Glowe, according to Rasvlach's instructions.

And down in Glowe already were Longhella and Pietro, Diderik and Wenzel—no wolves in the forest as Rasvlach had surmised. Wolves deployed elsewhere, positioned in market place, harbour and main street.

No wolves in the forest; only persons in the forest being Ludmilla, and Heraldo going from tree to tree, from place to place, calling out her name again and again once he'd reasoned Rasvlach had pulled himself away and was finally gone.

He called her name a hundred times and had yet to find her.

Ludmilla hearing him, though a long way off; Ludmilla trying to spit out the gag, loosen her bonds. Could do neither. Arms burning beneath the ropes Rasvlach had tied so tightly about the tree he'd placed her against. All the sounds she tried to make softened into non-existence by the gag so soaked in saliva it threatened to clog up her mouth for good, and so she stopped. Tried to breathe slow and calm. Pfiffmaklers out here looking for her. Heraldo out here looking for her, and would never stop until he had her found.

But Jesus and Mary, she was cold, chilled into immobility; hours since she'd been tied to this tree, hands and feet dull appendages no longer seeming part of her.

And oh Lord, she was tired. Her head nodding forward every now and then, pulled back each time into wakefulness by the rip of hair from her scalp, hair loosened from its plaits and tangled into the rough bark of her pillory, tethering her to what life she had left. She wasn't sure how much more there might be of it but she wasn't, as Hulde had surmised, about to go down without giving it everything she'd got. She wriggled within her bonds, purposefully moved those lumps of hands and feet so the rope burned into them, brought back some sensation. Pain essential if she was to keep herself awake long enough for Heraldo to find her.

And he would find her.

He had to find her.

She just had to wait a little longer, and a little longer, live through one minute and then the next and the next.

And then the snow began again, slow and gentle, skipping down through the canopy above her like fluttering moths. Memory in her of a night not long after she and Heraldo had taken to each other's beds and plighted troths, a night when Heraldo had nudged her awake, thrown a blanket about her shoulders, taken her hand in his and lifted her up, opened the flap of their tent.

'Only look,' he'd whispered, and so she had: saw the darkness fluttering and shifting with a million white-winged mayflies brought alive for that one night to meet and mate, as she and Heraldo had just done; mayflies swirling up and about and around the glimmerings of the Pfiffmaklers' fire so thickly the glowing embers could no longer be seen.

'One night they're alive,' he'd told her, 'and tomorrow we'll be walking through the snow-drifts of their bodies. But for this one night, my love, they are the most alive they will ever be. And that's how I feel about you. If I only had one more day to live, then I would choose to spend it with you.'

And I you, Ludmilla murmured, lips chapped and cracked, beginning to bleed. Head nodding forward once more, hair pulling at her scalp, ripping free. Ludmilla letting it be. No more strength in her to lift her head.

Come soon, my love, or I'll spend my last day without you.

Ludmilla alone in the huge dark forest of Jasmund, in the pure white snow.

Ludmilla's eyes closing.

Ludmilla having oh so little time left.

Thank God, thought Mergim. *He's gone for it. He's actually gone for it.*

Mergim having to slow his pace to allow Philbert and Kroonk to keep up.

Come on, come on, he wanted to shout at them; one person's pace rarely another's, and certainly not that of an age-raddled pig. It seemed an aeon before they got themselves to Glowe and an intrusion, an insult, how life there was carrying on as normal, its inhabitants going about their daily duties without a care. Mergim wanting to shout: *look out, citizens, you've a wolf amongst you!* Which of course he could not. Their plan, his plan, dependent on everything being kept on a low footing, on Mergim delivering Philbert up to Rasvlach as desired and gaining the information needed as to the whereabouts of Ludmilla before she froze to death. And she would freeze to death.

Snow had begun to fall again as they went.

Snow that would cover her over, and any tracks in the forest.

Mergim sweating despite the newly falling snow.

Mergim worrying.

Rasvlach deciding on the pier for the handover, and Mergim hadn't thought on that.

Had covered everywhere but the pier that was too open, too public, too clear a risk; cursing himself.

It seemed so obvious now.

Rasvlach would have gone down the day before and ordered himself up a boat ready to take himself and Philbert away. No need to chop his head off the moment he had him. And what better place than in the middle of the Baltic where he could do what was needed, stuff Philbert's head into a sack, shove the rest of his body into the water.

No one any the wiser.

Godammit, godammit. I've buggered it all up, Mergim was thinking as he threaded himself through Glowe's meagre streets, Philbert and Kroonk close behind him; the three passing through the market place where women were haggling over the prices of this piece of fish or that, this bunch of vegetables or another; the market place where Mergim had reasoned Rasvlach would demand the meet.

Got to give the Pfiffmaklers a sign, he knew, saw Longhella hovering at the edge of the crowd, raised his head towards her, caught her eye. Couldn't be sure if she'd got the message. And no time now to haver, to overthink. Pier only a few yards away, and Rasvlach standing right at its end. Rasvlach with one boot already on the boat tethered to the pier by a single rope already loosened, ready to let fly.

'It's me and you,' Mergim murmured to Philbert. 'I'm not sure we can count on the rest. I've miscalculated. I've misplaced them. Are you ready?'

'I'm ready,' came the stoic reply. 'Let's get it done.'

Mergim marching up the pier towards Rasvlach, at all times keeping Philbert and his pig behind him, stopping short of Rasvlach by several yards.

'We had a bargain,' Mergim said to Rasvlach. 'I hope you mean to stick to it.'

Rasvlach benevolent, Rasvlach assured, Rasvlach maybe even smiling somewhere within his grizzled beard grown greyer and larger since Mergim had last seen him.

'A bargain's a bargain,' Rasvlach said, with consummate cheer. 'You keep up your end, I'll keep up mine. Let's see the goods.'

'Tell me where she is,' Mergim demanded, Mergim blustered, fighting the urge to look about for Pfiffmaklers, to not tip his hand.

'Get them in the boat,' Rasvlach countered, Mergim holding out an arm to stop Philbert moving too soon.

'You don't need the pig,' he said, imminent hysteria on his lips to be arguing over such details. 'Let her stay. She's no part of the bargain.'

What are you doing, Mergim?

Rasvlach looking curiously at him, curling his lips, seeing weakness, smelling doubt, poking a stick right at it, unable to resist.

'I don't think so. Could do with a right good feed. Think I'll gut that little pig runt of his right in front of his eyes. Cut her up, cook her and eat her. Gnaw down on her bones. Pork always a favourite of mine.'

Not that it was.